Praise for *Once Around the Track*

"McCrumb has become the bard of motorsports. . . . There are literary references in *Once Around the Track* as well as literary touches, jokes, lore, tall tales, innuendoes, and subplots. . . . It's very entertaining and, as usual for McCrumb, most informative."

—*Asheville Citizen Times*

"It's only fitting, perhaps, that an acclaimed Southern writer should put a feminine face on NASCAR. And Sharyn McCrumb's new novel, *Once Around the Track,* is a beguiling tale. . . . A heartwarming story that celebrates loyalty and love of racing cars."

—*Richmond Times Dispatch*

"This book is populated with strong female characters, and McCrumb's detailed descriptions of the pit crew at work are so strong you can almost smell the motor oil. Readers will be happy to add McCrumb to their list of must-reads."

—*Booklist*

"A perfect summer read—fun, entertaining, and light as a sea breeze."

—*Georgia Times-Union*

"Well written and fun . . . character-driven . . . entertaining and well-researched."

—*Creative Loafing* (Charlotte, NC)

Praise for *St. Dale*

"Funny, smart, a must read. I loved it!

—Lee Smith

"A triumphant joy throughout, a *Canterbury Tales* with speed."

—Ed McBain

"A wild ride! Sharyn McCrumb has done it again."

—Ward Burton

"Wave the checkered flag, 'cause this one's headed for the victory lane! McCrumb's latest should attract a large and varied following."

—*Library Journal* (starred review)

"Wonderful characters, richly drawn stories . . . McCrumb has produced another winner!"

—*Richmond Times-Dispatch*

"This book may be to NASCAR what 'O Brother, Where Art Thou?' was to bluegrass."

—*Johnson City* (TN) *Press*

"A present-day, blue-collar comedy dealing with spirituality, stock cars, and shaky lives . . . one of McCrumb's finer achievements."

—*Denver Post & Rocky Mountain News*

"Chaucer meets NASCAR . . . *St. Dale* is just plain fun."

—*The Anniston Star*

"An incredible tribute to a lifelong friend."

—Junior Johnson, legendary NASCAR driver

"Sharyn McCrumb is a powerful novelist. She has assembled a marvelous collection of characters, and all their stories are fascinating. Yet everything comes together as a novel that is full of magic and laughter, wonder and love."

—Orson Scott Card

"Sharyn McCrumb is the Dale Earnhardt of Southern literature—outrageous, original, and unstoppable. *St. Dale* is a wise and wonderful journey honoring an American hero."

—Emyl Jenkins

"*St. Dale* reminds us that we can see the Divine anywhere, if we are willing to look. I loved it."

—Barbara Hall

"An incredibly enjoyable read. *St. Dale* is a novel that could very well be true, and Sharyn McCrumb tells the story like no one ever has."

—Kyle Petty

"Required reading for anybody who still mourns Number Three—or who wonders what the fuss is about."

—*Kirkus Reviews*

"McCrumb craftily combines the life and death of Dale Earnhardt with her fictionalized account . . . unusual and moving."

—*Romantic Times*

"St. Dale is funny, breezy and easy to read, but it's also well-researched. . . . McCrumb knows her stuff."

—*Georgia Times-Union*

Praise for Sharyn McCrumb and Her Novels

"One of our most gifted authors . . . There is no one quite like her among present-day writers. No one better either."

—*The San Diego Union-Tribune*

"No one writes a ballad, tells a tale, spins a yarn better than the lauded lady from Shawsville."

—*The Roanoke Times*

"McCrumb writes with quiet fire and maybe a little mountain magic. . . . Like every true storyteller, she has the Sight."

—*The New York Times Book Review*

"McCrumb draws you close, makes you care."

—*Los Angeles Times*

Once Around
the Track

Once Around
the Track

SHARYN
McCRUMB

KENSINGTON BOOKS
http://www.kensingtonbooks.com

To Ward Burton

76:9

You have been my friend. That in itself is a tremendous thing. I wove my webs for you because I liked you.

—Charlotte to Wilbur in *Charlotte's Web*

KENSINGTON BOOKS are published by

Kensington Publishing Corp.
850 Third Avenue
New York, NY 10022

All Kensington titles, imprints and distributed lines are available at special quantity discounts for bulk purchases for sales promotion, premiums, fund-raising, educational or institutional use.

Special book excerpts or customized printings can also be created to fit specific needs. For details, write or phone the office of the Kensington Special Sales Manager: Kensington Publishing Corp., 850 Third Avenue, New York, NY 10022. Attn. Special Sales Department. Phone: 1-800-221-2647.

Kensington and the K logo Reg. U.S. Pat. & TM Off.

ISBN-13: 978-0-7582-0779-1
ISBN-10: 0-7582-0779-4

First Hardcover Printing: June 2007
First Trade Paperback Printing: June 2008

10 9 8 7 6 5 4 3 2 1

Printed in the United States of America

CHAPTER I

Once Removed

"Have you found him yet?" The voice on the cell phone was shrill and insistent, but then it always was, even for the most trivial of messages. Clients were notoriously impatient people, and she billed them accordingly.

Suzie Terrell looked out her windshield at the kudzu-covered hillside overlooking a ramshackle collection of buildings that could hardly be called a town. Next to the narrow concrete bridge spanning what was surely nothing more than a creek was a battered tin sign, emblazoned with checkered flags and bearing the bullet-riddled legend: MARENGO, GEORGIA: HOME OF BADGER JENKINS, WINNER OF THE SOUTHERN 500.

"I think I'm on the last lap," she said wearily, and clicked off the phone.

As an Atlanta lawyer, Suzie Terrell had had her share of bizarre commissions—suing the dog's plastic surgeon came to mind—and this latest directive from a group of women investors would probably make the short list of *stories to tell at dinner parties after four drinks*. It promised to be quite an adventure.

Find Badger Jenkins.

Who the hell—? When she received the assignment, she had dutifully looked him up on the Internet, and an instant later the name appeared on her computer screen, accompanied by an

image of a glowering but handsome man in opaque black sunglasses and a red and black firesuit, positively robotic in his
well-chiseled perfection, possessing all the soulless beauty of a
state-of-the-art espresso machine.

Suzie stared at the scowling face for a few moments; then she
sank back in her office chair and muttered to herself, "Oh, great!
Now I have to go and make small talk with the Angel of Death!"

Further searches on the Internet turned up only vague hints as
to the current whereabouts of this alien being. Badger Jenkins, it
turned out, was a race car driver, currently unemployed, and a little older than NASCAR's current crop of drivers *(that is, he was
old enough to shave).* He was a native Georgian; he had won a
few races, raised his share of hell both on and off the track, and
was thought to be back home in some one-horse town called
Marengo, wherever that was. What Mr. Jenkins was doing these
days was anybody's guess.

Suzie had tried calling his business office in Marengo, but there
didn't seem to be one. The phone number, garnered from an out-
of-date Web site, turned out to be located in the Blue Tick Café,
and was answered by a drawling waitress named Laraine, who
claimed to be Badger Jenkins's second cousin once removed.

"Once removed?" said Suzie.

"Yeah, hon. Once removed out from under him in the backseat
of his car by my daddy and a loaded shotgun. I got grounded for
three months, but, boy, it was worth it. He wasn't but seventeen
himself that time." She sighed, savoring the moment. "Ol' Badger
was hotter than a two-dollar pistol back then. Tearing up dirt
tracks, leaving a trail of broken hearts and dented fenders. Face
like an angel, and hell on wheels. You ever seen one of them early
sports cards of him?"

"Er—no."

"Woo-hoo! It'd give you hot flashes just to look at him. There's
one of them cards I kept to this day that shows him with his firesuit unzipped to where you can see his curly little chest hair peep-
ing out, and those white pants so tight you could practically read
the Trojan wrapper in his pocket. 'Course that firesuit didn't have
pockets, as I recall, but you get my drift. And him settin' there

grinning and facing the camera with his legs spread-eagled wide apart, same as he sits in every picture I have ever seen of him right to this day. Like show-and-tell. I swear, try as you might, you can't help but look! Honey, if that boy was a mindreader, he could not walk past a crowd of women without limping."

"How . . . evocative." Suzie shuddered. "Perhaps you can help me. I am trying to locate Mr. Jenkins. I was hoping that you could tell me how to reach him?"

Laraine was silent for a few moments. Then she said, "Well . . . your best bet is the post office box. I think the rent on it is paid up anyhow. 'Course even if it isn't, Miz Todhunter the postmistress will give him the letters, anyhow. She's seventy if she's a minute, but she looks at him like a stray dog eying a drumstick."

"Perhaps there is a phone number where he could be reached?"

"Oh, he don't like us to give out phone numbers. Especially to bill collectors or ladies of a certain age, if you know what I'm saying. Badger says he's a race car driver, not a damn turkey baster."

"I have a business proposition to discuss with Mr. Jenkins," said Suzie, adding ice to her most lawyerly tone.

"Oh. Well, I reckon you can talk to his daddy then. That might get a message to him. Mr. Jenkins says he don't care if I give out his number to the older ladies. Reckon he's hoping he'll get some of the overflow."

But that hadn't gone well, either.

The old man who answered the phone had barely let her say her name before he launched into his spiel. "If you're calling about Clover Hoof, our prize Angus bull, why, his stud fee is five hundred dollars, payable in advance. He's a champion, he is. Won—"

"No, sir. It's not about the bull."

"Well, now, Keeper, our coon hound, ain't won no prizes, but he's the best tracker in three counties, no argument there, and his stud fee is fifty dollars cash money and the pick of the litter."

"Mr. Jenkins, I'm calling about your son Badger."

"Oh. Well, I reckon you'd better talk to him directly then," said the old man. "I don't know what *he* charges."

In the end, Suzie consulted a road atlas, left her office in Atlanta, and drove nearly three hours north into the red clay hills of Georgia, in search of Marengo, which, Laraine had assured her, was so small it was only on the map two days a week.

Now she had found it. Parking wasn't a problem, she told herself, as she surveyed the block of gently decaying storefronts subsiding into the hill of kudzu behind it. She seemed to be the only person in town. The two-lane blacktop was devoid of traffic, and the town's one stoplight was permanently set on a yellow caution light. In the minute business district, consisting of mostly empty buildings, the Blue Tick Café was easy enough to spot: a whitewashed cinderblock building with a big plate glass window, framed by two white flower boxes of red geraniums. Suzie surveyed the scene, looking for stray dogs. In case she had to order something in the diner, she could always eat the pickle, ask for the rest of the order to go, and then give it to some starving pooch with a cast-iron stomach.

Assuming her brightest Junior League smile *(the one that said "my teeth and my pearls are* both *real")*, Suzie Terrell stepped inside the café and beamed at the dishwater blonde behind the counter. "Are you Laraine? We spoke on the phone."

Narrowed eyes took in her pastel blue silk suit from Neiman Marcus and her Dolce & Gabbana purse. "Yeah, I remember. Is this about Badger?"

"Yes, it is. I represent a group of women—"

The waitress rolled her eyes and heaved a theatrical sigh. "His DNA's on file at the courthouse."

"No, that isn't it. My clients want to offer him a job. Driving a Cup car."

A Cup car. Three weeks ago that term would have mystified her, ignorant as she was of all things NASCAR. Just because you were born and bred in Atlanta didn't mean you acquired knowledge of stock car racing by osmosis. After all, what they called the Atlanta Motor Speedway was, in fact, in Hampton, Georgia, some thirty miles south of the big city. Suzie Terrell had never been there. In fact, where stock car racing was concerned, she had cherished her ignorance. Now here she was in an even more remote and savage place—Marengo, Georgia, teetering on the edge of the world—awaiting the arrival of the town's one celebrity: Badger Jenkins, race car driver and local satyr.

She cast about in search of small talk that she could make with the creature when he did appear, but quickly abandoned that idea—after all, how many one-syllable words could you string together?

Maybe it would be better just to get right down to business. A group of female investors in Atlanta has secured funding, and—God knows why—they wanted to field a NASCAR team with an all-female crew except for the driver, because there are no woman drivers at Cup level, the "major league" of motorsports. And they had chosen Badger Jenkins as their designated driver. Oh, well, she supposed that if the genders were reversed, no one would question the logic of their choice. *Why not get a pretty one?* That had been the underlying theme of male employment criteria for millennia.

And if those sports cards were any indication, Badger Jenkins certainly was a pretty one.

His face was a perfect intersection of lines and planes—the straight nose, the cleft chin, eyes the brown of Colombian coffee. *The better to drown you in, my dear.* . . . Ancient eyes that seemed to hold the sorrows of the world. Saint's eyes.

Oh, Badger Jenkins had won the gene pool, all right.

In those beautiful eyes it would be easy to read complexity and depth where none might exist. To build him a soul and then proceed to fall in love with it. The oldest of biological traps.

That was exactly why *pretty* wasn't a safe commodity. *Pretty* is coral snakes and lightning bolts and the elegant spirals of plague DNA. She thought that to see such perfection in a human figure ought to trigger a signal in your brain that said: *Run!*

Well, Suzie told herself, she was only the attorney for the business deal. She wouldn't have to work with him. All she had to do was make him an offer on behalf of her clients. So what if he was handsome? He probably had an IQ of room temperature and the ego of a Turkish sultan. Spending an hour in conversation with this warrior angel would give her a tale to dine out on in the party circuit for months to come. Since she had to talk to him, she might as well enjoy it.

She had managed to impress Laraine with the magnitude of the offer to Badger—the possibility of another chance to drive in NASCAR, and with some misgivings, the waitress had agreed to phone the news to Badger himself, *assuming that his cell phone got any reception out there on the lake.*

Suzie accepted a cup of coffee and a week-old copy of the *Marengo Herald,* and sat down in a booth to await further developments. After a few minutes of muffled conversation, Laraine announced that Badger himself would be along *directly,* which in the South could mean anything from five minutes to an hour and a half. Suzie nodded and continued to study the Vidalia onion recipes on page six of the paper. She sipped her coffee and wondered what Badger Jenkins would be having to drink if he did show up.

From the look of that menacing photo of him on the Web site, his drink of choice would be vodka and kerosene. She didn't see it on the beverage menu.

Directly translated to eighteen minutes and one free refill of black coffee before she heard a soft drawling voice say, "I understand you're looking for me."

Slowly, she lowered the newspaper—and kept lowering it.

The Angel of Death had apparently sent a cherub in his place. This boy—well, maybe not a boy, exactly; he wasn't very tall, but apparently he was as tall as he was going to get, because there were touches of gray in his brown hair. Was he thirty-five? Forty, maybe?

She looked into a pair of dark, earnest eyes that made her think that if the werewolf legend ever worked in reverse, so that a golden retriever could become human, he would look just like this sweet-faced boy: slender, handsome, and deeply sincere. In faded jeans, old work boots, and a T-shirt too worn for the logo to be legible, he stood there, as solemn as a guide dog, waiting to hear how he might help the lady. Was this Badger's younger brother, she wondered. His son, even?

"How do you do?" said Suzie, gearing up to convince yet another Marengo resident that she needed to see their local legend in person. "I am hoping to meet Badger Jenkins."

Solemnly, the were-retriever offered her his paw . . . er, his hand, and said, "Yes, ma'am. I'm him."

"No way!" She turned her exclamation of astonishment into a discreet cough as she struggled to regain her professional composure. Now that she looked at him she could see the resemblance between that fine-featured human face and the symphony of lines and planes that had been transformed into machine-like perfection in the motorsports publicity photos. Amazing what sports cards could imply without actually coming right out and saying it. The scowling six-foot Angel of Death, who looked like he ate kittens for breakfast, was apparently just a well-crafted media image of this angelic-looking kid from the backwoods of Georgia, who looked perfectly capable of giving his own breakfast to those aforementioned kittens. Go figure.

He nodded, still looking serious and deeply sincere, as if worried that his ordinariness had distressed her.

She motioned for him to take a seat opposite her in the booth. "I am Suzanne Terrell. I'm from a law firm in Atlanta, and I'm here on behalf of a group of investors to offer you a proposition." *Business proposition,* she corrected herself silently. *Business proposition!* She sighed. *Watch him pounce on that with a leering grin.*

But he was still looking at her with that earnest, faintly worried retriever expression, without a flicker of amusement. "Yes, ma'am?"

She stared into his sorrowful brown eyes, searching for some trace of irony or opportunism, but if it was there, it was masquerading as polite sincerity. *Boy, he's good,* she thought. *He almost has me fooled. And he has the most perfect, regular features. The camera would love him. You could probably sell beachfront property in Kansas with that seraphic face.* She kept staring at him for just a few beats too long, before some still-functioning part of her brain called the rest of her body to order, prompting her to return to the business at hand.

"The people who sent me want to form an all-female NASCAR team," she said. "Well, except for the driver, because there aren't any women drivers in Cup racing, or so they tell me. So they need one Y chromosome to round out the team, and they want it to be yours."

Badger Jenkins's brow furrowed. "What's that mean?"

"What?"

"That Y-thing ?"

"Ah. Chromosome. It means that they need a man to drive the car."

"Oh. But the rest of the team will be women?" He considered it. "Have to be some big ones then. Some of those pit jobs—like gassing and jacking—call for right much size and strength, you know."

Suzie didn't know, but she assumed that the people with the twenty million dollars had taken such things into account. "Well, this is all preliminary," she told him. "They just wanted to talk to you. To see if you're interested."

Badger Jenkins glanced at his watch. "Well, I might be," he said. "If it isn't a p.o.s. car."

"I believe it is a standard stock car," said Suzie. "A Ford, perhaps, or a Dodge."

Laraine, who had been hovering in the background, coffee pot in hand, giggled. "P.O.S. means *piece of shit*," she announced. "That was the problem with his last team, wasn't it, hon? They had an underfunded p.o.s. car, and they wanted him to stand on it, and 'course he wouldn't. Be crazy to've."

Suzie blinked. Apparently, when one comes to north Georgia, one should bring along an interpreter. Well, whatever all that meant, it wasn't her concern. Her mission was simply to arrange a meeting between the investors and their chosen driver. The rest would be someone else's problem.

Badger looked at his watch again, and she found herself faintly annoyed that the prospect of a NASCAR job—not to mention her own elegant self—did not seem sufficient to hold his interest. "I'm sorry," she said sweetly. "Am I keeping you from something?"

He looked uncomfortable. "No, I'm real interested in what you have to say, ma'am. It's just that the body shop closes at five, and I need to get there before Jesse goes home."

"Body shop? You mean, like car repair?"

He nodded unhappily. "Yeah. Only it's not a car I'm taking in. It's a turtle."

Suzie frowned. "I'm sorry. I'm not very familiar with racing terms. What is a turtle?"

Badger gave this question serious consideration. "Well," he said at last, "it's sorta like a lizard but with a hard shell."

"An actual turtle?"

"Uh-huh. This one is about so big." He positioned his hands to indicate something the size of a garbage can lid.

"Do you mean that you are taking a live turtle to a car repair shop?" She was sidetracked in spite of herself.

"Have to," said Badger as solemnly as ever. "I found it in the lake just as I was putting in to come here. Motorboat propeller had tore up his shell pretty bad, so I hauled him in and put him in the truck. I figured me and Jesse could fix him."

Suzie stared. "How?"

"Fiberglass. You know how to apply fiberglass for repair work? No? Well, it comcs in a close-woven mat, and you just mix it with resin and paint it onto the split part of the shell, smooth it down with a roller, maybe sand it down after it dries, and it'll just knit that shell right back up into one piece. Only take a couple hours, I reckon."

She was gazing into those drowned eyes again in bewildered fascination. "So you are going to spend the evening saving the life of an injured turtle?"

"Uh-huh." He glanced away. "Laraine, do you have any lettuce you were going to throw away? Figure he might get hungry while we're waiting for the stuff to harden."

Like one who is hypnotized yet still awake, Suzie saw her hand place itself on the young man's arm, and she heard herself say, "Do you need any help? I could come with you. Maybe bring you some dinner while you're working?"

"Well, thank you," said Badger. "But I expect you ought to be getting back to Atlanta before it starts getting dark. The roads aren't too well marked up here. But thank you for coming. And you can tell those folks I'd be glad to talk to them about driving."

He stopped just long enough to accept a plateful of chopped

lettuce from Laraine; then he was gone. Suzie stared for a few moments at the door to the café, and then, still dazed, she shook a
packet of *Sweet & Low* into her empty coffee cup and tried to
drink it.

From behind the counter Laraine was watching her with a pity-
ing smile.

Finally, Suzie murmured, "But he's so sweet. From what you
said, I thought he'd be some kind of leering, sex-crazed playboy."

Laraine shook her head sadly. "Oh, no, hon. You got the wrong
end of the stick. Badger ain't the motorboat. He's the turtle."

CHAPTER II

Drive My Car

ENGINE NOISE
Your Online Source for NASCAR News & Views

Wonder Women? *Engine Noise* is hearing that a new team is being formed in NASCAR—with a twist. The crew chief and pit crew will all be female. An all-woman group of investors, spearheaded by chemical heiress Christine Berenson, is supposed to be putting together this Ladies' Team for NASCAR Cup racing with the intention of running a full season beginning next year. The wheel man will be a guy, though, because they need a veteran Cup driver to add some experience to this novice team. Who will they choose as their token man? Berenson isn't ready to announce yet, and since *EN*'s prognostication skills are *rusty*, we might miss the *mark,* so to *ward* off all your questions, we say: "Don't *badger* us for an answer!"

#30

Christine Berenson tapped her computer screen with one perfectly manicured nail. "That last bit is in code somehow, isn't it?" she asked her visitor.

The big man leaned across the desk to read the *Engine Noise* article with its vastly premature, yet accurate, assessment of the new NASCAR team. Then he settled back in the leather visitor's chair with an enigmatic smile. "Of course, it is. In that last sentence the writer managed to work in the names of Rusty Wallace, Mark Martin, and Ward Burton—all veteran drivers who might conceivably be lured back into Cup racing if the right deal came along. Oh, and Badger Jenkins, of course. So they hedged their bets a little on who the driver would be, but they did come up with the right answer. They usually do."

She frowned. "How do they find out these things?"

Her visitor shrugged, seemingly unperturbed by this security leak. In the world of motorsports, the man was a cross between a rock star and the secretary of state. He knew everything and everyone, and in another sphere of influence, he had been an acquaintance of Christine Berenson for twenty years. They had served on several advisory boards together and had exchanged pleasantries at the usual charity events that pass for a social life among the moneyed classes. The man's current role was that of a friendly expert, giving her advice out of the goodness of his heart, because of their longstanding association. She thought of him as the Big Wheel.

"I wouldn't worry about it, Christine," he said. "*Engine Noise* just reports rumors, which means that word about your team has already leaked out from somewhere. At least this way you know that the news is in the wind. And it isn't such a worrying disclosure, after all, is it? You were planning to announce it soon anyhow."

"But how did they know?"

He shrugged. "People call in tips to the Web site, just for the hell of it, I guess. The people at *Engine Noise* talk to hauler drivers, waitresses, shop people. You've been looking for a place around Mooresville to locate your operation, aren't you? Maybe your real-estate agent blabbed. Or someone could have overheard your dinner conversation in a restaurant. But it will be common knowledge soon enough, once your NASCAR application is formally approved, so why fret about it?"

Christine sighed. "NASCAR application. You have to *apply* to join this sport, as if it were a country club."

"It is, in a way. NASCAR is the only privately owned sport in the world. You should be fine, though. They are chiefly interested in whether you intend to play by the rules and whether you can afford to compete. I don't think there's any question of that."

"No, I suppose not," said Christine. "But it is a rather unsettling feeling to know that one is being watched."

The man laughed. "Get used to it then! NASCAR is such a small world that you can dial a wrong number and still talk. But by and large, they're nice people, and if you need any advice, most of them will be glad to help you."

"Will they give me recommendations? Our biggest problem is that we don't know anybody. How do we find mechanics and fabricators and all the rest of the people we need?"

He raised his eyebrows. "Mechanics and fabricators. All female?"

"That won't be possible," she said, with the air of someone rehearsing a sound bite. "Behind the scenes we need good, qualified people regardless of who they are. I just need to know how to find them."

"Then hire a team manager who does know the sport, Christine, and then trust that team manager's judgment. The less you meddle, the better, I'd say, until you get a better sense of what you're doing. And don't expect to do a lot of winning in your first year of competition. It will take a while for all the components to jell, you know."

"But surely if we hire top-notch people . . . ?"

"Experience counts," he reminded her. "You specified an all-female pit crew. That will put you a few laps short on experience right there. They'll learn soon enough, I expect, but you mustn't expect too much too soon."

"What if the sponsors get impatient?"

He considered the point. "Winning is pleasant," he conceded. "But all in all, most sponsors would rather have a personable driver who is popular with the fans than an obnoxious winner who endears himself to no one. Ideally, what you want is a handsome nice guy who wins."

"Jeff Gordon."

He smiled. She was learning fast. "Exactly. If you could afford him. Which you cannot."

She sighed. "It would take the economy of a third-world country to afford him. Imagine our surprise when we discovered that."

"It's not like hiring a pilot, you know, Christine. You're not hiring a high-speed chauffeur. There's a lot more involved in the job than just driving the car. Your driver is a brand, an image. He can attract sponsors or scare them off. But tell me: Why Badger Jenkins?"

Christine stared. *"Have you ever seen him?"*

He laughed. "Almost all of him," he said dryly. "I once saw him change into his firesuit before a race. I can't say that the sight of any of them in skivvies does much for my blood pressure, but you might be favorably impressed."

She thought it best to ignore that remark. "Badger is certainly personable. Photogenic. People seem to like him. To us he seemed an obvious choice."

Her NASCAR mentor was silent for so long that she thought he wasn't going to answer, but at last he said, "You know, Badger has had a hiatus in his career. Spent some time between rides, which isn't a usual thing. Didn't you ask yourself why that was?"

"No. We thought we were lucky to have a chance to hire him. I suppose we chalked it up to Fate. But since you brought it up, tell me: Why was he available?"

He hesitated. "Well, Badger is a nice young man . . ."

"Oh God! What is it? Drugs? Alcohol? Girl Scouts? *Boy* Scouts?"

"None of the above, Christine. The word around the garage is that he's just a little laid-back, that's all."

"A race car driver? *Laid-back*? You mean he loses? He won't take chances?"

"Not at all. On the track he's a mad dog. He'll try to put that car in places I wouldn't try to fit a shoe horn. Oh, he's brave enough, all right. Except that I'm not sure it really counts as brave if you're so deep in denial that you think death is something that only happens to other people."

"Never mind that. You admit he's a good driver. I know for a fact that he's gorgeous. So what's the matter with him?"

The Big Wheel sighed. "Nothing is the matter with him—at least not by the standards of the old days in racing. But times change. Badger is an old-style Cup driver. Southern, fearless, and likable. If he had been around in the era of Cale Yarborough and Junior Johnson, he'd have been a champion. But now—"

"Now?"

"He just wants to race. He thinks that's what his job is. Drive the car. Then he'd like to go home. He doesn't work in the textile mill like some of the old-timers did on weekdays, but he definitely thinks he can have another life besides Cup racing. And he *can't.*"

"He can't?"

"Not in this day and age, Christine. He has to live and breathe racing. The team is his family. The job is his life. When he isn't involved in the mechanics of racing, he ought to be giving interviews, doing charity work, filming commercials, and generally keeping himself on the map of celebrity. Dating a movie star would be a nice touch."

She shuddered. "You make it sound as if we bought him, instead of just hiring him to race on Sundays."

The Big Wheel considered it. "We pay them a lot of money," he said at last. "And it isn't forever, you know. The career of an athlete isn't terribly long in most cases. Twenty years if he's lucky. Anyhow, if he doesn't want the job on those terms, there's ten thousand other guys who would crawl over broken glass to get it. You'd be wise not to let him forget that."

"Thanks. I'll do my best. But he *is* a good driver, right?"

"He's a natural. Now it's up to you to help him win."

"And how do I manage that?"

"Hire the best people you can find; pay them enough to keep them; don't meddle too much; let them know you appreciate them; and give them the wherewithal to win."

She smiled. "As simple as that, huh?"

He shrugged. "Well, it's like *diet and exercise*. Everybody knows how to do it. The question is: Can you make yourself do what it takes even when it isn't easy?"

"I guess I'll find out," she said.

Ralph Earnhardt. Marvin Panch. Benny Parsons. Bobby Allison. She had it now.

Julie Carmichael stuffed the scrap of newspaper back into the pocket of her jeans. She wondered how other people remembered phone numbers. Or license plates. Street addresses. It was the only advantage she could think of to her unconventional upbringing: every number to her was a NASCAR name and face, which meant that she seldom forgot a number or transposed the digits. The difference between 12 and 21 was Ryan Newman versus Ricky Rudd—you weren't likely to mix up those two. Her skill at remembering numbers was certainly useful, but it didn't make up for the rest of her bleak childhood.

She remembered all the Spam and pinto bean dinners . . . the smell of motor oil and gasoline that pervaded the small frame house and never quite went away . . . the bill collectors she'd been sent to the door to deal with, in hopes that a wide-eyed little girl could convince them to leave. Those were hard times, but Daddy always said they would get better. Prosperity was just around the next turn in the track, he used to say. Only it wasn't.

She had been an only child back in Rowan County, but she hadn't felt like one. The real child of the household had been Daddy's pride and joy—a hulking steel monster with a room of its own: the garage. For as long as Julie could remember, that car, or one of its predecessors, had taken precedence over her. All the spare time that Daddy could steal from his day job went into his relationship with that car—tinkering with it, racing it, repairing it. The car always got fed, got new shoes, got "doctored"—whether she did or not. Like some revered male heir, to whom its parents sacrificed everything in hopes that it would someday support them, the car was catered to, and the family often went without so that the monster's needs could be met. The car was their hope of prosperity. That had been the plan, certainly. That hunk of steel and plastic was supposed to win races, and ultimately carry them all away to some happily-ever-after beyond Victory Lane, and from there onto bigger tracks and grander rides, until finally they'd have a fancy house and enough money so that everybody could have new shoes and a second helping of meat.

Well, it hadn't worked like that.

Despite all the sacrifices, Big Brother the Car had never lived up to its promise, and Daddy had died too young to make it work or to wise up and try to do something else with his life. Julie decided that it was up to her to even the score between humans and machines, and she figured that cars owed her something to make up for the lousy childhood she'd had. Early on she had worked out a strategy to succeed. She treated herself like a car. She stayed as pretty as she could, because paint schemes matter, and she made excellent grades in high school to streamline her path to greater things. She stayed away from roughneck boys who would have constituted a detour in her life plan, and finally, she won a scholarship to Virginia Tech, where she'd studied automotive engineering with a fierce determination that allowed her no time for socializing or extracurricular activities. She graduated from Tech with highest honors, because she had pursued car knowledge like a bounty hunter going after a fugitive, which in a way she was. After graduation she had her pick of job offers, but instead of heading for a research and development job with one of the big car manufacturers, she had chosen to devote her talents to NASCAR.

Her advisor's jaw had dropped when she told him. "NASCAR, Julie?" he'd said. "How could you possibly choose that over an industry job?"

She'd smiled and said that she thought it might be an adventure, which was true. Industry jobs would always be there, but she thought she'd like to try stock car racing first. "Daddy would have been proud," she'd said primly, speaking of her family's racing tradition with a nostalgic pride she did not feel.

She still had nightmares about standing on the roof of an old sedan with a stopwatch in her hand, ready to time a car that hurtled past her at breakneck speed. She could still feel the dust in her throat and the chill of the night air on her bare legs. *Carmichael.*

Her father's folks had been of Irish descent. Maybe in an earlier time they would have been horse crazy, instead of obsessed with cars. Maybe this obsession with speed was bred in the bone. Sometimes she could feel it, too, but mostly she felt the rage of the slighted child toward the hated favorite. Now, though, she would be in charge.

We got him.
Christine Berenson held up the photo in front of her as if it were a mirror.
So this is Badger Jenkins.
As always with Christine Berenson, the professional reaction came before the personal one. She acknowledged that whatever his shortcomings educationally and socially, the camera obviously loved Badger Jenkins, definitely an asset in a world where money buys speed, because sponsors provide the money. Win or lose, a pretty boy in the driver's seat could bring in corporate sponsors, not to mention selling a million tee shirts, coffee mugs, and other assorted ritual items to his besotted admirers. Her advisors said that Badger Jenkins was a good driver—a *seat-of-the-pants* driver, all nerves and instinct—but she was more pleased that the other end of him was marketable. For business reasons.
Well, mostly for business reasons.
The face that looked back at her from the photo looked nothing like hers. It was a strong, masculine face that seemed composed of sharp edges—prominent cheekbones, a blade of a nose, a jutting jaw—even the brown eyes were piercing. It wasn't an angry face, though. Focused, perhaps. Determined.
Struggling to have a thought, Christine told herself with a wry smile, fighting the attraction of that face. He was, after all, just a race car driver. Imagine trying to make him sit through an opera.
She sighed. If their genders were reversed, she could keep him as a pet and no one would think twice about it, but women were denied that luxury. They were expected to marry someone even more powerful than themselves, and that usually meant someone older and more sharklike. This little one-trick pony would probably end his career in half a dozen years with two million dollars in

the bank and four concussions, and think himself both rich and lucky. No, you couldn't ally yourself with him on any formal basis. Idly, she ran her forefinger along the perfect jawline in the photo.

But he was undeniably handsome, in the same way that a thoroughbred or a Harrier jet is beautiful: perfection of design with no conscious desire to please. The man was looking away from the camera, absorbed in some private reverie of his own, indifferent to the effect those perfect features might have on the observer. He was too busy being himself to care what anybody thought about him—exactly like a stallion.

That's what he reminded her of: her first horse. That little bundle of nerves that was so beautiful and so much stronger than she was. She had to learn, by sheer force of will, to get the better of him by out-thinking him. It was a lesson that had served her well, and one worth remembering now.

This man looked as if he didn't care what anyone thought about him as long as he could do whatever it was he was determined to do. Win races, she supposed.

She wondered what it would feel like to be so unencumbered of the feelings of others. Certainly she had never known such self-possession. As far back as she could remember, the pressure had been there to be pretty, to be smart, to be pleasing to others. First Mummy had instilled in her the message that people only liked pretty girls, slender girls, smiling girls. And if she had doubted the truth of those early lessons, then half a dozen years of adolescence would have shown her the light, because to be an ugly duckling in the world of private schools and debutante parties was to experience hell on earth. The poor, chubby, frizzy-haired beast on her hall had swallowed a bottle of aspirin, had her stomach pumped, and then went away forever, giggling with relief and joy.

What would it feel like to exercise just because you enjoyed it, rather than in social self-defense? To befriend people because they were interesting, and not because they were useful? To live without second-guessing yourself every waking moment?

One might as well ask a thoroughbred. Certainly this pretty boy was not up to philosophical discussions. But that was all right.

She would do the thinking for the team, and she would see that he was treated well and kept happy. Just as she would have looked after a thoroughbred had the other form of racing appealed to her instead.

"But why would you want to invest in a stock car?" Tate had asked her, in mild bewilderment, as if she'd ordered oysters in May.

She had given him a vague smile and a little shrug, trying to formulate a polite response. It wasn't as if he actually *cared*. It was, after all, *her* money. "I don't know," she said. "Horses are so passé, I suppose."

He nodded, not really interested in anything she did, but as unfailingly polite as six generations of inbreeding could possibly make him. "Yes, one does feel that the sport is somewhat quaint in this age of lasers and space shuttles."

She nodded. They vaguely knew of people in northern Virginia who kept polo teams, and certainly Indy racing was fashionably daring in their social circle, but she rather fancied the idea of cars that looked like actual street vehicles and the reverse snob appeal of stock car racing. NASCAR was indeed a millionaire's sport, even if few people realized that fact. It was different. Christine liked being different, as long as she did not incur any social punishment for it. Stock car racing promised not to be boring. The other women with whom she had formed this venture all sounded so idealistic, talking about opportunities for women and automotive safety research, and she had murmured agreement with all these lofty goals, but really her motives were much more basic than that.

And it was *her* money.

Tate, making a noble effort to keep the conversational ball rolling, said, "Well, I suppose cars are easier to repair than horses."

She nodded, as if this had been a consideration. Then, amusing herself by coming as close to the truth as she dared, Christine had said, "And after all, darling, what is the point of owning a horse if you can't ride it?"

Badger Jenkins. Oh, yes.

*   *   *

Christine Berenson looked at the stack of reports on her desk and sighed. Who knew that starting a sports venture could be so . . . well . . . corporate?

She supposed that it made sense, really. Everyone knew that NASCAR was a multibillion-dollar business. The only family-owned sport in the world. But somehow the idea of investing in a form of entertainment obscured the fact that it was simply a business like anything else. With a grimace, she pictured the operators of the Roman Colosseum toting up their expenses for lion upkeep and arena personnel against the projected gate receipts of the games.

First, they'd had to line up sponsors, because you couldn't even play the game without twenty million dollars or so to bankroll the operation. It was amazing how many months of planning and meeting and schmoozing had to take place before the gentleman could start his engine. The race may go at 180 mph, but the preliminary phase went at a snail's pace. So much to plan and negotiate.

Find a suitable property to use as a race shop. They had decided to rent one in the vicinity of Mooresville rather than go to the extra expense of new construction, because, after all, one never knew whether the venture would turn out to be successful or not. Most of the race shops were within hailing distance of Mooresville anyhow, which meant that finding some suitable but vacant garage space was a feasible plan, and the personnel to run the operation would also be available locally.

She sighed, looking at the morass of papers on her desk. Stacks of job applications and résumés and letters of recommendation. Who knew how many people were required to run even a one-car racing team? She marveled at the figures before her. Anyone who thought that stock car racing was one man driving one car was decades out of the loop. The venture was beginning to remind her of the space program: a few people going up in high-tech machines, backed by a small army of engineers and technicians on the ground. Same with racing, apparently. The race shop, once established and outfitted, would house dozens of support personnel who would never even go to the speedways themselves. These "shop dogs" built the cars, refurbished old or damaged ones, engineered the motors, tinkered with body design to gain the best advantage for a given track, and did a dozen other things to ensure that the driver had the best car the team could afford to field. Engineers . . . fabricators . . . mechanics . . . secretaries . . . janitors . . . publicists . . . It added up to a lot of salaries. Who knew?

She had been vaguely aware of the need for a pit crew for the race itself—people to change tires and put fuel in the car—but this behind-the-scenes infrastructure of personnel had taken her by surprise, although she didn't know why it should have. Everything was complex these days. How naive they had been back when they had thought that securing the services of Badger Jenkins was the answer to all their problems. Now, she sometimes found herself thinking that he hardly mattered at all. Certainly his talent could not compensate for poor engineering, bad equipment, or a lack of research and development. That face would sell a lot of tee shirts, though. And it ought to lure in a fair number of sponsors that wanted a good-looking athlete to personify their products.

Every day she was finding out that she needed answers to questions that had never even occurred to her when the project began. Fortunately, she had seasoned advisors on board to answer those questions, but still it gave her pause to think of how little they had known about the logistics of it all when they began. There were questions that had never even occurred to them at the outset.

How does the pit crew get to far-flung race tracks like Sonoma or Phoenix or New Hampshire? And most of the races these days were well beyond driving distance from the greater Charlotte area, home of the majority of race teams. Where do you house them for race weekends, and who feeds them?

None of these minor problems of logistics had occurred to them when they began the team, but little by little, practicality had intruded upon the daydream of owning a human racehorse, and one by one, questions were asked and answered, often by courtly old gentlemen who seemed within a syllable of using the term "little lady" in their discourse. But however antiquated the men's world views, their advice had been eminently practical, and little by little, the answers fell into place, so that now, many months later, they could actually say that the team existed; that it was housed in adequate, if not luxurious, quarters, in Cabarrus County; and that it was staffed by competent professional engineers, mechanics, and other support persons necessary to the running of a race team.

This behind-the-scenes crew was, necessarily, predominantly male. This gender bias was unfortunate but essential, Christine thought with a sigh. Fielding an all-female team sounded charming and democratic on the face of it, but the truth was: one simply could not fill *all* the behind-the-scenes technical positions with women. Racing had for too long been an all-male domain, so that most of the current expertise, the hands-on experience of stock car racing, resided in male brains, and the fact was that one simply could not do without them. After a brief meeting and a careful examination of the cold, hard facts, the investors agreed that there was no choice in the matter. The behind-the-scenes personnel would have to be mostly male, and that's all there was to it. But the pit crew was the most visible part of the operation, anyhow, aside from the driver, and in that area they did have an element of choice.

She had called a meeting of her fellow investors to, the cliché made her smile, *bring them up to speed*. Technically, they were owners, too, but she was really the one in charge. Some of them just chipped in their money for a lark, believing that her venture was a good investment, and certainly were able to afford the loss if it wasn't. It was *fun*. A couple of the others were interested in the sport as fans, but they had promised to give her a free hand in the running of the team. But they enjoyed getting together, hearing about her adventures in this brave new world. Sometimes she felt like the star of a private reality show for millionaires: *Survivor: NASCAR*. But she didn't mind entertaining them, considering how much money they'd entrusted her with. And if she learned the sport well, and if luck was on her side, then in a little while nobody would be laughing at her. That was the important part of the enterprise. Badger was just a side bet with herself. The icing on the cake.

"I'm working on assembling a pit crew," Christine told the assembled gathering. "How hard can that be? Change the tires, put gas in the car, clean the windshield—"

One of the younger women raised her hand. "Actually, Christine, I read that race car windshields are tear-off sheets of—"

"I know," said Christine through clenched teeth. After all these months and all this work, how could they think she wouldn't know that? She forced a smile. "I was simply making a point. Thank you, Faye. But the premise is sound. Anyone of reasonable strength and agility can be trained to perform those tasks in a relatively short time—unlike the intricacies of engineering and mechanics, which take years of study and experience. Fortunately, people at the race and television viewers will see the pit crew and not the shop personnel, so in accordance with our intended goal, to the casual observer, the team will still look all female."

"Well, except for Badger," said Diane Hodges, the former Miss Texas who had married into Oil. "He could make my toes curl through a locked door."

A large framed poster of Badger Jenkins in his firesuit hung on the wall of the office. With one accord, the investors turned to study it. One or two smiled approvingly, and one of them said, "He reminds me of my grandson."

"Perhaps we should have tried harder to find a female race car driver," said the investor from Winnetka. "There's that girl at Indy—"

"We can't afford her," Christine replied with the assurance of one who has had this argument so many times that her response was a sound bite. "There are half a dozen women in the lower echelons of stock car racing as well, but either they are under contract to one of the big teams in development programs or they are out of our price range. Or both."

"I like Badger just fine," said Miss Texas.

"I'm sure that a lot of women will agree with you," said Christine. "That bodes well for our recruiting of new secondary sponsors. Companies who sell primarily to women will want an image that appeals to them."

"Oh, honey, he does."

"And remember that souvenir merchandising is a significant source of income in motorsports. Pretty faces sell tee shirts . . . hats . . . coffee mugs. The potential is huge. Even if he loses, we'll still win. But, of course, we want to win."

CHAPTER III

Hail to the Chief

Grace Buell Hoskins Tuggle hoped that the job interview wasn't going to include lunch, not that she minded a free meal, but from the looks of the ladies on the interview committee, every one of 'em about two ribs short of a shadow, she figured their idea of a noonday meal would be a lettuce leaf and an Ex-Lax pill. They were skinny enough to be drivers' wives for sure, but they looked a little too steely-eyed and Old Money for that.

Now back in the old days, when Daddy had been racing, the wives were whoever the racers had happened to marry back when they started out working in the factory or wherever, and their lined faces and plump bodies testified to a lifetime of hard work, starchy food, and infinite patience with race-crazed husbands. Grace, who was pleased that her initials also stood for *Grievous Bodily Harm,* but who preferred simply to be known as Tuggle, did not hold with fad diets and plastic surgery. In her opinion, if being a willowy size two got you a race car driver for a husband, then they ought to put warning labels on Slim-Fast.

Wheel men! Lawn jockeys with 800-horsepower egos. Fortunately, she was past the age to confuse *foolhardy* with *sexy,* which was just as well, because no driver worth his salt would listen to a pretty girl giving him orders over the head set anyhow. They'd listen to her, though. If they had any sense they would.

Her daddy had been a force to be reckoned with on the racing circuit, back in the days when North Carolina was the hub of the world—Hickory, Asheville, Wilkesboro, Winston-Salem. She often said that her blood type was *Hi-Test*. And then there were her two husbands—the driving one from her wild younger days, who had put her heart so far into the wall that she thought she'd never get over him. Well, she hadn't really, that was the truth of it. But at least she had learned from that experience that restrictor plates were not a bad thing for the human heart. Her second husband, Doyle, was a mechanic, and she claimed that she'd married him "for entertainment." He didn't take your breath away like the first one did, but he didn't make you want to put a hose to the exhaust pipe, either, so she reckoned it evened out—less joy, less sorrow. That's what getting older mostly meant anyhow.

Drivers. Like tigers. A lot of fun to look at, maybe even okay for a brief, wary encounter, but try to hold on to one and he will rip you to shreds. Well, maybe times had changed with all these West Coast pretty boys coming into the sport, but Tuggle didn't think so, and she rejoiced in the fact that she was too old to care.

She wondered if she ought to offer the benefit of her wisdom to this charmed circle of designer-clad ladies, but she decided against it. They were too old to care, too, whether they knew it or not. And maybe they were into the sport for philosophical reasons. An all-woman team. Well, whatever kept the sponsors happy.

She assumed an expression of polite interest, which on her bulldog features looked like a double-dog-dare, as she waited for the questioning to commence.

The regal one they called Christine began by saying, "Perhaps you could tell us a little bit about yourself, Grace."

Tuggle winced at the sound of her given name, sounding like a sermon title in the precise diction of this high-maintenance woman. "It's Tuggle, if it's all the same to you," she corrected her. "As for my qualifications, my daddy ran dirt track and Late Model Stocks around the region—wherever he could afford to go and still keep his day job. Back then family was about the only pit crew you could afford, so he trained me and my brothers early on." As if in answer to an unspoken question, she added, "They're dead now." She kept her voice steady—well, mostly steady—willing herself not to think about little Gary, dead in a rice paddy in Vietnam, and Cole, the daredevil, hitting the wall at Hickory in those days before fuel cells, when the word *fire* stuck in your throat.

"And I believe you raced yourself at one time."

She nodded. "They used to have Powderpuff Derbies, as they called 'em. Good for attracting a crowd to the track on off nights. Daddy said I was almost as good as Cole, but, of course, I quit that foolishness once I grew up. Keeping a marriage going is a dern sight harder than winning an old stock car race."

"Times have changed since those days," said one of the younger women in a not-from-around-here accent. "NASCAR is rocket science now. What makes you think you could manage a team in a sport dominated by engineers?"

"Well, I reckon you will have engineers," said Tuggle. "Strategy hasn't changed. Maybe the cars are better now, and NASCAR keeps adding rules as fast as folks can think up ways around 'em, but it's still the same old sport it used to be."

"Now, we realize that our aim of having an all-women team is a bit unusual."

Tuggle shrugged. "Well, it's not traditional, of course. Back in my day, the old-time drivers had a saying: *No tits in the pits.* But times do change, don't they?" She flashed a wolfish smile at the circle of frozen faces.

"Times do indeed change," murmured Christine. "We consulted various experts, you know—fitness instructors, physicians, engineers—and they seem to think that there's no reason a female pit crew couldn't do the job, providing that they were carefully chosen and properly trained."

"Likely as not," Tuggle agreed. Women came in all shapes and sizes, especially in these exercise-crazed days. She'd known a few gals who could bench-press tractors. Find some of them and there wouldn't be a problem.

"Of course, we will need someone to oversee the operation. I understand that is a customary to have a team manager and a crew chief, but we see no reason why a competent person couldn't do both those things as one job. What do you think?"

Tuggle thought she'd have to have had more than one Bloody Mary for breakfast to tell this group of wine and cheese ladies what she thought about anything. She needed the job, and if that meant agreeing to use St. Christopher's medals for hubcaps, she'd go along with it to keep the team owners happy.

"And we are already in negotiations with a driver. This one." With a proprietary smirk, Christine Berenson slid an eight-by-ten photo out of a folder and passed it across the desk.

Tuggle contemplated the picture of Badger Jenkins, who was looking smolderingly at the camera, his legs spread far enough apart for a prostate exam. She snorted, unimpressed.

"Yeah, I know Badger," she said. "He's all right. Good seat-of-the-pants driver."

Two of the investors glanced at each other, lips twitching. "We noticed that," one of them said.

Tuggle scowled. She didn't hold with people who treated drivers like cat toys. Or with drivers treating fans like that, for that matter. "*Seat of the pants* means a driver who can react quickly and handle things by instinct, whatever happens out there. A natural." She glanced again at the photo. "I can see how you might misinterpret that phrase, though, with this to go by. That boy keeps sitting like that, he's gonna get himself arrested."

"For indecent exposure?"

"For false advertising."

The investors glanced at one another, and then wisely decided not to pursue this line of questioning. "So, would you be comfortable working with Badger Jenkins?"

She considered it, knowing that the bosses wanted only a yes/no answer from her. What they really wanted was a *yes* answer as quickly as possible, but it wasn't that simple. Like any Cup driver, Badger had his good points and his bad points. The question was whether he was good enough to make putting up with the rest worthwhile, and more importantly, whether the team could get anybody better who was likely to be less trouble. On the whole, she thought that they couldn't.

Would she be *comfortable* working with Badger? Well, he was a sweet boy, no meanness in him, as far as she could see. He could be stubborn and he could show temper, but he wouldn't be a race car driver if that weren't the case. She did know Badger, and she believed in the adage "Better the devil you know than the one you don't." At least she knew where the trouble was. He might be a pussycat at sponsor events, but it practically took a cattle prod to get him to one. Sometimes he was so handsome it would take your breath away, but he might forget to shave for a day or two, and usually he schlepped around in old clothes that Goodwill wouldn't have taken off your hands. But skinny boys in firesuits looked like warrior angels. Badger *gift-wrapped* would sell some tee shirts, all right.

He could be slipperier than a weasel in getting out of things he didn't want to do, and he'd roll in to the track around midday on Thursday, unless you twisted his arm to show up earlier. You had to watch him every minute, or else he'd slope off to do his own thing—trout fishing, flying model airplanes, or Lord knows what. He thought that anything that wasn't spelled out in his contract was a personal favor on his part, necessary or not. And nobody could make him understand that publicity and interviews were important. She understood exactly why his previous team had let him go. She knew she'd have to have a come-to-Jesus talk with him at least once a week to keep him in line.

On the other hand, he wasn't a bad bargain as drivers went. He'd be sober when he needed to be. He didn't treat women like party favors. And he was a loyal friend who kept his word once he gave it. You could trust him—if you shouted at him enough.

She saw no reason to share his faults with the team owners. Badger would be her problem.

"Yeah," she said, "I reckon I can work with old Badger."

She heard several sighs of relief, and then one of the older women said, "And do you think Badger Jenkins will be able to deal with an all-female pit crew?"

Tuggle had thought about that. "Sort of like *Snow White and the Seven Dwarfs*? Only in this case, it'll be *seven* Snow Whites and *one* dwarf."

"I'm sorry, Ms. Tuggle . . . did you say *dwarf?*"

She waved away the question. "Figure of speech is all. He ain't that little—for a driver, that is. Mark Martin could have about driven a die-cast. I reckon Badger and I would stand nose to nose. 'Course I outweigh him," she finished cheerfully, ignoring the shudders of the scrawnier investors. She imagined them later pushing away untouched plates of salad. "But you were asking about temperament, weren't you?"

Several of the women nodded, perhaps not trusting themselves to speak.

"Well, it will mostly depend on how well they do their jobs, doncha know. A driver would be happy with a tribe of chimpanzees if they could get him out of the pit on four new tires in twelve seconds. You take much over thirteen, though, and a band of angels wouldn't satisfy him. So get me good people and don't worry about whether their booties were pink or blue."

There was another awkward silence while the investors exchanged more significant looks. Must be telepaths, thought Tuggle. Finally, Christine said, *"Find you good people?* But surely that is your task, not ours?"

"Well, you're the bosses," said Tuggle amiably. "Like you said before, most teams nowadays have a crew manager and a crew chief. It's the manager who hires the personnel, and the crew chief who makes sure they function smoothly as a team." Noting the dismay on the women's faces, Tuggle added kindly, "Of course, there's no law that says you have to have a team manager. They never bothered with such things back in the day. Why, Bill Elliott's crew was mostly his family, and he certainly did all right for himself, so I guess if you want me to handle both jobs, I can do it about as well as anybody. Hire the crew. Hmmm."

Handling both jobs would be more work, but it also meant more independence—one less person to answer to. Grace Tuggle prized independence above rubies, and she was even willing to work harder to maintain her autonomy.

"You'll need to pay me some more money to do both jobs," she said.

No point in being a damn fool about it, she reasoned. "I'll do both jobs for $950,000." That way she didn't have frighten them with the word "million," but crew chiefs didn't come cheap. To sweeten the deal, she added, "I can save us some money on the pit crew by hiring people who can do double duty."

"I thought we had to have seven over-the-wall crewmen."

Tuggle nodded. "Yes, but that's for race day. What's the point of hiring people who only work a day or two a week? If we get enough applicants for the jobs, we can hire the ones who also have another skill we can use. Say, a mechanic or a computer person, or someone who can also drive the hauler. That way we'll have fewer workers on the payroll and a more efficient team. We also need a tire specialist—well, we can probably train a likely candidate, within reason."

"What's a tire specialist?"

Tuggle swallowed a sign of exasperation. "That's the person who inflates the tires. Well, first we let the air out of the tire and refill it with nitrogen."

They stared at her in puzzled fascination. "With *nitrogen*? Why on earth—?"

"I don't know, but everybody does it. It's not illegal. Trust me, okay? And when you hire an engineer, ask him—*her*—why NASCAR teams prefer to run on nitrogen-inflated tires. And as for tire-soaking—"

"What's that?" asked Christine.

That was illegal. Most everybody did that, too, but she probably ought not to discuss it with people new to the sport. Tuggle took a long, fortifying breath; then she said, "Well, you want to wash the tires before the race to make sure they haven't picked up any bits of debris that could cause a blowout." It seemed plausible enough, as lies went, and no one questioned her explanation.

"So, you're saying that we can streamline the team and save money on salaries by hiring people who can do two jobs. But wouldn't such experts cost more?"

"Well, you have to have them anyhow. Shop jobs may take skill and experience, but anyone reasonably spry and willing can be taught to serve on the pit crew. We'll just hire the people who are willing to do both jobs at a salary we can afford to pay. That suit you?"

They nodded, looking relieved that she was looking out for the team's budget. It had been quite a shock to most of them to learn how expensive Cup racing was. A million dollars for a crew chief? More than twenty-five thousand dollars per race for *tires*? No wonder sponsorships were so expensive.

"What about equipment?" said Tuggle. "I take it we're not building the cars from scratch?"

"I got some advice about that," Christine Berenson said. "We're going to buy the chassis from . . . Oh, what is his name? I have it written down somewhere . . ."

"Never mind," said Tuggle. Four guesses would have told her what the name was, but it really didn't matter at this point. "And you're getting the engines from Hendrick?"

"However did you know? I believe that *was* the name."

Tuggle nodded. It had been an educated guess. Hendrick was a five-car race team with about 500 shop dogs at their disposal. If anybody could spare adequate engines for a price, it would be them.

"All right," said Tuggle, "so we buy the components and get our people to overhaul them. That ought to work." It won't win you a championship, she was thinking, but with reasonable skill on the engineers' part and a halfway decent wheel man, it ought to keep you in the game.

"And you've had your application cleared by NASCAR? Got assigned a number and all?"

They nodded. "Apparently you can't pick your own number," one of them remarked.

"Well, no. Teams are assigned numbers. Some of them not in use are still already taken," Tuggle explained.

"We wanted number 7."

"Taken," said Tuggle. "Both 7 and 07; both. Why did you want it in particular?"

They glanced at each other uneasily. "Well, there's a feminine product, Monistat 7 for yeast infections, and we thought—"

Tuggle's eyes glazed over as she tried to picture Badger Jenkins as the spokesperson for a yeast infection product. He'd have to carry pepper spray to the drivers' meetings. Thank God that number was taken by Robby Gordon, who already had a sponsor. She'd have paid money to see Robby Gordon's face if the yeast infection people had approached him about sponsoring his car.

"Twenty-eight would have been a good number, too!" said Diane Hodges, the former Miss Texas. "I think that pharmaceutical company with the birth control pill would have come on board if we could have got that number."

"That was Davey Allison's number," said Tuggle. "And Ernie Irvan's." Both Daytona 500 winners: one of them dead and the other so badly injured he'd never race again. No, you wouldn't see the number 28 back on a NASCAR track anytime soon, and she was glad of it. She wouldn't want to see anything disrespectful done with that number. She didn't want to jinx Badger, either. Repressing a shudder, she said, "So what's our number?"

Christine Berenson said, "NASCAR assigned us the number 86."

Tuggle tried not to wince. Not an auspicious number in Cup racing. It had been used fewer than a dozen times in the past thirty years, and never with any notable success.

"Isn't 86 a slang term for terminating something?" asked one of the women.

"Maybe they want to *eighty-six* a woman's team," another one said.

"It's just a number," said Christine, with the weary patience of one who has had this discussion often. "Randomly assigned, I expect."

"It's okay," said Tuggle. "It's as good a number as any. Better than some. At least it's not a number whose past would over-shadow you, like . . . oh . . . 22." 22. Now that was a number to conjure with. The legendary Fireball Roberts, who had died after a fiery wreck at Charlotte in the sixties; country singer Marty Robbins, who used to try to come in second because he didn't need the prize money; the respected and popular modern drivers Ricky Rudd and Bobby Labonte; and Daytona 500 winners Bobby Allison and Ward Burton. They all had driven the 22. She'd hate to have to compete with that reputation in her first season. At least it wouldn't take much to *eighty-six* the previous reputation of number 86. She said, "So if you've got enough money to buy engines and chassis, you must have a primary sponsor lined up."

"We do. A pharmaceutical company has developed a pill for women—you know, like Viagra. It's supposed to—"

"I know what Viagra does," said Tuggle, hoping to forestall the lecture. "For women, huh? What's this one called?"

"Vagenya."

"Virginia?"

Christine smiled. "Yes, it does sound like the way Southerners pronounce the name of the state, doesn't it? Actually, I think the makers may have been playing with the words 'virginity' and 'vagina,' but who knows where they come up with these peculiar names for drugs nowadays? Anyhow, since it is a women's team, the company decided that we would be a good place to advertise their product. So our sponsor is Vagenya, and our colors are royal purple and white."

"Um . . . purple," said Tuggle, trying to think of something to say other than what she was thinking, which was that if they decked Badger out in a purple firesuit with a Vagenya logo on it, he was probably going to have to beat people up in the drivers' meeting to stop the catcalls. "There's a brand of synthetic oil called Royal Purple. You might see if they're interested in being a secondary sponsor."

"Thank you," said Christine, making a note of the name. "That's exactly the sort of thing we need to know. As inexperienced as we are, I think we were very fortunate to get the makers of Vagenya to sponsor the car."

"Of course, it helps that Eugenia's father is the CEO of the company," said Diane Hodges with a wink and a grin.

Tuggle stared at the circle of satisfied smiles. They were pleased. They were smug. They had managed to snag a twenty-million-dollar sponsor for their new Cup team. Weren't they clever? Tuggle was thinking, *Oh . . . my . . . God . . .* She pictured drivers meetings. Fan sites on the Internet. Press interviews. But most of all she pictured having to be the one who tried to explain to Badger Jenkins what Vagenya was.

"And we can get free samples if you want some," said one of the investors happily.

Tuggle summoned a queasy smile. *Great,* she thought, *maybe I can swap it to Bobby Labonte for some of his Wellbutrin.*

Later that afternoon, Tuggle sat on the polyester bedspread in her room in the Mooresville Best Western and tried to figure out what had just happened. She had taken the job. She had just accepted responsibility for a multimillion dollar operation and a temperamental race car driver, all funded by a sponsor that she still couldn't mention with a straight face. There must be easier ways to make a living. Nothing she'd rather do that would pay a tenth of the salary, though, come to think of it.

Now she'd have to see about finding a place to live nearer to Mooresville, and then she'd have to begin the process of building a team she could work with. Well, she wasn't in the market for a Lake Norman McMansion, that was for sure. Lake Norman was the Beverly Hills of NASCAR: a community of upscale homes on a man-made lake north of Charlotte. Oh, they paid some drivers well enough—though merchandising and commercial ventures counted for more of their income than winnings—but compared to the lords of the wheel, crew chiefs as a rule didn't get obscenely rich in this sport. But if they didn't try to outspend the drivers, they earned enough to be set for life.

Crew chiefs who were really fortunate stayed around for a

decade or more, ultimately prospering enough to promote themselves to owners and start teams of their own. It would take considerable luck and consummate skill for such a thing to happen to
her. She wasn't counting on it. Just get through these first days of
building the team and see how it went from there, she told herself.

Or, as everybody in racing said: *One lap at a time.*

She was now the very first female crew chief in NASCAR Cup
racing, which meant that pretty soon word would get out—it
might be on *Engine Noise* already—and then reporters from all
over kingdom come would be tracking her down for an interview.
They'd be asking her all sorts of silly questions, more than likely.
Not the questions they'd ask a male crew chief, like what's your
strategy and which tracks do you think you'll have the best
chance of winning on? No, she'd get all the smarmy questions:
Would the team wear designer-made uniforms from Vera Wang?
Would they put Perrier in Badger's water bottle? Did she have any
NASCAR-themed recipes to share with the public? And now, God
help her, did she use Vagenya?

Crap. The onslaught hadn't even started yet and already she
had a chip on her shoulder. Tuggle didn't suffer fools gladly. She
understood why Tony Stewart had to be restrained from assault-
ing reporters who harassed him with stupid questions. She might
be tempted to deck one herself before the initial media frenzy was
over.

Everybody was going to think this team was a gimmick. A joke.
A bunch of know-nothing female amateurs teamed with a pretty
boy from Georgia. They weren't supposed to win. They were the
sideshow, and who would care, because, after all, the money in
NASCAR doesn't come from winning races, but from sponsor support and souvenir sales. Success in those areas was a given, thanks
to sexy little Badger, so the team's absence from Victory Lane
would hardly matter.

It mattered to her, though. And she thought it might very well
matter to Badger Jenkins, too. He might be a pretty boy, but he
was first and foremost a competitor. She had watched him that

last year he raced, on the team that fired him after a mediocre season. It had been an underfunded two-car team, and the driver of the team's other car was the owner's pet. The team's big sponsor was an RV manufacturer, and the nice young kid from Chicago who drove the RV-sponsored car happened to be the son of the owner of the biggest dealership for that brand of recreational vehicles. Naturally, that kid was first in line for everything, and Badger was the also-ran, getting the second-rate cars, the second-string crew, and a smaller share of the racing budget. Naturally, he did not do as well in competition as his teammate, because money buys speed, but instead of admitting what the real problem was, the owners chose to blame Badger. It was easier to replace the driver than to find another ten million dollars to upgrade the operation.

Watching Badger's struggles last season reminded Tuggle of an exercise pony in horse racing. An exercise pony is the horse used to train the promising young thoroughbred by running practice laps with him *and always losing*. Even if the practice pony has a good day and is actually going to beat the golden boy, his rider pulls him up short to allow the other horse to win. Constant winning builds up the confidence of the promising thoroughbred, but its effect on the other horse is not so good. Eventually, the unbroken chain of defeats crushes the spirit of the practice pony. Maybe he forgets how to win. Or he just stops trying.

Tuggle had thought Badger might be in some danger of becoming like that. In some of the later races last season, when he was well out of the chase and not even within hailing distance of twentieth place, he seemed to be coasting through races on autopilot. In racing parlance, *he wouldn't stand on it.* It hadn't been his fault, either. She had made careful note of the outcome of Badger's team in his last year's races, where they had finished and why. It was a litany of misfortune—thirty-six races, and in twenty-four of them he'd never had a chance.

Daytona 500 – penalized due to not securing lug nuts
Las Vegas 1– team changed motor, forcing him to start at the back

Bristol – hole in radiator caused overheating
Richmond 1 – was in top 15 until lug nut left off, lost 2 laps
Daytona 2 – backup car, started in back; by lap 18 was in top
    20 until rear tire went flat and went 58 laps down
New Hampshire – brake problems
Michigan – alternator failed
Kansas – brake problems after 50 laps, lost 12 laps

Tuggle thought that another season with no chance of winning would probably finish Badger's career; no team would want him, and he might lose heart for competition anyhow. It was hard to go out there and sweat through the danger and the discomfort of a race when you knew it was an exercise in futility.

She figured it was up to her to see it didn't happen that way. Owners never cared overmuch about the drivers they employed to race for them. Cup drivers were like shuttle flights to Charlotte, you could always catch the next one. There was nobody except her who knew enough and would care enough to save him.

The expendability of race car drivers—43 slots in Cup racing and 40,000 guys who'd kill for the chance to be there. She thought that might be why Cup champion Tony Stewart had adopted fifty ex-racing greyhounds. Sure he loved animals—he had a tiger, for heaven's sake!—but Tuggle also thought that he might have looked at those gallant canine racers in their cages, euthanized when their usefulness was over, and in the anxious brown eyes of his canine counterparts he would see himself and his fellow competitors. And so "Smoke" had saved the greyhounds, fifty of them—one for every single Cup driver and seven extra for the part-time field fillers. Oh, yes. Professional courtesy.

Well, she would save Badger. If those designer-clad checkbooks tried to treat him like a disposable greyhound, then she would make it her business to see that he did well, so that he could stay around as long as he wanted to. She hoped his future after racing would be one of peaceful retirement on his beloved lake or else perhaps a career in Hollywood or broadcasting, but whatever happened, she intended to look out for him. She didn't hold with putting down champions just because they'd outlived their use-fulness.

Of course, she thought, pursuing the metaphor, racehorses weren't put down upon retirement. They were . . . put out to stud.

Grace Tuggle started to laugh. Poor Badger! From what she had seen of the pit lizards who stalked Cup drivers, she'd bet that Badger would rather live in a cage at Tony Stewart's place.

Vagenya, indeed. They ought to be working on a cure for testosterone poisoning.

CHAPTER IV

Rosalind

In her more fanciful moments, Rosalind Manning sometimes pictured herself being interviewed by an earnest television journalist, who was leaning forward breathlessly and asking her, "But why, of all things, did you join a NASCAR team?" And Rosalind, perched on the black vinyl sofa under hot studio lights, would stare into camera number two and say, *"Because I hate my mother."*

Daydreams aside, Rosalind knew that such an interview would probably never take place, except possibly on the SPEED Channel where no one her mother knew would ever see it, and even then Rosalind would not be so forthright about her motives. She was, after all, her mother's daughter, with several centuries of patrician reticence bred in the bone. No matter how much she might resent her relatives, in many ways she was just like them. The family never discussed its personal conflicts with outsiders, much less on-air to the immediate world, but the fact that she would not broadcast her resentment did not make the statement any less true. She did hate her mother, and for precisely that reason she planned to deal the woman the ultimate insult: She would join the world of stock car racing.

Not that her mother had anything against sports. Rosalind had been taught to ride a Shetland pony before she could walk, and she had the requisite number of tarnished silver cups stashed in a closet somewhere, attesting to a youth spent competing in local horse shows. The family had several friends who were followers of Formula One racing, which was considered quite respectable, even in the best circles, probably because there was a large European contingent to the sport, or because the cars bore no resemblance to anything one might actually drive. Upper-class pursuits had to be archaic or frivolous to be acceptable; practicality was for the proletariat.

And American stock car racing? Her mother equated it with competitive bowling or even professional wrestling. She thought it wasn't a sport, and that the cars looked too much like personal vehicles to be interesting. Surely anybody could drive one? Rosalind, who knew quite a bit about the sport, could have set her mother straight on that. She had the little speech down pat for when the subject came up in conversation with acquaintances.

"Oh, so you think stock car racing isn't a sport, do you? You think that because you can drive a Chevrolet it's easy, huh? Fine. Let's see you get in your car and drive for five hundred miles without getting out, and the longest you can stop is thirteen seconds. You have to watch beside and behind you all the time, because forty-two other cars are coming at you at a speed of three miles per minute. And the temperature in your car is over a hundred degrees. The g-forces pull your body to the right while you are trying to turn the wheel to the left to make the turns; if you're not strong enough to maintain control, you go into the wall at one hundred eighty miles per hour, and if you are strong enough not to wreck, your body will feel like you spent three hours tumbling in a clothes dryer. At the end of every race the heels of both your hands will be solid blisters from fighting the wheel, and you may have burns on your feet as well if your suit doesn't protect you enough. You need the hand-eye coordination of a bomb technician, the depth perception of a sniper, the courage of a smoke jumper, and the strength and stamina of a rock climber. Oh, yeah, it's a sport."

She seldom got to deliver this speech in its entirety before her listeners' eyes glazed over, but she enjoyed the self-righteous glow it gave her to defend the downtrodden. She had never attempted to enlighten her mother with this lecture, however. Listening was not Mother's forte. She would let you rattle on until you ran out of steam, and then she would favor you with that superior little smile of hers and solemnly agree with everything you had said, in tones suggesting that you lined your hat with tin foil.

You couldn't tell Mother anything she didn't already know.

"Really, Rosalind," she would have said. "You might as well go off and join the circus."

Well, thought Rosalind, so she had. Joined the circus. Exactly. NASCAR: Brightly colored haulers assemble each week in an arena in a different town, a different state. Then on Saturday night or Sunday afternoon the "greatest show on earth" is performed for a cheering crowd of thousands, and when it is over, the workers break it all down and move it to another place to begin all over again the next week. The circus, indeed. Rosalind would like to have seen her mother try to explain that to the ladies in her club.

As satisfying as it was to horrify Mrs. Manning with her career decision, Rosalind wasn't joining a NASCAR team only to spite her mother. That was just the icing on the cake. Thanks to her father, she really was interested in the mechanics of the sport. From the time she could walk, "Daddy's girl" had preferred wrenches and pliers to dolls. Daddy had always been tinkering with some machine in his spare time—a remote-controlled airplane, the motor of his sports car, even a broken kitchen appliance. If it had gears or moving parts, it was fair game for Clifton Manning. Early on Rosalind had learned that the way to Daddy's heart was via a stream of alternating current.

How cute she had been in a little pink overall, with a socket wrench in each chubby fist, and an axle grease moustache. When she was in fourth grade, Rosalind's father had died of a stroke, and she had burrowed into her grief for a while by sitting out in Daddy's workshop, straightening the tools, and keeping the place swept, as if by doing so she could entice him into coming back.

By the time she recovered from her loss, Rosalind was as hooked on machinery as her father had been, or perhaps her interest was the result of a genetic legacy from him. She had stuck with her obsession through years of ballet classes, pony club meets, dancing lessons, and four years in an all-girls boarding school, where "shop" meant "Bloomingdale's" and "auto mechanics" was not an option in the curriculum. Despite her mother's best efforts at molding her into a young lady of culture and refinement, Rosalind's interests were unwavering. She used her allowance to subscribe to *Road and Track*.

It wasn't just her "unladylike" interest in machines that had caused the rift between parent and child. Rosalind felt that her entire existence was an affront to her mother's expectations. In perfect conformity to the corporeal dress code of her social circle, Mrs. Manning was a slender and elegant swan. Rosalind herself was more of a pouter pigeon: dumpy and neckless, with stubby legs and a matronly shape that resisted every program of diet and exercise her mother had imposed upon her in an effort to battle the inevitable. Even her mother's indomitable will had not been able to conquer heredity: Rosalind got her looks from her father's side of the family, but also her brains.

Her mother might not have minded so much about her intellectual pursuits if she had been able to look the part of her debutante. In a graceful and beautiful young woman, such an unlikely pastime as auto mechanics might even have passed for an amusing eccentricity. But dumpy little Rosalind was too earnest and awkward for anything she did to be fashionable. She didn't know what was worse: her mother's constant belittling efforts to change her throughout her adolescence, or the feeling of reproach and failure that she got when those maternal efforts finally ceased. She was not the daughter her mother had wanted. She hoped she might be the child her father would have approved of, but she would never know. She could only please herself and be satisfied with that.

When it came time for college, Rosalind had resisted her mother's halfhearted efforts to send her to a genteel finishing school. She had the grades and the aptitude for engineering and a trust fund to finance her independence, so off she went to MIT, where presumably ugly ducklings would be recognized as swans.

Okay, maybe even MIT didn't recognize her as a swan, but they did confirm her assumption that she was a damned smart duck. She aced her automotive engineering classes, and she seemed to understand motors in the same instinctive way that her Virginia forebears once understood their thoroughbred horses. Her mother had not been able to make it to graduation, because she had been on an antiques-buying tour in southern France that month, but she had sent Rosalind flowers, a card, and a graduation present: a gift certificate for a spa and diet ranch in Arizona. Rosalind sent a careful thank-you note to her mother, a somewhat more sincere letter to the administrator of her trust fund, and she resolved never to go home again.

She had moved to Mooresville shortly after graduation on the advice of some of her fellow students, North Carolinians who assured her that if she wanted a job with race cars, Mooresville was the place to go. She liked the town well enough, once she got over the urge to reach for an English/Mooresville dictionary every time she had to talk to somebody. It was easy enough to find people to talk to about things mechanical, which was about all Rosalind could talk about without self-consciousness, but she found that the employment prospects were another matter altogether. Despite her stellar qualifications—a stratospheric GPA from MIT— she found that race teams were not eager to employ an over-educated young woman as a member of the crew. In many ways stock car racing was still an old boys' network and a family business, where second- and third-generation family members worked in a sport they had been raised in. Rosalind found it difficult even to get people to talk to her, much less consider hiring her. A rich girl from Michigan with a fancy college degree was nobody's idea of a chief engineer.

Aside from her gender, her lack of experience was the most telling deficit she had. Book learning did not impress the powers-that-be in racing, many of whom had learned on the job without any higher education at all. In recent years that had changed dramatically, and now there was even a community college in Mooresville that taught people some of the jobs associated with a racing team, but experience still trumped diplomas in this world.

On the advice of one of the shop dogs she'd met in her job searches, Rosalind began volunteering with a Late Model Stock team at a small local speedway. The pay was nonexistent and the hours were long, but at least she got a chance to work with a race car. It was light-years from working on a Cup team, but, she reasoned, you had to start somewhere.

After months of interviews and applications, Rosalind had finally become discouraged, and she had begun to toy with the idea of packing up and going—well, not home, but elsewhere, anyhow—when Team Vagenya announced its intention of fielding an all-female team. The exceptions were noted in fine print. The driver would be male, as would most of the behind-the-scenes personnel, but Rosalind figured that at least the team had stated an intention of hiring women, which meant that they were her best chance at a job in Cup racing.

She had printed out yet another copy of her résumé, with its brand-new section of racing experience, and a few nonprofessorial references—the guys she had met at the little local speedway. Sure enough, a week after she'd submitted it, someone from Team Vagenya called to set up an interview, and Rosalind had calmly replied that she was available at their earliest convenience. She'd had to keep taking deep breaths to keep from squealing into the phone, which would have been a first for her, and perhaps the most feminine thing Rosalind Manning had ever done, except that she didn't do it. As always, Rosalind was grave and deliberate. Grace under pressure was a prerequisite in this intense and dangerous sport.

She had been surprised and not overjoyed to find that the crew chief and team manager were the same person, and that the person was also female: Grace Tuggle, a bulldog of a woman who had both the bloodline and the experience to work for a NASCAR team.

In Rosalind's experience, when it came to giving another woman a break, women were not as likely to do so as people might think. Perhaps they felt that being the exception made them special, or that favoring another woman would be taken as a sign of weakness. Whatever it was, Rosalind was cordial but wary of her interviewer. At first they had exchanged pleasantries, talking in general terms about Rosalind's background and interests. Rosalind felt that she acquitted herself well enough during that initial phase. She was no good at small talk, but then neither was Grace Tuggle.

"MIT?" Tuggle had said, looking dubiously at the résumé as if she wanted to check the references of the references.

Rosalind decided not to apologize for attending MIT. She responded with a slight nod and tried to look as if she didn't particularly care if Tuggle hired her or not. Well-bred indifference was a Manning family tradition, and generally it served them well.

Tuggle frowned at the neatly word-processed résumé. "You don't think you're a tad overqualified to jazz up cars?"

"I think practical experience is always valuable," said Rosalind carefully. "You'll see that I put in some time at the local speedway as well. I enjoyed it." This was not entirely true. Physical dexterity did not come naturally to Rosalind, and like most people, she did not enjoy things she did not do well, but it had been educational, and she appreciated that aspect of the experience.

Tuggle's answering grunt could have meant anything from wholehearted agreement to open skepticism. Then she said, "We already have a chief engineer. Two of them, really. Julie Carmichael got that job. She's an engineer, too, but she has more racing chops than you do. And on an unofficial basis, she'll be working with Jay Bird. Do you know that name?"

Rosalind nodded. A year ago she might not have known who Jay Bird was, but after months of hearing NASCAR junkies talk about the sport, past and present, the name registered with her like an electric shock. The man was the patron saint of jackleg mechanics—not a formally trained engineer, but someone who had grown up in the Carolinas with stock car racing and who knew motors as instinctively as a migrating bird knows south. He had been a force to be reckoned with in NASCAR garages for three decades, and more than one Cup champion owed a debt of gratitude to the mechanical genius of Jay Bird Thomas.

"But he'd have to be nearly eighty!" said Rosalind, blurting out her last thought instead of all the reverent ones that preceded it.

Tuggle nodded. "He is, but he still knows more about race car engines than all the diploma jockeys in the world. And I didn't say he was the chief engineer. He's strictly around to advise us in an informal capacity—and we're damned lucky to get him."

"Yes, of course you are. How *did* you get him?"

"He's Julie Carmichael's godfather. Courtesy title, you understand. Neither one of them is the type to go to christenings, but he was her dad's best friend, so he's been like family to her all her life. Hell, on the strength of that I'd have hired her if she didn't know a socket wrench from a nail file."

There was no arguing with the logic of that. Rosalind thought she would have done the same, but she still wanted a job with Team Vagenya. "Okay," she said, "Carmichael is going to be your chief engineer. I don't blame you for that, but I still want to come on board. Just because I'm overqualified doesn't mean you shouldn't hire me in some other capacity."

"Like what?"

"Engine builder? Engine specialist? I know my way around motors. I know how to read spark plugs. I know the gear ratios for most of the tracks. You'll need a different setup every week, and your chief engineer might appreciate some expert assistance in other areas as well."

Tuggle balanced a pencil lengthwise on the end of her forefinger. Rosalind wondered if the job hung in that balance. She willed herself not to breathe as the silence lengthened and the pencil wobbled. Finally, Tuggle said, "We can't pay the fancy salaries that engineers would get in industry. I suppose you know that?"

Rosalind said, "Money is not the deciding factor."

"Figured it wasn't." Tuggle wouldn't have known a designer handbag if it bit her on the arm, but without even intending to, Rosalind exuded an unmistakable aura of *expensive*. She let the pencil fall from her outstretched finger to the desk; then she looked up. "Engine specialist, then," she said. "You talk to Julie and Jay Bird. See if y'all get along. See if your skills mesh with theirs, and if you have the same sort of thoughts about what kinds of setups we need for each race. If you think you could be a productive part of that team, then come back and tell me, and we'll put you on the payroll."

Rosalind did not quite trust herself to speak. She nodded her thanks. Fortunately, she was not into personal power or ego trips about titles. She would be content to let Julie Carmichael oversee the shop dogs and do the interviews with sports journalists. Crew chiefs were celebrities in their own right in today's NASCAR. Chad Knaus and Tony Eury, Jr. probably had more fans than some of the drivers. Rosalind didn't want that kind of notoriety. She liked machines better than people anyhow. It was better this way.

On her way out, she remembered to thank Tuggle and to shake her hand. She was proud of that.

A couple of days later, Rosalind went to meet with Team Vagenya's chief engineer and with the legendary Jay Bird Thomas, who had forgotten more about race car engines than most people would ever know. Working with him would be an honor. Rosalind hoped they would like her; in her experience, people mostly didn't, but she intended to do her best to be agreeable. She did Google Julie Carmichael and Jay Bird, looking for some clues about their backgrounds and interests. How did people talk to strangers in the days before Googling?

They were expecting her. Rosalind walked into Julie Carmichael's office at team headquarters with a brittle smile and ice water in the pit of her stomach. Julie Carmichael was a lanky woman about her own age, with horn-rimmed glasses and a hank of brown hair bound in a long braid. She wore designer running shoes, faded jeans, and a plaid flannel shirt over a vintage Davey Allison tee shirt. Beside her, with his nose buried in a technical manual, was a sweet-faced old man with jug ears and a fringe of white curls around a shiny bald pate. He peered up at Rosalind through rimless bifocals and twinkled a welcoming smile.

The small office, which had beige cinderblock walls, a tiled floor, and a curtainless metal window, looked as if it were a converted classroom, furnished from the Used Office Furniture Depot without much regard for style or ambiance: a faux wood and steel desk and table half buried under books and piles of paper, a large black-rimmed clock, and a collection of die-cast race cars from previous years in NASCAR. On a white erasable bulletin board was a photo of the 86 car (without Badger) and a computer-generated banner that read VAGENYA TECH.

Rosalind shook hands, belatedly remembered to smile, and nodded toward the sign. "Cute," she said. "This is the engineering headquarters for Team Vagenya, but the sign is also a pun on your alma mater, isn't it?"

Julie nodded. "Virginia Tech. Right. And Tuggle tells me that you graduated from MIT."

Jay Bird Thomas looked up from the manual he had been reading, and said, "How do you spell that?"

Rosalind felt a ridiculous urge to curtsey, but she didn't. "Same way they spelled it when you guest lectured there, sir."

The old man looked pleased. "That was back before your time up there," he said. "Nice bunch of fellas. After my lecture a bunch of us spent half the night in a bar trying to figure out an alternative to restrictor plates. Wore out the batteries on my calculator."

"Wish I'd been there to hear that discussion," said Rosalind.

"What would your solution be?" asked Julie. She pulled out a chair and indicated that Rosalind should sit down.

An alternative to restrictor plates. Rosalind had given some thought to that question already. Everybody in racing groused about restrictor plates, the metal plates that restricted the air flow to the carburetor preventing the car from going over 200 mph, in an attempt to keep the cars from going airborne. It was a safety precaution, enacted in the 80s after Bobby Allison's car achieved lift-off at Talladega and nearly took out a grandstand full of spectators. The plates served their purpose of restricting speed on super speedways of Talladega and Daytona, but they also prevented cars from pulling away from the rest of the field, so that a race tended to be a clump of closely packed cars all going about 190 mph: If any driver lost control or tapped another car, the result could be a chain reaction wreck that could take out half the competitors. Finding a safe, workable alternative to restrictor plates was the holy grail of racing engineering.

"What would I propose as an alternative to restrictor plates?" said Rosalind. "Well, there are a lot of alternatives that would produce the same results. You could mandate a smaller carburetor, or an engine with less horsepower, but those changes wouldn't solve the problems. I might go to the speedway package they're using on Busch cars. The blade across the top of the car, and then set the spoiler at about seventy degrees instead of the fifty-something setting that Cup is running. It makes the car more stable and knocks the engine down about twenty-five horsepower." *Too much information.* Rosalind stopped short and tried to gauge their expressions. Was she being a knowledgeable professional or a hopeless geek? "Er—what would you do?" she asked Julie.

"I might reduce tire size," said the team's chief engineer. "Cup, Busch, and Truck all run on twelve-inch wide slicks that are normally pretty sticky. It seems to me that if you reduced the tire size to eight or ten inches, then the cars could not negotiate the turns at two hundred miles per hour. That would make driver skill a greater factor in super speedway racing again."

"Yeah, but it would be easy to overdrive the tires," said Rosalind. "Might even increase wrecks."

Jay Bird shook his head. "If they go to smaller tires, the teams would have to put more downforce in the cars. Plus, drivers would have to brake going into the turns. I'm not saying it wouldn't work, I'm just saying it would tee-totally change the way they race those super speedways, and I'm not sure that's what anybody wants. Seems to me, if you do all that, you're just duplicating the truck series—big heavy clunkers with no restrictor plates—'cause they can't go fast enough in the first place to need 'em. Neutering the cars."

Julie nodded. "Well, there are no easy answers. So what would you do, Jay Bird?"

The old man didn't bat an eye. "Considering the current crop of Cup drivers? I believe I would sedate every driver whose last name starts with *B*. That ought'a do it."

Julie shrugged. "Couldn't hurt." She grinned at Rosalind. "So what do you think? Do you want to join this wacko team?"

"Yeah, I do," said Rosalind.

Jay Bird peered at her over the top of his bifocals. "Why? Start-up team full of amateurs. You're not one of those Badger groupies, are you?"

"No, sir. He's a decent driver, and I respect him for that, but personally? No. Handsome jocks are not my thing. I want to join this team because I want the experience, and to be honest with you, NASCAR is still largely an old boys' club, so it's hard for a newcomer to break in. And if the newcomer is a woman, then breaking in is next to impossible. I thought this team was my best shot. I didn't care who your driver was. I just figured this is the one place that my gender would be an asset rather than a liability."

"Fair enough," said Julie.

"But it's really an honor to be able to work with Jay Bird Thomas, too."

The old man waggled his eyebrows. "So you'll work for free then, will you?"

"No. But it's not your money anyway, so I doubt if you care," said Rosalind.

"You're right, he doesn't," said Julie. "He just wants us to pull at least one victory out of the hat to show that old boys' club what we can do. Now how do you suggest we do that?"

Rosalind shrugged. "Same way the old boys do it. Cheat."

CHAPTER V

Finding Your Marks

*W*ell, *it would probably be better than working for the food page of* The Charlotte Observer. *Probably.* Too bad the pay wasn't better, but at least the hours were.

Melanie Sark knew that there were lots of people in the world—70 million, in fact, if you believed *Sports Illustrated*—who would clutch their hearts and faint with envy at the thought of getting a job as a publicist to a NASCAR team. To get paid to attend races. To get up close and personal with an actual Cup driver— as part of your job. Oh, sure, a dream come true. But not to her it wasn't, because she wasn't a NASCAR fan, and neither were any of her colleagues in journalism, as far as she knew. The glamour of this line of work would be lost on them, which meant that gloating would not be among the perks of her new job.

Her fellow journalists would ask her the same questions they'd pose if she had just taken over the editorship of *Shoppers Weekly*: How much does it pay? *(Not a lot);* What are the hours? *(Erratic, as far as she could tell, but less arduous than that of a newspaper reporter);* What are the perks? *(Well, attending NASCAR races, if that happened to appeal to you, but she couldn't suddenly start pretending that it did.)*

Sark had already thought out her response to the polite cynicism of her acquaintances: *plausible enthusiasm.* No, she wasn't doing it because she wanted to go to stock car races, and no, she didn't have a jones for runty little guys in firesuits. The point, she would tell them, was that the job would offer valuable experience in public relations, and it might lead to a more prestigious gig—Hollywood, perhaps, or a corporate position in industry, which would really pay well. Making something look good was the name of the game, whether you hyped a car, a new movie, or a race car driver, so it didn't matter where she started out, as long as she performed the task with skill and creativity.

The NASCAR job would be a hoot, she would tell her colleagues. Surely she'd soon be able to regale the gang with tales of excess on the Redneck Riviera (aka Lake Norman), and stories about Thunder Road prima donnas behaving badly. *Stay tuned,* she would tell them, leering.

She took the job. There was never any doubt that she would. Diversification looked great on a résumé, and she was still young enough to get away with it and pretty enough to have a good shot at any job she really wanted. She had a good academic record, a modest legacy from her grandmother to use as a safety net, and two older sisters to deflect her mother's lust for wedding planning and grandchildren. Sark was out to see the world before age, career demands, or Mr. Right put an Invisible Fence around her life.

She had already worked in the publications office of her university, spent the obligatory year in New York working for a fashion photographer, and worked as a publicist for a minor music company, whose main claim to fame had been a group called "The Okay Chorale." Then she'd tried her hand at newspaper reporting, but the "assigned beat" system of a metropolitan daily had soon bored her, especially since the reporters with the least seniority got the most mind-numbing assignments. The zoning board. *Oh, please.* Taking a job as a NASCAR publicist was a small price to pay to escape that; during some of the interminable board meetings she thought she might have gnawed off her own foot to get away.

She had seen the story about the all-woman NASCAR team before it had even made headlines. One of the guys in the sports department had been bruiting the news about as his current favorite joke, but Sark had not been amused. NASCAR was a notoriously all-male enterprise, and on principle she applauded an injection of diversity into the mix. It had been easy enough to get the sports guy to give her the contact people, once she'd managed to convince him that her interest was opportunistic rather than journalistic.

She had e-mailed her résumé to the team, and by the time they called her for an interview three days later, she had put together an impressive portfolio of fashion photographs, zoning board stories, and record company press releases.

Christine Berenson had studied the work samples with clinical interest, and then she'd taken a long look at the slender girl with long cognac-colored hair and an expression of impish intelligence. At last she said, "And just what experience do you have with stock car racing?"

There it was. Sark knew she couldn't bluff her way through that one. She had done some reading on the subject—at least enough to know that Jeff Gordon and Robby Gordon were not brothers—but she thought it best not to feign an interest or an expertise that she did not have.

"I'm eager to learn," she said, with what she hoped was an enthusiastic smile.

Christine Berenson's expression was noncommittal. "Well, your credentials seem satisfactory, and your photography is quite good. How exactly would you suggest we promote Badger Jenkins?"

Sark's smile wavered. The name of the driver had not been made public, and while she had tried to memorize as much as she could about forty-three race car drivers who were just names on a page to her, she did not recognize this name, and not a single fact about him surfaced in her consciousness. She pretended to weigh the options, while she grasped at what few generalizations she had gathered about the mystique of stock car racing. "Well," she said at last, "I think that race car drivers are the modern equivalent of . . . of . . . knights in shining armor. People see them as brave warriors, risking their lives in a kind of mechanized jousting tournament. I think I would focus on that nobility of spirit."

Her prospective employer's eyes widened, and for an instant

her lips twitched. "Ah. Badger Jenkins as knight in shining armor. How very unexpected. But our researchers tell us that there are some thirty million female fans of NASCAR, and perhaps that is exactly the image that would appeal to them. Interesting."

They talked a bit more, and Sark continued to be fortunate in her answers, so that by the time the interview was over, she felt confident of having landed the job. She left with Christine Berenson's promise that she would hear from them soon.

That evening, Sark had a dinner date with Ed Blair, a freelance writer who specialized in articles for local magazines and occasionally even scored big with a national publication. Over dessert she told him about her new job prospect, careful to keep her tone light and ironic, displaying the elitism of a journalist, certainly of a sophisticated person well beyond the lure of stock car racing.

"It should be a hoot," she said, toying with her crème brûlée.

Her companion stared into his coffee cup for a moment, deep in thought. "You know," he said, "it could be quite an opportunity as well. You'll have the inside track on a NASCAR team. And a notorious one at that. The all-female team. Who knows what goings-on you'll get to see? It should be a satirist's dream. I doubt you'd even have to exaggerate. You ought to keep a diary."

"Why?"

"Well, so that you can write it all up at the end of the season. Surely this ladies' team won't last more than one season, so you'll be out of a job by December anyhow. Then you can shop this article to a national magazine like *Vanity Fair* and make good money. You might even get a book deal out of it."

"*Vanity Fair?*" Sark blinked. "What kind of article?"

"Oh, you know, something hip and sarcastic. Knights of the round track, or redneck cowboys, or something like that. Get the tone right and it would be a great story. It should almost write itself. How hard can it be to make fun of stock car racing?"

No argument there, she thought. "But how would I get a national magazine to look at it?"

Ed Blair smiled. "Keep in touch, Sark. When you're ready to shop the piece, I'll make a few calls. I'm sure we can convince somebody to take it. NASCAR is becoming quite a cultural phenomenon, you know. They've just purchased some land on Staten Island to build a speedway in New York. That will put the sport on the national radar more than ever."

Sark thought it over for a few moments. "All right," she said, "I suppose it couldn't hurt anything to keep notes, if I get the job. And if I get a good offer for an article, why not? Especially if I'm unemployed at the end of the season. Just don't forget you promised to help me shop it."

He raised his coffee cup in a mock toast. "Here's hoping you get the job, and lots of dirt along the way."

When the job offer came a day or so later, Sark accepted it with more enthusiasm than she had expected. She didn't even mind that the pay was not astronomical. After all, she told herself, in a way she would be working two jobs at once.

Laraine set a pile of clean shirts on the bed next to the old brown suitcase. "Fresh out of the dryer, hon," she said. "But I still don't see why you have to move up there. I thought you hated Mooresville. You said the air feels like cotton candy in the summertime."

Badger Jenkins was sitting on the floor, cradling his helmet in his lap, seemingly oblivious to the process of packing. He nodded sadly. "It does," he said, without looking up. "But they'll expect me to be around, and I figured I ought to go. Help set up the team."

She nodded. That was a good sign. Impress his new employers with his dedication before fishing season or apple harvest or some other local distraction lured him away again.

Laraine set the shirts in the suitcase, next to several pairs of patched and faded Levis that she thought would be better off in the rubbish bin than in the suitcase. She looked around the sparsely furnished cabin, wondering what else he would want to take, but he seemed so lost in thought that she hated to ask him. *Not the dramatic Badger Jenkins racing poster taped to the refrigerator.* She'd always suspected he kept it there as a joke. *Not the old racing trophies on the mantelpiece, surely. Not the shot-*

gun or the fishing rods. Not the eight-by-ten color picture of the former Miss Georgia-USA, who was also the former Mrs. Badger Jenkins—speaking of things that should go in the rubbish bin, if you asked her.

She paused for a moment, with a dingy pair of socks in her hand, and looked at him, marveling as she always did at the difference between the stud on the NASCAR poster and the slight, earnest fellow on the floor, hugging the helmet. *Pictures don't lie,* she thought, but those firesuit shots of Badger certainly weren't within hailing distance of the truth. A collection of Badger's racing posters graced the wall of the diner, and sometimes when Laraine hadn't seen Badger in person for a week or so, even *she'd* start believing that the fellow in the picture was real—tall, wise, and powerful, and sexy as hell.

Then one day he'd turn up for lunch, looking like a lost Boy Scout in ratty old jeans and a tee shirt two sizes too large, and in two heartbeats she'd forget all the impure thoughts she'd had about him that wouldn't bear repeating even on Confession Sunday, and she'd feed him a double helping of everything, and then forget to charge him for the meal.

He put her in mind of a stray puppy sometimes—lost and helpless, and so intent on his own concerns that he barely noticed all the times loving hands rescued him from one mishap or another. It wasn't that he was ungrateful, exactly. Just oblivious. Whenever life seemed ready to flush Badger Jenkins down the toilet, something or someone always did turn up to save him, and he never seemed to wonder about his charmed life. Maybe you couldn't if you were a race car driver. Maybe you had to believe in a luck that was stronger than steel and more reliable than gravity. How could you go out there and risk your life on a race track if you didn't believe that?

She folded another tee shirt *(This one said, "No Fear!" Laraine thought they ought to make one that said, "No Common Sense!")* and stole another glance at him, but he was still taking no interest in the preparations for his own departure. Like a child being sent off to camp. He'd thank her when she was done and hug her good-bye with all the sexless abandon of a little kid, but she wasn't sure if that constituted gratitude as the rest of the world understood it or not. If she hadn't done his laundry and the packing, somebody else would have. That's the way the world worked for Badger, fair or not. Somebody would always look out for him; a dozen self-appointed crew chiefs steered him through life, just as the real ones had kept him on-track in the race car.

Another thought occurred to her. "Have you got somebody looking out for the cabin while you're gone, hon?"

He nodded absently. "Yeah, Paul down at the Bait and Beer said he needs a place to stay while they're rebuilding his house. Wood stove caught fire, you remember."

Laraine nodded. She did remember. Someone else's disaster turned into Badger Jenkins's luck, just like on the track, when Johnny Benson or somebody had cut a tire, and the resulting caution had allowed Badger to pit just before he would have run out of fuel. His whole life was like that, it seemed to Laraine.

"I'm only charging him four hundred dollars a month," said Badger, brightening at the thought.

For house-sitting? thought Laraine. But she didn't say anything. That was another thing about Badger. Just when you thought he had no more sense of self-preservation than a baby bird, he'd come out with something so shrewd and calculating that you found yourself wondering if the whole innocent thing was just an act. She never could figure it out. Maybe Badger wasn't that macho robot from the racing posters, but that didn't mean the real guy was any easier to understand.

And why do we love him so much? she wondered. He is handsome enough, but no more than a hundred other guys anywhere you look. He's kind when he remembers to be, but he can break your heart, too, by forgetting a promise or letting you down at the last minute. What is there about him that makes everybody stick to him like bugs on a windshield? There was a saying around Marengo, generations old: "Nobody ever got anywhere by loving a Jenkins." Lord, that was true. But it didn't stop people from trying, anyhow.

And in Badger's case, it wasn't the money or the fame. Oh, maybe it was for some people. There were plenty of folks who liked to brag about knowing a guy whose cardboard likeness stood in the grocery store aisle, as if that was anything to crow about, if you asked her. And there were always women who—in the words of that song—would *wonder how his engine feels.* But for the people who really mattered, it wasn't starfucking, it was genuine devotion. And you never knew how he felt in return or even if he noticed the charmed circle that protected him—all the old friends who answered his fan mail, fixed him hot dinners, and guarded his privacy from reporters and clueless fans. Laraine's own self-appointed task was to present Badger to outsiders as the macho stud people expected NASCAR drivers to be.

You just went on doing things for him and not expecting anything in return but a soft-drawled thank you, when he remembered, and for some reason that was enough.

Whatever it was, you never got over it, she thought, as she went on sorting socks.

CHAPTER VI

Badger Meets the Owners

The occasion was part business meeting and part happy hour. The Walter Raleigh Conference Room at a newly remodeled hotel near the new team headquarters had not been festooned with balloons and streamers, because, after all, motorsports was a male-oriented business, but there was a fifteen-foot copy center banner that read WELCOME BADGER JENKINS in large red letters.

The team hierarchy and its sponsors had gathered to meet their driver.

Just inside the door, a small table draped with a purple table-cloth held an arrangement of flowers and an assortment of name tags, including one decorated with purple ribbons that simply said BADGER. Along one wall stood a long buffet table, which held an assortment of wines and several party trays of finger sand-wiches and vegetables and dip, all strategically positioned around an enormous sheet cake featuring a photo of Badger rendered in icing, and checkered flag–patterned paper napkins. On a smaller table nearby, the staff had stacked 100 eight-by-ten color photos of Badger, and a plastic cup full of felt-tipped pens in case anyone missed the point that he would be expected to autograph them.

Deanna, the secretary in charge of securing likenesses of Badger for the occasion, had been in a quandary about what image of him to select, because all the firesuit photos of him linked him to his previous racing teams. Team Vagenya had not yet had a chance to get new photos made of him in their own distinctive purple regalia. Deanna had considered getting portraits of him in what she thought of as "civilian clothes," but in those shots she felt that he lacked the sexy ferocity of his NASCAR incarnation. The one taken at a charity golf tournament, for instance—sad, really. In that one, Badger was wearing jeans and a red polo shirt, putter in hand, and grinning at the camera like a tourist who has just found the all-you-can-eat buffet. Not his finest hour, image-wise, she thought.

Deanna personally liked photos depicting Badger scowling, or at least looking focused and determined, and these were mostly candid shots of him walking beside the race car or being interviewed at the track. In the end, she plumped for cropping one such photo into a close-up shot of his face in profile, so that only a bit of the blue and white firesuit showed, and you couldn't read much of the sponsor lettering on it anyhow. In the picture, some reporter had stuck a microphone in Badger's face, and he had tilted back his head, seeming to consider the question with the earnest sincerity of a general making a tough decision about some approaching battle. She loved that photo, because in it he appeared reassuringly strong and yet so gentle. His dark eyes caught the light, and his feathery hair was brushed forward until it nearly touched his eyebrows. The firesuit even looked like the tunic of a knight. Sir Galahad might have looked like that, she thought, so brave and reverent that it made your heart turn over to look at him.

Just having a photograph of Badger pinned to the filing cabinet beside her desk made Deanna feel safer, as if no one would dare to steal paperclips from a workspace watched over by such a powerful, yet compassionate being. Because of that image, she began to feel that she knew and loved Badger even before she saw him in the flesh.

In the end, after much consideration, she decided to please herself with the photo selection, and the "Galahad" picture was the one she chose. With any luck she could get him to sign a copy for her, too; then she could tape that one up on the filing cabinet next to her desk to look at when she was feeling besieged. She might even frame it. A signed picture would be an even more potent charm of protection. Badger Jenkins, her very own knight in shining armor—and to think that she almost *knew* him!

Suzie Terrell, the attorney who had first approached Badger about driving for the all-female team, was his minder for the afternoon's event, not exactly his advocate, but certainly, at least in her own mind, charged with seeing that he behaved, and even more that he was treated professionally and not imposed upon. Perhaps it was ridiculous to suppose that a prosperous group of grown women would behave at all improperly toward a male business associate, but Suzie knew that the proximity of celebrities affected people in peculiar ways. Otherwise normal, sensible individuals could become quite pixilated in the presence of someone famous. Suzie didn't know why this was, but she had seen it often enough in connection with the stars of Atlanta society: the occasional movie star; Atlanta's Braves and Falcons; and of course, passing musicians, artists, and other cultural luminaries.

People acted as if celebrities did not have feelings to be hurt. *"Boy, you played lousy in the game last week!"* or *"You're so much prettier on television."* Many people seemed to think that the maxim "the customer is always right" applied to creative people as well as to retail establishments, and that this gave them license to order the celebrity around. *"Here, sign this book for my nephew. I've written out what I want you to say,"* or *"Sing a few notes of your hit song for me."* Suzie thought that attitude was the modern equivalent of bear-baiting; the poor celebrity was tied to the stake of public opinion and mauled to death by autograph hounds. But the scalp hunters were the worst. All those people who wanted to brag that they'd hugged somebody famous—or more, if they could manage it. Did people go home and boast to their friends about the fact that they'd hugged a celebrity, and if they had slept with one, would that, too, have become a source of bragging rights? Sometimes after an evening at the sort of party that throws social lions to the jackals, Suzie would feel like going home and showering in Lysol to get rid of the taint of celebrity-baiting.

But sophisticated people were expected to know better than

to behave boorishly toward the famous. Surely these well-to-do women would be more sophisticated than to misbehave around Badger? No, there were nearly a dozen of them. The odds were too great that there'd be at least one idiot in the bunch. She resolved to stay within earshot of the guest of honor, just in case he needed rescuing.

Badger had made an effort to be presentable, she decided. He was dressed in jeans, of course, and clunky brown work boots that might have added a grace note to his height, but he had put on a crisply ironed sport shirt instead of a tee shirt, and he was even wearing a silk tie, although the way he kept tugging at his collar suggested that he had mistaken it for a noose. He carried a gym bag, and she wondered what he'd thought it necessary to bring. He had trotted along beside her as obediently as a guide dog, prattling happily about nothing in particular. He didn't seem nervous, but as they approached the conference room, he touched her arm. "I need to find the men's room," he said.

Well, thank God you're not going to pee in the punch bowl, she thought. She nodded, somehow managing to keep a straight face, and she stationed herself in the hallway outside the men's room to wait. Three minutes later, a man emerged from the rest room, and Suzie had to look twice to make sure it was him.

He had put on the new team firesuit over his street clothes.

Suzie stared. He looked taller, stronger, wiser—more important somehow. Noticing her sudden loss of composure, Badger smiled. "Yeah," he said, "firesuits are magic, aren't they? Nobody can say no to a guy in a firesuit."

"Did they ask you to wear it?" she stammered.

"No, but I figured they'd expect me to look like a race car driver."

Suzie nodded. "Well, I guess you won't need your name tag."

It was a good psychological ploy, she thought. Maybe Badger was more shrewd than she'd realized. The suit had royal purple sleeves, collar, belt, and trousers, while the chest area was white and emblazoned with the logos of NASCAR and various sponsors, such as Sunoco, the official gasoline of NASCAR, and thus everyone's sponsor. In the center of the chest, at diaphragm level, was the large logo of the principal sponsor: an embroidered red heart and the slogan *Vagenya Is for Lovers!*

The get-up should have been silly, Suzie thought. A grown man standing in the hall of a corporate building dressed like Buck Rogers, but Badger was right: A man in a firesuit was a vision of power and nobility. She didn't feel like laughing. She had to keep telling herself that it was just Badger, to keep from feeling that she was in the presence of some transcendent being. *Firesuits.* She wondered if medieval knights got the same mileage out of suits of armor. She thought that probably they did.

"You've already got the job," she told him. "You know that. They just want to meet you. They'll probably be very excited about it. I expect some of them will want your autograph, or to have their pictures made with you."

Badger nodded earnestly. "That's kinda usual."

"I expect it is. You're right about the firesuit. . . . It's perfect for photo opportunities. The corporate people are just going to eat this up. Are you ready to go in?"

"Sure," said Badger. "If there's anybody there who's really important, maybe you should give me a heads-up, though. I'm not too good at recognizing names. I'm always meeting people like TV stars who think I ought to know who they are, and I never do. I wouldn't want to hurt anybody's feelings."

"I'll stay close by," said Suzie. "Anything else?"

"Well, you could keep some Sharpies handy in case I have to sign anything."

"Oh, I think you can count on having to sign things. I'll carry the Sharpies." She touched his arm, wondering how she ought to word what she had to say before they went in. "Umm . . . Don't take this the wrong way, Badger. I don't mean to be rude, but is there anything I should know about you?"

He stopped. He had a way of tilting his head back and looking at you through narrowed eyes as if you were a long way away, and his expression was always one of earnest sincerity, as if every comment, even "pass the salt," required his undivided attention. "What do you mean *anything you should know*?" he asked.

Suzie sighed. "This is awkward," she said. "Look, I'm on your side. I want you to do well, so I thought I'd ask if there was anything I should watch out for. Are you, say, allergic to seafood, or afraid of dogs, or—"

He considered the question, and when he finally smiled he did not look amused. "So you really want to know if I have trouble holding my liquor or if I'm susceptible to pretty girls, or maybe worst of all, if I'll be rude to VIPs when they get pushy, right?"

Suzie blinked, perhaps because a career in law had sheltered her from too much plain-speaking about anything. "Well, that pretty much covers it," she said, trying to sound nonchalant.

"I've been through this before," said Badger. "I could probably drink anybody there under the table, if I had a mind to, but I can take it or leave it. And since I prefer to drink with my friends, I think I'll stick to punch at this event. Now, pretty girls . . ." He gave her a wolfish grin. "Well, ma'am, I think the ones here will be over my age limit, and as for the rest: If I have to fight 'em off, I'll be polite about it. It's the firesuit. What does that leave?"

"Pushy people?"

"Right. Look, I was raised to be nice to people if at all possible. I'm not naturally touchy. I'll put up with a lot." He shrugged. "There's only forty-three Cup rides, and I want this job. They can rib me about my accent or call me a redneck, you know. Whatever. I'll take it in stride. But if somebody wants a fight with me bad enough, he'll get one."

"I hope that won't happen," murmured Suzie, who was more relieved than she sounded. Despite the rising tone of menace in his last statement, Badger's reply had been as good an answer as she could have expected, all things considered. She didn't know much about the fine points of auto racing, but she figured that in order to go out there at blinding speeds and face the inevitability of wrecks and the danger of life-threatening injuries, a driver had to be running on high-test testosterone, which meant that behavior problems came with the territory. If he could control his actions, that was all that could be hoped for.

"I don't think you need to worry," she told him. "We're a mostly female team. Besides, this is just a business meeting masquerading as a social occasion."

Badger nodded. "In my experience, social occasions most always are," he said. He reached for the door handle. "I'm ready."

They entered the room to a momentary hush as the assembled guests looked toward the doorway, followed by a collective gasp as everyone simultaneously recognized the famous and handsome Badger Jenkins, their newly hired wheel man. Or perhaps it was just the magic of the firesuit. Badger had been right to wear it, Suzie thought. If a plumber had walked through that door in the firesuit, he would have been heralded as the conquering hero. Whatever it was, Badger had a captive audience from the moment they saw him. The gasp of recognition gave way to scattered applause and a babble of voices, all talking at once and saying much the same things: *"Isn't he adorable?"* . . . *"Such a talent!"* . . . *"Shorter than I expected."*

That about summed it up, thought Suzie, trying not to smile. Adorable, talented, and vertically challenged. To his credit, Badger affected not to overhear any of these comments; certainly he showed no reaction to any of these sentiments. With an affable grin and an appealing veneer of diffidence, as if "meet and greets" would be his favorite thing in the world, if only he weren't so shy. Badger eased his way through the crowd of admirers, alternately shaking hands and hugging his well-wishers. He had perfected a genial one-armed hug that managed to seem friendly without giving the recipient too much encouragement. Sometimes he'd wink at someone who was standing too far away for a hug or a handshake. Charm personified. She wondered if he had been born with charm or if he had studied his technique as painstakingly as he'd learned driving techniques. Watching him was an education.

When someone pointed a camera at him, he obligingly went on point, smiling happily for the camera as he posed with his new best friends, the total strangers on either side of him. To his credit, the party guests seemed delighted with him. He played the part of a gregarious celebrity very well. Suzie wondered how he really felt about it; surely such poise had not come naturally to a backwoods boy from Georgia. She resolved to ask him if she ever got another chance to speak to him in private.

Dutifully, she hovered at Badger's elbow, ready to bring him a drink, supply a name, hand him a Sharpie, or to make herself otherwise useful to the guest of honor. Thus, she was probably the only person who noticed that his responses were not only perfunctory, but identical. He said almost the same thing to every single person. Of course, in fairness, almost every person said the same thing to him, so perhaps there were only so many variations that one could make on "Thank you. How kind of you to say so." Anyhow, he was such a handsome, unassuming guy that it didn't much matter what he said. Just the smile would have been enough for most people.

Badger had also perfected the art of scribbling his name on whatever was handed to him without seeming to notice that he was being asked for an autograph. He'd simply scrawl his name, hardly glancing at the paper, while he kept on talking to the women crowded around him. You didn't even have to *ask* him to sign his name. Any photo of himself, any die-cast model of a car he'd ever driven, or any other racing-related item that a Sharpie would write on—hat, tee shirt, coffee mug—he would sign if the item were thrust at him, never interrupting the flow of his conversation.

It took the embarrassment out of the situation, Suzie decided. The fan was not required to formally request "the great man's" autograph, and Badger was spared the awkwardness of being fussed over or seeming to demand deference. He seemed no more arrogant than a ticket taker, accepting pieces of paper, "processing" them, and then handing them back without ceremony. It was a graceful maneuver, she decided, and she wondered if all the drivers were similarly skilled in celebrity.

Badger also had his sound bites down pat: a modest, cheerful, patient litany of platitudes. He was honored to be a part of the team; he couldn't say how well they'd do in the season, but he would certainly try his best; and no he didn't think he was the most skillful driver *ever*, but it was mighty kind of the lady to say so.

He's good, thought Suzie. He could be in politics. Then she remembered that senators outnumbered Cup drivers, and she decided that one didn't keep a Cup ride without the consummate skills of a politician.

In a momentary lull of adulation, Deanna, the secretary, touched his elbow and pointed to the stack of Badger likenesses in a letter tray on the table. "We thought people might like to have signed photos of you," she said. "I know I would. If you wouldn't mind?"

"I'd be honored," said Badger, taking the proffered Sharpie from Suzie and reaching for a photo from the top of the pile. He winced. "Oh, *this one*. You know, I never was too partial to that picture of me."

Deanna sighed. "I think you look wonderful in that shot. That solemn, dedicated look on your upturned face, and the way the light hits you. Like an angel in a stained glass window." She willed herself to stop babbling.

"Yeah," said Badger, as if he hadn't heard a word she said. "I remember when they took that shot. We had just finished a three-hour race. I came in second, and they just swooped down on me with the microphones and the camera and all, and, Lord, I had to piss so bad I thought it would come out my ears. . . . Who do you want me to make this out to, sweetie?"

Deanna summoned a wan smile, "Oh . . . just sign it," she murmured. There was always eBay.

Christine Berenson and several of the more important party guests waited until the frenzy had subsided somewhat before they attempted to converse with the star of their team. "Such a joy to see you," said Christine, pressing her cheek against Badger's. Since they were the same height, this was not difficult. She nodded affably to Suzie. "I think you know everyone," she said to the lawyer, but she recited the names of the gaggle of socialites in her wake and beamed while each of them hugged Badger, some with considerably more determination than others. Suzie thought she detected a slight reduction in the voltage of his enthusiasm. His smile seemed a bit more perfunctory, and he had begun to look restive. Perhaps he was an introvert, after all. He did spend a lot of time alone fishing on that lake back home. Being effusive to a room full of strangers must have been quite a drain on his reserves of cordiality.

Christine had drawn Badger aside for a private talk. "How do you like the decorations for the reception?" she asked.

"Real nice," said Badger without a glance at any of them.

"There's one item I particularly wanted to show you. A piece of racing memorabilia that someone gave to me when I started the team. What do you think?" A metal chair against the wall held a cheaply framed two-by-three foot poster labeled *"The Winston-Charlotte Motor Speedway–May 17, 1987."* It was a group photo of NASCAR drivers in firesuits, with Neil Bonnett, Terry Labonte, Dale Earnhardt, Bill Elliott, and Richard Petty kneeling in the foreground, and fifteen equally illustrious drivers standing in two rows behind them.

Badger said, "That's a dirty poster."

"What? It seems in mint condition to me."

"They did a clean version of this poster, after they caught it, but this is the original one. Look." He put his finger on Neil Bonnett's right ear.

When Christine knelt down and peered closely at that part of the photograph, she realized that directly behind Neil Bonnett's ear—but not entirely obscured by it—was the erect penis of Tim Richmond, dangling out of his white and red firesuit, while he stared into the camera with careless bravado.

"Tim Richmond was pretty wild," said Badger. "Great driver. Died of AIDS. That was before I got into the sport, of course."

If he had expected her to be horrified by revelations about her X-rated poster, he had underestimated the corporate she-wolf. Looking distinctly unshocked, Christine gave him a long, appraising stare below the belt, leaned close to his ear, and whispered, "Tell me, Badger, how do you think you measure up to Tim Richmond?"

Now he was shaking hands with one of the few men present at the reception, the silver-haired husband of a regal older woman

whose silvery dress matched her hair. The couple had been per-
suaded by Christine to make their furniture company a minor
sponsor of the car despite their own genteel misgivings about the
sport of stock car racing. Now that the object of their dubious investment had materialized, the elderly gentleman took the opportunity to question Badger as if he were a customer service
representative instead of a famous Cup driver. "It certainly costs a
lot of money to put that palm-sized decal on your car, young
man."

His wife nodded emphatically. "It certainly does. Daylight rob-
bery."

Badger hesitated for a moment, perhaps wondering if the couple were joking, but apparently he decided they weren't. Summoning his "aw-shucks country boy" look, he said in his most
mellifluous drawl, "Well, ma'am and sir, if it was up to me, I'd be
happy to slap that decal on there for you for nothing, but you
know I don't really have anything to do with it. The owners set the
prices for sponsorship, and I reckon they spend most of that
money seeing that I don't run out of tires or have to use second-
hand parts. Since I've been in the hospital a time or two from
going into the wall from a tire blowout or wreck due to a faulty
part, I guess my life pretty much depends on a well-funded car. So
I sure do appreciate your help in keeping me safe."

The man sniffed. "Our decal is on the side of the car. The only
time it shows up on television is if they show a close-up of your
car, and the only time they do that is if you are in the top five."

His wife gave his arm a playful smack. "Oh, stop it, Lewis!" she
said. "This poor boy's life is at stake. If you want a bigger ad, then
give him more money." She enfolded Badger in a motherly hug.
"And you be careful out there, honey, you hear?"

"Yes, ma'am," said Badger.

With a proprietary hand in the small of his back, Christine
steered Badger away from the elderly furniture manufacturers.
"Nicely done," she whispered to Badger. "Before they leave, I'll
talk to them about increasing their sponsorship."

"I just told them the truth," said Badger, edging away from her.

"Well, you might want to resist the urge to do that. The man by the punch bowl is the representative of Vagenya."

Badger blinked. "Senator Allen?"

"Not Virginia! *Va-gen-ya*. Our primary sponsor. You know, the drug for women that—oh, never mind." She patted his arm and smiled. "Just try not to discuss it. By the way, perhaps you and I could have dinner some time to discuss the direction we want to go with this team."

Badger nodded solemnly. "Tuggle and I would be happy to talk to you about that, ma'am."

Christine opened her mouth to say that Tuggle's presence would not be required, but something in his eyes made her think better of it. *So he wasn't an innocent little redneck, after all*, she thought. *He's like a fox cub. If* cute *will get him what he wants, he'll use it, but if not, he can bite with the best of them.* Interesting. Motorsports was more complicated than it seemed in all sorts of unexpected ways.

Then they were within hailing distance of the pharmaceutical company representative, who hastily set down an overfull glass of wine in order to shake hands with Badger. "Charlie Conley, Badger. Pleasure to meet you." His eager expression suggested that he had a pocketful of die-cast cars, but if so, he didn't produce them.

"How you doin'," said Badger, whose retriever affability always made him look glad to see anybody.

"We're really excited about sponsoring your car this year, Badger," said Conley. Then he winked. "No pun intended."

"Glad to have you on board," said Badger. "I hope we have a real good year."

Someone had come up with a camera and motioned for Badger and Conley to pose together, which they did with equally perfunctory smiles and hardly a break in the conversation.

"Well, we'll be cheering you on. We're even getting a skybox at Charlotte. People at corporate will get a thrill out of meeting you."

Badger nodded. "I'll be there." He managed to sound as if he had been ordered to take a machine gun nest singlehanded— bravely resigned to his fate, but determined to do his duty. It was an endearing expression, Suzie thought. You'd trust Badger with your life and not think twice about it.

Conley smiled. "You know we had another idea that you might get a kick out of, Badger. In a couple of weeks we're going to be doing a pharmaceutical trade show to kick off Vagenya—you know, show the world our new wonder drug. And we were thinking it would be just a great attention-getter to have you there."

Badger's genial smile began to tighten at the corners, and he stood very still.

"We haven't really thought it all out yet," Conley went on. "There are half a dozen possibilities, I think. Of course, we could have you sign photos. I know you're used to that, but we were thinking—and, you know, Badger, this is just off the top of my head here, but I was thinking . . . good-looking stud like you, boy . . . What about a kissing booth? Wouldn't that be a hoot?" He winked and leered.

Badger's expressionless stare did not waver. He did not move a muscle.

Happily unaware of the effect of his little suggestions, Conley went barreling on. "And we'd have a slogan, something like . . . oh . . . *If You Haven't Got Badger, Try Vagenya.*" He turned to Suzie, as if noticing her for the first time. "What do you think?"

Suzie was spared from telling him what she thought, because at that moment, Christine Berenson, who had not been privy to the discussion, glided in, wineglass in hand. She took Badger by the arm and led him away toward another clump of guests. She waited motionless beside him until the chattering died down, and then, still clutching his arm, she announced to the group, "You know, Badger is not only a great driver, he's also something of a humanitarian. When Suzie here visited him in his hometown, he had just rescued a large injured turtle from the local lake. A motor boat had cut its shell, and he actually saved its life."

Her listeners responded with a suitable assortment of oohs and aahs and a few seconds of muffled applause. One large woman in flowered silk who was either an animal lover or an opportunist hugged Badger again, professing her admiration for his noble efforts.

Badger bore all this attention with a modest smile, but he wasn't forthcoming with any information about the rescue, so that finally Christine was forced to ask, "And how is the turtle?"

Solemnly, Badger Jenkins said, "Why, ma'am, he was delicious."

Suzie Terrell's smile had turned into a rictus by the time she had managed to steer Badger across the threshold of the reception room and out into the hall. He was still trying to wave as she slammed the door behind them.

"Wal," he said, "I don't know about that Vagenya guy . . ."

"Shut up!" she hissed.

"No, I'm serious," said Badger. "I try to be as accommodating as I can to the team sponsors, but I gotta tell you, that kissing booth idea of his just made my skin crawl. There ain't no way I'm doing that. You tell them, all right? It's not in my contract, stuff like that. Not even close."

Suzie waved away his concerns about the Vagenya schemes. "You *ate* that turtle! You ate that poor defenseless, endangered— *What is wrong with you?*"

He shrugged and began to walk off down the corridor, but she ran after him and grabbed him by the elbow. "You barbarian!" she hissed. "How could you?"

Badger shrugged and tried to pull away, but she tightened her grip on his arm, and when he saw tears spring into her eyes, he sighed and patted her shoulder. "Okay," he sighed. "I didn't eat the turtle. He's fine. Jesse down to the body shop is keeping him right now, and my buddy Paul is building him a little pen at my lake house with a little spring-fed pool for him to swim in. If the vet ever says he's well enough to go back in the lake, we'll turn him loose next time I get down there, and if he doesn't ever get fit for the wild, I reckon I'll just keep him around."

Suzie stared. "Then why did you tell them that you'd eaten him. Did you want those women to think you were a Neanderthal?"

He nodded unhappily. "Sorta," he said.

"But *why*? They pay your salary! Don't you want them to like you?"

He thought about it. "Well, to tell you the truth—not too much."

When her horrified expression did not waver, he shook his head. "Come on," he said softly. "Let's get out of here, and I'll explain it to you on the way out."

"I can hardly wait to hear it," muttered Suzie. "Has your medication worn off? Is that it?"

"Look, I like animals, okay? Always have, from the time I was a little kid. And I know that ladies are real soft-hearted when it comes to animals—well, from a distance they are, anyhow. I mean, you try to keep a raccoon in the bathroom or a garter snake in your sock drawer and they'll sing a different tune, but they like to *think* they like animals. You know, in the abstract."

"Uh-huh. So?"

"So you told them about my big wounded turtle, and they were getting all misty over it, and the next thing you know they'd want to know what its name was, and then they'd try to send little presents for it. Turtle booties or something. And then they'd want to come *see* the turtle. Somebody would tell a reporter and a cutesy story would turn up in a tabloid, and then five hundred fans would send me turtle key chains, turtle tee shirts, turtle *everything*. And then they'd try to get Turtle Wax to sponsor the damn car. Then everybody would want the thing brought to the track. One time Junior Johnson's sponsor made him race with a live chicken in a cage in his car. Don't think any of us will ever forget that. I'm not taking any chances on having a damn turtle for a copilot."

"Okay, but did you have to say that you'd eaten it?"

He shrugged. "Well, it saved a lot of argument. It's a snapping turtle, anyhow, so he's not exactly sociable. You ever see a snapper the size of a garbage can lid? This boy bit the tip off a broom handle one day. Anyhow, by telling that lie, I didn't have to hurt those ladies' feelings by telling 'em they couldn't come by to see my turtle."

Suzie smiled sweetly. "Yes, I expect a lot of women want to see your turtle, don't they?"

He shrugged and looked away. "That Christine woman sure does," he said. "I need to keep my distance from her."

Her last remark had reminded Suzie of another matter she

needed to mention to Badger. "By the way, speaking of seeing your turtle, I think the team wants our new publicist to write a feature article about you in your natural habitat."

His brow furrowed. "What's that mean? They wanna come to my house?"

"Well, yes, but not to your place in Mooresville. They want to send someone back to Georgia to see where you grew up. You know, the life and times of Badger Jenkins."

"Follow me around and all?"

"Right. Take photos, put together a little human interest story about you. Would that be all right?"

He shrugged. "I don't mind, if she doesn't get in my way. I don't want to spend my day off sitting around being interviewed. But if I can do my fishing and all while she asks me stuff, it'll be all right."

"Good. I'll have the publicist call you to decide on the particulars. Her name is Sark."

He nodded solemnly. "And does she want to see my turtle?"

Suzie did not trust herself to reply.

CHAPTER VII

Daydream Believer

Taran Stiles reread the online notice in *Engine Noise* for the third time. *All-woman pit crew* . . . That bit of information interested her somewhat, but what really caught her attention—what held her so spellbound that her luncheon cheeseburger cooled into a puddle of grease in its wrapper on her desk—was the other bit of information tucked in the article. Unable to contain her emotion at this momentous news, she let out a yelp of joy, right there in the office.

Matt Troxler, in the next cubicle, rolled his chair back until he could see her computer screen. "What is it now, you silly git?" he asked, in tones suggesting that he didn't want to know. "A long-lost Tolkien manuscript discovered?"

"No," said Taran, "it's my other obsession. NASCAR."

"NASCAR." Troxler shuddered. "Couldn't you just chew tobacco, dear?"

They'd had this discussion so many times that each of them could have argued the other's position, so Taran didn't bother to respond to his salvo. "A new team is hiring Badger Jenkins to drive for them. I'll get to see him again!"

Troxler raised his eyebrows to indicate incredulity and nodded toward Taran's work space, adorned with a Badger Jenkins mouse pad; a poster of him in his blue firesuit; a fierce-looking Badger in dark sunglasses on an official NASCAR coffee mug; and her computer screensaver: a candid shot of Badger Jenkins leaning on his race car with a look of fierce determination on his perfect features. *(Troxler called that pose "Badger Erectus.")*

Taran had the grace to blush. "I mean a chance to *really* see him," she said. "He has been holed up in that Fortress of Solitude of his in north Georgia, and he hasn't even been interviewed on the SPEED Channel in months. I miss him. But—oh, I feel so guilty, Matt!"

"Really? Why? Have you been buying his garbage on eBay?"

"No, I feel guilty for wanting to see him back out there. It's so *dangerous*. When he was racing I worried about him all the time."

Troxler sighed. "You could always watch something else on Sunday afternoons," he said.

She nodded. "Sometimes I did. When he was in that awful car last season, and he kept having mechanical problems and getting so many laps down—you know what I'd do? I'd put *Gladiator* in the DVD player, paused on the scene where Russell Crowe is in the arena fighting the tigers, and then I'd watch the race. And when it got too painful to watch—when Badger was a couple of laps down, fighting to keep the car out of the wall or having mechanical problems—I'd push PLAY on the DVD and watch the movie instead. Somehow it hurt less to watch Russell Crowe being mauled by tigers than to watch Badger wrestling with that awful car, but I still felt like I was seeing the race. I worried about him so much."

Troxler sighed. Since his own hobby was an appreciation of modern dance, he couldn't really relate to this fever pitch of anxiety on behalf of one's hero, but he knew that Taran was desperately sincere about it. Propped up against the poster of Badger was a ceramic leaf inscribed with a Bible verse: Psalm 91:11: "For He shall give His angels charge over thee, to keep thee in all thy ways." Taran, he knew, was not particularly religious, but just as there are no atheists in foxholes, he supposed that maxim might prove equally true of devotees of race car drivers.

"Taran, you don't know him," he reminded her gently.

"I do," she said. "I got his autograph at the Atlanta Motor Speedway, and then last year he did a signing at an auto parts store.

There weren't many people there, and I shook his hand and he smiled at me, and said, 'Hey, sweetie.' "

Troxler sighed. "And you didn't get your name legally changed to that? I marvel at your restraint. Is he married by any chance?"

Taran made a face. "He was," she said. "To a former Miss Georgia-USA. Very pretty, if you like the type. But she wasn't a NASCAR fan; she said it was like joining the circus, having to fly somewhere every weekend to sit through a hot, noisy car race. So she dumped poor Badger for a billionaire developer of beachfront condos. Can you imagine?"

"It boggles the mind," said Troxler solemnly.

"I know. I don't think he ever got over it, either. Anyhow, I worry about him so much. I hope he'll be all right with this new team. It can't be as bad as the last one. Women are more attentive to detail than men."

"Women?"

"Uh-huh. Did I tell you? The whole team except for the driver is female. The article online said they were looking to hire pit crew personnel."

Troxler smirked. "Well, I suppose if you really wanted to look out for your precious race car driver, you'd join the team so that you could look out for him personally."

The look on Taran's face told him that he should have put more sarcasm into his tone, because her expression had taken on that rapturous look of martyrs and undermedicated saints who are about to give their all for the Cause.

He hastened to add, "Of course, I'm sure it's very specialized work, pitting. Or crewing. Or whatever they call it. I don't suppose you can just volunteer."

"I think you can," said Taran. "There aren't many women in the business. They'll probably train the people they hire." Idly, she tapped a few letters on the keyboard, making Badger's face vanish from the screen, to be replaced by an official-looking document: her résumé.

"But you're an electrical engineer, Taran. Surely the pay cut would be the fiscal equivalent of skydiving."

"I expect so," said Taran. "But I do have a parachute. I invested wisely in tech stock and sold them just in time. I could afford a year on minimum wage."

Troxler sighed, wondering why it was never that easy to persuade people to do things that you actually *wanted* them to do. "You're quite sure about this?" he said.

Without looking away from the screen, Taran nodded. "If they accept me, I'm gone."

"Um, look, Tare . . . I think it's great for people to want to follow their dreams and all, but I don't want to see you throw a good job away for a pipe dream. You don't think that this job is going to lead to a relationship with this driver guy, do you?"

Taran stiffened. She was staring at her screen saver—that impossibly beautiful photo of the stern man in the firesuit and sunglasses with his cleft chin and his perfect, perfect nose. Reflected in the screen's shiny surface was a dim image of her own face— with its thin lips, freckled nose, and pale, too-small eyes, that radiated not beauty but intelligence. No, there was nothing about her that would make Badger Jenkins even slow to a walk if he passed her on the street. Unless she could somehow make him realize that no one could ever love him as much as she did.

"No, Troxler," said Taran softly. "I know nothing will come of this. I'd just like to meet him is all."

Matt Troxler nodded, pretending to believe her. "Okay," he said. "Well . . . that's good. Umm, then can I have your stapler?"

Taran waved away the stapler. "Sure. Whatever. Take it now. But go away. I have work to do."

And she did have work to do, but she didn't do it. Instead, she logged on to the Badger Jenkins unofficial fan Web site *(Badger's Din)*, the address of all of her best friends, none of whom she had ever met. At least once a day, the several dozen people who constituted Badger Jenkins's most loyal and hopeless supporters would log on to hash over the latest rumors about their idol's NASCAR career, or to alert each other to the mention of his name in news articles. Sometimes one of them would have a thirty-second encounter with Badger at a scheduled appearance, and then a breathless account of What He Said to Me *("How you doin', sweetie . . .")* would be posted and endlessly discussed. The account was often accompanied by a fuzzy digital photo of Badger gazing pleasantly into the camera lens, flanked by a beaming fan in the transports of religious ecstasy. So you knew what some of your fellow disciples looked like, but not their real names, because the women tended to use aliases, like *Lady Badger* (wishful thinking), *Badgeera,* or *Short Track Gal,* while the male fans called themselves things like *FastDrawl* or *Bonneville Bill.*

Some of the guys had an annoying habit of digressing into harangues about pro football or their mostly nonexistent sex lives, and they tended to "flame" any adoring female who dared to make syrupy comments about Badger's perfect nose or his golden brown eyes, but all in all, the folks at *Badger's Din* were the only people in the world willing to discuss day after day, *ad nauseum*, the fascinating topic of Badger Jenkins.

Is this new team any good? What is his new number? Sponsor? Has anybody seen any new Badger gear? Ordered a hat or a tee shirt? How is Badger's turtle doing? Every day they danced around in a ring and supposed, but Badger never ever replied or took any notice of them at all. They didn't expect him to, really. They became friends, and sometimes their own discussions of snowstorms, sick children, and job issues took such prominence on the site that one would almost think they had forgotten that Badger was the reason they were there.

But now their personal lives were forgotten, and they were all abuzz with the news of Badger's new team. An all-female team! *Is it true that Miss Norway is going to be one of the pit crew? Had they hired a beautiful Vegas blackjack dealer as a tire changer?* Rumors were rife. One of the posters had a friend whose son was dating the daughter of a NASCAR mechanic, and so she had it on very good authority that . . . Except the rumors never turned out to be true somehow.

Taran sat with her fingers poised over the keyboard. She was going to tell them that she would be trying out for a spot on the pit crew of Badger's new team. She would have the inside track. She would befriend their revered driver. The news she reported would not be a miasma of rumor; it would be actual team business. For once Badger's fans would know the facts—even before

Engine Noise got the scoop. She took a deep breath, but she didn't push down any keys.

She hadn't actually gotten the job yet. Why get this bunch all excited about a mere possibility? The guys (especially *FastDrawl*) would tease her mercilessly and make bets that she wouldn't be chosen. The female *Badger's Din* members would be more supportive, but their very enthusiasm would be annoying, too. They would ask her every day—no, *twice* a day!—if she had got the job yet. And once she had it, they would ask her a thousand questions a week.

What was he wearing? What does he eat for lunch? Can you get him to personalize a team hat for my nephew's birthday?— And, worst of all . . . *When can we visit?*

Oh, yes, they would want to visit. Taran would suddenly become the Queen of the Damned, the high priestess of the *Din,* and the dearest friend of several dozen cyberstrangers with agendas. They would want passes to Cup races, permission to attend practices. Oh no! They would want to meet Badger. To have dinner with Badger. To become *pals* with Badger. They would consider Taran their personal ambassador to Planet Badger. *Can he come to my company's annual picnic? Can we have a tour of his motor home? What's his cell phone number?*

Taran shuddered. She could not possibly tell them what she was up to. No, she would go ahead and try out for the pit crew, without telling any of her friends in NASCAR fandom. All right, they were her friends, sort of, but her first allegiance was to the man himself. She resolved then and there that if she were chosen to serve on Badger's pit crew, she would have to keep it a secret from the *Din.* Oh, she might tell them some things, a tidbit here and there, just because she knew that they loved Badger, too, but she wouldn't tell them how she came by her information. And when all her tips turned out to be completely accurate, she would gain the respect of everyone, even the odious *FastDrawl.*

Taran nodded to herself. It was the only sensible course of action. Now, having made her decision, she took a deep breath and began to type:

Hi Guys! Great news about Badger's new ride! If
anybody hears anything about the team, I hope we
hear it here first! Can't wait! Badger 4-Ever,
Mellivora.

That was Taran's name on the site: Mellivora, the honey badger. She was proud of having come up with that.

CHAPTER VIII

Badger Meets His Crew Chief

"Hello, Badger. Remember me?"

"Yes, ma'am," said Badger meekly. She looked at him, standing there in his tatty jeans and an old Talladega tee shirt. On the wall directly behind him hung a framed poster of Badger Jenkins the Race Car Driver in his firesuit and opaque shades, leaning against the race car with a look of sullen insolence on his chiseled features. As usual, she could find no resemblance between the powerful man on the poster and the shy-looking kid in front of her. When Tuggle entered the team office, he had stood up. Now he was looking at her with all the solemn deference of a nine-year-old called on the carpet in the principal's office.

Tuggle's stern expression did not change, but inwardly she was gratified that despite his fame and money, Badger at heart had remained a well brought-up country boy, to whom manners were second only to breathing. Good. He'd live longer. "Just make it Tuggle," she said gruffly. "You know we're going to be working together."

He gave her one of those smiles that could melt asphalt, and his dark eyes burned with earnest fervor. "It is my honor to work with you, ma'am," he said, in a golden baritone that dipped every vowel in molasses. "I'm going to give this team one hundred percent."

"Boy, you can't even count that high," said Tuggle. "And you can dial back that drawl, too. That accent is your get-out-of-jail free card, but it won't be working on me."

His eyes widened a bit, but he contrived not to react to this speech.

"I know about you," said Tuggle. "I've heard tell. We've not worked together, but the racing world is a small town, and everybody knows everything, so we're going to have a little talk now, and you'd better hope we don't have to have it again."

He nodded, expressionless, and she couldn't tell whether he was still all polite obedience or whether he was mad as hell but holding it in for the sake of the job. Well, she didn't care either way. Whether he took it easy or fought her tooth and nail, things were going to be done her way, and that was that. She knew that some of the team would look at that Christmas tree angel face of his and melt, but it left her unmoved, except as a warning that here was a pretty boy who had cruised through life in neutral on account of that doll baby face. Well, she wasn't buying it.

"As wheel men go, you're not half bad, Badger," she conceded. "You came up on dirt track, and that's in your favor. Means you can drive a loose car without taking out half the field. That'll help some. And your instincts are good—you don't swerve when you can't see; you don't throw the race to win a grudge match against some other driver. Put you in a race car, and I got no complaints." She saw him begin to smile and she held up her hand to forestall his relief. "*But*—there's more to this job than seat-of-the-pants talent. And that's what we need to talk about."

The smile faded. "Yes, ma'am?"

"Anybody can drive a damn car." His jaw tightened at that remark, and she knew she would get an argument out of him about that. Deserved one, too. It wasn't true—*not* anybody could drive a car, not the way they drove in NASCAR. It wasn't like a run down the local interstate. It took the courage of a teenaged rhinoceros and the hand-eye coordination of a sniper. You couldn't learn it much past childhood, either. Most of the successful drivers had started out in go-carts about the time their six-year molars came in; because if you waited for your wisdom teeth before you started racing, you would never be good enough.

Badger had started young, and he had what it took to be great—except that he wasn't a corporate type, and in today's sport, that flaw was fatal. Her only hope was to berate him into co-operation. It was a gamble, but she thought it was worth a try. His previous teams had all tried to reform Badger, using everything from bribes to threats, but nothing they did had ever worked. She thought the unvarnished truth was worth a shot.

She took a deep breath and let him have it. "You have the at-tention span of popcorn, boy. And you are either bone lazy or too overconfident to live; I can't figure out which. I don't much care. You're what they call a prima donna, and with a team full of women, that is the last thing I need. Yeah, I heard about you with that last team you drove for. You acted like they paid you by the hour with no overtime. They practically had to tie you to a chair to see you other than on race days. I heard. They fired you, too, remember."

She saw his eyes glisten, and she felt the comforting words rise up in her throat, but she choked them back. Hell, she wanted to hug him, poor little thing. Oh, but she knew better. "Don't look at me like a whipped spaniel, either, boy. Your mother died when you were born. Yeah. Everybody knows that from the press kit in-formation. *Poor old Badger.* And ever since then those mournful brown eyes of yours have made every woman over the age of twenty want to baby you to make up for it, with the consequence that you have been getting away with murder all your damn life. So I'm just putting you on notice, Pretty Boy, that this act of yours will not be working with me, understand?"

"I hear you," he said softly, his face as expressionless as milk. He was good, though. She had to concede that. He could do "earnest sincerity" better than a damn cocker spaniel.

"I expect you do hear me. I'm talking loud enough. Just get it through your head that I expect you to do a proper job and to work as hard as the rest of us. You be here when I tell you to be here, and you put us first. Not your business deals or your fishing buddies or your daddy's tractor problems, or whatever the hell else you come up with that interferes with the running of this team. *Do-you-understand?*"

She saw his jaw tighten, and on each cheek there was a spot of color in an otherwise ashen face. Tight-lipped, he nodded.

"Fair enough," she said. "You know, Badger, I believe I would be your momma if you were still young enough to take a belt to. Except that you're no little kid. Hell, you're older than Jeff Gordon, and sometimes you look hotter than a two-dollar pistol. And posters of you like that one"—she nodded toward the firesuit photo—"can make even me think thoughts about you that would melt the decals off that race car. Except that I know better than to confuse the paint job with what's under the hood. *You ain't him.* You never saw the day, boy. Well, in real life you're not him, anyhow. But maybe if you learn to work with me instead of fighting me every step of the way, you can be him on the race track. I'd like you to make me believe it's that stud on the Technicolor poster that's driving my car. Will you try to do that?"

He nodded, taking deep breaths like he figured breathing in was better than letting any sound come out right now.

"Well, all right, then. We have a deal." She took a deep breath. One hurdle down, another big one to go. "Did anybody tell you who the sponsor is?"

Badger's face brightened. "Yeah. I'm real happy about that."

Tuggle blinked. "You are?"

"Why, sure. Richmond and Martinsville are about my favorite tracks, and I'm a big fan of the Hokies in football. And there's King's Dominion . . ."

Tuggle digested this information. Then she nodded, not even surprised, really. "The Hokies. Virginia Tech, right? Badger, do you by any chance believe that your race car is being sponsored by the Commonwealth of Virginia?"

"Well, sure. Somebody in the front office mentioned it to me. Isn't it great? I'll be honest with you: I was surprised. You'd think they'd want to sponsor Elliott Sadler, though, wouldn't you? On account of him being from there. Or maybe Jeff Burton."

"Well, I think I can explain that to you, Badger. What they told you was that the sponsor is *Vagenya.* Yeah, I know it sounds about the same when you say it, but they didn't mean the state. Vagenya is the name of a new drug, and the pharmaceutical manufacturer is our team sponsor."

"Vagenya," said Badger, thinking hard. "Never heard of it."

"No," said Tuggle, "I don't expect you would have. But since you're driving for those folks, you'll probably get asked about it in press interviews."

Badger assumed an expression that he probably thought of as crafty. "Y'all want me to say I use the stuff?"

Tuggle's lips twitched. "That won't be necessary, Badger. Thank you all the same."

"*Vagenya,* huh?" He savored the word, probably trying to commit it to memory. "Va-gen-ya. What does it do, anyhow?"

She hesitated. "You have a meeting coming up with the team publicist. Since it's her job to prep you for media interviews, I think I'll let her explain it to you."

Badger's amiable countenance clouded over again. "A meeting when?" he said. "I'm pretty busy this week."

Tuggle stared at him expressionless for a long moment waiting for him to blink, and when he did, she said, "You've already forgotten what I just told you, haven't you? You will not give this team lip service instead of full cooperation. You will give us one hundred percent, or else the only drug you will need to worry about is Preparation H, because I will shove my foot so far up your ass . . . Now, get over to the shop and see do they need you."

Without a word, Badger turned on his heel and left the office.

Deanna, the secretary who had been hiding in the photocopy room, crept back out when she heard the slamming of the office door. She was in her early thirties, and on her desk was an old Badger Jenkins coffee mug, bearing a photo of a younger Badger with his hair in an Arthurian pageboy, wearing a blue firesuit reminiscent of a knight's tunic and leaning against a wall with such a reverent expression that he lacked only the horse and sword to look like Sir Galahad.

"Wow," she said. "I can't believe you talked to him like that. He's so famous."

"I'm trying to keep him that way," said Tuggle grimly.

"But you were so mean to him. When you said all those harsh

things, his eyes glistened, and I was afraid he was going to cry. It was all I could do to keep from bursting into tears myself. I just wanted to hug him."

"More fool you," said Tuggle. "That boy needs to straighten up. Being pretty might help you win fans and sponsors, but the rest of this sport is pure Type A male and it's run by corporate piranhas. They won't put up with his shenanigans for one second. Time somebody told him so."

"Do you think he listened?"

The crew chief sighed. "More or less," she said. "I reckon I'll have that speech down by heart before I'm done giving it, though."

Deanna looked thoughtful. "I've got some items here that fans sent in for him to autograph, and he always says he doesn't have time . . ."

Tuggle gave her a look.

The secretary shook her finger at the framed firesuit poster of Badger Almighty. "All right, Pretty Boy," she said. "Sit your ass down at the conference table and sign those hero cards *right now*."

Tuggle nodded. "Keep practicing," she said. "I'll shoo him back in here when we're done at the shop and you can tell him that for real."

The secretary sighed. "Yeah, but I'd rather hug him."

CHAPTER IX

The Dominatrix

Badger Jenkins didn't think anybody would recognize him in the Mooresville Wendy's. Maybe Jeff Gordon and Dale Earnhardt, Jr. got mobbed everywhere they went, but most of the other drivers, when they weren't wearing firesuits, were relatively anonymous. Although if you were going to be recognized anywhere, it would be in Mooresville, the epicenter of behind-the-scenes racing. Desperate fans on the prowl for NASCAR stars had even been known to mistake local plumbers and lowly shop dogs for Busch drivers, and anyone with a beard could pass for Martin Truex. Even Elliott Sadler. If your autograph book bore the inscription "Casey Caine," that was a good sign that the blue-eyed young man in the coveralls at the Waffle House had not, in fact, been Cup driver Kasey Kahne.

Since Badger wanted an uninterrupted ten-minute lunch, he had kept his sunglasses on, just in case. He didn't have much time to eat. They wanted him at the shop in the early afternoon, and he had got busy with phone calls—it was always something—so now he figured he had only a few minutes to wolf down a burger, and then he'd better get over there, to keep Tuggle off his case.

He had just lifted the oozing burger for another bite when a scraggly woman in starling black slid into the other side of the booth. "Badger Jenkins," she said. "Nice to meet you. I don't have much time." She set her cell phone down on the table next to his

French fries and scowled at her wristwatch as if it were directly responsible for her shortage of time.

He had no idea who she was.

A fan? Badger set the burger back down on the wrapper and summoned a wan smile. He eased the Sharpie out of the pocket of his jeans and glanced around for something to autograph. It wouldn't be the first paper napkin he'd ever signed for a fan. This woman seemed more than a little flaky, but you got used to that after a while. "How're you doin'?" he mumbled, as if her intrusive behavior were completely normal.

The woman eyed the Sharpie with a sneer. "Oh, I don't want your autograph," she said.

He blinked. She didn't look like somebody who would be a fan of his. After a while you could sorta tell who favored whom in racing fandom just by the way they dressed and talked. Come to think of it, he couldn't even hazard a guess at which driver would attract the likes of her. Well, okay, if he *had* to guess, he'd say she'd be a *Kevin Harvick fan*. Harvick was a Californian, and a little unconventional himself. Yeah, that would fit.

The scraggly woman could have been any age between thirty and fifty—and as plain as she was, nobody would have cared which. Her helmet of dyed crinkly black hair framed a moon face with skin the color of library paste, raccoon eye shadow, and carefully penciled-in lips colored clown red. She wore some kind of sleazy, shiny black outfit that might have cost a lot, but if so, the designer was probably somewhere yelling "Gotcha!"

Badger didn't mind plain, dowdy women, as long as they didn't lunge at him. He tried to be nice to everybody, and generally he succeeded, but he had hoped to eat his lunch in peace. So he sat there waiting for her to say what she wanted, and he hoped it wasn't "Kevin Harvick's cell phone number," which he didn't know anyhow.

"Badger, I am Melodie Albigre, and I'm affiliated with Miller O'Neill Associates," she said, as if that explained everything.

He blinked. If she was expecting a lightbulb to go on in his brain, she'd have a long wait coming. Badger knew all the Cup team names, one or two law firms, a couple of sponsors, and maybe a dozen or so rock groups, but as best he could recall, none of them was named "Miller O'Neill."

"It's a management firm," she said.

Badger adjusted his expression to reflect "shrewd and business-like." He was good at facial expressions—like a German shepherd, contriving to look serious and wise in the presence of about-to-be-dropped food. Whether any concomitant thought ever accompanied Badger's appropriate demeanor was a matter of considerable speculation. He ventured a comment: "*Management.* You mean like . . . apartment buildings?"

"No. I do not." She didn't look like a fan. She wasn't smiling or simpering or fishing NASCAR cards out of her purse. She reminded him of a particularly stern grade school teacher he'd once had, one whose pet name for him had been "Insect."

"Miller O'Neill manages celebrities," she informed him briskly. "And race car drivers. I am quite well known. I'm surprised you haven't heard of me." She contrived to make it sound as if that were his fault. "I do a bit of everything. I write grants, set up television shows. Anything, really. We need to discuss your future—insofar as you have one, Badger."

"Shrewd and businesslike" was congealing into "annoyed," but Miss Albigre was unmoved by her listener's reaction. "You need help," she said briskly. "I heard that you have been hired by the new women's Cup team. Congratulations. You have been given a second chance, and you need someone to make sure that you make the most of this opportunity. Someone to generate prospects for you. Commercials. Endorsements. Because you're *not* famous, you know, Badger. You're not Jimmie Johnson. And you're certainly not getting any younger. You'd better secure your future while you can."

Badger shrugged. "I do all right," he said.

"Really?" She had that you-gave the-wrong-answer look that he remembered from sixth grade. "Do you? What provision is there in your contract for, say, appearance fees?"

"Uh. Well . . ." He tried to smile. "I don't exactly have everything we agreed on the contract spelled out in writing in the contract. I just give my word."

She rolled her eyes. "*Idiot.* How many times have *you* gone into the wall? No contract, indeed! You obviously need somebody to manage your career."

"I'm just not sure I can afford—" Badger's cheapness was legendary.

Melodie Albigre gave him a chilling smile. "You won't be able to afford anything if you keep going as you have been. But don't worry. Miller O'Neill pays my salary. It will all come off the top where you won't miss it. You're certainly lucky that I am between projects at the moment, aren't you?"

Badger felt as if the floor were tilting. "Uh . . . well."

"Of course, you are. That's settled. I can handle everything. I will see that you make lots of money. And you'll need it, won't you?"

"What?"

In a failed-to-spell-cat-correctly voice, she said, "Well, there's just a rumor going around that a development corporation is planning to put a retirement community on that north Georgia lake you're so fond of. Golf course. Two hundred condos. Tennis courts. Roads. I'm surprised you hadn't heard. But perhaps it isn't a done deal yet. You might be able to buy the land yourself, I suppose. If you could afford it." She eyed him critically. "You may be a hard sell in a promotional sense. You're not very sexy, if you ask me, but I suppose there are people who'd like you. Hicks and old ladies, maybe."

He tried to speak, but there were too many conflicting thoughts battling for precedence in his head, so that his only response was a feeble croak of alarm.

The human steamroller nodded, as if she spoke croak fluently. "Leave it to me," she said. "Now, I need your cell phone number, your home number, a team number where you can be reached . . . Is there anything in your life you don't want me involved in?"

"Uh, I guess not."

Looking back on it later, he thought that a portion of that conversation had been skipped over. The part where Melodie Albigre should have asked him if he wanted a manager, and if he was actually consenting to be bossed around by her without limitation.

He was sure that he would have said no. But she didn't ask. She just rolled over him like a Sherman tank en route to Berlin, and before he knew it, he had acquired a manager he hadn't known he needed. It was like getting a fairy godmother, he supposed, if your fairy godmother could be a dowdy, bitchy woman who didn't much like you.

If Badger had paid more attention to the vampire movie he saw once at the county drive-in, instead of trying to exchange bodily fluids with his date of the evening, he might have found one of Miss Albigre's questions quite familiar. "What don't you want me involved in?" According to folklore, you had to invite a vampire into your residence or else they could not cross the threshold. And while Melodie Albigre was certainly not a vampire, whatever she was, he had just invited her in. But at the time he was not apprehensive about the arrangement. He had someone to run his life and make money for him, practically for free.

He began to scribble all his phone numbers on the paper lining of the Wendy's tray, and for the first time in their brief acquaintance, Melodie Albigre smiled.

CHAPTER X

Tryouts

ENGINE NOISE
Your Online Source for NASCAR News & Views

Hearts Like a Wheel? Look out, Badger. We hear
you're going back into a Cup car, and your car number will be 86. We don't know who your primary
sponsor is, but it ought to be Amazon.com, because
that's who your team is going to be: *all Amazons.*
Yep, you heard it here first, folks: The "adorable"
Badger Jenkins has been captured by an *all-woman*
racing team. Woo hoo! Looks like he's going to be
the "lucky dog" in every race. Pit crew tryouts are
this week at the team headquarters in Mooresville.
Hot pass, anyone?

"Are you nervous? I am!" Taran Stiles whispered to the burly
woman beside her.

The big woman shrugged. She was wearing an extra-extra large
Darlington tee shirt, and she had used red yarn to tie her greasy
blond hair into a limp pony tail. She didn't look like fear played a
big part in her life. "Nothing to stew about," she said. "Either you
make it or you don't. There's plenty of other teams, you know.
Plenty of better paying jobs, for that matter."

Well, that was true, thought Taran. She had investigated the matter online for several weeks now, and she had learned that some of the Busch pit crew members even worked for free, or for expenses, anyhow. Cup racing at least paid pit crew a salary; less than she had been making in her corporate cubicle, but she reasoned that she ought to go out and have adventures while she was still young. The cubicle would still be there when she was too old for wilder endeavors.

She still couldn't believe that she was actually in Mooresville. It was only a small town north of Charlotte but to true racing fans, Mooresville, North Carolina, was the center of the universe: headquarters of many of the race shops, home to some of the Cup drivers, and the site of the Dale Earnhardt Incorporated building, the legendary Garage Mahal of the Intimidator himself. It was also the current residence of Badger Jenkins. According to *Engine Noise,* he had left his fishing shack at the lake in Georgia and moved to Mooresville to be close to his new team. He might even be here today. Taran shivered. And all she had to do to be allowed to stay here was to do well on the pit crew audition.

At first glance the race shop yard looked like the setting for cheerleader tryouts: fifty women in shorts and tee shirts milling around or chatting in small groups, waiting to be told what to do. Closer inspection, though, would definitely rule out cheerleader tryouts. Some of these women could have been linebackers, and several of them looked old enough to have daughters in high school.

There was no doubt about who was in charge, though. The stern-looking woman in an official team windbreaker with the word "Tuggle" embroidered on it was stalking around the yard, eying the prospective crew members as if they were horses and she was the buyer for Alpo. Judging by her scowl, she didn't seem unduly impressed by what she saw. Occasionally, though, she would stop and talk to one of the women, and then make a notation on her clipboard for future reference.

This is it, thought Taran. *My one chance to work with him.* For luck today she had worn her best Badger Jenkins tee shirt, the one from his former team, commemorating his winning of the Southern 500. The one he had actually signed for her one blazing afternoon in Atlanta, when she had waited in a sweltering line for what seemed like forever just to get thirty seconds of his time.

He had been sitting at a metal card table in front of the souvenir trailer, looking much less formidable in jeans and a polo shirt than he did in his firesuit. When at last it was her turn to enter The Presence, he had glanced up at her through opaque sunglasses, Sharpie marker poised for signing, his expression as solemn as that of a child.

She had set the gray tee shirt down on the table next to a stack of eight-by-ten team photo cards and the half dozen brightly feathered fishing lures, which had been gifts to him from other people in the autograph line. Fans liked to bring drivers tokens of their affection, except, of course, that they had no idea what to give their idols. Who knew what drivers were really like? You mostly relied on what it said in the team-generated press releases. So, for lack of better information, fans tended to believe the clichés in the driver biographies published in motorsports magazines or on team Web sites. Civil War buff Sterling Marlin was given military books and old bullets; Tony Stewart, the animal lover, received toy tigers; and handsome bachelors like Kasey Kahne probably got a lot of phone numbers, perfume-soaked fan letters, and more intimate offerings that wouldn't bear thinking about. The fan gifts of choice for Badger Jenkins were items related to freshwater fishing, since everybody knew that he was a country boy who lived on a lake in north Georgia. Hence, the fishing lures—small, portable, inexpensive, but appropriate tokens of a stranger's affection. No one ever seemed to realize that the cliché present was the one everybody else had thought of, too, and that Badger was likely to have drawers full of fishing lures. Still, yet another fishing lure was probably better than the other typical fan offerings: homemade clothing, badly drawn amateur portraits based on sports card photos, or pictures of the pet that was named after him (Badger the cat, Badger the gerbil). Some guy had a Web site featuring a NASCAR cartoon in which Badger really *was* a badger.

When Taran finally reached the front of the line she had taken a deep breath, hardly trusting herself to speak to him, and said, "Could you sign this for me, please?"

He had nodded. That was one good thing about NASCAR drivers. They pretty much would sign anything. Your shirt *(sometimes with you in it)*, a photo, a die-cast car, your arm. Whatever. It was all the same to them. She'd heard that some drivers would only sign sanctioned items produced by the companies with which they had merchandising deals, but for the most part, the guys were really nice and would autograph anything you handed them. Word went around among the fans about who was difficult and who wasn't. By all accounts, Badger wasn't.

He had spread out her gray tee shirt on the table in front of him, and with a fine-point Sharpie marker, he had begun to inscribe his name on the fabric above the transfer image of his face. Taran wondered what it would be like to see people walking around wearing pictures of yourself on their shirts. Possibly creepy, she thought. He was probably used to it, though. Anyhow, he didn't seem to mind.

Taran had spent the half hour in line trying to think up just the right thing to say to him. Should she ask him about fishing, or wish him luck in the race, or tell him how wonderful she thought he was? What could she say that he hadn't heard a dozen times in the past thirty minutes? She watched the letters of his name seep into the gray cotton shirt, thinking that she had only seven letters left to say what would have taken her a day to fully express.

Finally, when he had finished inscribing the "s" in Jenkins, he handed back the autographed shirt. His hand brushed against her fingertips, and to her horror she heard herself blurt out, "I love you."

Badger froze for an instant, looking up at her with no expression, and then, solemnly, even sadly perhaps, he nodded.

Oddly enough, she thought that he seemed to understand. She had not said it happily or seductively. She had said "I love you" as if it were the symptom of an ailment, which it probably was. Those three words, in that particular tone of voice, had meant: *I know you're a total stranger, but I adore you, anyhow, so much that it hurts. . . . I carry more pictures of you in my wallet than I do of my family members. . . . I start crying even before you wreck. . . . I worry too much about you, and too little about me. . . .* and most of all, *I feel really stupid right now, but I can't help myself.*

And he really did seem to understand that her words were not so much a compliment to him as they were a description of her own emotional confusion. She felt the blush begin to spread across her face, and she turned to stumble away before she could compound the embarrassment by bursting into tears. Behind her, she heard a soft drawling voice say, "You take care now." And he had sounded as if he meant it.

For weeks thereafter she had thought she'd never be able to face him again, but finally the memory of his gentle response overrode her shame, and she found that she cared about him more than ever. She bought more posters, a key chain, and another coffee mug, and she posted glowing accounts of his racing performances on his unauthorized fan site *(Badger's Din)*. She had told him she loved him, and he hadn't laughed or rolled his eyes or *anything.* He was a Nice Guy. And Taran Stiles would have died for him, anytime, anywhere.

That autograph session in Atlanta had been more than a year ago, and her devotion to Badger Jenkins remained undimmed. And now here she was, on the verge of becoming his coworker.

The thought of Badger Jenkins made her so nervous that she felt her throat tighten and her stomach churn. She might really get to know him as a friend—if she could ever get up the courage to speak in his presence, that is. Surely she could do something on this team. The ad said that they would train people. She wasn't very hefty, but she did work out to try to build up her muscle tone, and to counteract the effect of having a desk job. Okay, maybe carrying a 70-pound tire with Olympic agility was out of the question, but she could probably hold up signs or something.

They were hiring the personnel for seven jobs today: jackman, gasman, catch can, front tire changer, front tire carrier, rear tire changer, and rear tire carrier. Apparently, you didn't have to tell the judges (or the employers or whatever they were) which job you were applying for. You just jumped in and did what they told you to do, and in the end they chose people for whatever spot they thought they'd work best in. That was fine with Taran. She'd do anything to make this team.

They had been given an hour's worth of preliminary instruction in the various duties of a pit crew. Each woman had been given the opportunity to use the Impact Wrench to tighten the lug nuts on a practice chassis, to lift the tires into place, and to pump up the jack for the tire changes. The instructors explained that the team needed people with physical strength, agility, and the coordination of a dancer, to stay out of everyone else's way. They also needed grace under pressure and the ability to work quickly in noise and haste without getting flustered. It seemed like a tall order, but none of the jobs struck her as intellectually difficult, only physically challenging. She supposed that practice would help.

There were seven slots for over-the-wall pit crew—the only people allowed near the car during a pit stop. You could have lots of people behind the wall, she'd learned, but only seven can enter the pit stall itself: two tire changers; two tire carriers; the jackman who hoists the car up for the tire changes; the gasman who refuels the car; and someone called the catch-can man, who simply stood at the rear of the car to the left, holding a container to catch the overflow of gas during the fill-up. That last job seemed to require the least strength and agility. Taran thought she might have a shot at the position.

She didn't think that any of the applicants were particularly outstanding at any of these tasks, though, of course, some of them were stronger than others. There was a good deal of fumbling. People running into each other. Everything taking much longer than it should have. Taran thought she still might have a good chance to make the team.

She looked around at her fellow applicants, thinking that some of them would be her teammates if she was lucky enough to be chosen, and she might as well start trying to make friends with them. The tanned redhead nearest her looked to be in her late twenties. She wore a Celtic design T-shirt, and her auburn hair was bound in a long braid that hung halfway down her back. Her thin-lipped frown didn't look especially friendly, but Taran told herself that the woman might just be nervous from the pressure of competition.

"Isn't this exciting?" Taran whispered. "Getting to work with Badger Jenkins!"

The woman sniffed and rolled her eyes. "I thought this was supposed to be an all-woman team," she said. "I don't see what we need *him* for."

"Oh, because there aren't any women yet cleared to drive in Cup. Nobody this team could afford, anyhow. My name's Taran, by the way." She held out her hand, still determined to be friendly.

The woman ignored her hand, and said grudgingly, "Reve Galloway. I work in a fitness center in Monterey. Thought this might be fun. Not that I know anything about auto racing, though. Except that there seem to be damn few women involved. I thought I'd like to help change that."

Taran nodded. She knew that the pit crew people would have many different reasons for applying, and as long as they weren't going to be tiresome zealots about their causes, that was fine with her.

"Why are you out here?" Reve asked her.

Taran hesitated. *Because I love Badger Jenkins and I want to keep him safe.* Somehow she didn't think the truth would sit too well with a political Amazon. She shrugged. "Beats typing," she said.

Reve shrugged. "What doesn't? So you're a racer girl, huh?"

Taran blushed. She ought to be used to being teased about it by now. The past few years had been an endless succession of smart remarks from her coworkers about her *addiction,* of NASCAR put-down e-mails forwarded to her by mischievous acquaintances. And then there were the gag gifts. Christmas, birthday, somebody's trip to a flea market or a Dollar Store—all occasions to present Taran with another teasing reference to her hobby. She received Tony Stewart coffee mugs and Matt Kenseth mouse pads. Jeff Gordon posters and Jimmie Johnson notepads. Ryan Newman pencils and Kurt Busch key chains. Apparently, her bemused friends did not understand that NASCAR has teams just as football and basketball do, that the driver is the focal point of the team, and that nearly every racing fan has a favorite driver. Giving a Jeff Burton coffee mug to a devoted Badger Jenkins fan was a waste of money, and if in gift-giving it is the thought that counts, then such a gift would indicate no thought at all. Taran, who never wanted to hurt anybody's feelings, would always thank the giver for the gift, no matter how much they snickered as they were presenting it to her. Then she would drop the offending item off at Goodwill on her way home.

Oh, yes, by now she was accustomed to obnoxious remarks about her NASCAR hobby, but she did think she might escape such treatment at a NASCAR-related event. Apparently not.

"Yes," said Taran, summoning a tepid smile. "I'm an electrical engineer, but also racer girl. What brings you here?"

Reve shrugged. "I told you. Sisterhood. Plus a chance to travel a bit. Maybe I'll get a TV gig out of the experience. I guess you don't have to like this sport to be able to lift a tire."

"Well," said Taran, "it might help."

Reve had noticed Taran's Badger Jenkins tee shirt. "So you are hot for this driver guy?"

"I admire his work," said Taran primly. She certainly wasn't prepared to discuss the catalogue of Badger's attractions with a supercilious stranger.

"I admire his ass," said an older woman behind them.

"How can you tell?" asked another applicant. "He's so wrapped up in that firesuit, he might look like a plucked chicken underneath it all."

Several more women contributed their own graphic opinions concerning the finer points of Badger Jenkins's anatomy, but Taran did not participate in the discussion. Her feelings for Badger were too sacred to be made sport of. She tried to tune out their banter and focus on studying her fellow applicants, trying to figure out which of them would fit each position, and guessing what had motivated them to come.

Several of them looked like they worked in gyms or taught physical education somewhere. Fitness trainers, maybe. One jolly-looking girl with cropped hair and the look of a field hockey player was reading *Paradise Lost* while she waited; Taran supposed she was a college student.

Now, with orientation over, the applicants were being grouped together in various configurations to see who worked well with whom, and all the while overhead video cameras recorded the action for future analysis by the team manager. Taran tried to remain inconspicuous, because she wanted a chance to observe the action one time before she had to do it herself.

"All right, crew!" yelled Tuggle, waving her clipboard over her head for emphasis. "Now we're going to see what you can do under pressure. We're going to bring the car in here for an actual pit stop." She pointed to the seven women nearest to her. "I want you, you, and you—and you four—to be the pit crew this time. The rest of y'all—watch! Your turn is coming up."

She turned back to the seven applicants. "Before we start, go into the garage and find a fire-retardant helmet and a fire-retardant suit that fits you, and gloves and what-not. I assume y'all know that pit crew personnel wear protective gear, as does the driver. We can't do much to protect you from getting run over—and from time to time that does happen, unfortunately—but we can minimize the risks to you from other things that can go wrong."

Someone in the crowd called out, "Such as?"

Tuggle favored them with a grim smile. "Oh, let me count the ways," she said. "Fire is the big one, obviously. The gasman is dumping fuel into an extremely hot vehicle. Sometimes you get a fire. Or a tailpipe can spurt flame, and if you happen to be standing in its path . . . Hey, where are y'all going?"

Nearly a dozen prospective employees had suddenly decided that they weren't quite crazy enough to work on a NASCAR pit crew. Smiling nervously, they raced each other for the gate.

Tuggle took the defection with a philosophical shrug. "Well, you all need to be aware of the risks," she said. "We do everything we can to ensure your safety, but this is not volleyball. People do die in stock car racing—and not just drivers."

She paused while a few more applicants went sane and broke for the exit.

"But we do provide helmets and these nice fire-retardant suits, and you'll be wearing one even in practice." She smiled encouragingly at the diminished pool of would-be team members. "But please bear in mind that those fire-retardant suits are only fireproof for eight seconds—Well, thank you all for stopping by . . ."

Another ten women suddenly remembered a pressing engagement.

Tuggle surveyed the remaining applicants, who were eying her nervously, waiting for further revelations. She grinned at them. "Well, I think we have now weeded out all the people who aren't crazy, so the rest of you, let's get on with this exercise."

They were all novices, and Tuggle wanted them to err on the side of caution, so she didn't bother to tell them that cars used in pit practice normally had their main fuel tank filled with water, with a dump valve installed to dump the water on the ground before they go on to the next round. The engine in practice sessions is run off a small tank installed inside the car, about the size of a two-gallon jug, so that the team can practice filling and emptying fuel, without the waste and danger of spilled fuel, which would create hazardous conditions, especially for amateurs.

Three of the first seven women chosen for the first test had thought better of volunteering, so Tuggle selected replacements and sent the group off to get fitted with protective gear. The remaining applicants murmured uneasily to each other, and the crew chief studied the papers on her clipboard while she waited for the first team to get ready. Finally, they emerged from the shop, outfitted in cast-off suits scrounged from various teams.

"Our colors are purple and white," Tuggle remarked to no one in particular. "But we're still waiting for the official suits to arrive. It will help when we know the sizes of the crew members chosen for the positions, you know."

She nodded to one of the mechanics who was lounging in the doorway of the shop, and he signaled to another mechanic who was stationed at a corner of the building. Suddenly, the purple and white 86 car came roaring around the side of the shop building and screeched to a halt in the designated "pit" area.

The seven hopefuls converged on the car and set to work. The driver, dressed as if it were race day, muffled in a firesuit and a helmet that showed only his eyes, sat there tapping his gloved fingers on the steering wheel, perhaps in dismay at the awkward performance of his would-be pit crew.

Taran knew that the average pit stop in Cup racing—changing four tires and refilling the fuel cell—took about thirteen seconds. This practice stop was reminiscent of the bygone era before Leonard Wood of the Wood Brothers racing team had thought to streamline the process—back in the early fifties, when pitting took five minutes, and drivers got out and walked around while they drank coffee. There was a lot of fumbling, and the jackman couldn't seem to get the car high enough, which considering the way the front end was tilting was probably a good thing.

Grace Tuggle watched the proceedings with the regretful air of someone forced to witness a train wreck. But she didn't yell. When the interminable pit stop finally ended, many dropped tires and some spilled fuel later, she simply nodded, and made some more notes on her clipboard.

She waved the car away, and it zoomed off around the parking lot, behind the shop building and out of sight again. Then she called seven more women forward to repeat the exercise.

Taran was in the third group to try out, and she felt that she was a little more prepared than the first teams simply because she'd been able to observe their mistakes. She was also confused on one particular point.

"All right," said Tuggle, "you know the drill. We're going to assign you duties. Watch how you function as a unit. Film your performance. Speed counts. Accuracy counts. *Everything* counts. Any questions?"

Tentatively, Taran raised her hand. "Who's driving the car?" she asked.

Tuggle glared at her, took an exasperated breath, and then snapped, "Our driver is Badger Jenkins, a veteran Cup driver who has won the Southern 500. Any *other* questions?"

Taran's hand went up again. *"Who . . . is . . . driving . . . the . . . car . . . now?"*

This time Tuggle's look of annoyance turned to a thoughtful

appraisal of the meek but persistent young woman. After a few moments, she said, "I told you. Badger Jenkins."

"Yeah, but that's not him," said Taran.

There were a few gasps from the other applicants, but only a silent stare from Grace Tuggle herself. At last with a grudging smile, she said, "You can't see nothing but his eyes, and you had less than a minute to see them, and you weren't close. What makes you think it wasn't Badger?"

Because I know those eyes. They've stared at me from my screensaver, from my coffee mug . . . from every NASCAR Nation *program I ever Tivoed . . . from a hundred daydreams . . . I know his eyes.*

Aloud, she said, "The helmet is higher above the steering wheel than it ought to be. Guy's too tall to be Badger."

Tuggle squinted at her for a long minute while nobody moved. "What's your name?" she said.

"Taran Stiles." She could feel the other women edging away from her, in case a blast of wrath was forthcoming from the crew chief.

Tuggle nodded, and made a note on her clipboard. "Well, Taran Stiles," she said, "as it happens, you are correct. The driver for today's exercise is Tony Lafon, one of our shop dogs, and he is indeed taller than Badger. You're not. Generally, we want big people on pit crew, but occasionally it helps to have a runt around. So if your physical skills are as good as your powers of observation, you might make the team. Now get going, you seven!"

Afterward, Taran marveled at how nervous she had been for a job that paid only a fraction of what she had been making in the corporate world. She had never thought of herself as a particularly athletic person, and heretofore her competitive instincts had been confined to making the highest score on the exam, but during the tryouts she found herself trying harder than she ever had in any physical activity. The girl who had been content to coast through required courses in physical education suddenly demanded that her body respond like a well-oiled machine, because she *wanted* this job.

And she got it.

Someone from the team had called her the next day to tell her that she was now a member of Badger Jenkins's pit crew. Well, they didn't put it like that, of course. They thought of themselves by number and sponsor and owner. The 86 car; Team Vagenya. To the front office, Badger was just a cog in a money-making machine, but he was what mattered to her. For a fleeting moment she wondered who else had made the cut. Well, she would find out soon enough. There was a team meeting at the end of the week, the beginning of the long process of getting a bunch of novices ready for competition at the highest level of motorsports. First, though, she had to call Matt Troxler back at the old office and tell him that his worst fear had been realized: He had talked someone into a NASCAR career!

Taran went in that Friday to meet her new teammates. Later, she wondered if all randomly assembled groups of people constituted an assortment of types resembling the cast of old war movies. There was Taran herself, the dreamy romantic, who was the catch-can person. Reve Galloway, the gruff crusading fitness worker from California, was the gasman, because she was strong enough to lift a seventy-pound container of fuel.

The hockey playing student reading *Paradise Lost* at tryouts turned out to be a Texan named Cass Jordan—she also brought a book to the team meeting. It turned out that she had been on her high school wrestling team, and she could still bench-press calves. She was Team Vagenya's new jackman.

The front tire carrier, Jeanne Mowbray, was the only girl in a family of construction workers from Ohio, so carrying a heavy tire was not a novelty to her, or to her counterpart, rear tire carrier Sigur Nelson, a flaxen-haired farm girl from Minnesota, who looked as though she was only working in Cup racing until her application to be a Valkyrie was approved.

The two tire changers were less striking physical specimens, because they did not have to lift the tires. The skill they had was not strength, but the dexterity to manipulate the lug nuts and the drill. The oldest of the over-the-wall gang was forty-one-year-old Kathy Erwin, granddaughter of a Carolina racing family. She knew both Tuggle and the team's chief engineer Julie Carmichael, so there was some talk that she got the job through her connections, but even if that were the case, she was exceptionally fast at tire changing, so it hardly mattered.

The second tire changer, Cindy Corlett, was a small, serious girl with a pixie face and long, tapering fingers.

"Are you a mechanic?" Taran had asked her in disbelief.

The dark-haired girl had smiled and shook her head. "Musician," she said. "Bluegrass fiddle. I'm good with my hands, you see."

"But why on earth would you want to change tires on a race car then?"

"I guess I come by it naturally," said Cindy. "Back in Ozark, Arkansas, my family was always about two things: picking and racing. I decided I'd like to try both. My daddy is just thrilled to death about this. I promised to get him a hot pass to Bristol."

So there they were, with a spectrum of backgrounds and home states, each with a different reason for being on board, and each with a second skill to benefit the team. When they weren't needed on pit crew, they would drive the hauler, work as a mechanic, serve as the computer technician, assist the fabricators—there were many talents needed to field a stock car. It made sense to hire people who could serve in more than one capacity. Taran would be the computer person.

She hoped that she would become friends as well as coworkers with this collection of strangers, and that she would be a valuable member of the team. Taran had never been much of a joiner, and she tended to be shy around new people, but she thought that having a common goal might make it easier for her to connect with the rest of the crew. She didn't think she'd ever get over being intimidated by Tuggle, but she did hope that sooner or later she could find the courage to say something to Badger Jenkins. Something besides "I love you." Surely he had forgotten about that.

CHAPTER XI

Get Shorty

"I'm supposed to do sports card shots of *him*?" Melanie Sark lowered her camera and peered at the young man in the purple firesuit who had just entered the studio door.

"We don't call them that in motorsports," said Tuggle. "Folks say *hero cards*."

Hero cards? Sark stared at her. "I would rather swallow my tongue," she said.

Tuggle shrugged. "Just a figure of speech. 'Course you might want to remember that it is a dangerous sport."

"Yeah, we could call them idiot cards."

"How about *autograph* cards?"

"Fine. Autograph cards." She glanced again at the young man loitering out of earshot in the doorway, talking on his cell phone. "All right, how do you expect me to do an autograph card for *him*? He's the size of a mailbox!"

Tuggle shrugged. *You could tell that this girl hadn't been in motorsports very long. What was she used to? NBA players? Badger wasn't even unusual for a Cup driver.*

"This is NASCAR," she reminded the new team publicist. "At Speedways, you always want to watch where you step."

Sark wrinkled her nose. "Dog poo?"

"Jeff Gordon." Tuggle held out her hand at about shoulder

height to illustrate the point. "Now on the autograph cards, we'll say Badger is five foot seven."

Sark smirked. "Why don't you say he's the Emperor of Japan while you're at it?"

"Well, they might be about the same height," Tuggle conceded. "He's got a beautiful nose, though, Badger does. He ought to write his Welsh ancestors a thank-you note for that perfect bone structure. You should see some of his old autograph cards. He photographs well. And it's all in the camera angles. You can make him look tall."

"Yeah, if I stand in a drainage ditch. Okay, thanks for bringing him over. You can have him back in an hour." She peered doubtfully at the young man in the doorway, who seemed to be waiting for permission to enter. "Will I need an interpreter?"

Tuggle smirked. "Just listen slowly—he's from Georgia."

Badger Jenkins turned around and around, surveying the empty building lit with studio lights. "How you doin'?" he said, extending his hand and summoning his brightest smile.

Sark lifted the camera and took a step backward. "Save it, Frodo, I'm not into this sport. I just needed a job, all right? And apparently my job is to make you look good, so that you come across as a combination of Superman and Tom Hanks." Her tone of voice indicated the magnitude of that task. "Let's do the photos first, okay? We can work on the interview after that. Five minutes ought to suffice for it. Stand there with your arms folded. That'll be the car shot."

With a puzzled frown, Badger looked around at the empty studio. "But there's no car here," he said.

Sark rolled her eyes. "*Duh.* I'll take the shots of you first, and then digitally I'll paste in shots of the race car behind you. That way I can fudge a little. Put you in at one hunderd percent, maybe paste the car in at eighty."

"Why?"

"So you'll look bigger." She peered at him through the lens. Assuming the eager-to-please expression of a Westminster show dog, Badger faced the camera with a pasted-on smile. Sark sighed and lowered the camera. "Lose the smile, sunshine," she said. "You're supposed to look tough, aren't you?"

Badger nodded, relaxing his features into a solemn, slightly baffled expression.

"The light in his eyes is the sun shining through the back of his head," muttered Sark, supplying the caption to the imaginary photo. This would be a perfect episode to include in her notes for the secret article. Height fraud in NASCAR. Or the art of illusion in sports photography. She would jot down a few particulars later, but now she had to get on with a more pressing assignment: making Badger Jenkins look imposing.

"You look about as scary as cottage cheese," she told him. "Try again."

As she knelt on the floor a few feet in front of him and lined up his image in the viewfinder, the transformation took place. Badger put on his dark sunglasses, sat down on a stack of tires, and assumed his characteristic pose—leaning forward slightly; legs spread wide apart; tapered, sinewy hands clasped at belt level; with an expression of stern intensity ennobling that chiseled, perfect face. He had the calm of one who knows he is the most dangerous thing around and the stillness of a coiled spring.

Sark blinked. Where the hell did *he* come from? The diffident and affable Badger Jenkins had vanished, and in his place was a warrior angel, beautiful and terrible to behold. He took your breath away. And he looked a foot taller than Badger really was.

"Da-amn," she whispered, looking up over the camera, half expecting to see the real Badger standing off to the side of the room, but no, it was him sitting there on the stack of tires, like Hollywood's idea of a combat general—handsome, strong, and damn near irresistible.

He had enough sense not to move or speak or break the pose. Without a word, Sark clicked the shutter, adjusted the angle, snapped again. Scarcely daring to breathe, she spent the whole roll on that one pose, at slightly varying heights, angles, distances, chasing the play of light across the planes of his face, and trying to imagine an expression in the blank stare behind those shaded eyes. After a few minutes she almost forgot who he was, or that he was an ordinary and pleasant young man who drove cars for a living. She usually spoke to her subjects as she photographed them, offering up encouraging pleasantries to make them hold the pose or to elicit a more confident expression, but this time she was silent. What could you possibly say to *him*?

At first she had considered telling him to alter the pose, thinking there was something improper in his spread-eagled stance, and resolving that if he insisted on flaunting his "package," then at any rate she wouldn't look. She looked.

Boy, it was hot in that room. Must be the studio lights, she thought, wiping the sweat from her forehead with the back of her hand. Badger didn't seem to be affected, though.

He tilted his head back. "Are we about done? They want me to practice a couple of laps."

The spell was broken, or almost. Badger pulled off the sunglasses, waiting to see what else she wanted, and once again he was an ordinary guy, impatient to get back to work.

"Uh . . . I need to talk to you to get some material for the press release." Sark's voice sounded hoarse even to her. She took a deep breath and set the camera down on the floor. "Just a couple of questions . . ." *But* not *the questions that had been uppermost in her mind,* she thought.

Badger said, "Really? You want to talk to me for the press release?"

"Yeah. Why?"

"Well, nobody ever has before. They just tell me to get lost, and then they write whatever they feel like saying."

Sark frowned. "Well, how would they know what the facts were?"

"Facts?" said Badger. He shrugged. "One of 'em told me once that I was the blank screen that everybody ran their own movie on. It didn't matter what I was really like. What does that mean?"

Sark thought it over. It wasn't Badger people believed in. It was the guy she had seen in the camera lens. The one who didn't exist. "Well," she said. "I guess there are a lot of people out there who think you're the guy they see in the photographs. They think you're tall and wise and wonderful, and that you'd be the best friend in the world. Like a guardian angel, I suppose. If you ever called them, they'd buy a new answering machine tape and save the one with your voice on it forever. Maybe some of them imagine you telling the boss to get off their case, or showing up at their house for a backyard cookout so that the neighbors will fall dead from envy."

He got the idea, so she didn't say the rest of it. *Women want you to beat up their abusive boyfriends, or take them away from a humdrum life, or just point to them in a hotel lobby and say, "You." That's all it would take. And some people would be happy just to shake your hand, and they'd treasure that memory forever.*

Badger sighed. "They shouldn't put me on a pedestal," he said.

"You could use the extra height," muttered Sark.

"I wish I was that guy. I wish I had the kind of power they think I have."

"Maybe you don't have to be, Badger. Maybe it's enough that people have something to believe in. Anyhow, let's do the best we can on this interview, so that we don't disappoint them." She motioned for him to sit down in the plastic chair near the work table.

"I'm not too good at quizzes," said Badger. "What do you want to know?"

"Well, I suppose I can get all the basic stuff from NASCAR.com or by Googling you. Previous racing stats, for example."

"I wouldn't know them off the top of my head," said Badger. "Fans often do. Amazing what they can reel off at the drop of a hat when I can't even do it myself."

Sark consulted her notes. "Height. Weight. I can fake—er—*look those up*, too. Marital status. Says here you're married to . . . um . . . a Miss Georgia . . . *Desiree* . . ."

Badger shook his head. "Not anymore. Dessy was an ambitious girl. She was headed for the big time, and she decided I wasn't it. She was right about that. She has her heart set on being a spokesmodel, or maybe a letter-turner on one of those daytime quiz shows. Too rich for my blood. So we sold the big house, and she took most of the money and moved to Florida. I wish her the best." He brightened. "I'm okay, though. I kept my fishin' shack on the lake. I like it there."

Sark made a note: *Dumped by Gold Digger*. She gave him an encouraging smile. "Hobbies. Fishing?"

"Animal rescue," said Badger. "I don't have any formal training or nothing, but I just never could stand to see anything suffer. When I was a kid my daddy hit a doe with his truck, and we found the fawn standing there by the side of the road, so I bundled it up in my coat, took it home, and bottle-fed it 'til it was big enough to be turned loose again. I guess that's what got me started. And I had an owl that had got a wing shot off by some hunter who was either careless, drunk, or mean as hell. Kept him in the house." He grinned. "Dessy wasn't any too happy about that. You ever try to get owl shit out of a Persian rug?"

"No," said Sark. She drew a line through *Dumped by Gold Digger* and wrote beside it *Ideological Differences*. "Okay," she said. "Let's get to the silly stuff. What's your favorite song?"

"'Georgia on My Mind'," said Badger without a second's hesitation.

"Oh. The Ray Charles version?"

"Who?"

A glimmer of suspicion flickered in Sark's brain. "'Georgia on My Mind'." How do the words go again?"

Badger sighed. "I'm from Georgia, okay? That's supposed to be my favorite song."

"Whereas your actual favorite song is?"

He shrugged. "Can I say the National Anthem, then? When they sing it before the race, I swear I tear up every time."

"Okay, forget music. Favorite food?"

Badger looked uneasy. "What am I supposed to say?"

Sark shuddered, considering the possibilities. *God knows*, she thought. *You're from the rural South*. Aloud, she said, "Grits?"

"Well, not my favorite. But I do like 'em every now and again. One time in New York I ordered them, and they charged me fifteen dollars for them as a side dish. Called it *polenta*."

Sark considered writing down "polenta," but thought better of it. "Don't you know what your favorite food is?" she asked.

"Yeah, but that's not the point, is it? That's one of those gimmick questions that's supposed to tell fans what kind of guy you are. For your image. Like maybe if you're from Wisconsin, you say cheese, or if you're sponsored by a cereal company, you name the cereal. Or maybe if you want people to think you're macho, you say buffalo in bourbon sauce."

Sark tapped her pen on the notepad. "Just tell me, okay? What is your favorite food? Say anything. I don't care!"

Badger sighed. "Bologna on Wonder bread," he said. "And tomato soup."

"Fine!" said Sark. She wrote down *buffalo in bourbon sauce*.

The rest of the interview went along placidly enough, highlighted by Badger's heartwarming stories of bottle-feeding orphaned fawns and the rescue of his giant turtle. Sark thought she could make quite an appealing press kit out of an expurgated version of Badger's life story—minus a few DUIs and youthful escapades, that is.

She checked the notes on her clipboard. There was only one more matter to cover. "They asked me to talk to you about our sponsor," she said, fighting to keep the irritation out of her voice. *Why me?* she thought. *Surely there's somebody higher up the totem pole who could handle this.*

Badger had assumed his earnest retriever expression again. "Oh, yeah. That drug. They said I might have to talk about it in interviews some time."

"Well, I expect it will come up," said Sark. "So they want me to give you some pointers in how to deal with it."

"How about I say I take it regularly and that it works?"

Sark took a deep breath. "You really have no idea what the sponsor is, do you, Badger?"

"Some kinda drug."

She chose her words carefully and said them slowly to make sure they sank in. "Vagenya is a drug to enhance sexual desire. In women."

Badger frowned. "I thought that was illegal."

"I'm sorry?"

"Is that the stuff guys drop in ladies' drinks to knock 'em out?" He squirmed in his chair. "I sure never needed to do that."

Suddenly, she had a flash of what a media interview with Badger might be like. She would have to go with him. She would have to devise a signal for *shut up*. She would make him memorize sound bites. Oh, hell, was it possible simply to hire a Badger impersonator? No, probably not. He was one of a kind, all right. She would have to prepare him for all possible contingencies, and step one was explaining to him just what product his race car would be advertising. Oh, boy.

"No," she said carefully. "You don't put Vagenya into a woman's drink. It's . . . um . . . Do you have Mark Martin's cell phone number?"

Badger's eyes widened in bewilderment for an instant, before he realized who had sponsored Mark Martin. "Oh," he said. "Like Viagra, you mean."

"Exactly."

"Oh." He digested this information for a few anxious moments. "And that's gonna be my sponsor, huh?"

"Right."

"So people are gonna give me a hard time about it."

Sark sighed. "Some of them might." She repressed a shudder, as she pictured the unauthorized tee shirt slogans. The cartoons on Web sites. Leering woman fans holding up signs at the races: BADGER JENKINS GETS ME HOTTER THAN VAGENYA.

"But I don't have to say that I use it myself?"

"No. Please, no."

He brightened at once. "Well, that's good! Then all I have to say is that it's a good product and I hope it helps people who need it." He pulled a box of breath mints out of his pocket and held them up as if posing for the camera. "It's a good product and I hope it helps people who need it," he said in tones usually used by finalists in the Miss America pageant. Then he resumed his customarily goofy grin. "Was that okay?"

Slowly, Sark nodded. Now that she thought about it, the combination of Badger and Vagenya might actually work. In interviews, Badger would assume his most earnest guide dog expression and repeat his catchphrase with a worried frown of sincerity every time the subject came up, and only the truly heartless would give him grief about it. Of course, there were a lot of truly heartless people in sports media, but even they would get bored and stop baiting him up after the umpteenth repetition of Badger's earnest sound bite. If you continue to taunt someone who bears your torment with dignity and grace, eventually the tormenter is the one who looks bad.

Something else might happen, too, she thought: a backlash of sympathy. People said that when Mark Martin first acquired Viagra as a sponsor, the teasing was merciless, but he was so calm and serious about the matter that soon people began to respect him for having the guts to drive for such a potentially embarrassing sponsor and for taking all the taunts with such grace under pressure.

Maybe the same thing would happen to Badger with the Vagenya sponsorship. Maybe this new need for gravitas would reveal a whole new dimension to his personality. She glanced over at Badger, trying to picture him as a dignified elder statesman of Cup racing. He had opened the plastic breath mints box, and now he was tossing a mint into the air and trying to catch it in his mouth.

The dignified elder statesman of Cup racing. Yeah, right.

CHAPTER XII

Once Around the Track

"I don't think this is a good idea," said Tuggle, but she could see by the looks on the women's faces that it would be pointless to argue further. Still, she had to try. "You ladies hired that boy to race. Not to give y'all pony rides."

One of the socialite types pouted prettily. "But it's our money," she said. "And people keep asking me if I've gotten to ride in the race car yet, and I'm tired of telling them *no*."

"And as you pointed out, Tuggle, we did hire him. It's our car and our team. I don't think this little adventure is too much to ask for people who are making all this possible." Christine Berenson did not raise her voice, but there was stainless steel in every syllable.

Tuggle took a deep breath, swallowing a few sarcastic comments that would have been hazardous to her employment status, and scowled, wondering if further wrangling would be a waste of breath. It probably would be, but she figured she owed it to Badger to try. They were partners, her and him. Crew chief and driver. *"It's like a marriage,"* she often said. *"Lots of hassling, no sex."* She might be hard on him, in terms of what the team needed from him, and she certainly never cut him any slack, but that didn't mean she'd let anybody else treat him like a hired hand.

She tried again. "But you see, it's his day off. He was planning to go home to Georgia. Something about his dad needing him on the farm . . ."

"Well, we need him here. Anyhow, it won't take long. There are only ten of us, and at the speeds those cars go, he should be through in an hour at most, surely."

"So that's settled," said Christine. "See about getting a passenger seat fitted in a spare car, and tell Badger that we are so looking forward to this."

Tuggle sighed. *Hell to pay*, she thought.

She had been right. Badger Jenkins wasn't happy about it. "I'm not supposed to hafta be at the track on Thursday," he said when she told him. "I got things to do."

"There's ten of 'em," Tuggle said. "Every one of them was born with more money than sense, and they're all spoiled rotten. Do you want to try to tell them why you won't do it? 'Cause I tried already, and I got nowhere."

Badger sighed and ran this hand through the bristles of his cropped hair. "You tried to tell them no?"

Tuggle's voice softened. Sometimes when Badger got that mulish look on his face, he reminded her so much of her long-ago first husband that it made her heart turn over. Maybe if they'd had a son, her and Johnsie. *And wouldn't that have been fresh hell,* she told herself, but her voice stayed gentle from the thought of it.

"*Did I tell them* no? 'Course I did, boy. They paid me no never mind. But, like they said, it wouldn't take but an hour or so of your day. I guaran-damn-tee you'd spend longer than that trying to talk them out of it."

Badger turned to look at her, innocence radiating from guileless brown eyes. "They want to ride around the track in the race car wi'me—one at a time."

"That's right." Tuggle smiled. "They said they thought it would be *exciting*."

Badger nodded solemnly. "I expect it will be," he said.

The shop dogs had grumbled about the extra work they had to put in to modify the race car, but after all, it was being done for

the big wigs, so there wasn't much point in complaining about it.
Everybody knew that it would have to be done, nuisance or not.
You keep the owners and the sponsors happy, or you don't have a
job at all. The racing community is the size of a village, and if you
prove difficult to work with, pretty soon you won't get hired by
anybody.

The bosses wanted to take a ride-along with Badger, and that
was that. Since race cars are strictly one-man vehicles, they had to
make some modifications to accommodate a second rider. Even
the bosses wouldn't want them to waste time and money mon-
keying around with one of the actual Cup cars, so what they
needed for this dog-and-pony show was a car that looked like an
actual contender but wasn't, so they built one. By taking the chassis of an old race car and putting a new body on it, they produced
a cargo cult version of a race car that looked good, despite the fact
that it didn't run as fast as a primary car. It would go fast enough
for civilians, though. When you are hurtling around in tight circles, the difference between 150 and 180 is negligible, especially if
you are screaming at the time.

The passenger seat would be as good as the one on the driver's
side, with one major difference: The passenger seat would not be
custom-molded to the rider's body measurements, while the driver's
seat, conforming perfectly to Badger's size and shape, would fit him
like a glove. Tuggle said that even with ten different riders, the
passenger seat wouldn't be a problem, because all the would-be
riders were pretty much the same size and shape, anyhow. "Put a
dress on the damn jack and use that for your measurements," she
told them. "That ought to work."

"Gotta alter the setup, too," one of the mechanics said. "Have
to allow for the extra weight of the passenger."

"Not all that much weight," said Tuggle, thinking of the stick-
figure women. "But figure an extra hundred pounds or so. And
make it very drivable—not real loose, not too tight. Don't worry
about maximizing speed. They'll think they're going fast enough
by the time he hits one fifty, I'll bet. But I want that car to handle
like a dream. We don't want the boy losing control of the car with

serious money on board, all right? They want a thrill, but they sure as hell don't want a wreck."

"What about a head rest on the passenger side?" the mechanic asked.

Tuggle thought for a moment. "No," she said carefully, "might cause a vision problem for the driver. Better leave it off."

The mechanic started to argue. "But without that head rest—" Then he caught the crew chief's carefully neutral expression, and a slow grin spread across his face. "Okeydokey, ma'am. You're the boss. No passenger-side head rest, boys."

"One more thing," another shop dog called out.

"What's that?" said Tuggle.

He grinned. "Can we come watch?"

Early Thursday morning at Lowe's Motor Speedway was turning into a hot, sunny day, and the place was already a bustle of activity in preparation for the weekend races. At the edge of the track, the newly modified race car sat gleaming in the morning sun, awaiting its masters and commander.

The prospective passengers had all arrived together in a minivan, which they drove right through the tunnel and up into the infield of the speedway. They had tumbled out of the van, still holding Styrofoam coffee cups and chattering nineteen to the dozen about their forthcoming adventure. They had more cameras than a Mitsubishi press conference. A few moments after their arrival, they had surrounded the car, like a gaggle of meerkats. Tuggle had insisted that each woman be outfitted in a firesuit and helmet for their own protection—as well as to make them hot, uncomfortable, and as awkward as possible going in and out the window of the vehicle. She didn't want them to enjoy this command performance too much, and if they came away from it with a greater respect for Badger's skill while working in difficult conditions, so much the better.

After a close but clueless inspection of their newly painted ride, the bosses amused themselves by taking turns photographing each other with the race car in the background, while they assured each other that the firesuits did not make them look fat.

"Before we take any more shots, maybe we should wait for Badger," one of the older ladies said as another camera clicked.

Sark, who was also on hand to make sure that at least some photos turned out well, smiled reassuringly. "Most of us are shooting digital, Mrs. Wagner," she said. "So we'll never run out of film. Now, stand closer together and smile!"

After half an hour or so of posing and chatter, Badger Jenkins stumped out of the hauler, where he had been holed up, ostensibly talking about technical matters with members of the team, but really drinking bottled water and grousing about this additional chore. What was the world coming to when women actually wanted to ride around in race cars instead of pleading with you to stay out of the thing yourself?

If he was still annoyed about it, though, it didn't show when he emerged from the hauler. His angelic face wore its usual expression of smoldering seriousness, and the opaque sunglasses ensured that his expression would give nothing away. The firesuit did wonders for his image: He actually looked taller when he was wearing that thing. He looked, in fact, wise and powerful and devastatingly competent. Even Tuggle, who knew better, was impressed by the sight of him.

He shook hands solemnly with each of the waiting passengers, and when most of them insisted on hugging him, he bore that with grave politeness as well, although Tuggle noticed that he kept his hands at his sides and endured the embraces like a child ambushed by maiden aunts. She supposed that celebrities had to become accustomed to being hugged by people who didn't realize that they were total strangers, because they felt that they knew *you.* Any Cup driver too squeamish to put up with such familiarity would be branded by fans as temperamental and stuck-up, so most of them did endure it with good grace. She didn't envy them that part of the job. Tuggle wasn't close to many people, and she reserved the right to choose who she'd hug and who she wouldn't. Come to think of it, she couldn't name a single person that she would hug voluntarily.

She took a long look at Badger. Well, maybe one person . . .

Whether or not Badger minded the embraces of his starstruck employers and their guests, he was polite about it, and he even posed for pictures longer than Tuggle thought he would. She noticed, though, that during the staging of the photos, he didn't put his arm around anybody. Badger didn't talk about feelings much, so you got into the habit of observing his body language for cues to his emotions. The fact that he was careful not to touch any of the guests meant that he was none too pleased to see them. In each photo he stood between two ladies, arms at his sides, facing the camera dead-on, with a look of proud intensity. The women on either side of him might have been trees for all the notice he took of them.

"*Hercules and the villagers,*" muttered Tuggle.

"What?" said Sark, who had been deputized to snap the official group portrait with her own camera and then with half a dozen others belonging to the ladies. There was talk of posting the photo on the team Web site, which meant that she would have to get everyone's name and do an accompanying write-up as well. "Did you say *Hercules*?"

Tuggle nodded. "That's what he looks like," she said. "Badger. Like some Hollywood hero posing with a passel of anonymous walk-on types in the cast for the publicity photos. Like he's the star of the movie."

Sark shrugged. "Well, isn't he?"

"Maybe so. But I have a suspicion that those women don't think he outshines them. Remember they're rich and prominent their own selves. I reckon they think of him as a cuddly pet they picked up at a dog pound. I just hope two things. One, that they don't insult him, or hug him anymore for that matter. He'd hate that just as much. And two, that he remembers that one of these mud hens signs his checks."

"*Insult* him?" said Sark.

"Oh, you know how people are about race car drivers. They might think it was cute to call him a redneck or say that he was dumb. You know how city people are about anybody who doesn't live in a concrete anthill. Or they might make the sort of raunchy remark to him that they themselves would never put up with coming from a man."

"Well, a lot of people think sexual harassment is a one-way street," said Sark. "I doubt if any of them would consider a sexual proposition to him as an insult. These women are all rich and well-preserved. Maybe they'd think he'd be flattered if they hit on him."

"More fool they then," grunted Tuggle. "He's got more pride than sense, does Badger, and they'd better show him some respect."

Sark put the camera back up to her eyes, waving for the group to pack in closer together. A tall storklike blonde used this instruction as an excuse to slip her arm around Badger's waist and pull him closer. "I always wanted a boy toy!" she declared.

Badger's smile did not waver, but Sark noticed a glint in his eyes that had not been there before. She snapped pictures in rapid succession, varying the shots by changing her angle and proximity to the subjects, rather than by giving them any further instructions on how to pose. She thought they'd better get the photo session over with before things got any worse. "He sure photographs well," she murmured to Tuggle.

"He damn well better," said Tuggle. "There's a couple thousand guys can drive a race car, and only forty-three slots in Cup, give or take a Bodine. Back in my daddy's day you could look like a small-town insurance agent and make it out there, but not now. Not anymore." She remembered a photo taken at a motorsports banquet back in the early sixties—half a dozen of the greatest drivers of the time posed together, all heavy-set, middle-aged men in loud sports jackets. They were indistinguishable from any small town newspaper photo of the local bigwigs; any school board grouping, any Moose Lodge membership portrait would have looked the same. Not anymore, though. Now there were drivers with image consultants and maybe even makeover specialists, for all she knew. Most of the young ones could pass for movie stars these days, or at least for country singers. Well, not the Busch brothers, of course. Sometimes talent did take you places without any help from charm or beauty.

She raised her voice and gestured to the crowd. "One more shot with Badger, folks, and then it's time to get this show on the road. You'll be riding one at a time, couple of laps around the track, and remember that the only way in or out of the car is to crawl through the window. I would also ask that anyone who has heart problems or a tendency toward motion sickness to please excuse themselves now." She paused and scanned the crowd. One older woman pulled the helmet off and shook an equally hard helmet of tight gray curls. Tuggle nodded her thanks. "All right," she said. "Who's going first?"

Badger surveyed the eager passengers with solemn intensity; then he grinned at the blond stork who had called him her boy toy. "You look brave enough to take it on, ma'am," he said, motioning her forward. "Heck, you could probably do the driving yourself, Miz—what was your name again?"

The woman bridled at the unexpected praise. "Katharine-with-a-K," she said, patting her hair. "You want me to go first, honey? Well . . . maybe just once around the track."

Tuggle and Badger looked at each other for a long, silent moment in which volumes of information were exchanged between crew chief and driver. Asked and answered.

Then Badger smiled at Katharine-with-a-K. "Well, ma'am," he said, "I reckon we'll get started." He ushered her over to the car. "I'd open the door for you, but like Tuggle said, there isn't one, so why don't you climb on in the window there and let's get started."

In one graceful movement, he swung himself up and through the driver's side window, making the process look easy, but his passenger's awkward clambering on the other side of the car suggested otherwise. She bumped the helmet trying to go in head-first, straddled the window frame, and then hung there for a moment with one leg outside the car until one of her cohorts put both hands under her dangling foot and boosted her in.

"Puts me in mind of Michael Waltrip," Tuggle murmured to Sark. "Tall, gangly people have a hell of a time getting into race cars."

"What worries me is how much trouble they'd have getting back out in a hurry," said Sark. "If they had to."

They exchanged looks, and with some trepidation, they turned to watch Badger begin the first ride-along.

Badger hit the ignition switch and then the starter, but there was a further delay while Tuggle went over to make sure that Katharine had fastened the safety harnesses correctly. When this was done, she put up the passenger side window netting, tapped the car, and stepped back, waving Badger on.

With a roar the car leaped forward and they were off. When the car was far enough away so that you could hear again, Sark said, "Well, at least he knows what he's doing."

Tuggle sighed. "That's what I'm afraid of."

Katharine-with-a-K had been thrilled that the sexy little race car driver had chosen her as his first passenger. Maybe her not-altogether-joking remark would lead somewhere later on. Too bad he couldn't keep the firesuit on while he did it. Somehow, despite the fact that there was a part of her mind that knew better, she had envisioned the ride-along as a chance to get better acquainted with Badger. She spent the last few seconds before take-off trying to think of some pleasant remarks to make to a race car driver as they whirled around the track, but now she realized that she needn't have bothered, because the helmets they wore and the engine noise prohibited conversation. The words would have stuck in her throat anyhow.

As they plunged into breakneck speed (she hoped that adjective wasn't too appropriate), she tried to focus on the details of the experience that were not as she had expected. She had envisioned her experience of speed to be similar to the sensation of traveling in a fast car, say, on the autobahn, only more so. Perhaps the landscape would be more blurry. But she discovered that moving forward at nearly three miles per minute on a circular track proved to be nothing like zooming along an interstate. She had very little time to worry about her visual impressions, because the rest of her body was experiencing peculiar effects that she had not even considered.

Some force seemed to be pinning her back against the seat, making it difficult for her to move. The phrase *swimming in mo-*

lasses flashed through her mind. She tried to concentrate on the proper technical term for such a phenomenon. *Gravity? No. Inertia? No. Paralysis? Incontinence? Hubris? Stephanotis?* No, that last one was a flower. She realized that her brain was just throwing out long words now, too overloaded to manage anything resembling critical discernment. She struggled to zero in on another impression. There was something strange about the scenery. What would you call it? *Immediate.* That was it.

She discovered that if you looked straight ahead through the windshield, the view was not blurry at all. It was as clear as a photograph. Except for the peculiar paralysis she was experiencing, she might not even realize—*oh, wait* . . . if you turned your head just enough to look through the window netting on the side . . . suddenly it looked as if someone had put the world into a blender.

Perhaps if he slowed down just a teensy bit. She tried to raise her hand to tap him on the arm, and then she decided that at 180 mph this might not be such a good idea, even if she could have managed it, which seemed not to be the case.

Katharine found that her thoughts were not quite keeping pace with the speed of the car, and also that each observation that ran through her brain was now punctuated with an expletive, as in: *Oh shit, I'm pinned back against the seat and can't move. . . . Oh, shit, the landscape isn't a blur straight ahead, it's perfectly clear so that I can see exactly which wall we're about to slam into. . . . Oo-oooh, shit, here comes a curve and I'm leaning into it and I can't straighten up. . . . oh shit . . . leaning to the right more and more . . . and the wall is awfully . . . and my head is . . . oh shit oh shit oh shit . . .*

Given the fact that NASCAR fined people $10,000 for saying swear words on-air, that thought expressed aloud could have constituted a most expensive conversation, except, of course, that no one would hear it. Not even Badger, as it happened, because her throat did not seem to be working. She kept opening and closing her mouth like a fish, while Badger, as intent upon the track as an automaton, seemed to have forgotten that she was there.

He certainly seemed calm enough, as if orbiting a track at 180 mph was like a morning commute to him, which it probably was.

The waiting passengers stood well back from the track as they watched the car whip past them in a blur. At Turn One they let out a collective gasp. The blur hurtled down the straightaway, faster and louder than they had anticipated. Oh, they had been told the speed and they had been issued earplugs, but somehow the mere recital of facts and figures did not translate into this rush and roar before them. It was loud. It was blindingly fast.

As the car dove into Turn Two, one of the women tapped Tuggle on the arm indicating that she was trying to speak. It shouldn't be possible to shout *meekly*, but the worried woman managed it. Round-eyed with fright, she pointed and mouthed, "Isn't he going awfully close to the wall?"

Tuggle's reply was drowned out as the car sped past them again, but they all caught the phrase "hitting his marks," whatever that meant. The car surged on, leaping for the wall at every curve.

Bugs to a windshield, thought Sark, and wished she hadn't.

"But Katharine's head is poking out the window, through the netting!" shouted one of them, jiggling Tuggle's arm.

"And she's next to the wall!" shouted another one. As she mouthed the words, she inclined her head and used her open hand to pantomime the proximity of the wall to the passenger side of the car.

Tuggle held up a circled thumb and forefinger to signal "okay," but she couldn't quite manage the reassuring facial expression to go with it.

Moments later, someone thrust a note into the crew chief's hand. It said, "Tell her to sit up straight."

Tuggle nodded solemnly, keeping her eyes on the car. Pointless to attempt conversation over the engine noise. Later she would explain to the ladies about g-forces; that is, that Katharine could not sit up straight without breaking several laws of physics. And those same laws of physics meant that her head was going to poke out of that window whether she wanted it to or not, which, odds are, she didn't.

She was going to have to give him hell for this temperamental display, of course, scaring the money people like that, but she had to admit to a sneaking admiration for the boy's skill. Badger was one hell of a driver, all right. He could put that car close enough to the wall for his passenger to strike a match against it, but she wasn't really in any danger of being smashed into the concrete. Well, unless he blew the right front tire, of course. Then all bets were off. But that shouldn't happen in so few laps. Probably.

After what probably seemed like an eternity to the passenger, the race car screeched to a halt. Ride over. Half a dozen people had rushed to the passenger side to extricate a whimpering, semi-conscious Katharine through the window, so Tuggle sidled over to the driver's side and leaned down for a word with Badger.

"Smart aleck," she said, mouthing the words and trying not to grin.

Badger lifted his visor, and yelled, "Who's next?"

As it turned out, nobody was.

CHAPTER XIII

Creative Engineering

Tuggle was outside the garage, smoking her second allotted cigarette of the day when Deanna from the office turned up at her elbow, looking worried.

"The oddest thing just happened," she said. "It may be none of my business, but I just thought I ought to tell somebody."

Tuggle nodded, wondering why Deanna had bothered to walk over to the garage instead of calling her cell phone. The day was cold and windy, and the secretary had come out without her coat, so she kept shivering and hugging herself to keep warm. Tuggle hoped that Badger hadn't made a pass at her or something. Surely not. That wasn't his style. She figured he was the type to act sweet and clueless until desperate women attacked *him*. Considering the Badger shrine that surrounded Deanna's desk, any sexual harassment between those two would definitely be going in the other direction. "Something wrong?" Tuggle asked through a plume of smoke.

"I don't know," said Deanna. "The racing business is so crazy, it's hard to know when anything is wrong, because we still haven't come within a mile of *normal*."

"Point taken. What's going on?"

"A little while ago, this woman walked into the office, plumped her laptop down on the conference table, sat down, and started talking on her cell phone. And then she told me to get her some coffee! I said we were fresh out and that I'd go and get some, and I came right out here to tell you about it. Maybe you're not even the right person to tell, but you are the team manager, as well as the crew chief, so . . ."

Tuggle stared at the end of her cigarette, digesting the information. "A woman invaded the office. Hmmm. Not a reporter?"

"No, they do identify themselves. And now that the gender story is old hat, we're not exactly news, are we? Nobody thinks much of our chances to make it into the Chase."

Tuggle tried again. "Fan stalker?"

Deanna hesitated. "She wasn't at all impressed by being in a racing office. She didn't even glance at the posters of Badger."

That was a bad sign. Fans could usually be shooed away with a signed photo, but this one sounded like trouble. Tuggle tried again. "Did she look like an ex-wife or something?"

Deanna considered it. "Well, no," she said slowly. "I don't want to be rude about her, but I've seen the other drivers' wives, and she doesn't look like one of them. Not unless Badger is less concerned with looks than any other man on the planet."

Tuggle grunted. "He was married to a Miss Georgia, so if this one is as homely as you say, I think we can rule out a romantic angle. I suppose she could be a process server, but I don't know that any of us is getting sued. Badger seems to be behaving himself pretty well, as drivers go. Did you ask her who the hell she was?"

"She told me. I'm just not sure I believe her, because it's the first I've heard of it. She claims that she is Badger's *manager*."

Tuggle digested this information. "Badger," she said at last, "does not *have* a manager."

"Well, that's what I thought," said Deanna. "But unless she's a reporter or a fan stalker, then apparently he does now. A scarecrow in a shiny black dress, fishnet stockings, and stiletto Jimmy Choos is roosting at our conference table, and she's got an attitude that could scour a cast-iron skillet."

Tuggle grinned. "I'm glad you aren't planning to be rude about her, Deanna."

The secretary pursed her lips. "She ordered me around," she

said. "She treated me like a *servant*. I don't care who she is, I don't work for her. Anyhow, I thought I ought to tell you she'd moved in. Do you think I should ask Badger about it?"

"Yeah, that would be a big help. This woman sounds like she could eat Badger for breakfast." Tuggle ground her cigarette into the dirt. "I'll come with you and see what we've got here."

They walked back to the office without speaking. Deanna was a shy young woman who dreaded the whole idea of conflict, even if she was merely an innocent bystander, and the thought of an impending confrontation made her too nervous to think up any small talk, especially with the crew chief, who was a bit abrupt at the best of times. Tuggle, on the other hand, was on point, as always, mapping out possible strategies for the current situation, so focused that she had nearly forgotten that there was anyone walking beside her. *An interloper in the team office. Peculiar.* She hoped that all this was simply a misunderstanding, but her lifelong experience with motorsports and a bred-in-the-bone cynicism made her seriously doubt it.

Sure enough, the conference room was under siege by a black-clad woman who was staring at the screen of her laptop and tapping her pen against her presumably empty Team Vagenya coffee mug, which she had appropriated from a nearby counter. Tuggle stood for a moment in the doorway, sizing up the intruder, deliberating on how best to proceed. Probably not a fan, Tuggle decided. Of course, it was hard to tell for sure these days, because fans could be absolutely anybody from the president to the latest rap star, but this woman looked to be more business than pleasure. Fans generally walked around the office of a race team looking awestruck and touching things reverently. Tuggle studied the woman for a moment: unfortunate hair, Wal-Mart rock-star clothes, definitely not an ex-wife or an old girlfriend, unless she had fallen on exceptionally hard times since her days with Badger. If Tuggle were forced to guess, she'd have pegged the woman as a relative of Badger's from a side of the family they didn't talk about, but apparently this apparition was claiming to be his manager. *Managing Badger.* What a concept. What experience would prepare you for that? Keeping a troupe of spider monkeys in your living room? This ought to be interesting.

"Something I can help you with?" said Tuggle.

The woman held up her empty coffee mug, but Tuggle's cold stare made her think better of the gesture. She lowered it again, with a philosophical shrug.

"Now, just exactly who—"

Unfortunately, the woman's cell phone rang just as Tuggle spoke, and she found herself waved into silence as the woman snatched up the phone. "Melodie Albigre here. Oh, hello, Nicole. What have you got for me? Grand opening of an auto parts store? Kyle can't do it? Well, when? Where? Okay, what's in it for Badger? How much? Tell them to double it and I'll see what I can do. Get back to me." She set down the phone with a sigh of exasperation and turned back to the computer screen. Then she seemed to re-member that she was not alone, probably because Tuggle had moved to within inches of her chair and was peering into her face with all the interest of someone observing an exotic animal build-ing a nest in the backyard.

The woman had the grace to blush. "I don't believe we've met," she said. "I am your driver's personal manager. Melodie Albigre of Miller O'Neill Associates." She whisked a card out of the case of her cell phone. Tuggle made no move to take it. "And you are?"

"I am the team manager and the crew chief, and this happens to be our conference room that you have commandeered without permission." Her tone suggested that they had the Mooresville police on speed dial.

The woman ignored this salvo. "Ah," she said, "you are Grace Tuggle. I have certainly heard of you. So you are the other person who has to manage Badger—in a manner of speaking."

Tuggle scowled. "Nobody told me that Badger had a *personal manager,*" she said, contriving to pack several tons of contempt in the words, making it sound as if "personal manager" were the sort of job that required a pole and a leather bikini.

Ms. Albigre regarded the crew chief for a moment with the spec-ulative gaze of someone who is trying to decide whether or not the snake is poisonous. "I just came on board," she said, peering at the screen of her laptop. She tapped a few keys. "I will decide what personal appearances Badger will make and I'll negotiate the fees, that sort of thing."

"Badger has a contract with this team," said Tuggle. She spoke so softly that one had to strain to hear her, but she gave the impression of someone who was a heartbeat away from bellowing with rage. "He has certain obligations spelled out in that contract, and those duties are not subject to negotiation. Of course, if he doesn't want the job . . ."

If Tuggle had hoped to intimidate the interloper with the threat of her client's dismissal, she was to be disappointed. Without a flicker of alarm at the prospect of Badger's imminent termination, Ms. Albigre said, "Did Badger actually sign a contract for once? He's the handshake type. Hopeless. Well, if there is one, I'll need to see a copy of it, I suppose."

"He has already agreed to our terms," said Tuggle. "He did sign an agreement."

The manager nodded. "Yes, in crayon, I expect. I still need to see it, so that I will know precisely what his obligations are. Then I can go from there."

Tuggle took several deep breaths and her eyes bulged, but the explosion did not come. Miraculously, the woman's laptop was not thrown across the room, and the cell phone stayed on the table in one piece. Finally, in strangled tones the crew chief managed to say, "Deanna, get this—get *Ms. Albigre* a copy of the driver contract, please."

The secretary gave a quick nod and scurried out of the room, relieved to be given an excuse to flee. When she was gone, Tuggle said, "We like Badger. He's a good man. He can be tricky to work with, though."

Melodie Albigre nodded. "Impossible, I expect," she said. "I imagine that working with him is like trying to keep fifteen kittens in a laundry basket."

Tuggle stared. "I thought you said you just started working with him. How would you know that?"

The woman smiled. "Well, he is a race car driver. There are certain traits common to most of them. Being difficult is certainly one of them. But, actually, I had Badger tested. Have you ever heard of the Myers Briggs–personality test?"

"Nope."

"Really? You should check it out, especially since you have a number of employees to supervise yourself. It's quite a useful tool." The Albigre cell phone went off. Its owner glanced at the caller number, wrinkled her nose in distaste, and went on talking. "We at Miller O'Neill like to give that test to all of our new clients, so that we can determine what style works best in dealing with them. It divides people into four categories—thinking or feeling, perceiving or judging, introverted or extroverted, and so on."

Tuggle smirked. "So you classified Badger, did you?"

"Verified an educated guess," said Melodie. "I was already pretty sure what he would turn out to be—because quite a lot of athletes are. He's an ISTP."

"The motor oil?"

"Not STP. I-S-T-P. It is a classification of personality traits. It stands for introverted, sensation, thinking, and perceiving."

"Gobbledygook," said Tuggle. "What does it mean?"

She shrugged. "Oh . . . I suppose you might sum it up as *Billy the Kid in a good mood.* Badger lives in the moment; loves action and danger; hates schedules, authority, and routine of any kind. He doesn't mean to be difficult or inconsiderate. It's just the way he's made. He's good with machinery, though, and while he generally has the attention span of stoned ferret, he is capable of focusing for hours on end on something that really interests him."

"I could have told you that," said Tuggle. "On a race track he is zeroed in like a laser."

"Exactly. But in, say, a classroom where they're teaching American History, he would be bouncing off the walls. Probably was, in fact. I don't imagine he did very well in school."

Tuggle's eyes narrowed. "Wait a minute. You're not thinking about giving him drugs, are you?"

"No, of course not. You can't dope a racehorse." She paused to consider a stray thought. "Or neuter him, more's the pity. We just wanted to know how best to communicate with Badger, that's all."

"A two-by-four upside of the head?"

"Tempting," said Melodie with a grim smile. "In case you're interested, it's no good berating him or shouting at him. He will simply shrug it off. And if you read him the riot act, he will promise to reform. He will even mean it, but that's only good for about four days, and then he reverts to being his old self."

"Which brings us back to the two-by-four," said Tuggle.

"Considering the head injuries he has sustained over the course of his career, you probably shouldn't joke about that," said Melodie primly. "I expect those accidents made him worse, but I'm sure he was always like this to some extent. ISTPs love excitement and danger. Managing Badger requires firmness and persistence. Whoever nags him the most wins his time—temporarily. He tends to give his attention to the person who demands it the loudest."

"Yeah, but I'll bet he'd hate you for it."

"Apparently not. ISTPs tend to be fairly good-natured. But that point is irrelevant, to me in any case. I am not here to be his friend. Badger Jenkins is a project to be managed, and I intend to manage him as efficiently as possible."

"More power to you," said Tuggle. "If he's fool enough to put up with you, I won't stand in your way. Just don't interfere in my operation here, and don't schedule Badger for anything that conflicts with the needs of this team. And one more thing—"

"Yes?"

"Why the hell are you using our conference table as your office?"

At "Vagenya Tech," as the chief engineer's office was now called by everyone on the team, Julie and Rosalind were brainstorming with Jay Bird.

When Rosalind had said, only half in jest, that the way to win a race was to cheat, she had been oversimplifying a basic premise of motorsports. NASCAR made rules intended to even the playing field, so that no team had any particular advantage over the others. Racing teams tried to find loopholes in those rules, or else they tried to come up with equipment modifications not yet banned in the sport. This would work briefly, and then NASCAR would discover the infraction and devise a new, more stringent rule to cover it. Jay Bird called this artful dodging an endless game of Whack-a-Mole: find a new outlet, get slammed by the inspectors, look for a new way out. One of NASCAR's legendary drivers best summed up the teams' position on unauthorized modifications when he said, "There are two types of racers: cheaters and losers."

"Creative engineering" went all the way back to the beginnings of the sport, and it ranged from something as simple as fabricating the car's bumpers out of Styrofoam to reduce its weight to something as complicated as restructuring the entire chassis slightly off-kilter in order to minimize wind resistance.

The patron saint of creative engineering was Smokey Yunick, the legendary racer and mechanic from Tennessee, who back in the sixties tried all sorts of gimmicks to circumvent NASCAR's racing regulations. Once he drove his Chevelle at Daytona with an eleven-foot fuel line snaking its way back and forth in an intricate maze between its fuel cell and the engine. That illegal gas line held six gallons of gasoline in addition to what was in the fuel cell itself, which would have given him an incredible advantage in the race—nearly an extra hundred miles of racing before he needed a pit stop. The second helping of gas might have won the race for him, except that he got caught. A new NASCAR rule about gas lines followed immediately.

Since then it had become more difficult to bend the rules. Stock car parts had to conform to templates—molds that specified the exact size and dimensions of a given part or piece of hardware down to a thousandth of an inch. Cars had been penalized for having the wrong size screw on a part in the engine. Getting caught with a nonstandard modification could cost you in fines, result in the suspension of the crew chief, and get the car sent to the back of the line for the start of a race. NASCAR was trying to close all the rat holes it could. They inspected the race cars each week, impounded them at some tracks between the last practice and the start of the race, and then at the end of each race, NASCAR officials inspected the top five finishers and then another car from the race chosen at random. The inspectors looked at the engine, the ignition, the fuel tank, the body of the car, and they even inspected the fuel for additives. The game of cat and mouse was becoming increasingly harder for racers to win, but that didn't mean that anybody had stopped trying.

Julie threw a crumpled ball of notepaper at the shelf of die-cast race cars. "We are a one-car team," she said. "We do not have the benefit of multicar testing at various tracks and pooling the results. We do not have five hundred shop dogs to build cars from scratch. We do not have a wind tunnel."

"Well, that's not exactly news," said Jay Bird. "You knew that when you took the job."

"That doesn't make me feel better," said Julie. "You were supposed to come up with a miracle, Jay Bird."

The old man chuckled. "How about we dress you two up in spandex and fishnet tights and send you out to bars to pick up crew chiefs?"

"Only if Tuggle needs a ride home," said Rosalind. "I'm not into the bar scene."

"Neither are the crew chiefs, I bet," said Julie. "Come on, you guys. Stop kidding around. We need to think up a miracle here."

"An *affordable* miracle," said Jay Bird. "That makes it harder."

Rosalind sighed. "How's this for cheap? We reduce the size of the mesh on the window net. That will let less air into the cockpit and cut wind resistance. Not much, but in qualifying a hundredth of a second makes a difference."

"How about an air dam under the car to channel the air straight back?" said Julie. "The bottom of the car isn't covered by template, so it isn't even illegal."

"Doesn't have to be," said Jay Bird. "You let an extra blast of air hit that spoiler from underneath, and your boy will be an astronaut instead of a race car driver. *Liftoff!*"

"He's right," said Rosalind. "And we can't modify the spoiler, because it *is* covered by template, but maybe we don't have to channel all the air straight back. Maybe we could fiddle a compromise between the need for downforce and the channeled air. It doesn't have to be an all-or-nothing proposition."

They both looked at Jay Bird.

"It's worth a shot," he said. "But just so you know, this idea has been tried before."

"By whom?" said Rosalind.

Jay Bird sighed. "By everybody who can spell NASCAR. But let's give it a shot anyhow. We have to start somewhere."

CHAPTER XIV

Wild Ride

The diner wasn't hard to find, provided that you didn't blink between the sign that said WELCOME TO MARENGO and the one that said Y'ALL COME BACK NOW, Y'HEAR. After the three-hour drive from Charlotte, Sark was glad that the designated meeting place served coffee and came equipped with an indoor toilet. She was in need of both.

She wondered why Badger had told her to meet him at the diner. Probably because even with directions, you couldn't find the way to his house without a trail of breadcrumbs. Badger's fortress of solitude in the Georgia outback was the stuff of legends in NASCAR. By meeting him in town she could simply follow him out to wherever it was that they were going. He had not yet arrived. She knew what his car looked like from having seen it parked at the race shop—a silver Chrysler Crossfire with a Georgia vanity plate that read "Badger 1." (Probably his idea of a play on words *Badger won,* get it?) But "Badger 1" was not parked in front of the diner, and Sark wondered what she ought to do if he had forgotten his promise to show her around on his home turf. Hunt him down, she supposed. After making the three-hour drive from Charlotte, she wasn't about to give up without a fight.

She pushed open the door to the diner, and found herself staring right into the calf brown eyes of Badger Jenkins; but in this case, it was simply because the life-sized poster of him had been placed on the wall facing the door. The place was empty except for a blond waitress behind the counter, presumably the curator of this shrine to Marengo's one celebrity.

The walls were plastered with NASCAR photos of Badger Jenkins, all dutifully signed in Badger's loopy scrawl, and a glass display case sported a collection of die-cast cars, all presumably former rides of Badger dating back to his salad days in the Busch series. On the wall behind the cash register were the non-Badger photos, a collection of publicity stills from former customers who had been passing through fame and Marengo simultaneously. A couple of minor country singers were represented, as well as a pro football player, the weather girl from an Atlanta television station, and several other NASCAR drivers, looking menacing in their firesuits and sunglasses, presumably friends of Badger who had come to town to go fishing with him and to have their visits forever commemorated by a signed eight-by-ten glossy on the pine-paneled wall of the diner. In one of the photos, a younger, curvier version of the waitress snuggled up to an unshaven, shaggy-haired Badger, and they both smiled happily at the camera—not posed smiles, but two really happy people caught in a golden moment.

"Excuse me," Sark said to the waitress, whose plastic name tag said "Laraine." "I'm here to meet Badger Jenkins. Have you seen him?"

Laraine smiled and went on putting sugar packets into little plastic containers. "Sure. Every inch of him."

"I mean today. I'm the publicist for Team Vagenya. He was supposed to meet me here for an interview." Sark looked at her watch for effect. "I drove down from Charlotte."

Laraine began to wipe down the countertop with a wet rag. "I expect he'll turn up," she said. "Did he promise you? Did he give you his *word*?"

Sark hesitated. "He agreed to the time and date," she said at last.

"Oh, *agree*." Laraine had finished with the sugar packets and was now scrubbing the counter. "Badger will agree to anything to get women to stop hassling him. You ought to know that by now.

But he sets a store by giving his *word*. If you actually want him to do something for you, you need to make him give you his word. Then he's bound to go through with it."

"He had better go through with it," said Sark through clenched teeth. "I take the team photos, and I wasted a whole day to do this. If he doesn't want to look like the Creature from the Black Lagoon in every publicity shot for the rest of the season, he'd better haul his ass in here real soon."

Laraine eyed her suspiciously. "Don't you have his cell number?"

"Of course, I have it! But my cell phone doesn't get any reception out here. I suppose I could use a pay phone. If there is one."

Laraine sighed and picked up the telephone, punching in one number. "There's only one provider within range of here," she said. "I guess that's not the one you've got. Well, seeing as how you're with the team, I guess I can call him for you. I got him on speed dial," she explained to the testy visitor. "Of course, if he happens to be out on the lake where his cell phone won't work, then you'd just better hope he remembers, because nobody can reach him when he's out there."

"Yeah, but he has to come to shore sometime, and then he'll wish he hadn't," said Sark.

"Everybody says that," said Laraine. "It's water off a duck's back."

Sark had a sinking feeling that she had made a three-hour drive for nothing. "Does he do that to people a lot? Stand them up?"

Laraine went on wiping the counter with a rag. "He doesn't mean to," she said at last. "He's good-hearted, just a little impractical. When people ask him for things, he just hates to say no, and when it comes to his time, he's liable to promise more hours in the day than there actually are. Plus, he really wants to spend most of his time alone out there on the lake. I think he'll turn up for you, though, what with you being with the team and all. It's mostly journalists who slip his mind. He honestly does not see the point of bragging about himself for public consumption. He'd be a much richer man if anybody could make him see the value in publicity."

"I have tried," said Sark grimly.

Laraine nodded. "Like trying to teach a pig to sing, isn't it? Look, why don't you pick a place and sit down while I phone him, and then I'll bring you some coffee."

Sark kept studying the racing posters of Badger that adorned the diner's walls until she decided which one that she hated the least. *(Badger minus the sunglasses, wearing a goofy smile, and holding up a can of motor oil as if he had found it quite delicious. Sark always liked the Vagenya driver better when he wasn't pretending to be a comic book hero, and in her current mood, the more ridiculous he looked, the more it pleased her.)*

She slid into the booth beneath that goofy motor oil photo, musing again on how strange it was that images of someone she actually knew could constitute a *décor.* Badger posters. Badger clocks. Badger sofa throws. Of course, there were certainly worse examples of human commercialization. The real merchandise monsters were NASCAR's two most popular drivers, Jeff Gordon and Dale Earnhardt, Jr. The range of products bearing their names and likenesses was downright frightening. Toothbrushes. Shot glasses. Valentine candy. Christmas ornaments. Mouse pads. Bath mats. She supposed that there were actually people who decorated their houses in NASCAR driver motif—there was rumored to be a Badger bathroom somewhere in Ohio—but from her outsider perspective, the resulting décor didn't bear thinking about. If she'd had to live amidst such a theme decoration, she would have felt that she was trapped inside a TV commercial.

To his credit, Badger himself seemed oblivious to these commercial tokens of fan loyalty. If he turned up at the shop and you happened to be wearing, say, a Badger Jenkins tee shirt, he affected not to notice. She thought that was a good strategy. It avoided embarrassment for everybody. Any other reaction on his part would have been asking for trouble. If he had acted pleased to have people sporting his likeness on their chests, he would have seemed conceited, and if he made fun of it, he would come off as an arrogant ingrate. Ignoring all Badger-themed merchandise was by far the most diplomatic way to handle the situation.

While she waited for Marengo's favorite son to arrive, Sark

sipped her coffee and looked over her notes, so that she would know what sort of questions to ask him. In her experience, the more you knew about somebody, the better the interview was likely to be.

According to the biographical material, Badger was a lifelong resident of the county, and he had grown up on a farm that had been in his family for five or six generations. He was an only child whose mother had died when he was born. According to the articles, he had been part Cherokee, which gave Badger a Native American heritage in which he took great pride. He'd been raised by his father on that family farm in the hills north of town, where he had spent a seemingly idyllic childhood in country pursuits, most notably hunting and fishing on his beloved lake. He sounded like Tom Sawyer, Sark thought. Or possibly Conan the Barbarian. She wondered what a typical day with him would constitute. Nothing likely to appeal to a city girl, she supposed. Fortunately, anticipating this, she had worn an outfit that would have served her well on a hike in Yellowstone: khaki pants, hiking boots, and a tan windbreaker over a Team Vagenya tee shirt. In the trunk of her car she had stashed a snake bite kit, mosquito repellent, and bottled water.

She was making notes on her list of possible interview questions when Badger turned up, about twenty minutes late, with his usual nonchalant grin. "Sorry about that," he said.

She gave him a bitter smile. "Oh, don't mention it. I've just been enjoying myself here in the shrine of St. Badger." She indicated the phalanx of posters bearing his likeness that surrounded them. "And here you are in the flesh. Should I kneel?"

He pursed his lips and did that little head jerk that meant the remark had stung. "Laraine put those things back up when I got this new ride. She says it's good for business. Anyhow, I didn't mean to be late. I didn't forget. I got stuck behind a logging truck going over the hill where you can't pass."

Sark raised her eyebrows. "Safe driving? From *you*?"

He nodded. "If you get a speeding ticket, all it costs *you* is a hundred bucks or so, but if I get a speeding ticket, all hell breaks loose, and the press never lets me hear the end of it. You ready?"

Sark gathered up the pile of press releases and scribbled index cards and stuffed them back into the large purse that served as her briefcase. "Where are we going?"

"Figured I'd take you out to my fishing cabin on the lake. Let you see my natural habitat."

"Okay," said Sark, who had been expecting this. "Shall I ride with you? Let me get my camera gear out of my car." *And my change of clothes and my snake bite kit,* she added silently. You couldn't be too careful around lakes.

"Well, we'll be headed west from here, and there's a shortcut back to the interstate north from there, so it would save you time if you just took your car, instead of having to come all the way back down here. Why don't you just follow me?"

Sark stared at him. He was serious. "Because you won the *Southern 500* at Darlington," she said.

"Not in that old pick-up truck, I didn't," said Badger.

"Yeah, well . . . driving is driving. I've heard that Dale Earnhardt, Jr. and Jeff Gordon have sometimes tried without notable success to keep up with *you*."

He grinned. "Aw, I told you, I try to be a good boy off the track. Come on." He jingled his keys and headed for the door, stopping to give Laraine a bear hug on his way out; then he strolled out to the parking lot.

"Well, how hard can it be to follow him?" Sark wondered aloud. "It's just a two-lane blacktop country road."

Laraine nodded. "That road sure has a lot of curves, though. Some steep hills, too, every now and again."

"Exactly," said Sark. "That ought to slow him down. Badger will probably be the perfect person to follow. Where driving is concerned, his ego must be rock solid. I don't suppose he feels the need to show off by speeding down ordinary roads to prove how macho he is. *I'm sure I'll be fine."*

"That's what everybody says," muttered Laraine, but Sark was already scurrying out the door, fishing in her purse for her sunglasses.

Badger was waiting in his truck revving the engine when she emerged from the diner. As Sark walked to her car, she took a precautionary look at Badger's license plate, just in case they got sep-arated by traffic. *(In Marengo?)* Oh well, it still wouldn't hurt to know the license number. Red trucks were certainly not at a pre-mium in north Georgia, and it would be reassuring to know for a fact that you were following the correct one.

It took her a moment to realize that the Georgia truck tag was a vanity plate, because it consisted of a series of numbers, much as standard-issue plates did. But to someone who had been study-ing Badger Jenkins's biography for several days now in prepara-tion for this interview, the numbers were indeed significant. They were the numbers of cars he had driven in the early days of his ca-reer.

She was sitting there behind the wheel thinking how endear-ing that license plate was—sentimental without being too boast-ful. (He could have had one that said "Champ" or "NASCAR 1" or some such slogan of self-importance. Well, he did have such a slo-gan on his Crossfire, but she supposed that was in keeping with his celebrity image around Charlotte. Here among the home folks he'd probably be given no end of grief for such pretensions. Be-sides, such a tag would be a dead giveaway to fans that the truck belonged to Badger, but she didn't suppose that there were all that many Badger Jenkins groupies roaming around in the vicinity of Marengo. Except, perhaps, Laraine.)

Sark was so intent upon her meditation on the tasteful vanity plate that she was completely unprepared for the abrupt takeoff of the truck she was supposed to be following. Badger screeched out of the diner parking lot in a red blur, headed north on the two-lane blacktop that was only "Main Street" for about a hundred yards, before it became a country road again, at which point they would probably make the jump to light speed, Sark thought wryly.

Was he trying to lose her? The little turkey. She gritted her teeth and peeled out after him. Fortunately, there was no traffic on the road, because Badger's truck was now a red dot receding into the distance. She couldn't afford to lose him. She didn't know where she was going. If he made a turn up ahead past a curve where she couldn't see him, she'd never find him again.

Why had she not thought to obtain a county map? Or at least verbal directions from the waitress.

Because she had not expected her host to be such a macho jerk, she answered herself.

Well, he could be as difficult as he chose, she was sticking with him. Grimly, she hunched over the steering wheel and mashed the accelerator into the carpet, not trying to overtake him, but at least determined to keep him in her line of sight.

Once she glanced down at the CD player, deciding that music might calm her nerves; although at their current speed, *The Ride of the Valkyries* would be the logical choice. When she looked up again an instant later, she saw that Badger's red truck was even farther ahead, so she had to accelerate again to close the distance. After that, she kept both hands firmly on the steering wheel in the "ten o'clock and two o'clock" position, and she didn't take her eyes off the road for an instant. In fact, she decided that blinking was not even a good idea. Badger knew the road, every curve, every rise—but she didn't. She also noticed that he seemed to accelerate going out of a curve, while she slowed down well before she reached it and did not resume her normal speed until she was back on the straightaway. Maybe she should try it his way, she thought.

She kept both hands on the wheel and hung on for dear life, but she stayed with him.

A few miles farther on, when she discovered that Badger didn't bother with turn signals, either, she gave up taking unnecessary breaths, so intent was she upon following the road at the greatest possible speed. He was turning left. *Ah, his specialty.* Fortunately, when he made that course change, he was far enough ahead to allow her time to slow down and to make the turn in relative safety. She had thought that she might try to remember the route just in case she did become lost, but after that first turn, she lost track of the road changes they took, and at some point she realized that she couldn't possibly find her way back to Marengo on her own. They had been going too fast for her to read the route numbers or to memorize the left and right turns. She must not lose him.

Finally, after what seemed like hours, but was actually only twenty minutes or so, Badger's red truck made one last left turn and headed up a dirt road, churning up clouds of red dust in its wake.

Almost there, thought Sark, easing her grip on the steering wheel so that her knuckles no longer showed white. She knew that later on her arms would ache and probably her head as well from the tension, but just now she was able to ignore any physical symptoms by focusing on exactly what names she was going to call Badger as soon as she was on solid ground again. And while she was at it, how would he like a face full of mosquito repellant?

After another jarring mile or so up the dirt road, dodging ruts and washed out places, the brake lights on the truck glowed red, her cue to slow down, although the expanse of greenish brown lake up ahead would have tipped her off that they were coming to the end of the ordeal. She eased the car to a stop a little way away from Badger's truck, let out a sigh of relief, and rested her head for a moment against the top of the steering wheel. Anybody who followed Badger Jenkins down a country road ought to have St. Christopher's medals for hub caps.

The red truck had pulled up in front of a glass and cedar A-framed house that most NASCAR fans would have recognized as Badger Jenkins's fishing cabin. Although not large by celebrity standards (Sark was no expert, but she thought it might run to 3,000 or 4,000 square feet), it was well-maintained and even stylish. She had been half-expecting something thrown together by Badger himself out of recycled chicken coops, but this place looked as if an architect, or at the very least a local construction company with a set of plans from a magazine, had constructed it.

The cedar cabin, surrounded by a vast multilevel deck with benches and geranium-filled planters at each corner, sat on a little knoll facing the lake, where an equally well-constructed boat dock sported Badger's motorboat, a canoe, and a little green rowboat, that last vessel presumably for duck-hunting expeditions.

Sark got out of her car and slammed the door, with blistering words hovering on her tongue, but before she could utter a single withering syllable, Badger had run up and enveloped her in an exuberant hug. "You did good!" he said. "You kept up with me. I thought for sure I'd have to pull over and wait for you."

Sark stared at him in momentary disbelief, and then she felt her annoyance melt away in a glow of pride. *I did good?* she thought. And then she realized that she had indeed performed well; he had not managed to lose her in the Georgia outback. If the drive out to the lake had been a test, she had passed it.

I kept up with a NASCAR driver, she thought with an inward smirk of satisfaction. She must write up this episode for the exposé article that she would write at the end of the season. Perhaps the adventure was a bit upbeat for an otherwise critical piece, but she wanted to be able to boast of her accomplishment to the world at large. Besides, she thought that with the proper slant she could use the anecdote as a criticism. Maybe the incident would serve to point out that fast driving wasn't really all that difficult— that any reasonably coordinated person could do what Cup drivers did if only they put their minds to it.

Her good humor restored, she studied the landscape with a more benevolent eye. The lake was quite large; it curved past a tree-lined peninsula and went on for several miles, as far as she could tell. There was no one else in sight, perhaps even no one for miles.

"So this is your fortress of solitude," she said to Badger, sighting the lake through the viewfinder of her camera.

"This is it," said Badger. "Beautiful, isn't it?"

Wet, anyhow, thought Sark, who preferred her bodies of water to be encircling Caribbean islands. It was a greenish brown lake encircled by pine trees, hardly Yellowstone. Why was Badger so crazy about this place? Most of the other NASCAR drivers lived on an even bigger lake near Charlotte—Lake Norman. Why not just move there?

"It's nice to have this place to come back to," he said.

"Do you own the whole lake?" she asked with a note of surprise in her voice. It wasn't that NASCAR drivers didn't make good money—heck, Jeff Gordon could probably have bought Lake Erie if he'd wanted it, but Badger was not in the top tier of Cup drivers.

"Oh, no," said Badger. "It's a man-made lake, you know. I own most of what you see here, but the rest—around the bend, half a mile or so away—belongs to a couple of local landowners. And there's a state game preserve adjoining it, too, at the far end."

"So no close neighbors. I suppose it's peaceful here," said Sark.

"That's it," said Badger happily. "Peaceful. It's not that I don't appreciate the interest that people take in me and my racing career, but sometimes I just need time to be by myself, you know?"

Sark nodded. "I imagine things can get pretty hectic for you," she said.

"It sure can," said Badger. "Sometimes the clamor seems to be nonstop. Why, just now on the drive out here, I got four calls on my cell phone."

She snapped a picture of the lake, framed by a stand of pines at the water's edge. "Well, I suppose that's the price that—*You what?* You got four calls . . . You mean just now, driving out here?"

"Yeah."

She took a deep breath, in lieu of shouting, and lowered the camera so that she could glare at him directly. "Do you mean to tell me that while I was following you out here—at a pace, I might add, that prevented me from taking deep breaths or even blinking . . . at a speed that no sane person could possibly maintain on the Bonneville Salt Flats, much less on a two-lane country road with curves and hills . . . And for the duration of that absurdly dangerous drive, you are telling me that *you were talking on a cell phone?*"

"Well, yeah," said Badger, serenely unconscious of self-incrimination. "But you gotta remember that I grew up here. I know these roads pretty well."

"But I don't!"

"I know," he said happily. "That's why I was so tickled that you kept up with me. And in that cheap little car, too. You were great. Now, come on. I'll show you around."

Deciding not to press the point, Sark trailed after him. So much for her triumphant feat of driving skill. She had been hanging on for dear life, scarcely daring to breathe, and he had been talking on his damned cell phone. Okay, maybe race car driving was a little more difficult than she had been willing to admit. Mentally, she excised that section from her article.

She still wondered if he had driven so fast to test her, or if he was simply oblivious to high speeds through years of racing at two or three times those speeds. She decided that she was reserving judgment on whether or not he was a jerk.

Badger seemed to have a standard routine for hosting visitors, probably a habit born of having to entertain so many journalists and TV crews over the years. First came the tour of the lake, when Badger, at the helm of his motorboat, with the life-jacketed guest installed in the prow, buzzed off to the far end of the lake, and then slowly worked his way back to his own property, pointing out items of interest along the way. At first Sark thought she would go to sleep and fall in the water, while murmuring, "Nice tree. Nice rock. Nice shrub." But dutifully she took pictures along the way, most of them incorporating Badger into the foreground of the shot. She thought she might have taken some good feature-story portraits: Badger in his natural habitat, looking at ease and princely on his beloved lake.

By the time they had wended their way to the end of the lake and were halfway back to where they started, an odd transformation had taken place. The lake really *was* beautiful. At first she had thought that it was a glorified mud puddle in the middle of nowhere, but she had resolved to be polite about it. However, somewhere along the way, his enthusiasm had infected her, and she had begun to see the land as Badger himself must be seeing it. Suddenly, without quite knowing how or why, she *got* it.

The landscape was a tapestry of the brilliant blues of sky and marsh and lake water, the sere browns of dry grass and leafless shrubs, of tall dark pines, and the silver-tipped branches of the maples in arabesques at the water's edge. She saw it as a protected place where wild things could find peace and refuge. She looked over at Badger, who was guiding the boat as effortlessly as he had maneuvered the curves of that country road.

And for now, thought Sark, *one of them has.*

While Badger tied up the motorboat at the dock, Sark took more photos of the lake, the cabin, Badger and the boat, Badger framed against the surrounding hills. She had decided to start a team archive in case any publications needed informal shots for feature articles about Badger's life away from the track.

"Where's the turtle?" she asked when he had finished securing the boat.

Badger pointed to a fenced-in enclosure near the woods. "In there asleep. His shell is still healing up. Fixing him up was a lot more complicated than we thought. Once I got him to the body shop, Jesse called the local vet, who is a fishing buddy of his, to make sure we did it right. The vet came over and checked out the turtle to make sure the membrane thing under the shell wasn't broken, which it wasn't. That was good—less chance of infection and all. Then he cleaned the wound and put on a wet dressing to keep it from getting infected. Gave him some antibiotics, too, every day for a month, which I paid for. Good thing I'm working again."

Sark felt a pang of journalistic disappointment. Turtle surgery in the body shop would have made a great human interest story. "So you didn't use fiberglass in the body shop to fix the turtle?"

"Oh, we did. Just not until a couple of weeks later, after the wound had healed up pretty good and the layer above it had started to harden. Then we took him back down to the shop and fixed him a patch with fiberglass boat materials and waterproof epoxy."

"Can I see him?" asked Sark, peering into the shady enclosure through the camera viewfinder. Just visible in the shrubbery was the shell of an enormous turtle.

"Just don't get too near him. You wouldn't like him much close up. He is a humongous snapping turtle, and he's got the disposition of Kevin Harvick. He lunges at you, and he's faster than you'd think a turtle could be. He could take your finger off in a heartbeat."

Sark grinned. "The turtle or Harvick?"

"Either one, I reckon," said Badger.

"If the turtle is so fierce, then how do you handle him?"

Badger shrugged. "I get along with most animals," he said. "I guess they know I'm on their side. Anyhow, animals are easy. You can mostly figure out what they want. Sometimes with people it's hard to tell."

As they walked back toward the cabin, Sark said, "I was in a grocery store the other day and I saw a sign that reminded me of you."

"That doesn't sound too good," said Badger. "Ham? Or vegetable section, maybe?"

She laughed. "Well, not quite the vegetable section. It was the flower and plant department. The store had a bonsai tree on display, and in front of it was a sign that said: PLEASE DO NOT TOUCH! I'M REAL! From what I've seen of your adoring public, I thought that the team ought to have a sign like that made for you." She looked at him appraisingly. "Do you *mind* being hugged?"

"Well, it's okay when little kids do it."

Sark tried to keep her astonishment from showing. She had been expecting the typical macho answer, something to the effect of "I don't mind being hugged by pretty girls or movie starlets." But children? Go figure.

"I suppose that people feel they know you," she said. "They've followed you in racing for years, and seen you on TV in their living rooms so many times. I guess that they care so much about you that they forget that to you they are strangers. To them you are one of the family."

Badger nodded sadly. "They don't mean any harm. It's nice of them to take an interest."

Sark's cynical soul recoiled in disbelief. Could he really be so disingenuous? She said, "What about the ones who take too much of an interest, Badger?"

He hesitated, and she thought he might be considering feigning ignorance, but she forestalled that response with a no-nonsense glare that said he'd better not try playing dumb. He might not be able to quote Shakespeare (or even *spell* Shakespeare), but since he had been a handsome man for a couple of decades now, she was pretty sure he'd know the difference between admiration and lust when he saw it.

"Well, okay," he sighed. "Off the record. If I think that a woman has"—he grinned to show he was being facetious—"*designs on my honor*, I have this one-armed hug that I use. It keeps them from . . . um . . ."

"I get it," said Sark, repressing a shudder. "How strange that you should have to worry about things like that instead of being able to concentrate on driving the car."

Badger nodded. "Don't forget, though, that there are a lot of people who can drive a race car. The Busch guys are good, and most of the truck guys would do just fine in Cup. There are even some fellas on local tracks who just never got the right breaks, and they could do my job, too, some of 'em. So the forty-three of us in Cup are pretty damn lucky to be where we are. Some of that success is due to popularity with the fans. Best not to forget that."

He's not as dumb as he'd have us believe, thought Sark. Maybe innocent is just part of the act. He's shrewd about business and probably about charming people, too. She decided that she'd think over all that later for the article she'd be writing about the real Badger Jenkins in her exposé of Cup racing.

Still, she had to concede that he was right in his assessment, and she was grudgingly pleased that he wasn't being an arrogant jerk about the public adulation he received. He did realize that to some people anybody in a Cup ride was a hero. Some of his success came as much from luck as from talent. But his humility did not change the fact that people routinely invaded his personal space without a qualm, and no matter how kind he appeared to be, she still couldn't believe that the intrusiveness of it didn't bother him.

"But fans putting moves on me, or being pushy, it doesn't happen as much as you'd think," he said quickly, as if reading her thoughts.

"No?"

"No. You learn how to deal with it. At the track, you know, when I'm in my firesuit and sunglasses, I can project an attitude of *leave me alone*. I don't smile at people, and I walk quickly, without slowing down for people waiting for autographs. Then people just know to keep their distance. I learned that trick from Dale Earnhardt himself."

Sark blinked. "You didn't try to hug *him,* did you?"

"'No, I did not try to hug Dale Earnhardt," said Badger, scowling. "I mean that I watched how the Intimidator carried himself, that's all. I noticed that nobody ever approached him unless he allowed them to. He had an attitude that was bulletproof. I watched how he did that, and I started trying to do it myself."

Sark gave him an appraising stare. There was nothing remotely intimidating about Badger. He had a perfect profile and cameras practically melted when you took his picture, but in real life he was small and cute, and above all harmless-looking. "I can't see how that tactic would work for you, Badger," she told him. "You look like a lost puppy dog. Now, Dale Earnhardt, from the pictures I've seen of him, could come across as truly fierce, but—no offense—you could not possibly pull that off."

With a sigh of resignation, Badger pulled his sunglasses out of his pocket, slid them on, and stood up. In an instant, his perfect features hardened into a blank-eyed, tight-lipped mask of cold rejection. He folded his arms, raised his chin a little, and stared at her, waiting.

Sark's objections stuck in a dry throat. The affable country boy had vanished and in his place stood a stern and powerful stranger whom nobody would argue with. She wasn't going to, anyhow. He might as well have been shouting, "Get the hell away from me." She remembered that first time she had done a photo session with him. He had looked formidable then when he posed, but this was leagues beyond that; now, he radiated an icy grandeur that would stop you in your tracks. *How the hell did he do that?*

"Oh," she said, and it came out hardly more than a squeak.

Badger nodded. "And I'm not even wearing the firesuit. You add that to the sunglasses, and people generally don't mess with me."

"Well, that was certainly educational," said Sark briskly. "Take them off again, please."

They walked up the steps of the deck toward the front door of his cabin. "I had a guy renting this," he told her, fishing in his pocket for the key. "But he got his place fixed up, so it's all mine again. I don't get to come back as much as I'd like to, though."

He pushed open the door and waved her inside.

Having seen the outside of the fabled "fishing shack," Sark was not surprised to find that the pine-paneled interior was equally well-kept and nicely furnished with Shaker-style furniture in oak and cherry wood and overstuffed sofas flanking a large stone fireplace. The walls held an assortment of trophies—but not the sort that Sark had been expecting. Instead of racing memorabilia, there were fishing rods, mounted game fish and deer heads, and framed art prints of ducks and deer in woodland settings.

"Where's all your NASCAR stuff?" asked Sark.

"My daddy's got most of it," said Badger. "He's got boxes full of stuff in the basement. My Darlington trophy was in the middle of his dining room table last time I looked."

"That must make for interesting dinner conversations," said Sark.

"I guess," said Badger. "We don't talk much. And I gave a lot of my old posters and a couple of old trophies to Laraine for the diner." It suddenly seemed to occur to him that she might be asking for a reason. "Do you want anything? I think I have some die-cast cars in a drawer here."

Sark smiled. "All I want is your time, Badger." She felt a small pang of guilt, because she knew that wasn't true. This interview would be grist for two articles: the feature story for the team and the exposé she planned to write at the end of the season. *Well,* she told herself, *he probably is a jerk. I just haven't found out how yet.*

When Sark got back to Charlotte that night, she found an e-mail from her journalist pal Ed Blair, asking her to report on her progress with Team Vagenya.

> How is Project Badger coming along? Didn't you
> have an interview with him this week? Learn
> anything interesting?

I went down to visit him in his natural habitat today. Whatever it is that Alexander the Great and Moses and, for all I know, the Lone Ranger . . . whatever they had, he's got it. And I'm not talking about sex appeal (for a change.) Spent five hours alone in the woods with him and felt absolutely no vibrations on that frequency, either way. But what is magical is the focus—that quality that makes him an incredible race car driver, I guess. . . . He's *there.* Absolutely, perfectly, 110% THERE. The world is a desert island, you and him. He'll talk about anything. He'll listen. No games, no bragging, no ego. I think all of us were like that when we were about twelve, before we started caring about social status, and appearance, and all the facades of the adult world.

If it is possible to be twelve at heart but fully adult in intelligence and understanding, he's it. What Peter Pan might have really been like, or maybe Siddharta en route to becoming the Buddha.

He's not dumb, either. He just lives in his body, and I live in my head, so there's a different frequency. But he's really nice. Wish I knew how he managed to grow up and not be a jerk.

So you spent the day with the Buddha in the wilds of Georgia, did you? What exactly does that entail? How does his engine feel? Surely you've found out by now!

Got a tour of the lake and his lake house, and met the turtle. I don't know how his "engine feels." Nothing happened. Probably because I do not own a tiara and a sash proclaiming me Miss Something-or-Other. Beauty queens are more his speed. He's not a jerk about it. He was just raised to think that women should be high-maintenance trophies, and that as long as other guys envy you, compatibility doesn't matter. Poor guy. He's really very sweet, though. I was surprised. Of course, the problem with not being a teenager anymore is that one has no second gear anymore, so I'm quite afraid that some day he will hold that sexless hug of his for a heartbeat too long, and I'll instinctively reach for the stick shift and find out "how his engine feels," as you so colorfully put it.

You seem to be using a lot of automotive metaphors lately. Is the job getting to you?

Possibly, Ed. I am very susceptible to atmosphere. The lake was rather picturesque, and he certainly cares about the place. His fishing shack is not exactly a hovel, either. It's a nice A-frame, furnished with clean, modern pieces in natural wood.

Decorator?

Ex-wife, perhaps. But it is possible that he has taste, you know. I enjoyed having an uninterrupted afternoon to talk to him. By the way, I got him to talk for ten minutes about "Do they know how much we love them?"

About what?

You know . . . the adoring fans that NASCAR drivers have. He steadfastly ignored *(and I did not bring up)* the pit lizard sign in the equation. He talked about how no matter how rushed or mad he was, he would never ignore a child. How he came to the sport from humbler beginnings than most guys, and that he had vowed never to lose his head over the money or the fame. Says he never thought he was better than anybody else.

Someday I'll get a couple of Heinekens down his pretty little throat, and then I'll ask him about the dark side of the Force. Wonder if he has ever succumbed. The way he looks, I'd put money on a bet that he has given it up to somebody, somewhere, but I don't think it's a regular sport with him. He has to know that there are people who salivate at seeing the number 86. . . . He chooses not to notice. I suppose it saves awkwardness . . .

If I were him, I'd notice if pretty ladies were hot for my bod! I'd have a basket at the track to collect hotel room keys.

I'll bet you would, thought Sark, logging off. Maybe most guys would. But she was pretty sure that whatever Badger's vices were, lust was not among them.

CHAPTER XV

Shop Talk

The team was having another pit stop practice at the shop, but Badger was not on hand to help. He wasn't required to be, of course, but sometimes he had dropped by just to encourage them and to see how things were going. Today, though, his personal manager had commandeered him to make a public appearance at the grand opening of an auto parts store. The team knew about this because Deanna, who had been dispatched by Ms. Albigre to get more of Badger's autograph cards as a rush job from the printer, was still grumbling about it to anyone within earshot.

"She misspelled the name of the sponsor on the sports card," Deanna told Sark, who had wandered in to use the fax machine. "I told her, and she said she didn't care. She said they were in a hurry."

Sark sighed. "This is all new to me, but her idea of publicity certainly differs from mine. A few days ago I got a call from a turtle rescue program, asking if Badger would film a public service commercial for them, so I relayed the request to Melodie, and she said, 'What's in it for Badger?' "

"I think a turtle rescue ad would be great publicity for him," said Deanna. "Is he going to do it?"

"I don't think she even bothered to tell him about it. No percentage in it."

Deanna made a face. "I just hate the way that woman talks to him, Sark. I mean, she may be a genius, for all I know. Although with her spelling . . . but anyhow, she shouldn't talk to Badger the ways she does, as if he were a mangy old dog. I wish there was somebody we could report her to."

Sark nodded. "How about Amnesty International?"

Badger was led away to dazzle the auto parts store customers with his boyish charm *("How ya doin', sweetie?"),* and practice went on without Team Vagenya's official driver. One of the shop dogs was again subbing for Badger, and the pit crew drilled on tire changing while Tuggle timed them with a stopwatch and shouted instructions. After half an hour of precision drill, the crew chief turned them loose for a break while she went to talk to a journalist. The hot and sweaty crew headed for the shop where there were apples and granola bars on the counter and an ice-filled cooler stocked with a selection of soft drinks and bottled water.

The tall young man who had been Badger's stand-in for the practice dug a Diet Snapple out of the cooler ice and looked at it appreciatively. "This is way better than the guys' teams," he said. "They mostly just put out a loaf of Wonder bread and a package of bologna. And regular cola, if they think of it."

Taran smiled. "That would suit Badger," she said. "I think that's what he lives on, anyhow."

The substitute driver shrugged. "Yeah, but he works out. And that junk food jones of his may be an act for all we know. In private, he may eat plain salad and scrape the butter off his fish. Most Cup drivers are pretty fanatical about their health—or at least about their looks."

"Well, whatever he does, it works," sighed Taran, glancing at the poster of Badger taped to the wall of the shop.

Tony shrugged. "He's a talented guy," he said. "But he's lucky. They all are."

Taran looked at him more closely. "You're the one who drove the car for our pit stop practices on the day of tryouts, aren't you?" she said. The name tag sewn on his firesuit said "Tony." It wasn't a Vagenya firesuit, though. It was an old one, probably from a time when he'd raced at local speedways somewhere. Almost everybody in racing started out that way.

The dark young man nodded. "I'm just a mechanic, so that was kind of a thrill. Me driving Badger Jenkins's car. Even if it was just fifty yards to a pit stop. They told me somebody spotted the difference."

"Yes. That was me."

He looked disappointed. "How'd you know it wasn't him?"

"Oh, not because of the driving," said Taran quickly. "You did a great job. Really. It was the eyes. Badger has very dark, sad eyes. You can't mistake them. Anyhow, yours are blue."

Her explanation did not seem to comfort him much. Tony said, "Plus, he's rich and famous, and I'm just a shop dog."

Taran thought it would be both impolite and insincere to agree with the patent truth of this statement. Besides, he wasn't so bad. Tony Lafon was a good three inches taller than she was, and therefore that much taller than Badger himself. He had dark straight hair offset by the fair skin and blue eyes that people associated with Ireland. Tony didn't have Badger's perfectly chiseled features, but he looked like a nice, bright guy, and he was certainly easier to talk to.

Taran said, "Well, maybe Badger is more successful than you are, but you look about ten years younger than he is. Are you? Yeah, I thought so. You still have time to make it as a driver. If that's what you want. Is it?"

Tony looked up at the handsome, stern face of Badger Jenkins staring down at him in airbrushed perfection from the Team Vagenya poster. Some guys got all the breaks. "It's all I've ever wanted," he said. "Ever since I was a kid, I've been watching racing, and working as a mechanic anywhere I could, and driving at the local tracks in southwest Virginia. You know, the little Saturday night tracks where they raced trucks or Late Model Stocks, and you had to go door to door to the local businesses to get your own sponsors." He sighed. "You want to believe that working so hard on the local level will someday get you into Cup—and sometimes it does."

"Of course it does," said Taran. "That's how Badger got started."

Taran knew every detail of Badger's rise to the exalted ranks of Nextel Cup. She could recite the date and place of every victory Badger had ever achieved in Cup racing *(there hadn't been that many of them to date)*. Although she had not memorized the string of little Saturday night triumphs he had amassed in the lower echelons of stock car racing, she could probably name more of them than Badger himself could, and she did know every racing category, every track, and every number under which he had competed. Her own car's license plate was a vanity plate, but people seldom realized it, because it was just his initials, BJ, followed by 7781, 77 being the number of the car he had once driven in local Late Model Stock racing, and 81, his number in his first season in the NASCAR Busch series.

"Badger was lucky," Tony said again. "There was a guy at his local track who was getting too old to do any racing himself, but he still wanted to be in the game, so he sold the equipment to Badger and stayed on to help him learn the ropes. Badger was a natural—I'm not saying he wasn't good—but there are a heck of a lot of guys who are good that never get past Late Model Stocks."

"So you decided to work for a Cup team instead?"

Tony nodded. "I figured it would be a good way to make connections within the sport. Racing is in many ways just a small town. What about you?"

Taran sighed. "You'll laugh," she said.

"Try me."

"I'm the team flake. Everybody else is doing it for the experience, or for a feminist cause, or because they're just crazy about stock car racing. But not me. I'm the fool who is crazy about Badger Jenkins." When she said it, she was watching him carefully to see if he was having trouble wiping a smirk off his face, but he had simply nodded and given her a look that might have been sympathetic.

"Guys in firesuits," he said, unwrapping another Granola bar. "A lot of people mistake them for Superman, I guess. I've seen it dozens of times. But why Badger in particular?"

"It sounds ridiculous," she sighed. "I was dating a guy who got me interested in NASCAR, and he was a Mark Martin fan. He kept telling me to pick a driver, so that it would be more interesting when we watched the races together." She stopped for a moment, remembering Rob, one of the company's electrical engineers. A nice enough guy, she supposed, if you liked Italian food and watching *Stargate* on the Sci-Fi Channel, which was okay. She just couldn't see doing that for the rest of her life. Besides, Rob looked like a mild-mannered frog in steel-rimmed glasses, and Taran thought that a permanent relationship with him would put you in the fast lane for old age. She decided that Rob himself had probably been born forty. But she'd always be grateful to him for introducing her to motorsports. He liked to watch the races with a clipboard of statistics at hand: Which driver had previously won at this track? Whose team seemed to be consistently good lately? Who had done well in practice and qualifying? As an engineer herself, she found this sort of scientific approach interesting, but since racing was, after all, a form of entertainment, she felt that Rob's joyless method of analyzing the race left much to be desired. She wanted to care who won: to hope for his success, rather than to coldly predict it with an assortment of dispassionate statistics.

"He wanted you to pick a driver so that watching racing with you would be a competiton," said Tony. "I'll bet he thought you'd go for Jeff Gordon. He's really popular with women and kids."

"No," said Taran. "He knew better than that. I'm an electrical engineer. He figured I'd go for the intellectual type."

"Ryan Newman, then. Engineering degree from Purdue."

"Right. And I do like Newman, but I don't think choosing a driver is necessarily a matter of logic. You don't cry over somebody just because he is the mathematical favorite."

"Well, some people might," said Tony. "But mostly not, I guess. People usually choose a driver who reflects their interests or their background. Home state, sponsor identification, looks—something. And then there are the people who won't root for a Ford driver, or who hate anybody in a Chevrolet. There are a lot of sides to take in this sport."

"I know," said Taran. "Every week is like a football game with forty-three teams on the field."

"So how did you come to pick Badger instead of Newman or Kenseth? Was it when he won at Darlington?"

Taran sighed a little, remembering. "No. It wasn't when he won at all. I remember they interviewed him before the race, and he looked kind of shy and self-deprecating, and—Well, I know this is going to sound strange, but his accent reminded me of my grandfather. He died when I was seven, and he wasn't real old. It was a car wreck. But anyhow, I heard Badger's voice, and it was like hearing my granddad, I just felt like I knew him."

"How did he do in the race that day?"

"He wrecked. Well, somebody wrecked *him*. And I just lost it. I was so terrified that I had jinxed him by liking him. He had a concussion, and I remember I kept checking *Engine Noise* all week to see how he was doing. Anyhow, by the time he got well and was back in the car—he missed one race, I think—I had gone online and bought a tee shirt, a coffee mug, and two key chains. I was hooked. Badger was it."

Tony nodded. He'd heard similar stories from fans before. "So what happened to Rob?"

Taran shrugged. "We stopped watching racing together. He said I was too emotional. I guess it's hard to concentrate on your chart of statistics when the person beside you is alternately shrieking and crying. So that was it. I didn't miss him, though. I had Badger."

Tony smiled. "It must have been a thrill for you to actually meet him."

"Oh, no," said Taran, shuddering at the memory. "It was ghastly."

It had been a few days after Tuggle had selected the Team Vagenya pit crew, and Badger, having finally finished giving interviews and having his picture made with the sponsors and owners, had finally come along to practice. He went down the line, shaking hands and introducing himself to his new teammates. When he got to Taran, he stuck out his hand, smiled like a movie star, and said, "How you doin'?"

And she had backed away from that outstretched hand as if it had been holding a switchblade. She had just wanted him to go away.

It certainly wasn't how she had pictured her first meeting with her driver. Once she had been chosen for the team, she had re-hearsed the moment in her mind a hundred times, in every possi-ble variation. From *"How do you do, sir? Such a pleasure to meet you,"* to *"I'm sorry? I didn't catch the name,"* to wordlessly throw-ing herself in his arms, while imaginary violins swelled to a stun-ning crescendo and the team practice yard dissolved into a field of wildflowers. But nowhere in her wildest imaginings had she pictured herself backing away from her beloved Badger in abject terror.

But she had.

Now why was that?

She had given it a lot of thought since then. She wasn't sure that Badger had even noticed her confusion. As she was backing away, Reve had put her hand into the small of Taran's back and gently pushed her forward again. She managed to croak a feeble hello, and Badger shook her hand and moved on.

Since then she had relived that moment another hundred times or so, wishing that you could get instant replays in real life. At least she'd have a second chance. They were teammates. Sooner or later she might calm down enough to actually converse with him.

She had tried to figure out exactly why she had panicked. *Well,* she told herself, *it isn't every day that you meet your screensaver.* Badger was shorter than she'd imagined, but otherwise he looked pretty much like his photographs, so that wasn't the reason for her dismay. Perhaps it was simply the pressure of that first meet-ing, because to her, anyway, it mattered so much. With most peo-ple you meet you can simply be yourself, and either you hit it off or you don't, and it's no big deal either way, but Badger was the SAT and an EKG rolled into one: a human exam, and if she failed it, the chance might never come again.

They had probably chatted for a minute or two, but the voice in her head was chanting "Don'tletmesayanythingstupidDon'tlet mesayanythingstupid" so loudly that she could no longer remem-ber what either of them said.

"He was wearing the firesuit, wasn't he?" asked Tony.

"And the sunglasses," said Taran. "It was terrible. I wanted to run."

"You didn't, did you? He's a pretty laid-back guy, you know. One of the nicest drivers in the bunch."

"I know," said Taran. "I'm starting to get over it. Lately when he comes around the shop for practice or just to stop by, I can talk to him a little bit without feeling faint." She smiled to show that she was kidding—almost.

"I wonder what that feels like," said Tony. "To be so famous that people are afraid to talk to you."

"I don't think he knows," said Taran. "He never seems to notice, anyhow."

Tony tossed his Snapple bottle into the recycle bin. "I think they want us back out there," he said. "Reve is waving at us."

Taran finished the last of her water. "Well, good luck with your driving. I hope you get your chance."

"Sometimes I do some driving on a week night at the local track. Late Model Stocks. I have a friend who lets me sub for him sometimes, and I'm working on getting a couple of local sponsors so I can have my own ride. Maybe you'd like to come out sometime and watch?"

Taran nodded. "I'd like that," she said. She was thinking, *The more I learn about racing, the more small talk I'll be able to make with Badger.*

In Julie Carmichael's office, otherwise known as Vagenya Tech, the team engineers were busy as usual, trying to stay one jump ahead of the NASCAR watchdogs.

"In the old days," said Jay Bird, "there were a lot of tricks we could have used to modify the car."

"Like what?" asked Rosalind.

"Lighten the roll cage. We used to replace the thick steel bars of the roll cage with lighter-weight exhaust pipe. Can't do that these days, though. NASCAR checks the roll bar thickness with an ultrasonic tester right there in the pits."

Julie explained to Rosalind, "They have a little handheld unit and they put a little jelly on the end of the sensor and put it up against the roll bars, and it reads the thickness on the digital display."

Rosalind was aghast. "But you can't lighten the roll bars, anyway!" she said. "In a wreck, that roll cage is what protects the driver. You could get Badger killed if you circumvent the safety measures."

"Badger wants to win as bad as we do," said Jay Bird. "I'll bet you wouldn't catch him complaining."

"He might be too macho to complain," said Julie, "but Rosalind is right. We can't risk him getting hurt."

Jay Bird was philosophical about it. "They'd probably catch us, anyway. What about having a little panel in the floor board that you can slide open to diffuse some of the air from underneath the car?"

"Everybody does that," said Julie. "Like lowering the motor mounts. Done that."

"Okay," said Rosalind, "here's an idea. Suppose we attach sensors to the car to transmit information back to us about the fuel mileage, the wheel revolutions per minute, and maybe the transmission gear selection? That would help."

"It's called *telemetry*," said Julie. "It's illegal."

"Oh," said Rosalind. "I'd better reread the rule book again."

Jay Bird said, "What about traction control?"

"Now I know *that's* illegal," said Rosalind. "It's akin to telemetry, really—installing sensors to detect the amount of wheel spin, and then regulating the amount of power being transmitted to the tire. NASCAR outlawed that, didn't they?"

"Big time," said Jay Bird. "Get caught with that on your car and they say they'll ban you from the sport for life."

Julie closed her notebook. "This isn't getting us anywhere," she said. "Let's just keep on doing all the dull but legal stuff we've been doing to make the car better. We'll keep fine-tuning everything."

CHAPTER XVI

Speed Week

ENGINE NOISE
Your Online Source for NASCAR News & Views

VAGENYA SLIM?—Well, what do *you* think the 86 team's chances are to make the Daytona 500? *Engine Noise* is betting that by race time Sunday they'll all be back in Mooresville watching the show on television. The legendary **Jay Bird Thomas** is acting as the team's godfather, but we think they'd be better off with a fairy godmother. With a magic wand. Boogity! Boogity! Boo!—Still, the team is in Daytona this week, getting ready to qualify for the Great American Race. Since they are a start-up team without a previous top 35 standing or champion's points, they'll have to make it in by having one of the fastest times of all the wannabees. So they'd better hope that Badger doesn't—*dare we say it?*—run like a girl!

Hey, Ed, Sark here. I finally made it to Daytona with Team Vagenya, and I'm taking notes like crazy. I'm beginning to think I need to write a book instead of just an article. If people don't know racing it would be hard to cram all this information into a couple of thousand words.

Yo, Sark! You're in Daytona already? I thought the race wasn't until next Sunday?

It is next Sunday, but you wouldn't believe how much we have to go through before the race. It's not even guaranteed that we will race. First there's qualifying, which I thought I understood. You know, cars go around the track a couple of times and whoever has the fastest lap gets the pole, and second fastest is next, and so on. Well, for the Daytona 500, they don't qualify like that.

So, enlighten me. Basketball is my sport. What do your car boys do at Daytona? Poll the audience? Call a friend? Convene the College of Cardinals?

Nothing so simple. They do the normal two-lap time trial on the first day, but that only determines who gets the inside and outside pole positions. Everybody else is still in limbo.

Limbo, Huh? *Then* they call the College of Cardinals?

No, then they hold two 125-mile qualifying races on the Thursday before the race on Sunday.

Two races? How do they decide which contenders race in which race?

Do you really want to know, Ed? Try reading an IRS tax form, and if you find that riveting, then I'll explain all the fine points of qualifying to you. Anyhow, suffice it to say that Badger is in the first qualifying race, and if he finishes in the top fourteen, he will take his place in the lineup behind the pole sitter.

That sounds dull, but coherent, anyhow.

It gets worse. There are also champion's points, provisional entries, and God only knows what else, but anyhow, we're not eligible for any papal dispensations or whatever you have to have to get into the race free. We have to get Badger in with a fast car, which, please God, he does not wreck during the qualifying race.

So now you're praying for Badger? I'm touched.

Listen, a lot of talented and dedicated women have worked pretty damned hard to get him out there, and if he gets this team in the race I'd be willing to put a statue of him on my dashboard.

Sounds like he's made a convert. And is Badger being a saint down there in NASCAR land?

He's working his ass off. We all are. What he does on his own time, I don't know.

Shouldn't you be finding out? For the article, of course.

I'll try. He has an autographing Thursday morning. Maybe I can ask him then. I'm supposed to be his minder for the afternoon, because the Dominatrix is busy (I told you about her). Maybe she has to have dialysis to change the antifreeze in her veins. Gotta go. Wish us luck.

If anyone had told Taran Stiles that she would someday spend a whole week inside the Daytona International Speedway, and that not once would she even bother to log on to the *Badger's Din*, much less boast about her adventures, well, she wouldn't have believed it. Here she was, living the dream, and she wasn't going to tell the people who would envy her most. In fact, the week had been so hectic that she couldn't even be bothered to read what they were saying about the forthcoming race.

Anyone who thought that stock car racing was not a team sport had better not say it to her face this week. People on *Badger's Din* used to talk about racing as if it was all up to Badger, but now Taran knew for a fact that it wasn't. Before he could go out there and qualify in one of Daytona's preliminary races, an army of support people had to do their jobs, and he couldn't succeed unless they were very good at their jobs, too. It was an intricate web of trust and dependency. The pit crew had to hope that the engineers and mechanics had set up the car so that it would perform well, and the engineers and mechanics had to hope that all their hard work would not go down the drain if the pit crew screwed up their part of the operation. And assuming that all of them did everything right both in the shop and in the pit, it all depended on Badger driving well and being lucky enough not to get wrecked by somebody else's mistake on the track.

The first practice at Daytona was a nerve-wracking experience for Taran. There were a fair number of people in the stands, and enough people were milling around the infield to populate a county fair. Taran thought it was hard enough to do her newly learned job without all these strangers watching her. It unnerved her that the garages provided for the Cup teams had one glass wall, so that anyone walking by could stand there and watch what was going on. She knew that the observers were probably just interested well-meaning fans, but the idea of being observed by strangers still made her uneasy. She felt that she was too much of a klutz in general to want an audience.

She was still standing there in a daze when Kathy Erwin, the team's front tire changer, shook her by the shoulder, and said,

"Stiles, quick—before it's Badger's turn to practice. We forgot to bring one of the parts we might need this afternoon. We need you to go over to one of the Childress teams and see if you can borrow one. You need to hurry."

"What part is it?" asked Taran.

The tire changer told her.

Moments later, Taran was standing at the tool wagon of the 31 car, trying to explain her errand to a harassed-looking man in orange coveralls. "We just want to borrow it, if you have an extra one."

The wiry man leaned in closer and cupped his ear so she wouldn't have to shout. "What was it you wanted again?"

Taran had it down pat. "A left-handed smoke shifter," she said triumphantly. "If you can spare it."

The guy in the orange coveralls sighed and shook his head. "We only brought the one," he said. "But I tell you what, why don't you go see if the 21 car has one to spare? I believe the Wood Brothers actually invented that tool. They're bound to have an extra one, don't you think, boys?"

Those of his fellow crew members within earshot nodded solemnly. The Wood Brothers. The 21 car. They all agreed that it was Taran's best bet, and off she went.

She threaded her way through the crowd of crew members getting ready for their car's turn at practice, trying to ignore the roar of engines and the people watching from the stands, all of whom were, she felt, looking directly at her. At the Wood Brothers' garage she restated her mission to another busy man in coveralls.

"Can't help you," he said, and turned away.

Desperation made her bold. "But I thought you people invented the left-handed smoke shifter!" said Taran, clutching at his arm.

The crewman sighed and looked down into the face of an earnest little idiot who was on the verge of tears. Sure she was a new fish, but he figured that race week would be enough of a hassle for her as it was. And Badger was a good guy. They went way back. Old Badger had enough to contend with, what with that embarrassing sponsor of his. He didn't need any hysterical teammates to boot. "Look, kid," the crewman said, "there's no such thing."

"What?" Taran strained to hear him over the waves of sound from crowds, engines, and loudspeakers.

"I said there's no such thing as a left-handed smoke shifter. It's an old joke. Crews pick the most gullible new team member and send them out to borrow nonexistent tools. They're back there laughing at you. Go back and get ready for the practice."

It took a moment for the sense of this speech to sink in to Taran's already panic-stricken and distracted brain, but finally the phrase *they're laughing at you* hit home, and without a word, she turned away and began to trudge back to the Team Vagenya garage stall. Practical jokes were not her idea of the best way to build camaraderie within the team, but she realized that NASCAR was still a man's world, which meant that the rules were different—and not necessarily harsher, either. The society of women had its own form of hazing, but usually they did it behind your back, and they never let you in on the joke.

Maybe the team thought she was the joke, Taran thought. Everybody knew how she felt about Badger. Oh, not the real Badger, but that ethereal creature in the firesuit that he sometimes became. Maybe that was why they had singled her out for torment.

She went back to the space allotted to the 86 car. Fortunately, everybody was busy, so they missed her arrival. She had been dreading the pointing and snickering. Then she saw why no one was paying any attention to her. A rookie's car had got loose in Turn Four and hit the back of another car. It wasn't Badger—always her first thought—but everyone's attention was now focused on the track where the two cars had stopped.

Suddenly, Tuggle was at her side. "Damn rookies," she said, nodding toward the track. "Look, go ask the guys if they brought the shrinker-stretcher from the shop. We may need it."

Taran blinked. "Wh-what?"

"The shrinker-stretcher. It's a tool," said Tuggle.

"Oh, I'll just bet it is!" said Taran. "Well, for your information, I have already fallen for that stupid trick once today. I'm not going to go on any more wild goose chases for nonexistent parts just to amuse this team. It's mean!" She put her hand over her mouth to stifle the sobs and ran off in the direction of the restroom.

Tuggle stared after her open-mouthed. "What the hell?—Hey, Erwin, got a minute? Go ask Tony if we brought the shrinker-stretcher."

It's a small part used to get the dents out of sheet metal, in case the car gets banged up out on the track. Kathy Erwin, who knew that, ran to the garage to check.

The team spent most of Speed Week in a frenzy of activity, getting the car ready; making sure they knew what they were supposed to do; and tripping over reporters, who wanted fluffy feature stories about the "girls' team." They had all been warned to be as bland and noncommittal as possible—and to make no personal comments about Badger.

One afternoon when they were in the garage area of the Daytona infield, during a rare moment of inactivity, Tony Lafon appeared, carrying a digital camera, and said, "Can somebody do me a favor?"

"I take pretty good pictures," said Taran. "What do you need?"

He handed her the camera. "Great. Hold this. I'll be right back!"

"Nice guy," said Cindy. "He's spotting for Badger Sunday, isn't he?"

Taran nodded. "He drives on some of the local tracks around Charlotte, so he knows what to say during races."

"He drives? Is he any good?"

"I think so," said Taran. "But I don't think he can afford good enough equipment to prove it."

Tony reappeared just then wearing a white firesuit with blue sleeves, emblazoned with a Sunoco logo and lettering advertising a local furniture store. On the belt at his waist was the name "Tony Lafon" embroidered in blue. The outfit was not on par with the elegant custom-made firesuit that Badger wore, but it still had the magical effect of making Tony look taller, handsomer, and extremely important.

"I wanted to get some pictures of myself for my portfolio," he said. "And maybe to do an autograph card for local events."

"Sure," said Taran. "Where do you want to go?"

"Well, since there aren't too many people around this afternoon, I was thinking Victory Lane." He said it warily, as if he expected the statement to be met with peals of laughter, but everybody just nodded, seeing the logic of the suggestion.

"Come on," said Taran. "If we take twenty or thirty shots, there's bound to be one you can use."

Victory Lane at Daytona is a large barred enclosure with a small set of bleachers facing a stage, whose white backdrop features the words "Daytona International Speedway" under a smaller design of multicolored flags. They walked from the garage area to the building that adjoined the Victory Lane enclosure, and a cleaning man obligingly let them in and pointed them to a door that opened into Victory Lane.

"How do I look?" asked Tony, as Taran positioned him on the stage under the word "Daytona."

"Important," said Taran. "Why don't you stand over there beside the reflective glass wall of the building? If I angle the shot correctly, I can get the reflection of the track itself in the glass behind you."

"That would be great," said Tony.

About five minutes later, Taran was on the fifteenth variation of Tony in the reflection shot, when the tourist trolley arrived.

The Daytona International Speedway is a tourist attraction every day of the year. People come from all over the world to see the mother church of American racing, and part of the experience is getting to circle the track in a coupled caravan of open trolleys while a guide recites a running narrative of speedway history and information. One highlight of the tour is when the carriages go up on the steep banking between Turns Three and Four for perhaps fifty yards, enabling the tourists to experience the thrill of actually riding on the same part of the track where the race is run. After that the tour takes a five-minute break in Victory Lane—major photo opportunity.

This time when the guide unlocked the gate to Victory Lane, the crowd of tourists surged into the enclosure, whereupon sixty people simultaneously spotted the miraculous vision within: *a*

NASCAR driver in a firesuit. As one, the horde of squealing spec-tators, which included a group of local schoolchildren, sprinted toward the exalted being posing for publicity pictures. Taking this as a signal that photos were indeed permitted, they encircled the driver and began clicking away. Others hung back, digging into pockets and purses for pens and scraps of paper on which to cap-ture the celebrity's autograph.

Tony bore up under this wave of adulation with remarkable grace and poise. He posed for pictures with anyone who wanted, and he motioned for all the fourth graders to encircle him so that he towered about them like an amiable Godzilla, smiling for a phalanx of amateur photographers. He shook hands and ac-cepted hugs from admiring strangers, while Taran stood by won-deringly, and so totally ignored by Tony's newfound admirers that she might have been invisible. He signed hats and hands and pieces of notebook paper. And posed for still more pictures.

And no one ever asked who he was.

After five minutes, the guide herded his charges back to the trolley to continue the tour, and waving their last farewells, the happy tourists climbed back on board and sped away up the track.

"Wow," said Taran. "That was amazing. They treated you like you were Jeff Gordon."

"It's the firesuit," said Tony. "It's magic."

"Yeah, I believe it. So . . . do you want to go over to Lake Lloyd? I could get some shots of you walking on water."

When they got back to the 86 garage area, they were still laugh-ing.

By Thursday, Tuggle had grudgingly pronounced them as ready as they were going to get. They hadn't seen much of Badger. He had been whisked here and there, filming a NASCAR commercial with a couple of other drivers, giving interviews for the sports media, and renewing his acquaintance with all his old friends from his former days in Cup racing. He was due to turn up again late Thursday morning for the first autographing session promot-ing the Team Vagenya merchandise.

"I still don't see why we agreed to this autographing," said Sark with a worried frown. "Badger has the qualifying race this afternoon, doesn't he?"

"He does," said Tuggle. "That's a couple of hours later."

"But shouldn't he be focusing on that? He can't even get into the Daytona 500 unless he does well in this race. Why distract him?"

Tuggle shrugged. "Because these days, being popular is just about as important as winning. It impresses the sponsor, and it's easier to achieve than a first-place finish."

"But shouldn't he concentrate on his actual job? He has to go around that track at two hundred miles per hour."

"He'll be fine," said Tuggle. No point in telling the publicist that to the bosses it didn't much matter whether he was fine or not. They could always get another wheel man.

Sark shrugged. Hers not to reason why. Because it was Badger's first autographing as the Team Vagenya driver, they wanted her to photograph the event and to do a write-up for the team Web site, and so she would. Logistics were someone else's problem. Sometimes Badger reminded her of Boxer the horse in *Animal Farm*: a hardworking simpleton exploited by the pigs of management. That observation might make an interesting sidebar for her exposé.

The lot where the souvenir trailers were parked—row on row of brightly painted vans, emblazoned with drivers pictures and team colors—reminded Sark of a state fairground. Here were the same kitschy souvenirs—the tee shirts, hats, and teddy bears—that you saw at the fairgrounds, and the same milling crowds of sartorially challenged sightseers. Only here, instead of the tattooed lady and the sword-swallower, people waited in line to meet a Cup driver. The difference, thought Sark, was that tattooed ladies and sword-swallowers made a living by letting people gawk at them, while presumably Cup drivers had better things to do. She resolved to make a note of that analogy for her future *Vanity Fair* article on the racing world. Ed Blair had called her on her cell phone that morning to ask how it was going.

"It's not as outrageous as I expected," she'd told him. "I've told you most of it in my e-mails. I know they haven't been very detailed, but I've been too busy to write much. Everybody is pretty nice, though."

"Keep digging," he'd said. "You can make anybody look stupid if you put your mind to it."

She eased her way through the crowd to the little wooden table where Badger sat ready to meet his public. He was wearing a purple Team Vagenya cap and tee shirt and a pair of faded Levis. She had expected to see him in his firesuit, but considering what a hot day it was, she supposed that his present outfit was a sensible choice, and the advertising logos meant that he was still promoting the brand.

A legion of race fans, predominantly female, stood in a disorderly line, cameras at the ready, waiting for the signal to surge forward. The signing had been an open invitation. Some drivers— possibly even Badger himself, for all she knew—were so popular that you had to get a ticket hours in advance just to be able to stand in their autograph line, but the team representative who had set up the event had not realized that Badger's star shone quite so brightly, so all comers were welcome. It promised to be a free-for-all, because he could only stay for half an hour, and there seemed to be no way to accommodate the crowd in that length of time.

"Hello," said Sark, bending down close to his ear. "I'm here to cover the event for the team Web site, and to provide moral support for you."

"Thank ya so much," drawled Badger, wiping his forehead with the back of a sweaty hand. He sounded both heartfelt and shy— and he had the sunglasses on, which at first glance transformed him into that fierce and sexy creature she had seen through the camera lens. Even Sark, who knew better, felt her pulse quicken for an instant, before she remembered that it was only Badger.

No wonder his line is mostly female, thought Sark. Aloud, she said, "I see you've got your water bottle and a bunch of Sharpies. Anything else you need?"

He shook his head, but his smile seemed to waver, and he glanced warily at the throng of giggling women. Sark remembered a Discovery Channel program about ancient Greece that featured the *maenads*: crazed packs of women who ran through the Hellenic forests tearing to pieces anyone they encountered. She wondered if this event might be a modern version of that ritual.

"Maybe you ought to stay close," Badger said softly. "It can get a little rocky sometimes. You never know."

She stared at him, wondering what sort of moral support he might require of her. Bodyguard? Bouncer? *Significant Other* Impersonator? "What do you expect me to do?" she whispered.

"I dunno," said Badger. "People get carried away sometimes. Whatever needs doing, I guess. You'll know." He waved a Sharpie at her and winked. "I reckon I'm ready."

Sark watched the signing ritual with all the fascination of an anthropologist observing an arcane tribal worship ceremony. Badger seemed to be both deity and sacrificial lamb. She found it interesting that the age and body type of the driver did not often correlate with that of his followers. She wondered if anybody had ever done a study on it.

One slab-faced older woman near the front of the line was wearing tight red shorts over ham-sized thighs and what must have been an extra-extra large Badger Jenkins tee shirt. She was so enormous that she could have carried Badger as a purse, thought Sark.

There ought to be a rule, Sark decided, *that if you outweigh your driver by a factor of two, then you ought not to be allowed to wear his apparel.* (This rule, she reflected, would cost the delicate and diminutive Kasey Kahne whole legions of his fans.)

She watched with interest to see what Badger's reaction would be—the ex-husband of a former Miss Georgia, contemplating *(ha!)* his biggest fan.

The massive woman set an autograph card on the table in front of him. Her earnest expression was almost menacing. Without cracking a smile, she said, "You're doing good work, Badger. In Pennsylvania we think the world of you."

"I appreciate it," said Badger solemnly, signing the card with his customary scrawl. "I reckon I need all the help I can get."

He handed back the card with a reassuring smile of thanks, and the woman took it, visibly relaxing at the reassurance of his smile. She hesitated for a moment, then said, "Badger, I know you're busy, but can I get my picture taken with you?"

He nodded. "Come around," he said, motioning her forward, and almost before the words were out, the woman had handed the camera to her friend and stumped around behind the table. Badger did not get up, which was just as well, Sark thought, considering the size differential. He'd look like the Dalmatian standing beside one of the Budweiser Clydesdales. Oblivious to the effect of their posing in tandem, the woman leaned forward and grinned, while Badger smiled "professionally" at the camera. Then— just as the friend snapped the shutter—Badger's biggest fan swooped down and enveloped him in a predatory hug that made Sark think of a praying mantis eating her partner after mating. *Click!*

The woman giggled. "Now I can go home and tell my friends that I hugged Badger Jenkins!" she said.

Before Sark could say or do anything, the woman and her friend hurried away, chattering happily about this escapade, hoping aloud that the picture would turn out. *Better hope Badger will be visible at all,* thought Sark, wondering if there was anything she could or should have done. Obviously she needed to be more vigilant than she had realized. Badger didn't seem perturbed, though, which rather surprised her. She didn't for a moment suppose he enjoyed it.

After that incident, she watched Badger with interest, waiting to see some trace of a grimace cloud that handsome little face, some smirk of derision perhaps that such a rough beast would have the audacity to embrace him—but his expression did not change. He simply smiled at the next person in line as if nothing had happened, and Sark felt herself sigh with relief. She hadn't wanted Badger to be the kind of man who would ridicule a woman for not being pretty. With a rueful sigh she remembered her own initial reaction to the bearlike woman, and she wondered if in his place she would have been as gracious as Badger was. She told herself that his poise came from years of practice, but she didn't altogether believe it. She considered the unlikely possibility that the handsome jock really was a nice guy. *Nah*. There had to be some other explanation. Media training, maybe.

Still, sincerely or not, he had done a kind thing. That poor woman probably would go home and boast for years about her triumph: *She had hugged Badger Jenkins. And, look, she had a picture to prove it, and he was just as nice as could be about it. Not stuck-up at all.* Perhaps in the months to come she would come back to the track and stand again in his autograph line, this time with that treasured photo for him to sign: further proof that she had hugged him. She had really hugged him.

Sark marveled at the magic of a meaningless gesture. She had lost count of the times Badger had hugged her, or Tuggle, or Julie Carmichael, and no one paid any attention to it. Badger was a hugger; he did it with all the abandon of a child, if he knew you. He was much more reserved around strangers, of course, and around fans, who were simply strangers who didn't know that they were, but he seemed to think of the team as his family, and if you were in his path when he was happy or sad or coming or going, or whatever, then he hugged you. No big deal.

But it *was* a big deal to these people, waiting in line with their photos and their official Badger Jenkins souvenirs. Sark thought that it seemed discourteous somehow to be unimpressed by gestures that other people would consider a rare privilege. How disconcerting to meet people who thought that Badger Jenkins was a great and wonderful man, and who would have saved forever a Styrofoam cup he had drunk from. And yet she had his cell phone number on speed dial. People have been killed for less, she supposed.

She wondered how Badger could stay afloat in this tide of adulation. Did celebrities begin to believe that their garbage was valuable, that their lightest word should be embroidered on samplers, that they were better than anybody else? To his credit, Badger didn't seem to think so. Well, Tuggle would never have let him get away with it for one thing. Perhaps the best favor that one can do for a celebrity friend is to periodically tell them to get over themselves. That, and to resolve to still be just as much of a friend when the luster of celebrity fades and the spotlight shines somewhere else.

She saw now why that would be such a hard thing to bear—to go back to being nobody, after *this*. And Badger was just . . . well, *Badger*. In the grand scheme of things, he wasn't all that famous, and still he had worshippers. What if he were really, most sincerely famous? The thought of being a member of the posse of Dale, Jr. or Jeff Gordon made her shudder.

The signing went on relatively calmly after the large woman went away. As the minutes passed, Sark found herself classifying the different types of admirers who stood in Badger's autograph line. Most of the people were just nice (if misguidedly starstruck) folks who were thrilled to be in the actual presence of a NASCAR driver. They wanted to shake his hand, to wish him well, to get his name affixed to a piece of paper—so that they could go home and brag to their neighbors that they had met *the* Badger Jenkins, and that he was just as nice as could be, no airs about him *atall*.

The line wasn't just a procession of the faithful, though; it was liberally sprinkled with "dealers." People who made a living getting minor celebrities to sign photos and other memorabilia that they would then resell in shops or online for a tidy profit. The more unscrupulous ones simply faked the signature—a necessary ruse, perhaps, if the customer wanted, say, Johnny Depp, but hardly necessary in the world of NASCAR. Drivers were nice guys. Most of them would oblige anyone who asked politely for a signature, provided that time was not a factor. In order to get their money's worth, sponsors saw to it that their drivers made many public appearances, which meant that obtaining their autographs was mostly a matter of perseverance and scheduling.

Dealer types were generally male, brisk, and unimpressed by the experience. Badger's signature on a photo might mean ten bucks to them, if they were lucky and if a true fan from faraway participated in the online auction. The dealers would attend the race and stand in every possible driver's autograph line, hoping to get enough signatures to make their speedway visit profitable. Getting an autographed photo from the likes of Badger was all well and good, but the dealers' greatest wish was to have the good fortune to run into Little E. or Jeff Gordon, the rock stars of Cup racing. A signature from either of them would cover the entire cost of the weekend. But you couldn't count on the availability of the superstars, so to pass the time the dealers staked out the small fry. They treated Badger with the curt efficiency of a remora preparing to clean the teeth of a very small shark: a necessary process for both parties, but only barely worth the effort.

If the dealers were blasé about the experience of meeting him, the true fans more than made up for it with their unbridled—occasionally semihysterical—enthusiasm. *Fandemonium.* Sark handed out tissues to more than one woman who burst into tears simply because Badger had touched her hand when he returned the autograph card. She began to wish she'd brought a supply of paper bags along so that she could hand them out to the overwrought and say, "Breathe into this!" (And occasionally when a fan became too saccharine and sloppy in her adoration of Badger, Sark felt like using a paper bag herself, for quite another purpose.)

There ought to be a happy medium, she thought, between the businesslike dealers and the gushing maenads. She thought Badger deserved more respect from the former and a good deal less adulation from the latter.

Who the heck was Badger Jenkins, anyhow? Rock star? Hero? Dream lover? Meal ticket? Favorite son? Star athlete? Big brother? There seemed to be as many answers to that question as there were people in line.

Occasionally, a giggling woman would thrust a cell phone under his nose and order him to say hello to her friend back home. *"Donna's your biggest fan. Just say hello to her. She'll die, Badger. I swear she will."*

Badger always managed to say a cordial sentence or two into the phone, and the response was a sometimes audible shriek. He usually concluded the conversation with, "Yes, ma'am, I'm really him. Thanks for being a loyal fan." He called them all *ma'am,* which Sark thought might be more an estimate of age than a term of respect. There were more requests for a hug, but he managed to evade them.

Sark began to feel sorry for the driver. Being loved can be more of a burden than a blessing. People have built you a soul, and if you run afoul of their expectations, they will turn on you with the ferocity of wild dogs. Dealing with one's public was harder than it looked, she concluded. Being handsome helped, because it meant you didn't have to say much to win them over, but a calm temperament and a seeming openness with strangers would prove invaluable also. She began to regard Badger with increasing admiration. There was more to being a race car driver than skill behind the wheel. Badger was damned good. He sent everyone away happy.

The line wound on, one gushing fan after another.

Often besotted maidens wanted to give him things—a photo of their cat whose name was Badger, or perhaps an amateur portrait of him they'd done themselves, which generally looked more like Bela Lugosi than like Badger himself. Other admirers embroidered pillows with his number and team colors; they brought him hand-tied fishing flies "for the lake" and homemade soap. They presented him with pots of raspberry jam, which they'd personally prepared in little jars affixed with handwritten labels, often including the telephone number of the giver. *Some hope,* thought Sark. Others wrote worshipful, badly rhymed poems about him, which they bestowed on him on parchment with carefully lettered calligraphy and a Dollar Store frame.

Badger accepted all these earnest offerings with solemn thanks, and with a few words of admiration for anyone so talented as to be able to produce such a thing, because *he sure as heck couldn't do anything as original as that . . . thank you so much . . .* and the givers went away happy. After a while Sark began to detect a particular tone of voice in his expressions of gratitude. When he said "Thank ya so-ooo mu-ucch" in a particular drawling way, she decided that it meant he was being given something he didn't want. That was useful to know. She filed the information away to see when she would hear it next. Mostly, though, he was kind and polite to people who meant well, and they felt that they had made a real connection with their hero with their gifts of soap and poems and homemade jam. Sark wondered what became of those things afterward, and she resolved never to try to find out.

And then there were the kids. Badger loved kids. He'd peer

down at a bright-eyed eight-year-old clutching anything from a napkin to a lug nut, and he'd strike up an animated conversation with the child while he scribbled his name on the proffered item.

"How you doin', buddy? You a big race fan?" Man to man, as if they were both the same age, which in some ways, thought Sark, they were.

Sometimes the child was too shy even to mumble a response, but Badger never seemed to mind. He went on being friendly and charming until the child stopped looking terrified.

Then near the end of the line a little tow-headed kid in a Dupont tee shirt set down a Jeff Gordon hat in front of Badger and waited for him to sign it.

Sark held her breath. As far as she could tell, Cup drivers wholeheartedly agreed with the Supreme Being that the number one commandment was *Thou Shalt Have No Other Gods before Me*. She'd heard discouraging tales of drivers refusing to sign even their own team-themed merchandise if it was an unlicensed product—because drivers received no royalties from homemade fan items. And here was a kid expecting Badger to sign a product honoring *another* driver? She pictured an ensuing tantrum, and wondered if she ought to snatch the Gordon hat off the table and hustle the kid away before he precipitated a public relations nightmare.

Before she could decide what to do, Badger picked up the Gordon hat and scribbled across the brim with his black Sharpie. "There you go, buddy," he said with a smile, handing the item back to its delighted owner.

When the child had walked away, Sark leaned in close again to Badger's ear. "Wow," she said softly. "You signed a Jeff Gordon hat. I cannot believe it."

"Well, he's a kid. I couldn't disappoint him," said Badger. "I can't sign any Earnhardt stuff, though."

"Why? You don't like the Earnhardts?" asked Sark.

"Naw, that's not it," said Badger sadly. "I just can't spell it."

The little boy had put on his signed cap and was waving good-bye from a few feet away. Sark peered closely at the hat, and sure enough, scribbled on the brim were the words "Jeff Gordon" in Badger's unmistakable rounded scrawl.

Sark could never decide if Badger was a complete innocent or the shrewdest person she knew.

She glanced at her watch. Time was nearly up, and the last two fans in line looked like trouble. They were young enough and skinny enough not to look completely ridiculous in their skimpy halter tops and barely-there shorts, but dyed-blond hair and ferret faces heavy with mascara and glitter blush weren't Sark's idea of sexy. She doubted if it was Badger's, either, but since he had done all right on his own today, she decided to wait and see how he handled the confrontation—Sark was sure there was going to be one.

Sure enough, the one wearing the most eyeliner sashayed up to the desk and leaned over it, giving him the full effect of her cleavage.

Sark wrinkled her nose in distaste. *Pit lizards.* The term, which she herself had only learned this week, had probably been coined before these two little newts had even been born, but they were quite representative of the species: slithery and predatory. Like the rest of their kind, they lurked around drivers' habitats in hopes of ensnaring one. Wives loathed them, and the crew either pitied or ridiculed them, according to the nature of the crew member and perhaps to the attractiveness of the individual lizard. It was universally acknowledged, though, that their appreciation of motorsports was similar to lions' fondness for the watering holes of zebras: voyeurism disguising darker motives. Today this pair of lizards had apparently decided to prey on Badger.

Repelled more than fascinated, Sark backed away toward the Porta-John, hoping that when she'd finished, the two creatures would be gone. She heard more giggles as the girls took out cameras and whispered in each other's ear. What were they offering him, anyway: a choice or a twofer?

And it happens to him all the time, she thought. How many times a day? A dozen? A hundred? How could such avid attention not go to his head? How could he not think himself God's gift to mattresses? How could he sustain a relationship with anybody in the face of such temptation?

She hurried toward the Porta-John, out of earshot of the arch conversation taking place at the signing table, acutely aware of her own embarrassment. Somebody, she thought, ought to be ashamed at what was taking place; odd that she, the innocent by-stander, should be the one who felt it. The other thing she felt was a bizarre, almost maternal protectiveness toward Badger. She wanted to yell, "Leave him alone! He's not a piece of meat." But surely that was a feminine impulse. Surely it was the essence of the male gender not to mind such an arrangement, even to revel in it. A free roll in the hay offered by a reasonably pretty girl who wanted nothing more? Why else would you want to be famous if not for perks like this? Did he feel like that, she wondered, or did the endless propositions make him feel slimed by the fetid desires of so many strangers? She wished she could think of a polite way to ask him.

Sark lingered in the toilet until the smell inside it was fraction-ally more distasteful to her than the sight of two attacking pit lizards in heat; then she stumbled out again into the sunshine, thinking that perhaps Badger would be expecting her to run inter-ference for him, to get him out of an awkward situation with no hard feelings on the part of the lizards, assuming, of course, that they were capable of such niceties. *Oh please let him not be suc-cumbing to their attentions*, she thought, and that notion almost sent her reeling back to the toilet.

Well, at least Badger wasn't married anymore, she told herself. Not that it would have mattered to his stalkers if he had been.

As she approached the table again, she noticed that Badger had his head tilted back and appeared to be listening attentively to one of the girls. Now he was nodding, with a mournful look in his dark eyes.

Uh-oh, thought Sark, hurrying back to her post.

"And she won't get her prescription filled," said the blonde. "She says it costs too much, and that taking it doesn't change the way she feels one bit. She says blood pressure is just a number.

But she has to work standing up for hours at a time on her shift at the mill. I tell her that can't be good for her, but she won't listen."

Badger was nodding sympathetically. "My granddad was stubborn like that," he said. "We lost him a year ago last spring."

"Really? Because he wouldn't take his medicine?" Tears were streaming down the young woman's face in little black rivulets of dissolved mascara. She dug in her tiny denim purse and fished out a creased snapshot. "This is my nana with her race cap on. See, it's one of yours, from your old team. I gave it to her for her birthday the year you won Darlington, and she just loved it."

Solemnly, Badger examined the grainy snapshot of a grinning old lady in a racing hat. "She needs to take her medicine, though," he said. "What's her name?"

The girl sniffled. "Dreama. D-R-E-A-M-A."

Badger took one of the autograph cards and wrote across the top: *Dreama, Please Take Your Pills. Badger Jenkins.* "There," he said, handing it back to the tearful pit lizard. "Maybe that will help. You tell her I can't afford to lose any fans." He shook hands with the girl and her friend, who now seemed much younger and less worldly than they had seemed before. "I have to go now," he said, nodding toward Sark. "They need me to do a radio interview or something."

The two women thanked him with moist smiles and as soon as they turned away, Badger got up from the table and hurried toward the motor home before anyone else could waylay him.

"That was pretty amazing," said Sark. "You were great."

Badger shrugged. "You get used to it," he said.

"No, you were great with everybody. You were kind and sweet. But what impressed me the most was that you made those two pit lizards forget all about hitting on you. How did you *do* that?"

He shrugged. "I treated them like people," he said. He ambled off, muttering something about Gatorade in the fridge.

Sark stared after him, wondering for the hundredth time whether Badger Jenkins was an old soul possessing great wisdom or a simpleton who was too dumb to be let out alone.

CHAPTER XVII

The Race Is On

"It's strange, isn't it?" said Sigur Nelson, the rear tire carrier. She was watching the thunderous crowd reactions to the driver introductions before the start of the race. "The driver gets all the fame and the glamour, and yet he's just one member of the team. He gets the private jet and the motor home and his picture on the tee shirts, and what do *we* get? A cattle car charter flight to the city where the race is being held, and half a cut-rate motel room apiece. And the pay! Don't even talk about that!"

"But Badger is famous," said Taran. "He doesn't even have his own jet and he rents that motor home, but he certainly deserves all that stuff."

"You think so?" said Reve. "Take an extra second on the pit stop a few times and see how well he does. Leave the cap off the brake line and see what happens to his points standings after the race. Nobody appreciates us, but we're important, too."

"I think Badger appreciates us," said Taran.

"I don't," said Reve, and Sigur nodded in agreement. "I think that to him we're the spear carriers in the opera of his life. I'd be surprised if he even remembered my name."

Taran, who had been nervous already, was now on the verge of tears. "Badger is always nice to me. He always smiles when he sees me, and he says, 'Hey, Sweetie.' "

"That's because he can't remember your name," said Sigur.

"You want to think he's kind. He is a handsome man, and because he is a rural Southerner, he is basically polite, just like Swedes. I think you cut him all kinds of slack on account of that. Pretty people always get extra credit just for winning the genetic lottery. I've never seen any evidence that he gives a damn about any of us."

"I don't see how he could stay humble with all the money, and the media, and the adulation of the fans. Of course he thinks he's hot stuff. But we work just as hard as he does to make this team a success."

Taran shook her head. "Badger deserves all of it."

Reve sneered. "Why? Because you think he's handsome?"

"No. Because he's the one who has to go out there and risk his life."

They had made it into the Daytona 500, qualifying for the Great American Race despite the predictions of half the motorsports pundits in the business, especially the self-appointed ones on the Internet.

Late Thursday night on the laptop in her motel room, Sark reported on the week's events to Ed Blair.

> Hey, Ed! According to Julie Carmichael, our chief engineer, "By the grace of God and the genius of Jay Bird Thomas," Badger Jenkins is now one of the forty-three entries in the Daytona 500. There is a great sense of relief and accomplishment here at 86 headquarters. But I think the real feeling is that, although Badger is an incredible driver, we were also very lucky.

> Yo, Sark! Glad to hear your team made the big race. Maybe I'll watch it while I read the *New York Times* Sunday afternoon. Did your boy win the qualifying race?

> Nope. Let me see if I can explain without making you sorry you asked. You can get in to the Daytona 500

by being one of the thirty-five top finishing teams from last year—but since the 86 team did not even exist last year, that was not an option for us. You can also get in by scoring one of the best times in the qualifying round. Or you can finish first or second in one of the races that determines who gets in.

I almost understood that, but then my eyes glazed over. So via which of these many choices did Badger & Company get in?

Well, that's where it gets even more complicated, Ed. One of the guys who got in on time trials also finished really well in the qualifying race, and since you don't need both of those ways to gain entry into the Daytona 500, that created an opportunity for next guy on the list to make it in, and so on. Anyhow, Badger did really well in the Bud 150, even though he didn't place in the top five. But there were a lot of wrecks caused by aggressive drivers, and he managed to avoid them, and then by some miracle, he did not have any engine problems or tire malfunctions, so partly by being a good driver and partly by being fortunate, he squeaked by, and after his competitors qualified in other ways, he was the last guy to make it in to the Daytona 500 on the basis of his qualifying speed. The team seems to be alternately thrilled and terrified at the prospect of being in the big race.

Well, thanks for that erudite explanation of the intricacies of stock car racing rituals, but hey, Sark, the next time I ask you a casual question like that, could you just say, "They decide that by examining chicken entrails." It would make just as much sense to me and it would save you a lot of typing.

See? I told you this sport wasn't for dummies!
Oops—I sound like a convert, don't I? Well, at least
it's all beginning to make more sense to me. I'll keep
you posted on our adventures.

I'll look for you in Victory Lane Sunday afternoon.

Yeah. That'll happen. I just hope he finishes before
the start of next year's race.

Badger got more requests for interviews after they had lucked their way into the starting lineup for the race. The press had a command center of cubicles and TV monitors in a large building in the infield of the speedway, and Sark had to usher Badger in for a press conference on Friday, where he stood beside Tuggle squinting in the bright television camera lights on the little stage at the front of the room. The fact that he had made the race was not the big story. The fact that the All-Woman Team had made the race—now, *that* was news.

"So what's it like to work with a handsome race car driver?" someone called out.

Tuggle shrugged. "Let me check with one of Kasey Kahne's people and I'll let you know."

Amid the laughter, she and Badger exchanged a high-five look. They had been expecting that question, and Badger himself had suggested that answer. They fielded the rest of the puff questions with equal ease, reserving the serious attention to the real questions about race strategy and team preparations.

The final question, directed to Badger by a smirking male sport writer, was also inevitable. "Hey, Badger! Tell us about your sponsor—*Vagenya!*"

Badger smiled. "I know your wife wanted you to ask us that, Bob."

"Tuggle, do you use Vagenya, or does Badger do the trick?"

Tuggle's scowl could have lowered room temperature, and Badger, eying her, shook his head sadly. "You boys are going to get me in trouble here. You know what a temper she's got."

When the delighted laughter died down, Badger assumed his earnest were-retriever expression, and said, "Vagenya is serious medicine, folks. If our advertising can bring it to the attention of people who need it, that's a good thing, isn't it?"

The respectful silence almost lasted long enough for them to make a graceful exit, but then a quick-thinking wag from *Sports Illustrated* said, "Well, if you crash into Mark Martin's Viagra car, they'll probably have to turn the hose on you to get them apart."

In an unspoken accord, Tuggle and Badger smiled weakly, nodded their good-byes to the assembled journalists, and left the room before the laughter subsided.

All in all, the questions had been entirely predictable, and they handled themselves well for a first team press conference. They had declined to hug for the cameras, and they had not allowed themselves to be baited into making incautious remarks.

"We did okay," said Badger.

"Unless they make up quotes for us," grunted Tuggle as they left the building.

The rest of the crew didn't see much of Badger before race day, prompting Reve to mutter about the *Upstairs Downstairs* nature of racing hierarchy. Drivers were treated like royalty, and the number of volunteers for the harem boggled the mind.

"They must think they're gods," muttered Jeanne, who had just seen a stunningly beautiful girl hit on a pit crew guy who looked like a garden gnome. And he wasn't even a Cup driver. She could not imagine the offers *they* got.

"When we can't find him, he must be somewhere screwing like a mink," said Sigur.

"Well, you'll never know," Kathy Erwin told them. "In the old days, this place could have topped Sodom and Gomorrah, but nowadays they tend to be more discreet."

"Most of the drivers are married," said Taran.

Kathy took a deep breath, struggled to keep a straight face, and mostly succeeded. "Yes, that's quite true, Taran," she said.

"Badger isn't married, though," said Jeanne. "He's probably buying his condoms by the case."

"You'll never catch him," said Kathy. "And since we have to work with him, believe me, you don't want to. It's none of our business. Just be glad he doesn't hit on *us*."

They were never able to find out what Badger was doing in his limited free time in Daytona, but they pictured him frequenting expensive restaurants in the company of movie stars far into the night, and possibly sleeping off a hangover beside said starlet on the race morning before the drivers' meeting.

All except Taran, that is. Although she would never have admitted it to anyone for fear of being laughed to scorn, Taran kept thinking of an illustration she'd seen once in a book on King Arthur, depicting the medieval squire on the night before his ordination, kneeling in prayer before an altar, his head resting against the hilt of his broadsword. She pictured Badger in his purple firesuit, helmet under his arm, kneeling in prayer in his motor home. She found this image so comforting that she resolved never to find out what he really did on the morning of a race.

But they were busy enough, anyhow, getting ready for the race, occasionally signing an autograph or posing for photos with passing fans, or shooing away journalists who were curious about the all-female pit crew. They spent long hours at the track, ate Granola bars and peanut butter sandwiches in the hauler, and trudged back to the hotel long after dark, too tired to do much besides shower and fall into bed, getting ready to do it all again the next day.

"I can't believe I'm really here," said Jeanne Mowbray, the tire carrier, on one of the rides back to the hotel. "When I was a kid back in Ohio, I lived next to the highway that the haulers took heading for the speedway up in Michigan. We'd get lawn chairs and put them up in a pasture alongside the road, and just sit there and watch those brightly painted haulers roll by. Nobody we knew even went to the race, but we'd listen to it on the radio. And we had seen the trucks go by." She sighed. "And now—I'm here!"

"There's an ocean out there somewhere," said Cindy Corlett. "I never thought I'd get this close to an ocean and not see it."

"I've been coming here since I was eight years old," said Kathy

Erwin, "And I'll tell you what my daddy used to tell me when I'd ask to go to the beach: *Just pretend you're in Vegas, honey.*"

"Well, if Badger wins, I'm going to the beach," said Cindy.

Kathy snickered. "If Badger wins, Cindy, the beach will come to *you.*"

Finally, Sunday arrived, a gray day of leaden clouds and cool temperatures, and an ocean of people all converging on the speedway, those that weren't there already, that is. Some of the spectators arrived in campers days before the race itself and spent Speed Week in a Mardi Gras of revelry. But for the pit crew Sunday was a dizzying combination of work day, final exam, and D-day all rolled into one. More than one of them had sent her breakfast swirling down the toilet before they set out for the track in the predawn darkness.

A few more hours of preparation, a pep talk from Tuggle, and they would be as ready as they'd ever be. From behind the stack of tires that she'd be changing in the race that afternoon, Sigur Nelson peered at a sturdy blond man wearing an orange Cingular NASCAR jacket. He was nodding solemnly at their crew chief, who was gesturing and talking to him in urgent tones that the pit crew couldn't overhear. Sigur blinked and looked again.

"Hey, Kathy!" she hissed. "What is Jeff Burton doing in our garage? Isn't he driving the 31 for Childress today?"

Kathy Erwin, the only crew member from a NASCAR family, took a long look at the visitor. "That's not Jeff Burton," she whispered back. "It's his older brother."

"The one who won Daytona a few years back?"

Kathy shook her head. "No. Not Ward. I'm pretty sure that's Brian Burton over there. He's the middle one. Instead of going to NASCAR like his brothers, he finished college and runs the family construction company."

"Oh. The smart one."

"Yeah, but he's also the one who won a slew of go-cart championships when the Burtons were kids. People say he's the best driver of the three of them."

"The best driver in the family did not turn pro?"

"It happens," said Kathy. "Dale's daughter Kelley was the most talented of the Earnhardt kids. Even better than Little E., they say."

Sigur digested this information. "They're not replacing Badger out there today, are they?"

"No. I think they're replacing his spotter. I haven't seen Tony around this morning, and yesterday at dinner he said he felt like he was coming down with something."

"He's allergic to shrimp," said Taran. "I warned him not to eat fried seafood at the restaurant last night. They use the same oil to cook everything. He says he'll be okay in a couple of hours, but Tuggle thought we ought not to take any chances."

"Brian Burton would be the perfect spotter for Badger," said Kathy. "He's smart, and he knows how to drive. I'll bet they've known each other for years. Badger used to go duck hunting with Ward. They all had similar driving experiences early on. And most important—"

"Are the Burtons from Georgia?" asked Taran.

"Virginia. But they sound a lot like Badger." Kathy grinned. "Boy, when those two get going, it's gonna sound like Navajo code talkers on our scanners. Oh, look! I was right. Tuggle is offering him one of our purple team jackets with the Vagenya logo on the back."

"Yeah, and he's backing away," said Sigur, stifling a giggle. "He must have heard of Vagenya, and he wants to keep on his Cingular jacket instead. Can he do that?"

"He's doing us a big favor," said Kathy. "As long as he keeps Badger out of the wrecks out there, I think he can do anything he wants."

In their purple Team Vagenya uniforms they stood on the pit stall, waiting for the madness to begin.

"Taran had better snap out of it," muttered Sigur. "Look at her standing there in a trance. You'd think we hadn't practiced this a zillion times. She's like a racehorse that can't focus because of all the distractions at the track. We ought to put blinders on her."

"She'll get used to it," said Reve. "It is rather overwhelming at first."

"But she's a race fan. She's a trained member of this pit crew. She ought to have known what to expect. More than I did."

"It's different in person," said Kathy Erwin, who had grown up on speedways. "Bigger. Louder. It's always daunting to people their first time. This track is huge. Give her a couple of minutes. She'll settle."

The countdown until the start of the race was certainly different from the practice days at the shop, and even later on the speedway itself when all you had to think about was doing your job as quickly and efficiently as you could. That had been difficult enough, but now the challenge was to perform with that same calm proficiency in the eye of a festive hurricane of color and noise.

The pageantry of race day was impressive enough viewed in miniature on a television screen, but when the full blast of it rolled over you in waves of team colors, engine roars, and the smell of leaded gas, the effect was numbing. More than one hundred thousand people were staring down at you, watching you work, while engines thundered. Air Force jets swooped low over the speedway in the flyover at the beginning of the race, and then all the pit crews lined up on the track, like spokes in a giant wheel, in a rainbow of team colors, to stand at attention while a famous singer—someone whose CDs you actually owned—sang the National Anthem.

"Who's that walking Badger to the 86?" asked Cindy, as she watched the procession of drivers heading for their cars. "I thought the wives escorted them. That doesn't look like a Miss Georgia to me."

"No, he divorced that one," said Jeanne. "Is it a dumpy scarecrow-looking woman? I think that's his manager. I hear they don't like her much around the front office."

"Did she kiss him?" asked Taran in a stricken voice.

"Nope. He barely looked at her," said Jeanne.

"Badger focuses," Kathy informed them. "A lot of drivers do that. Before the race even starts, he'll begin to block out everything but the driving. In his mind he is already on the track. He wouldn't know it if he had been walked to the car by the Bride of Frankenstein."

"He just was," said Tuggle, who had caught the tail end of the conversation.

All the fanfare of race day would have been distracting enough for the first few minutes, no matter which team you were with, but for Taran there was one extra element that she hadn't considered, and for a moment of fleeting panic, she found herself wishing that she had been hired on the pit crew of, say, Greg Biffle or Joe Nemechek, where this particular problem would not arise. But, oh no, *she* had to be the catch can for Badger Jenkins. *Her* driver. And to stand right there while he walked to the car . . .

Except it wasn't Badger.

Taran had got used to seeing Badger around by now—the little chicken hawk guy with the aw-shucks grin and the wave-on-a-slop-bucket walk, strolling around the shop in his baggy jeans and faded tee shirt. She had even had a couple of casual *(nice-day-isn't-it? How-you-doin'?)* conversations with him, and while it was true that when he tossed away his empty bottle of blue Gatorade, she had fished it out of the trash and kept it, she told herself that she could throw it away any time she wanted to. It was just that the plastic bottle looked rather nice with ribbons tied around the neck, holding a fistful of flowers or feathers collected on her morning walks. She had brought it with her to Daytona. For luck, she told herself. In the hotel room she had set it in front of her signed and framed eight-by-ten photo of . . . *Photo of whom?*

A stern-looking man in dark glasses and a purple and white fire suit standing in front of the race car.

It was one of the formal shots Sark had taken for team press releases, and in the photo a tall and handsome man stared at the camera. Embroidered on the chest of his firesuit, right beneath "NASCAR Nextel Cup," were the words Badger Jenkins, but the man in the photo certainly wasn't the affable little guy who wandered around the shop, eating beef jerky while he passed the time of day with the mechanics.

The man in the photo wasn't Badger: It was *him*. The guy she had watched in televised races and cried over when he wrecked and fantasized about for more nights than she cared to count. *The Dark Angel.*

And just as the race was about to begin that's who had walked past her and swung himself with practiced ease through the driver's side window of the race car. Taran froze, staring at this apparition, while the few remaining brain cells still on duty tried to assure her that the guy in the firesuit really was just little old Badger—only *gift-wrapped*. It didn't help, though.

"Will you snap out of it?" hissed Reve, nudging her in the side. "It's just Badger, for God's sake. He gets into his car through the driver's side window—just like everybody else from Georgia. Now we have work to do. Get over him!"

Taran nodded, still frozen, staring fixedly at the car, which was now proceeding around the track in those preliminary laps before the green flag signaled the start of the race.

"I'd advise you to get a grip on yourself," said Sigur. "Because, you know, if you do a lousy job on the pit stops, you could cost him the race. Would you want to have to explain that to *him*?"

Taran shivered, picturing herself cowering before the menacing presence of the Dark Angel in the purple firesuit. He wouldn't even have to scold her if she cost him the race. She would probably throw herself off the top tier of the grandstand in sheer mortification at the thought of failing Him. Somehow, the thought of laid-back little Badger telling her that her mistake was forgiven did not make her feel any better. She was pretty sure that when it came to winning races, the Dark Angel was always the being you would be dealing with.

Of course, his wrath wasn't really the point, was it? What really had Taran frozen in her tracks was abject terror. Suppose he got hurt out there? She was the one who had worried about him when he was just a face on a coffee mug, a stranger whose fate was completely beyond her control. She was the fan who sometimes cried during the National Anthem in sheer apprehension over what would happen to *her driver* once the race began.

This was worse.

Now that she actually knew Badger as a person, she was so afraid for him that she could hardly breathe.

She had thought that joining the team would lessen her anxiety because now at least she could keep an eye on things for him. In a small way she could even control aspects of the race car so that she could be sure that he was safe. When no one was paying any attention to her in the garage, she would check everything she could understand, which was nothing under the hood, unfortunately, but she checked tires for bubbles, lug nuts for cracks, harness fastenings for breakage. Surreptitiously, she also rubbed a thimbleful of dirt on the hood of the car. This was not illegal. She had checked the NASCAR rules. Nowhere did they mention dirt-rubbing. She just didn't want to have to explain to anyone who caught her that the dry brown substance in the plastic bag was sacred dirt from Chimayo, New Mexico, bought off a "shaman" site on the Web. The holy dust might protect Badger from harm out there—at least if any Navajo deities were officiating over motorsports rituals today.

Taran thought it was too bad that windshields were covered with tear-off plastic sheets, because a little holy water in the cleaning fluid couldn't have hurt, either. Later, it cheered her up immensely to learn that sometimes they did have to clean the Lexan windshield with spray and a towel, if they ran out of the tear-off sheets or if the tear-offs blew off during the race.

Some of the guys on other pit crews laughed at the idea of good luck charms—taping Bible verses to steering columns, or putting lucky talismans somewhere in the car—but as far as Taran was concerned, there were no atheists in the pits. If there were any omnipotent racing fans out there in the firmament, she wanted to take every chance there was of currying favor with one of them. All race fans knew that the one time Dale Earnhardt had won the Daytona 500 was in 1998 when a little girl had given him a penny for luck on race day, and he had glued the coin to the dashboard of his Monte Carlo. If such a ritual was good enough for the Intimidator, why shouldn't she use a little white magic to protect Badger? She didn't really care if he won or not. She just wanted him to be safe.

And as long as she was cultivating New Age spiritual pursuits, Taran wished she knew of some way to get the hang of astral projection, because an out-of-body experience would definitely have been an asset on race day. Taran had seen many races on television and half a dozen in person at various speedways in the Southeast, but until she joined the pit crew, it had never occurred to her that the one place from which it was impossible to view the race was trackside. And Daytona was probably the worst of the lot.

Daytona, a two-and-a-half mile track with thirty-one-degree banking in the turns, encircled an infield so large that it contained enough buildings to constitute a small town, even boasting a lake within its boundaries. In order to tell what was going on in the race, you needed a bird's-eye view of the action, afforded by a seat in a skybox or high up in the grandstands, or else the perspective of a battery of television cameras strategically positioned at the very top of the structure in order to capture a vista of the entire track at once.

Each team had a spotter positioned up there on the roof of the grandstand, giving the driver a bird's-eye view of the whole track. The spotter would warn the driver if another car was coming up on him. In the case of a wreck in which smoke might reduce visibility to a few feet beyond the hood of the race car, the spotter would tell the driver whether to go high or low to avoid any obstacles ahead. Sometimes the driver was running blind—at 180 mph—and then his life was in the hands of the spotter. If you were on pit crew, you could hear the spotter on a channel in your headset, and he was your eyes for the race, too.

The view of the pit crew, while immediate and thrilling, lacked in scope what it made up for in excitement. Cars roared by, and then vanished around Turn One, so that half the race went on behind them, on the far side of the infield, past a veritable village of buildings, crowds, trucks, and haulers, so that even if you turned around you would catch only brief glimpses of the race. All the pit crew could see was the few seconds of the race that played out as the cars swept past the pit stall.

Taran supposed that battles must be like that for infantrymen. All they can do is fight their little corner of the war, and then wait until the skirmish is over to find out the particulars of the con-flict—who won and who lost and why. She felt rather like a soldier herself. Surely a Cup race was as loud as a battle, and the same pressures were brought to bear on the participants: the tension, the feeling that you might fail your comrades through panic or in-experience or simply a lack of skill.

You were less alone than an infantryman, though. Always there were the voices in your headset, drowning out, for the most part, the roar of engine noise. The driver would relay his questions and comments back to the team, although Badger wasn't a particu-larly talkative driver. Tuggle talked to various team members to ask about the fuel situation, for example. Someone behind the wall was keeping track of fuel consumption; races had been lost at the finish line on the last lap when the car ran out of gas. It had happened to Dale Earnhardt once in the Daytona 500. Nobody wanted it to happen to Badger.

Hurry up and wait. If she'd had to sum up the feeling of being on a pit crew, that would cover it. There were the urgent voices, the pressure to be fast and accurate with millions of people all over the country watching you, and the noise and danger all com-bining to make the race feel like a three-hour reenactment of D-day. And above it all there was the fierce desire to be victorious, not for yourself, but for those who served with you, so that you could seal your bond of brotherhood in a struggle crowned with success. You would know that you did your part to ensure the win, and that your teammates valued you for your efforts. There would be more money paid to the winning team, but during the race itself, she doubted if anybody gave much thought to that. For the duration of that three-hour race, they were soldiers, wielding jacks and drills instead of rifles, to be sure, but soldiers nonetheless. Badger's life might well depend upon their skill, as much as if he had been a brother in arms. She felt that nothing she had ever done had mattered as much as this.

So for Taran the first Daytona 500 in years that she had not seen was the one in which she took part. The next day she would watch a recording of the television broadcast of the event, and from that she could piece together what had been happening at a given time in the race, and then she would try to summon up her own confused memories so that she could fit together the two perspectives into one coherent experience: what really happened, and what it felt like to live through it as it happened.

One thing that she was sure of, though. It had not looked or felt like the report of it that appeared on *Badger's Din.*

Badger's Din
Lady Pit Bulls "86" The Badger
by FastDrawl

Thank God it's over, folks. If you've been reading my lamentations since Thanksgiving because racing season was over . . . if you've heard me counting down the hours until Daytona . . . then you may be amazed to hear me thanking heaven that the race is history, but there it is, guys. I almost changed the channel. I couldn't take it.

They were awful.

If you want to measure Team 86's pit stop times, get a calendar.

Okay, spare me all your excuses, you bleeding hearts. Granted, the 86 is a new team with novice personnel. Granted, this is an equality gimmick as far as most people are concerned, but, folks, *we are not most people.* We are the diehard, tried and true, *whatever-he-drives-wherever-he-drives-it* fans of Badger Jenkins, and I submit to you that it is cruel and unusual punishment to make us watch him sabotaged and humiliated by this bumbling bunch of Hooters wannabees masquerading as NASCAR technicians. It scours my soul.

Badger is the man. He drives like greased lightning. He is the king of the redneck ballet out there—and to have to watch him brought low by his lousy support staff is more than I can endure. Can we take up a collection to get him some decent help? Or, failing that, at least some hotter-looking useless babes? *Is* there a Swedish volleyball team? My twenty bucks is in the hat for a new pit crew.

Taran read FastDrawl's article for the third time, wishing she had not decided to check on comments from her old Internet buddies. She had gone back to the hotel to check on Tony Lafon, who was still sick. Allergic reaction to seafood, he thought. He declined her offer to bring him dinner, and he was obviously in no mood for company. He had seen the race on television, and neither of them wanted to talk about that. After a few more awkward minutes, she left and went back to her room, wishing she had someone to talk to. That's why she had logged on to *Badger's Din.*

It had been more than a week since she'd visited the site, and she was so despondent after the race that she'd hope to commiserate with the faithful on Badger's unauthorized fan site. But instead of sympathy, she had found FastDrawl's screed, and now she was progressing from disbelief to shock to rage. He had no idea what it was like to be out there trying to do a job in thirteen seconds—*thirteen seconds*—with TV cameras zeroing in on you like snipers, and people barking orders into your headset, and having to worry about whether some car coming down pit road would lose its brakes or blow a tire and plow into you. Easy enough for that arrogant jerk FastDrawl to sit at home in his recliner, swilling beer and second-guessing the race, assuming that he could do everything better than the people who actually had the jobs. What was that quotation about critics? Teddy Roosevelt had said it, she thought.

Thank God for the Internet: All you had to do was type in a few keywords and you could find almost any quote you'd ever heard.

A few moments later she had found it, saved it with the copy command, and prepared to fire it point-blank at the smug little asshole at *Badger's Din.*

From Mellivora: Fastdrawl, who are you to criticize people who are actually trying to accomplish something instead of sitting on their butts critiquing life instead of living it? This is what I think!

It is not the critic who counts, not the man who points out how the strong man stumbled, or where the doer of deeds could have done them better. The credit belongs to the man who is actually in the arena; whose face is marred by dust and sweat and blood; who strives valiantly; who errs and comes short again and again; who knows the great enthusiasms, the great devotions, and spends himself in a worthy cause; who, at the best, knows in the end the triumph of high achievement; and who at the worst, at least fails while daring greatly, so that his place shall never be with those cold and timid souls who know neither victory nor defeat.

—Theodore Roosevelt

So, shut up, FastDrawl, as Badger himself would say, "You're a useless streak of widdle whose opinion isn't worth a bucket of warm spit." If you're going to root for Badger, support his team. If you're not, find somewhere else to be a blowhard.

Taran stayed online for a few more minutes, reading the crossfire between FastDrawl supporters and people who agreed with her defense of Team Vagenya. She found, though, that she didn't much care anymore what any of them thought. They didn't know Badger, and she did. They hadn't lived through a Cup race, and she had. All their endless paragraphs of speculation now reminded her of the work of some remote Pacific cargo cult, building a contraption out of sticks and vines and then expecting it to fly. They didn't understand anything at all. And she'd never be able to explain it to them.

She logged off. She was too tired to read any further entries, and too depressed to post any more comments, even to thank those who sided with her. Tomorrow they would be flying back to North Carolina, and there they would face a critic who *did* count, a critic who was quite entitled to point out how the doer of deeds could have done them better: Grace Tuggle—or worse—Badger Jenkins himself.

Taran decided to take another shower, so that Cass, her hotel roommate, couldn't hear her cry.

"Well, we sucked," said Tuggle, facing the despondent 86 team in their postrace analysis.

The pit crew and assorted other team members were back in Mooresville, sitting around the conference room table in various stages of misery, waiting for the crew chief to comment on their performance, not that they needed to know what she thought. The expression of disgust would be a mere formality, but it had to be endured. They would be watching the footage of the overhead view of each pit stop and analyzing each strategy call to see what they could have done differently. It would be unpleasant, but they all knew it was a necessary ordeal. They would never get better unless they knew exactly what had gone wrong before.

Taran had brought her own box of tissues to the meeting, and her swollen eyes and reddened nose suggested that this was her second box since the race; the others were maintaining a stoic calm, awaiting the storm.

"We sucked," Tuggle said again in that voice of preternatural calm that is worse than shouting.

"Aw, don't be too hard on 'em, Tuggle. They're new at it," said a drawling voice from the doorway. "And at least we qualified. That wasn't exactly a given, you know."

Nobody gasped, but nobody breathed, either. Badger and Sark were standing in the doorway, looking grim. Taran let out a stifled sob and buried her face in her arms.

"At least he isn't wearing the firesuit!" hissed Reve, elbowing her in the ribs.

He didn't have on sunglasses either, but he still managed to look intimidating to people who knew that his career and even his life had been in their hands—and that they had let him down. The fact that he was being nice about it only made it worse. Taran reached for another tissue.

"Come in, Badger," said Tuggle, indicating the empty chair beside her. "You, too, Sark. I'm sure the team would welcome your comments on their performance yesterday."

"Yeah," Reve muttered under her breath. "Nice to know he isn't on his yacht today, or out earning another ten grand signing his name somewhere."

"I'm not sure how you want me to write this up," said Sark.

Tuggle shook her head. "Smoke and mirrors," she said.

Sark nodded. *"We are a new team, and we view this first race as a learning experience. We value Badger Jenkins's expertise, and we are grateful for his patience as we learn the something-something of motorsports.* Like that?"

Tuggle sighed. "Whatever. Just don't say I said we sucked. . . . But we did."

"Well, at least we didn't come in last," said Jeanne, the tire carrier.

"Only because Badger had the good fortune not to wreck the car, and because Jay Bird and Julie's engine didn't give out during the race," said Tuggle. "But I'm sure you all know that apart from the DNFs who left the race in wrecks or with mechanical problems . . . apart from them . . . we were dead last, y'all. I assure you that you gave a lot of chauvinistic owners and sports writers a great deal of satisfaction with your performance."

That remark even silenced Reve, whose primary goal was proving that women could perform as well as men in motorsports.

Badger had poured himself a cup of coffee, and now he sat down next to the crew chief, looking gaunt and weary. Supposedly, drivers lose about ten pounds in a three-hour race. Looking at Badger this morning, no one doubted it.

"We'll look at the video footage in a minute," said Tuggle. "But before we do that, do you want to start us off, Badger?"

He stared into his coffee and sighed. "I wouldn't know where to begin."

"Well, we can start with you then. Your speeding down pit road cost us a lap. And this may be the crew's first real race, but it sure as hell wasn't yours, boy. We could have used that lap."

Taran raised a tear-stained face, ready to defend her hero. "It wouldn't have helped," she said in a hoarse voice that trembled on the breaking point. "I got the catch can stuck in the gas tank, and his having to come back to get that removed cost us a lap, anyhow." She looked at Badger pleadingly. "I'm really, really sorry."

The others exchanged uncomfortable looks, and Badger closed his eyes and held the coffee cup against his forehead. "It's okay," he said softly. "You didn't mean to. And it's not like any of the rest of us were perfect."

Taran wiped her eyes. "But I let you down."

Badger gave her a rueful smile. "You can't take all the credit for this defeat. We're a team. We all pitched in to make this fiasco."

The rest of the team nodded, but nobody would look at him.

"I left off a lug nut," said Cindy. "I had them taped to my arm, like you showed us, Tuggle, and one must have come off that time."

"And one time I let the jack slip during the tire change," said Cass Jordan. "I guess I had it at the wrong angle or something. Maybe I was more nervous than I thought I was."

Tuggle nodded. "And the rest of you did not make any howling blunders, but you were slow. I don't expect you to make a thirteen-second pit stop right off the bat, but I gotta tell you, you were putting me in mind of the days when drivers used to take five-minute coffee breaks on pit stops."

"When was that?" asked Sigur.

"Early fifties," said Kathy. "Leonard Wood of the Wood Brothers was the man who figured out that you didn't have to have a faster car if your team shortened the pit stop. And that's what we need to do, folks—shorten the damn pit stop."

"How?" said Reve.

"We stop screwing up," said Badger.

"Practice," said Tuggle. "We practice the moves until you can do them in your sleep. Until crowds and noise and cars whooshing by don't faze you anymore. We'll practice this afternoon after we finish here." She turned to Badger. "And as for you, boy, you need to remember that you are not calling the shots on this team. I am. You can give me your opinion, Badger, but the final call will be mine. Understood?"

"I know, Tuggle," said Badger. "But remember I'm not driving a school bus out there. My instinct is what makes me a Cup driver."

"I hear you," said Tuggle. "But either you start trusting me to plan the race strategy or you can take all the blame when we lose."

"Can we see the film now?" asked Sigur. "I'd like to know how we looked out there."

The others nodded in agreement.

Tuggle scowled. "Well, you weren't the Magnificent Seven, I'll tell you that. Roll the tape."

CHAPTER XVIII

Crying Up the Backstretch

"Badger has to do well in qualifying. At this track there's almost no way to make your way to the front if you start too far back."

"I'll keep my fingers crossed," said Taran.

"You'll do more than that," said Julie Carmichael. "You're going to help me make sure he does well."

"Why me?"

Julie smiled. "Because you never go home. Everybody else went back to the hotel an hour ago, and here you are still in the garage area tapping away on your laptop. Jay Bird is back in Charlotte with strep throat, and Rosalind is off doing an interview from some German journalist about being an MIT grad working in NASCAR. I need help right now, and you are the only person available."

"Okay," said Taran. "Help you how?"

Julie dropped her voice to a conspiratorial whisper. "We're going to soak the tires."

Taran blinked. "Are they dirty?"

Julie groaned. "You're almost as dumb as a wheel man, Taran. Don't you know what tire-soaking is?"

Taran shook her head. "No, but back at Atlanta that nice Mr. Baldwin in the next pit stall said that if I ever had any questions—"

"*No!* Don't mention this to a soul. Especially not to anybody outside this team." Julie dropped her voice to a whisper again. "It's not strictly legal."

The technical side of Team Vagenya had decided that the time had come for desperate measures. The race after Daytona had been at the California Speedway, a two-mile track, located in Fontana, California, about forty miles east of Los Angeles. They had not expected to do well at Fontana, and they hadn't.

As Tuggle explained to Team Vagenya's owners, "The California Speedway is an easy drive. The banking is never more than fourteen degrees; the track is a simple oval with no trick turns, and the track surface is excellent."

"Well, that sounds good," said Christine.

"Good?" said Tuggle. "It's a nightmare. For us, anyhow. It means all the drivers can perform well there, so Badger's ability gains us nothing. Remember that races get won by fractions of a second, and this race will be won by one of the big teams with fancy engineering and super equipment."

"Not us?"

"One of the Roush drivers," said Tuggle. "Bet on it. And it'll be a dull race, too," she added.

After the race, as they watched Jack Roush, aka the Man in the Hat, congratulating his winning driver in Victory Lane, one of the Team Vagenya owners was heard to remark that one might make more money betting Grace Tuggle's predictions than they'd make actually owning a Cup car.

The most memorable thing about Fontana as far as Taran was concerned was its proximity to Hollywood. Taran was stricken when she spotted the slinky blonde leaning against the 86, with her arms around Badger. "Who is that walking Badger to the car this time?" she asked indignantly.

"Malibu Barbie," said Reve.

The next race—Las Vegas—wasn't much better. One of the rookie drivers got loose on a turn and caused a wreck that triggered a chain of collisions, and the 86 car was damaged beyond repair. Badger sat out the last few dozen laps and finished thirty-eighth. Everybody was philosophical about that one. Wrecks happen. You just move on.

With the two winter west-of-the-Mississippi races out of the way, the Cup teams returned to the Southeast, heartland of stock car racing, for the Golden Corral 500, a mid-March battle at the Atlanta Motor Speedway. A fast, banked track located only a hundred miles from Badger's north Georgia hometown—everyone hoped that this would be the race that changed their luck.

"After all," said Taran, "Badger is a native Georgian. This will give the hometown crowd someone to root for."

"You mean, other than Bill Elliott?" said Kathy.

Even Taran had to admit that Awesome Bill, the 1985 Cup champion, who had twice won the Daytona 500, would outrank Badger as the favorite son at Atlanta, but to the folks back home in Marengo and to Taran, he would always be in first place. At least in Cup racing, she amended. Whenever she managed to get away from her duties with the team, Taran had been going to the local speedways to watch Tony Lafon race in Late Model Stocks. He hadn't won yet, but he seemed glad to have someone he knew to cheer him on, and someone to have dinner with after the race. She'd heard people at the track say that he was quite a talented wheel man, and Taran supposed that it was his driving experience that made him such an effective spotter for Badger in the Cup races.

Badger had arranged to get team pit passes for a couple of people from Marengo, and he had asked Laraine to walk him to the car before the race. Even Taran approved of that. Laraine had stopped by to visit with the pit crew that morning, bringing a basket of muffins from the diner and wishing them all luck. Badger had come with her, looking more relaxed and happy than they had ever seen him on a speedway.

"Well, she doesn't look like a Barbie doll," said Sigur. "Or like a driver's wife."

"Once upon a time," said Kathy. "Back before this sport was a glamourfest. My mom was a pretty lady, but she wasn't a centerfold. Laraine puts me in mind of her."

"I think she looks fine," said Jeanne. "To me she and Badger look like family. Same dark, sad eyes."

"I expect they are kin," said Kathy. "Badger says that in Marengo every home football game is a family reunion. She is closer to his age than the beauty queen was, but she looks classy in that watery blue silk dress, and she really does seem to care about him. Not about the publicity and meeting movie stars, but just about *him*. She's okay."

"*Almost* okay," said a scowling Reve. "When she was passing around the muffins, I went up to Badger and told him how much we all liked her, and he said, *'Yeah, she's a good girl. Too bad she doesn't look like a model'.*"

"And did you slug him?" asked Sigur.

Reve shook her head. "Wouldn't be a fair fight. I outweigh him. Besides, we need him to drive the car."

Badger had not qualified well at Atlanta. The team had drawn one of the last slots for qualifying, which meant that he went out on a hot track—generally not the way to nail a fast time. On the cool track not yet warmed up by the afternoon sun, earlier qualifiers were able to rack up higher speeds. So, lagging behind the leaders by only a few tenths of a second, Badger had started the Sunday race two-thirds of the way back in the pack—hardly an auspicious beginning, but winning was still possible, even from that far back. When the race began, Badger held his own, steadily working his way through the stream of cars until he was running tenth.

It was still early in the race, but those in the pit crew who were new to the sport began to cheer loudly, and it was obvious that they were beginning to envision themselves in the televised jubilation of Victory Lane.

"There's many a slip between the lip and the Cup," muttered Kathy Erwin, but no one paid her any mind.

She was right, though. Nothing drastic happened, really. Badger was tapped in one minor incident, but thanks to the resulting caution, he did not even lose a lap. He never blew a tire or developed engine trouble. He simply struggled to hold his place in the slipstream, losing a fraction of a second with every succeeding lap. Every so often his unmistakable drawl would come on, telling

Tuggle that the car was tight on the turns. Then they would wait for a caution so that they could use the pit stop to make adjustments. It didn't help, though. He just kept losing ground, a fraction of a second at a time.

It was one of those races that proceed without any particular drama, and unless you happen to end up in Victory Lane, it is not a memorable experience. They worked every pit stop they got to adjust the car so that it would handle better, but at best they were playing a game of catch-up, and in the end, everybody was relieved to see the race end, so that they could stop trying to fight the inevitable.

"It wasn't our fault this time," said Sigur, as they watched the red and white car take the checkered flag.

Kathy Erwin sighed. "Nobody cares whose fault it was. We all lost the race."

Badger's Din
The Lights Went out in Georgia

FastDrawl: Well, folks, I had high hopes for our man Badger at AMS when he was running up front, but this was a battle with long odds. I make it 52 to 1. Forty-two other Cup drivers, plus the 86 team's crew chief and pit crew all working to thwart Badger while he is trying his damnedest to win that race. That car handled like a cement mixer in a mudslide, and they never did get the setup right. It pained me to watch.

Lady Badger: They're getting better, though. At least he got up to tenth place, and he didn't wreck. I wish they'd interview him on camera, though.

Bonneville Bill: Hold the syrup, Lady Badger. Nobody wants to hear about Badger's beautiful eyes. I heard him on the radio after the race. He said: "The car was just way too tight all night long.

I got into someone during one of the incidents on the track and it knocked out the toe, and we had to make multiple stops to try and correct it, which cost us valuable time and track position. The Vagenya racing team worked hard all night to try and get the car dialed in, but it just never came. We were lucky that we were able to finish the race and finish as high as we did, especially at Atlanta."

Georgia Peach: Could somebody translate that, please? I'm a new fan.

Mellivora: *Dialed in* means "correctly adjusted." A dialed-in car is the ideal for racing. *Toe* refers to the direction in which the wheels are pointing. *Toe out* means it pulls to the right. *Toe in* means it pulls to the left. It's an adjustment made on regular cars, too. Sometimes, one side is in or out, making the car just plain hard to drive. The team did their best, like Badger said, but when he got caught up in that little wreck, it knocked everything out of whack.

FastDrawl: This isn't NASCAR Tech, Mellivora! The new fish can look up that information and stop wasting our time. Hey—I'm car shopping, folks. Does anybody know what kind of car Badger drives—off the track, I mean?

"Mellivora" typed in "A silver Chrysler Crossfire with a Georgia license plate that reads 'Badger 1'." But then she stared at the line for a moment, and pushed DELETE instead of SEND before logging off.

Now they were in Bristol, on the heels of a meeting with the team owner, who had not been happy with Team Vagenya's performance so far. After Atlanta, Tuggle had been summoned to the office of Christine Berenson for a discussion on the team's progress, or lack thereof. Tuggle had been expecting to be called on the carpet. Because the owners were new to racing, and because they were corporate types, they thought that throwing twenty million dollars at a problem would provide instant results.

"Surely after four races we ought to be doing better than this," said Christine, in a plaintive voice belied by her stern expression.

When she had entered the office, Tuggle had noticed that the framed posters on the reception room walls now showed pictures of the 86 car itself, rather than portrait shots of Badger in his firesuit.

"New teams take a lot of adjusting," said Tuggle. "There are a thousand things that can go wrong mechanically in every race. There's team skills. Communication with the wheel man. Meshing styles."

Christine heard what she wanted to hear. "Are you unhappy with Badger's performance?"

"No," said Tuggle, "he's a natural. Maybe we have to push him a little bit on practices and appearances, but he's a good man. He can't win without good equipment and a precision pit crew, though. Nobody could have done better."

"Because if you *are* dissatisfied with his work, we can certainly explore other options," said Christine. "Vagenya is quite disappointed that he did not go along with their kissing booth idea for the pharmaceutical conference. He needs to swallow his pride and be more cooperative."

"He's a race car driver," said Tuggle. "His pride is his roll cage— nothing makes a dent in it."

"He may have more pride than he can afford," said Christine.

"I wouldn't trade his pride for all the diligence in the world," said Tuggle. "He wants to win more than you do. He'll try to put that car into openings you wouldn't throw a tin can through, because he wants it so bad. Every time we don't give him a good enough car, I feel like we let him down. But if you give him half a chance, he will win or die trying."

"Well, if his performance does not improve, we may take advice elsewhere on measures that might help."

The discussion had not been productive. Owner and crew chief had remained civil to each other, but there had been no meeting of the minds. Tuggle went back and told the team engineers that if they had any miracles lying around, now would be a good time to use one. Julie, Jay Bird, and Rosalind talked it over, and they decided that, with very little to lose, they might as well soak the tires and see if they could get the pole at Bristol, where winning from behind mostly didn't happen. Meanwhile, they would try to come up with other gray-area technical refinements that might get past inspection.

Julie held up a metal canister of the sort that might contain turpentine or floor refinisher.

Taran frowned. "If it's illegal, then how did you get it?"

"I bought it at an auto store. Cost me fifty bucks a gallon, too. We should be able to do enough tires for the whole weekend with two gallons of this stuff."

"But if it's not legal—"

"Okay, it's not illegal per se," said Julie. "In go-cart racing you're allowed to soak the tires. That's why you can buy this stuff over the counter—as long as nobody finds out what you're doing with it."

"But what does it do?"

"Improves the tires' grip on the track. Makes for better control. If Badger can adjust to the feel of it. Not all drivers can. Like everything else, tire-soaking has a downside. Basically the stuff eats the tires. They don't last as long. But they're good for qualifying on. Should improve his time by a few tenths of a second, if we're lucky."

Taran blinked. "So . . . we're going to paint this stuff on the tires—like nail polish?"

"No, tire soak goes in from the inside out. We're going to put it *in* the tires for qualifying."

"How long does the soaking process take?"

"Couple of hours, I guess."

Taran shook her head. "Wait. That won't work. NASCAR requires teams to buy a new set of tires from them to qualify on, right? And they don't release that set until a few hours before qualifying. Usually there's just enough time to bolt them on and get into the two-hour tech line. So let's say that we get our qualifying tires about three to four hours before we get our turn to qualify. Then we're not in the shop. We're at the track with officials all over the place, so how are we going to soak tires without getting caught and ending up in big trouble?"

Julie grinned. "I thought of that, so I asked around. We're going to do what the big teams do."

Taran thought of asking which big teams she was referring to, but Julie probably wouldn't tell her, anyhow. "Okay," she said. "And what do the big teams do to keep from getting caught?"

"What do we do after we get the qualifying tires from NASCAR?"

"Well . . . we let the air out."

"Right. Goodyear mounts the tires with regular air, and after we get them, we deflate the tires and refill them with nitrogen, because tires run better on nitrogen than on plain air."

"Well, that's not illegal. . . . Is it?"

"No, everybody does it. But some of them also do something else. They have a small, portable nitrogen tank at the track to refill the tires, only that tank is halfful of *tire soak*. So as we refill the tires, we will be spraying soak inside the tire through the valve stem."

"What if you get caught?"

"Just don't let anybody from outside the team try to pick up the nitrogen pump. It'll weigh so much that they're bound to figure out that something is wrong."

"How did you know about this?"

Julie shrugged. "My dad was a race car driver, remember? He never made it to the big time, but he was serious about it, and I learned all the tricks tagging along after him. Back when I was a kid, the tire guy used to rub soak on the surface of the tire with a glove attached to a tube going to a bag of soak under his armpit." She sighed and fluffed her hair. "I'm glad those days are over. The nitrogen tank method is more reliable and less easily detected."

"And about a million times less gross," muttered Taran. "Are we going to have to do this on race day, too?"

"We can't," said Julie. "The thing about tire soak is that it deteriorates the tires. That's how it works. It degrades the rubber so that the tire sticks a little better to the surface of the track. That's fine for the two laps it takes for qualifying, but if you tried it in a three-hour race, the tires would disintegrate on the track. You could end up in the wall, or in a wreck, or just having to make green flag pit stops to replace them. But for a couple of qualifying laps here, that extra traction might be good for a couple of tenths of a second."

Taran nodded. She knew that sometimes three-tenths of a second was the difference between first place and fifteenth, so even the smallest advantage to gain the smallest unit of time mattered to a race team. She could see the advantage of that. "But what if they catch us?"

Julie shrugged. "Slap on the wrist, more or less," she said. "A fine. Whoever was caught doing the soaking gets booted from the track, maybe suspended for a few races. The trick is not to get caught, Taran."

"But it's cheating."

"I prefer to call it creative engineering. Everybody does it, Taran. And even if they didn't, it isn't as if we are on a level playing field here competitively, is it? The well-funded multicar teams get to test all their cars at a track and pool their results. We only get one shot. What's fair about that? Or say some car has a ten-million-dollar sponsor and one of the independent owner–driver guys has to take up a collection to buy enough tires to race. How can that be equal opportunity? Money buys speed. At least tire-soaking is relatively cheap."

Despite their efforts, Badger didn't get the pole, but he did qualify sixth, much to the delight of the team. When the race began, the 86 team's tires were all nitrogen-filled regulation tires. The only nonstandard modification was a bit of magic dirt that Taran rubbed on the hood of the car. Now it was all up to Badger's driving skills.

When the number 86 appeared in lights on the pole that

served as a vertical "scoreboard," the pit crew alternately hugged each other and screamed for Badger.

"It's the sacred dust from Chimayo!" screamed Taran. "I knew it would work eventually."

Less than a minute later, Badger's voice came over the headset. "This damn car is shaking like a sparrow in a snake pit."

"I hear you, Badger." Tuggle's voice was calm, as always. "Could it be a valve spring?"

A few more seconds passed in a tense cacophony of noise that registered as silence with everyone on the 86 team, because all that mattered right then was Badger's voice. Finally, he came back on, "Still shuddering, Tuggle. Hesitating."

"Try the ignition box."

After another interminable pause, Badger said, "That's it. Damn thing's gone bad. I'm flipping to the second one. Still shaking. The second box is bad, too, or else the switch is shorted out. It's totally dead."

There was a short silence while everyone thought things they couldn't say out loud with spectators' scanners tuned in. An ignition problem would trigger a misfire, causing the engine to begin losing cylinders. A car running on seven cylinders instead of eight would soon fall behind the rest of the pack. Even worse, the longer the motor was allowed to run on fewer than eight cylinders, the greater the chance that it would grenade the engine. If they couldn't fix it, they could be looking at a last-place finish.

Badger again: "It's skipping and popping. Sounds like hell. Missing."

Tuggle swore under her breath, then in an icy calm, she said, "Turn off the brake blowers."

"I'm dicing for the lead, dammit!"

"Well, you won't get it," muttered Tuggle. "You wanna bring it in now?"

He didn't have time to answer. In a matter of seconds the 86 began to lose its momentum. The loss of power caused his speed to decrease, and now instead of leaping ahead of the cars following him, Badger was fast becoming an obstacle in their path.

Somebody didn't figure that out in time to swerve completely out
of his way, and the resulting contact meant that they caught a caution. The collision was a minor one. Since Bristol was a short,
high-banked track, where the average speed was ninety miles per
hour, wrecks were not the terrifying prospect they had been at
Daytona. This was the NASCAR equivalent of a fender bender, and
given the 86's mechanical problems, the resulting caution was a
blessing.

"Bring it in, boy," said Tuggle, but Badger hadn't needed to be
told. He was on his way.

Taran was mentally composing a demand-for-refund letter to a
Navajo shaman when Tuggle's voice crackled over her headset.
"Stiles! You're the one with the electronics background, aren't
you?'

Taran turned to face Tuggle and nodded slowly, wondering why
that had come up.

"Good. When Badger comes in for the pit stop, I need you to
get into the car and fix that ignition problem."

"Can't he switch to the other ignition box? Oh, he already tried
that, didn't he?"

"He did."

"Could be a short under the dash," said Taran, picturing cir-
cuitry in her head. "No. Unlikely. I'll bet the switches are bad. I
could try changing the boxes manually. Be faster."

"Right. Good thing you know your stuff. And that you're little.
So get in there and fix the problem when he pits."

Taran blinked. *"In thirteen seconds?"*

Tuggle grunted. "Unless you can do it quicker."

Taran said nothing more, but her mind was still going faster
than the cars. In milliseconds she thought: *But how do I get into
the car? Oh. Same way Badger gets in. Only through the passenger's side window.* Around her the cars still roared. The crowd
still screamed. The voices in her headset chattered on. But to
Taran the world had just switched over to *slow motion* and *mute.*
For another couple of seconds she stared open-mouthed at the
swirl of cars streaming past, lost in thought.

Tuggle's voice roused her from reverie again. "Stiles, remember that a caution lap here at Bristol takes less than a minute, and a green lap is about fifteen seconds. Don't cost us this race."

Oh, good. No pressure.

The 86 engine sputtered as it came down pit road. Tuggle radioed Badger, "Turn the switches off when you come in, Badger. Taran can't change those boxes with the current on or it'll shock the crap out of her."

"Right," said Badger. "Hurry it up, though, y'all."

"We can't give you gas this time because Taran is the catch can." Everybody knew that they couldn't send a shop dog out to take her place, because that would mean more than seven people over the wall.

Badger cut the engine as soon as he halted in the pit stall. One of the team mechanics leaned over the wall and handed Taran a new red ignition box, which was about the size and shape of a brick. Dodging the jackman, fresh tires, and the tire changers themselves, she sprinted for the passenger-side window and dived in, landing with a thump straight on the floor—no passenger seat in a stock car, of course, just the driver's custom-fitted seat within the roll cage, and an empty space to his right. Badger's helmeted head turned to look at her as she fell, and she saw his eyes widen in surprise. Taran held up the new ignition box, and he nodded and looked away, as if he had forgotten she was there, so she set to work.

In her headset she heard the voice of the team spotter, "Pace car in one." It was Tony Lafon. The sound of his voice calmed her down.

Since the engine wasn't running during this pit stop, Taran was more conscious of the sounds of the rest of the team at work. Thirteen seconds to fix the ignition problem, and she had to do it accompanied by the high-pitched scream of the air guns zipping off the lug nuts, and the *thump thump thump* of the jack raising the car, pitching her at such a steep angle that she almost lost her balance. Badger reached out and put his hand on her shoulder to keep her from falling. She willed herself not to process that sensation. *Wham!* The jack was lowered, and the tire changers headed for the other side of the car to repeat the procedure.

"Pace car in two," said Tony's voice in her headset.

There wasn't anything particularly hard about fixing the ignition box problem, except, that is, if you were expected to do it in an idling car whose interior temperature was upward of 100 degrees. In a thirteen-second pit stop. Taran tried to ignore the roar of the other cars' engines and the shuddering as they sped past. She had to focus all her attention on the job. Because ignition boxes are bolted in with zeus fasteners, it would take too long to replace one by securing a new box to the dash, but fortunately, she didn't have to. All she had to do was take the plug out of the old one, put it in the one she brought in with her, and see if the engine fired this time.

It did.

Problem fixed. The roaring and shaking of the idling engine flustered her for a moment, but she took a deep breath, steadied herself against the dash, and tried to shut out everything except the task at hand.

"Pace car in three."

Running out of time.

Now all she had to do was secure the new box inside the car somewhere, by no means an elegant solution, but given the time factor, it was their best shot. She had thought about trying to tape the replacement box onto the two malfunctioning units mounted on the dash, but in the end it seemed simpler—and faster—just to zip-tie the new box onto the roll cage and get out of the car.

"Middle of three . . ." Tony's voice was taut with urgency.

Her hands were shaking, but she nearly had it. She was running out of time, though. Badger tapped on the dash and pointed forward. Taran barely glanced up, but she nodded vigorously, hoping that he understood her to mean, *"I'm working as fast as I can."*

Tony was shouting now. *"Pace car in four! Come on! Gotta go! Gotta go!"*

Another voice in her head. "Let him go, dammit!" That was

Tuggle, and with that tone of voice she could have parted the Red Sea.

"But, Tuggle . . ."

"Everybody back! Badger, go!"

Badger hit the throttle and scratched off as the shouting in their heads continued. Tuggle. "Gotta beat the pace car. Speed down pit road. *Do it!"*

The penalty for speeding on pit road is to go to the tail end of the longest line, but Tuggle must have figured that the penalty was better than going a lap down.

When the car took off, Taran was flung backward against the roll cage, scrabbling for balance, and resisting the urge to grab at Badger to keep herself from falling. At the pit speed of around thirty miles per hour, and then seconds later at nearly three times that, they burst onto the track.

From her vantage point on the floor, now facing backward, all Taran could see was the interior of the car and Badger himself, but for once he was not a comforting presence. Barricaded in his roll cage, wearing the full face helmet and the thick gloves, Badger looked like an alien in a science fiction movie. The banking of the Bristol track was nearly thirty-six degrees—horrendously steep—which meant that if she hadn't hung on to the bars of the roll cage, she would have been bouncing all over the car—or falling on Badger—which was somehow not as appealing at ninety miles per hour as she had once envisioned.

This is not how she pictured a ride-along with Badger Jenkins at all. In fact, in most of her fantasies, the firesuit morphed into shining armor, and the 86 had a mane and tail. But she had less than a minute to contemplate the unsatisfactory nature of *Take Your Stalker to Work Day,* because thirty seconds or so is all it takes to loop the half-mile track at Bristol Motor Speedway during a caution lap.

Afterward, she remembered those moments in slow motion, and there shouldn't have been time for all of it to have occurred, she thought. First, she heard Tony Lafon shouting, "Was that Taran that just went in the window? What the hell are you doing, Badger? Pit! *Pit! No-oow!"*

Taran felt a little spark of pleasure at hearing the concern in Tony's voice, which she hoped was on her account. The voices in her headset told her that her unscheduled ride along had not gone unnoticed for a second. Each pit stall has two NASCAR officials to monitor the team's activity: one stationed at the right front tire and one at the right rear. They weren't going to miss much. Especially not something as major as this. Badger had barely left pit road before the two frantic NASCAR watchdogs were radioing the tower to report the infraction.

"Crew member inside the 86 car!"

"Post the 86 car! Black flagged!"

Then the lord of the tower—NASCAR director David Hoots—delivered a much calmer response to the reporting officials: "Inspector, get with the crew chief on the 86 and explain to the lady the reason why NASCAR stock cars have only one seat. Then invite her and the Driver to the truck after the race."

A few seconds later, one of the watchdogs told him, "Message delivered to the crew chief of the 86."

Then it was Tuggle's voice again over the radio, "You heard them, Badger," she said. "Our NASCAR babysitters in the pit here are having a French fit." There was an infinitesimal pause, and then she said, "Did Taran get the box fixed?"

"Yes!" Taran and Badger both said it at once.

"Bring her in," said Tuggle. "She can get out and catch-can on this pit stop. Oh, and Badger, we're going to the red truck after the race."

"I hear you," said Badger.

Taran lived through the rest of the Bristol race on automatic pilot. Since the fixing of the ignition problem, Badger was "bad fast" as he would have phrased it, fueled probably by his frustration at having mechanical problems cost him time, and also by rage at having to report to the red truck over a miscue that was not his fault.

"It wasn't your fault," said Kathy Erwin, patting Taran on the arm. "The crew chief's word is law. You had no choice. Neither did Badger."

Tears shimmered in Taran's eyes. "What will they do? Yell at us?"

"No, they prefer sarcasm. And, of course, money."

"Money?"

"Oh, sure. That stunt will cost you a couple of thou, easy. Most expensive taxi ride you'll ever take."

Slug a fellow driver in a fit of temper after the race.

Wreck another car on purpose.

Flaunt the rules of the sport.

Red truck.

It used to be a red truck, so everyone still called it that, although now the vehicle in question was, in fact, yellow. NASCAR track headquarters. The dragon's lair. The principal's office. If you broke the rules during or shortly after the race, NASCAR officials would summon you to the truck for disciplinary action. They could fine you, suspend you, put you on probation. They could do anything they wanted. NASCAR is the only privately owned sport in the world. It's their way or no way.

They all went in together: Tuggle, Taran, and Badger. Somewhere the winner was celebrating his victory. Probably by now he had been escorted up to the glass-walled skybox high above the Bristol Motor Speedway, where two dozen journalists waited to interview the winning driver. But in the formerly red truck, nobody was smiling.

Taran felt like an eighth grader sent to the office to be punished. The big bear of a man in the rimless glasses looked at her sternly, and she felt the tears well up again. She pictured him calling her parents. Badger stood beside her, looking solemn and brave, but maybe also annoyed at being scolded when he could be out signing autographs for people who thought he walked on water. Only Tuggle remained unperturbed. She had greeted the man by his first name and made herself comfortable in the one available chair.

"What were you thinking?" the director asked her.

Tuggle smiled. "I suppose there's not much point in pleading not guilty."

"Not with two inspectors standing beside the car, no. Plus, I bet a few rows of spectators got some great pictures of the 86 car's extra passenger."

"We had to beat the pace car," said Tuggle.

"Why didn't you just shoot out its tires?"

Nobody laughed. In the red truck, sarcasm was not to be mistaken for friendliness—or for forgiveness. The director was not smiling, either. "This is a serious safety issue, people," he said. "An unprotected crew member in a race car is one monkey away from getting killed. I hope you all understand that."

Solemnly, they nodded.

"And a female crew person at that. If she had got hurt, we would be in for a public relations nightmare of Biblical proportions. And, you, Driver, would look like the biggest heel in the world of sports. Putting your ego over her well-being. For shame!"

"Sir! It wasn't his fault, sir." Taran's voice was barely a squeak.

"This isn't the army, crewman. And it was certainly partly his fault. I'm sure he noticed you were on board. He could have refused to exit pit road. A little something we refer to as a judgment call."

"He doesn't disobey my orders," said Tuggle.

"Well, then try to give him more sensible ones in future, Tuggle. If he didn't show more sense than he did today, I wouldn't let him drive a UPS truck, much less a Cup car." He sighed wearily. It had been a long weekend. At least Badger hadn't shoved anybody. Short tracks meant short-tempered drivers. There were a few other drivers waiting for their turn on the hot seat. "All right, you daredevils," he said. "There's enough blame to go around here, but I'm not of a mind to suspend any of you over this. Driver, you will be on probation, though, for the rest of the year."

Badger nodded mournfully, the golden retriever swatted with a newspaper. Tuggle's expression grew more stern, but she said nothing. Taran held her breath so that she would not sob.

They were ushered out of the truck so that the director could move on to the next matter demanding his attention.

"I'm sorry," said Taran, when they were once again outside.

"Nothing to do with you," said Badger quietly. "We took a gamble, that's all. I'm glad you weren't hurt."

"It's part of the deal," said Tuggle. "Just let it go. It all starts up again next week, you know."

"Well, at least they didn't fine us," said Taran.

"They will," said Badger. "They'll think about it some first, though."

"Fines are announced on the Tuesday following the race," Tuggle told her. "And they have to be paid before we can race again."

Then she and Badger walked away, talking shop, putting the incident out of their minds, while Taran stood there wondering how many minutes there were between then and Tuesday, because she knew she would agonize through every one of them.

On Tuesday, Taran was waiting at the shop when Tuggle arrived, carrying a Styrofoam cup of coffee and a bag of Krispy Kreme donuts. She offered the bag to Taran, who shook her head. "Go on," said Tuggle. "What will that be for you? Last night's dinner?"

Taran shrugged. Discussing dinners might lead to disclosures about throwing up. She wondered if Maalox counted as a meal.

"Have you heard anything yet about NASCAR's decision?"

"Yep, just now. Ten-thousand-dollar fines for me and Badger. Each. For you, twenty-five hundred."

Taran took a deep, moist breath, and nodded, digging in her purse for her checkbook. Twenty-five hundred dollars. That wasn't so bad. In her 3 A.M. nightmare, the penalty had been a firing squad. Besides, anything was better than not knowing.

"I don't suppose the team owners pay the fines for us?" she said.

"Nope," said Tuggle, dumping another sugar packet into her coffee and stirring it with a screwdriver. "They don't."

"Well, who should I make out my check to? The team, or NASCAR, or what?"

"The fines are paid," said Tuggle.

"But I thought you said—"

"Badger is paying your fine as well as his. Guess he figured he could afford it more than you could. Oh, jeez, you're not gonna cry again, are you?"

Taran took a deep breath and shook her head. "How can I ever thank him?" she whispered.

The next week's race was in Martinsville, Virginia, NASCAR's shortest track—without the steep banking of Bristol, but still a difficult track for passing. Heavy March rains canceled qualifying, which meant that Badger started in the back. He was lucky to start at all, since without a qualifying competition, slots in the race are assigned on the basis of owners' points from the previous year, and then past champions' provisionals, and finally the current year's drivers' ranking for the seven or so remaining places in the race. Badger started forty-second out of forty-three slots, and though he struggled all day to work his way forward, the half-mile track with its sharp turns kept him bottled up, as more and more cars fell off the lead lap. Finally, one of the young punks from out West, eager to get past him on the narrow track, tapped the bumper of the 86, and Badger fishtailed into the wall, ending the day with sore muscles and a car too damaged to make it back into the race.

"Is there a race in which you think you might do well?" asked Melodie Albigre. She had opened a small leather notebook and she sat with pen poised, watching Badger on the treadmill with clinical disinterest.

Badger wiped his face with a towel. He looked at her sharply to see if that remark had been intended as sarcasm, but Melodie's face bore its usual expression of businesslike boredom, as if he were an underperforming stock that she regretted having invested in.

Badger turned the exercise machine to a quieter speed. "There's a lot of factors in racin'," he said. "It's not just me, you know. I always try to win, but sometimes we don't have the car, and sometimes we run out of luck. It's seven o'clock in the morning, Melodie. Why do you want to talk about this here and now?"

He was already awake, of course, when she rang the doorbell at seven A.M., because he began his workout every morning at six, but he didn't much care to have visitors at that hour, especially not charmless ones determined to hold a business meeting before he'd even had his coffee, which, she'd informed him, she had no intention of making for him.

"I understand about the vagaries of the racing gods," she said. "I'm not asking you to do any fortune-telling. I'm simply asking you on which track in the next couple of months do you think you could *reasonably* expect to place higher than twentieth?"

Badger shrugged. "Darlington is a drivers' track. You can't buy Darlington with fancy engineering."

"Yes, and you've already won that one, haven't you? So I suppose that would be a safe bet. But it's in May. You can do well sooner than that, surely?"

He thought about it. "Phoenix, maybe. That one takes some driving know-how. It's got real tight turns on One and Two, and a dogleg going into Turn Three. I'd take my chances at Phoenix against anybody else out there."

"Fine." She consulted a printed NASCAR schedule the size of a credit card. "Phoenix, it is. That's in late April. I suppose it will have to do."

"What do you mean, 'Do'?" said Badger. "You're not betting on the races, are you? I think that might be illegal."

Melodie rolled her eyes. "I do not wager on sporting events. And if I did, I think Jimmie Johnson might be a safer bet than you are. Oh, stop looking daggers at me. I told you I wasn't your fan. I'm only here to get your business affairs in order. Now, before I go and do more important things, I need you to sign some papers."

"What papers?"

"Oh, just the usual dull merchandising agreements and things. Of course, if you'd like to sit down and read them—"

Badger looked at his watch. "I have an interview in an hour with the guy from the *Greensboro Record*."

She took a stack of papers out of her briefcase and set them up on the shelf of the treadmill, flipping off the machine as she did so.

"Hey! I wasn't finished!"

"Sign your name a dozen times and then you can run 'til you drop, for all I care." She handed him the pen and watched while he scribbled his name at the bottom of every page. "Thanks. I'll get out of your way now." She eyed his sweaty tee shirt and wrinkled her nose. "I could use some fresh air."

Badger's lips tightened, but all he said was, "Why did you want to know what race I was likely to do well in?"

She shrugged. "Just a deal I'm putting together. It's easier to impress people when you're not representing a guy who finished last. I'll be off now. Get back to your treadmill like a good little hamster."

Before he could reply she swept out of the room, closing the door behind her, just seconds before an empty water bottle hit it and bounced back onto the floor.

CHAPTER XIX

Relief Driver

"Congratulations," said Melodie Albigre to the half-naked man. "Only two laps down at the end. At least you managed to finish. Nice race. Wish I could say the same about your underwear."

Badger Jenkins, who had just stripped off his firesuit in the supposed privacy of the lounge of the hauler, wiped the sweat off his face with his forearm and glanced down at his faded blue boxer shorts. His eyes glittered with malice. "Well, I didn't figure on anybody seeing my underwear," he said.

She shrugged. She came the rest of the way up the steps into the lounge and sat down in the folding chair by the door. Badger had turned his back to her to finish dressing, but she was now peering at the screen of her PDA, which she contrived to find a good deal more interesting than an undressed race car driver. "Don't mind me," she said. "I'm just here on business. But, my, you are skinny, aren't you?"

He held up the water bottle against his forehead and closed his eyes. "I lose about ten pounds in a race," he said. "Maybe you should try it."

She ignored this salvo. "Well, as I said, although I'm sure there are women who would kill to take my place at the moment, or so they tell me, I'm simply here to talk about your schedule. I would

not have to be here if you bothered to return my phone calls."
She glared at him accusingly.

Badger scowled. "I was busy. I do have a job, you know."

"Yes, I just watched you doing it." She paused, letting her contempt go without saying. "You came in twenty-seventh. Nevertheless, we need to talk about what you're going to do tomorrow."

Badger finished pulling a purple Team Vagenya tee shirt over his head before he muttered, "I'm busy tomorrow."

Melodie gave him her "humoring the delusional" smile. "Indeed, you are busy," she said. "I have arranged for you to visit a local textile mill to sign autographs for the workers, who are apparently big NASCAR fans." Her tone implied that there was no accounting for taste.

Badger finished chugging his water, tossed the bottle into the trash barrel, and reached for another. "Tomorrow is Monday," he said, unscrewing the cap off the second bottle. "I'm off on Mondays."

"Right. The team does not require your services on Monday. However, I do. Now this appearance I have scheduled for you tomorrow—"

"I go back home on Mondays," said Badger. "Back to Georgia." He wasn't arguing. He was simply stating a fact with the calm certainty of one describing the action of the tides.

His personal manager was unmoved by this pronouncement. "Tomorrow you will be going to a North Carolina textile mill." She peered the screen of her PDA. "At noon."

Badger shook his head. "I didn't agree to that."

"I agreed on your behalf," said Melodie calmly. "I will accompany you to the event. Meet me at the team office at ten. Shall I drive? Yes, perhaps I should. I have the directions, and there are no left turns involved." She smirked at her little joke.

"Well, I don't want to go," said Badger. He was fully dressed now, and judging from the mutinous look on his face, he was seconds away from walking out of the hauler.

"But you will go. Your fee will be the standard one. Five thousand dollars an hour. Less our management percentage, of course."

"I told you, I—*what*?"

"Five thousand dollars an hour." She sighed. "It was the best I could do. After all, you're not Jeff Gordon. You're not even Jeff Burton."

Badger was still holding the cold water bottle against his forehead. He brushed a trickle of water away from his cheek. "How long do I have to stay?"

"Oh, an hour or so. I'll pick you up at ten. Try to wear something presentable."

"Like what?"

She rolled her eyes. "Well, God knows, Sunshine," she said. "Maybe I'll run you by the mall after we finish. Someone should see that you have some decent clothes. Too bad your beauty queen didn't stick around." With a faint sneer, she looked him up and down again. "Skinny *and* shabby. People will think you're sponsored by a charity for the homeless. Tomorrow then." She swept out down the steps and out of the hauler, just as her cell phone began to ring.

Badger sat down and contemplated the label of his water bottle, too tired to think what to do next. It had been a long, nerve-wracking race. They had never got the car dialed in, and he'd spent the entire evening fighting to keep the thing out of the wall on every turn. His arms and shoulders ached, and he had blisters down the sides of both hands from the rubbing of the wet leather of his driving gloves against his skin.

Tuggle came quietly into the room and sat down in the other chair. She closed the lounge door with her foot. She hadn't changed clothes yet. The lines in her face were deeper, and she looked like she hadn't slept in a week. No matter how many times she told sports journalists—and the team owners—that it took most of a season to pull together a competent team, it was still a frustrating experience to lose and lose and lose. It was always for a different reason: mechanical problems, wrecks, bad setups. There were a thousand ways to get it wrong, and Tuggle was afraid that they'd hit every one of them before they ever came close to winning.

At Texas and Phoenix they had finished in the mid-twenties. At Talladega, the other restrictor plate track besides Daytona, Badger had managed to come in twelfth, with the help of a multicar wreck that had managed to take out most of the big-money competitors. "Doing well by default," one sports writer had called it.

Now tonight at Richmond it had hurt to watch him out there struggling with a car whose setup was a disaster. On every turn he had fought to keep the car from going into the wall. Given the enormous g-forces working against the left-hand turn anyhow, she knew he must be sore and exhausted. And tired of losing. He hadn't needed that scarecrow manager of his berating him after that ordeal of a race he'd just endured.

"I'm sorry about the car," Tuggle said, patting his shoulder. It was as close as she ever came to hugging anybody. "They did their damnedest, you know. Just couldn't make it work."

Badger nodded without looking up. "I hope they get the hang of this real soon."

"We all hope so. They feel like they let you down. I'm sure every one of them would rather have the blisters on your hands than the feeling of guilt they're carrying right now."

"Tell them not to take it so hard," he mumbled. "It's all part of the game."

"I did tell them." She looked bemused. "Never saw a Catch Can cry before."

He tried to smile at that, but she decided there was more wrong with him than a lousy race. Technically, the rest of it was none of her business, either, and Tuggle was fanatical about minding her own business. She was fond of saying that if she saw someone drowning, she'd ask permission before trying to save him. But Badger was her responsibility for the duration of his contract, anyhow, and she figured that made him her business. An unhappy driver wouldn't be working at peak performance.

She wished she could just wish him good night and walk out, because she wasn't looking forward to the discussion, but instead, she said, "Listen, Badger . . . I heard the conservation that just went on in here. Do you want me to call a team meeting tomorrow?"

"What?"

She spoke slowly and carefully. "I'm saying that *if you want me to,* I can say I need you at the shop at noon tomorrow. For a team meeting."

"But tomorrow is Monday."

"Yes, Badger. I know that." She sighed. Subtlety was wasted on race car drivers. "You don't have to show up at the shop. I am offering an excuse to get you out of this gig at the factory if you are in need of a reason not to go."

He gulped down the last of the water and tossed the bottle at the waste can. Bull's-eye. Too bad basketball goals weren't a foot off the ground; Badger could have had a safer athletic career. Without a word, Tuggle dug another water bottle out of the ice in the cooler and passed it over to him.

The silence lengthened as Badger made a ceremony of unscrewing the bottle cap, tossing it into the trash for another bull's-eye, and taking a long swig of water. He kept sighing and looking away, and she thought for a moment that his eyes glistened. At last he said, "That appearance thing. I have to do it."

"Have to?"

"Yeah, she said I have to do exactly what she tells me to, or she'll quit managing me."

With great effort, Tuggle willed herself not to make the reply that was clawing at the inside of her throat. She contrived to look sympathetic, or at least noncommittal.

"Five thousand dollars," said Badger, staring at the wall. "My dad was a farmer. When I was a kid, that could have kept us going for a year. Even when I first started racing, that would have been a fortune back when I was racing Late Model Stocks."

Tuggle was no stranger to hard times, either, but she didn't think people ought to let the specter of famine intimidate them. "Yeah, I understand about poor," she said. "But these days five grand wouldn't buy you enough tires to get through qualifying, much less a race. It wouldn't get the jet off the ground. Some of your colleagues spend that much on dinner."

He groaned. "I know. I know that in my head. It just feels wrong to turn down money when I don't really have anything else to do, I guess. And I don't have a lot of endorsement deals like some of the younger guys."

Tuggle agreed with him on principle, except for the fact that if he did this gig at the textile mill, it would constitute a victory for Melodie Albigre, whom the entire team now referred to as his "restrictor plate," among other less civil epithets. NASCAR had a policy of fining drivers for using foul language in interviews, which prompted Tuggle to remark that expressing her opinion of Melodie Albigre would cost her ten thousand dollars.

"Okay," she said, "But the offer still stands. If she ever tries to make you do something you don't want to do, just tell her I've called a meeting. I'll back you up. Anytime. Day or night."

Badger nodded. "I hear you," he said.

"Look, Badger. You're famous. You're rich by most people's standards. Why are you letting her push you around?"

"She says this is my last chance. She's right. These days they're hiring nineteen-year-olds straight into Cup."

"Well . . . Kyle Busch, sure," said Tuggle. "But one shrub doesn't make a forest."

"It's the way of the world, Tuggle. Times have changed since I started out. And you never know how long a career is going to last if you're an athlete. I could go into the wall in the next race and never work again."

Tuggle said nothing. You couldn't argue with that. She couldn't even bring herself to say the names of the guys whose careers had ended that way. The thought of them brought a lump to her throat. And he had taken some hard hits in the past, no question about it. That was part of the reason that she wanted to protect him. He had become a celebrity by risking his life, and he had done so with grace and courage. She respected that. As far as she could tell, Melodie Albigre did not.

"Okay, point taken," she said at last.

"Yeah, so I need to think about my future. You know, you never save enough in your heyday, because you think it's going to last forever."

Tuggle grunted. "Tell me about it." She was a lot closer to retirement age than he was, with a lot less to show for it. That's why she'd needed this job. "Okay, I understand about the money, but why *her*? There are plenty of personal managers for athletes." *Ones that don't treat you like pond scum,* she finished silently.

Badger sighed. "I don't live up here," he said. "Well, I mean, I have a place up here, but I go home as much as I can. Between that and my driving schedule, I don't have a lot of time to be finding people to work for me. She showed up, and she's been really good. She says it would cost me fifty thousand dollars in salary to get someone to do her job, and she just works on commission."

But what has she done? thought Tuggle. Oh, there was the press release she sent to the local shoppers' weekly, with enough misspelled words to make even Tuggle wince. (Deanna had seen the original, which she had been asked to mail along with a team photo of Badger.) And she had got him a few minutes on a local TV sports show that aired at midnight Saturday night. And a few local appearances that paid a few thousand dollars, but, after all, Badger was a Cup driver—and there were only forty-three of them around—so such fees were hardly evidence of great ability on the part of his manager. If she had landed him a write-up in *Newsweek,* or a segment on *60 Minutes,* or a long-term corporate partnership worth millions, that might have made her worth putting up with—but for a shoppers' weekly and a textile mill gig?

Tuggle decided to let it go. Badger was worried about his future, and he was probably wise to do so. Scaring him wouldn't help. Privately, she resolved to monitor the situation. Perhaps Melodie was simply a semicompetent boor who liked to latch on to celebrities; if she was something more dangerous than that, Tuggle would have to decide what to do about it. A tire iron would be favorite, she thought.

"Look, Badger," she said. "I'm on your side. You know that, right? We may have our share of disagreements, but I won't stand by and see anybody take advantage of you, boy."

He nodded with that sad-eyed hound look of his. With a weary sigh, he hauled himself to his feet. "I'm going home," he said.

"Thanks for worrying about me. I know you're on my side. But I'm fine, really. I'm lucky to have her."

As she heard him exit the hauler, Tuggle muttered to herself, "Boy, you'd be better off swallowing a tapeworm."

The next morning at ten minutes to ten, a haggard-looking Badger turned up in the office and perched on the edge of Deanna's desk. He bore very little resemblance to the handsome daredevil in the posters surrounding him with mocking images of his idealized self. Without a word, Deanna went to the office refrigerator and took out a blue Gatorade, which she handed him in silent commiseration.

He accepted it with a feeble smile and took a few fortifying sips. "I'm meeting Melodie here," he told the secretary.

Deanna's sympathetic expression hardened into the one she usually reserved for cockroach sightings. "I know," she said, biting off every word. "She called and said she was on her way. She asked me to have coffee ready for her."

Badger nodded. He never interfered in interoffice dynamics. Opinion varied on whether or not he even noticed them.

Deanna said, "There's something else I need to tell you before she gets here. I guess you can't do it, but . . . Well, the Roush people called and asked if you could possibly do them a favor. One of their drivers was supposed to make a visit to the children's ward of a local hospital today, but their guy is not feeling well himself, and obviously nobody wants a driver who might be contagious going to visit sick children. I'm rambling, aren't I?"

Badger, who had closed his eyes, nodded.

Deanna took a deep breath. Sitting two feet from Badger always made her nervous. She'd tell her envious friends, *He's so macho I'm afraid he'll short out my birth control patch.* But she knew that such feelings were all in her head. Badger treated everybody just the same. "Well, anyhow, Badger, all the other Roush drivers are otherwise committed today, and so they phoned here asking for you. They wondered if you would go to the children's ward. The children are really looking forward to a visit from a NASCAR driver, as you can imagine."

Badger opened his eyes and sighed. "The *Roush* people called us?" he asked.

The secretary nodded. She thought she knew why he'd asked which team had called. If the team had been Hendrick or DEI, then the driver the children were expecting to meet might have been Jeff Gordon or Dale Earnhardt, Jr. Nobody would want to be the substitute who walked into a room full of kids expecting either of them. The howls of disappointment would be deafening. But Badger probably figured that he was as kind and personable and famous as the Roush guys—well, anyhow, he wouldn't be too much of a disappointment as a substitute.

"When do they need me?" he asked.

"Well, this afternoon," said Deanna. "At one o'clock. But I checked on the whereabouts of that textile mill you're visiting, and they are too far apart. You'd never be able to get to the hospital in time."

Badger nodded. He looked up at the black-rimmed clock on the wall behind the desk. Five minutes until ten. "Which Roush driver is sick?" he asked.

Deanna told him.

"He's a good guy," said Badger. "He's doing this for nothing, of course."

"Yes, I'm sure he is—or was. Before he got the stomach flu."

He ran his hand through the bristles of his newly cropped hair. "Yeah, he would. He's not rolling in money, either. Not yet, anyhow." He sighed. "Did you tell them I had another commitment?"

Deanna shook her head. "I told them I'd ask you and let them know."

"So you think I should do it?"

She gasped. "Oh, I would never tell you what to do, Badger. I just didn't want to make a decision without consulting you first."

"I appreciate that, Deanna." He sighed again. "I think I ought to go. Look, is there anybody around today who could go with me? Is Sark here?"

"No. She e-mailed her press release about the race and said she wouldn't be in. Almost everybody is off today. Well, Rosalind Manning is here. The engine specialist. She stopped in for coffee on her way to the shop, but she's not a publicist. She doesn't seem at ease with people somehow. I mean, she's polite and all, but . . ."

"She's smart, though," said Badger. "Went to MTA, didn't she?"

Deanna fought to keep a straight face. "MIT," she said. "But they're both found in Cambridge."

"Whatever. I just need somebody to carry the autograph cards and help me field questions in case any reporters show up. And, you know, keep me on schedule. I have a real hard time saying no to people, even when I know I have to."

"I'm sure she'd be glad to go with you," said Deanna, who wasn't sure at all, but she could not imagine anyone turning down a chance to spend the day with Badger. "If you were going, that is."

"Call them back. Tell them I'll do it."

"Do what?" said Melodie Albigre from the doorway. There was a dangerous lilt in her voice, and she was jingling her keys as if she might throw them at his head.

Deanna, who had picked up the phone and was in the process of punching in the number of the Roush office, gasped at the sound of the Restrictor Plate's voice. She started to replace the receiver, but Badger touched her wrist, and said, "No. Keep dialing, Deanna," he said. "It's all right."

Melodie made a show of consulting her watch. "We need to get going, Badger," she said. "You know what traffic is like on I-85 on weekday mornings."

Badger nodded. "I can't go," he said.

"What do you mean you can't go?" She swept into the room, her voice rising with every step she took.

Thank God for cordless phones, thought Deanna, scurrying toward the back room just as someone on the other end of the line picked up. She figured that as long as she was out of earshot she'd call Rosalind's cell phone, too, and tell her to get to the office as fast as she could. Badger needed rescuing.

"I can't go to the textile mill," said Badger, who was using his slowest drawl and wearing his most mournful retriever expression in hopes of averting the coming storm. "Something important just came up."

His manager's scowl suggested that she ate retrievers for breakfast. "Something came up, did it? Where is Tuggle? She can't
schedule practices on my day."

Badger hesitated. Tuggle would back him up. She said she would.
Any time he needed an excuse, she said, he could claim he had a
team meeting, and she'd swear it was true. He sighed. The hospital appearance would probably make the local papers, anyhow,
which meant that Melodie would find out sooner or later. Why
postpone her tantrum? Besides, Badger generally told people the
truth, anyhow. He was handsome enough to get away with it. In
his experience, people usually forgave him for whatever it was he
had done to piss them off. And if they didn't, well, there were always more people to replace them in his constellation.

"I'm filling in for a Roush driver at a visit to a children's hospital," he said.

Her eyes narrowed until they looked like knife slits in her
doughy face. "Why should you?"

"It's an emergency. They asked me."

"I see. And how much are they paying?"

"It's sick children, Melodie. I don't want any money for doing
it. It's the right thing to do."

She rolled her eyes. "You are so hopeless! When NASCAR finally dumps you, you'll be living in a packing crate and sharing
your last can of Alpo with one of the other has-been field fillers."

Badger's eyes glistened and he took a couple of deep breaths.
Finally, he said, "Maybe so."

For form's sake, Rosalind knocked on the already open door. "I
heard you were looking for me," she told Badger. "Deanna told
me about your appearance today. I'm ready if you are."

Deanna, who felt it was safe to return to the room now that re-
inforcements had arrived, rushed to her desk and began rummaging in one of the lower drawers. "Don't forget your autograph
cards, Badger! And I have a new box of Sharpies that you can
take."

"I'll take them," said Rosalind, eying Badger's Restrictor Plate
with a look that bordered on civility. She had overheard that last

exchange, and her expression suggested that she had not liked it. "We should get going, though. That signing is at twelve, isn't it?"

Badger and Deanna looked at each other, both remembering that he was scheduled to appear at one. "Yes!" they said in unison.

They turned to leave, but then another thought occurred to Badger. "Do you reckon they want me to wear m'firesuit?"

"Do it," said Rosalind. "Little kids love purple."

Melodie's cell phone began to chime. "I see I'm wanted elsewhere," she said, glancing at the caller ID. "Hopefully with someone who is cooperative, and therefore capable of being helped. I'll talk to you later." She swept out without waiting for a reply.

Rosalind picked up the stack of autograph cards and stuck out her tongue at the retreating figure of Badger's manager. She murmured to Badger, "Well, now that we've got the restrictor plate off your carburetor, go change into a firesuit, and let's go see some kids."

Rosalind drove her BMW, because oddly enough Badger didn't mind being chauffeured around by other people. She put him in charge of the directions, which had been faxed over from Roush headquarters.

"Do you want to talk shop?" asked Rosalind, when they were safely onto I-85 heading south. "I don't have much in the way of chit-chat. I'm an engineer. With all the social deficiencies that implies."

"Fine with me," said Badger. "I'm still tired from yesterday."

"Do you mind if I ask you a question first?"

Badger had leaned back and closed his eyes. "Shoot."

"Why do you put up with that fourteen-carat bitch who runs your life?"

He opened one eye. "Melodie? Oh, she's an expert. Got a college degree and awards and everything."

"Who told you that?"

"Oh, she did. She's not a bit shy about telling folks her qualifications. She's going to help me hook up some business deals."

"But surely there are lots of management people who could do that. Why do you put up with someone who treats you like a stray dog with mange?"

"I guess I'm used to it," said Badger. "Women always end up

treating me like that sooner or later. They say it's the only way they can get my attention."

"But doesn't it bother you? Tuggle would like to beat her with the jack handle, just from having to watch her hassling you."

Badger sighed. "Tuggle hassles me, too."

"Not like that, though. Tuggle is tough, but I think she likes you. She respects you, anyhow. But that woman acts like you're something she stepped in."

"Well, if she makes me rich, I guess it's worth it."

"Fine. Whatever," said Rosalind, who wouldn't have put up with such treatment for any amount of money.

"Well, like I said, I'm used to it. Can I smoke?"

Rosalind resisted the urge to brake or to take her eyes off the road to gape at her passenger. "You *smoke*?"

Badger shrugged. "Trying to quit. It's hard, though. Got started when I was twelve or so. I get real edgy when I try to stop. It keeps my weight down. So—can I?"

"Sure," said Rosalind, pulling out the ashtray for him. "I don't treat my car like a temple." She thought of a couple of smart remarks she might have made about the fact that he didn't treat his body like one either, but she decided not to say them. He had been harassed enough for one day. Instead, she said, "I'm sorry about the car."

"What?" said Badger. "It's nice. I like BMWs."

"No, I mean the race. I think the engine was okay, but that doesn't help if they can't get the rest of the package right."

Badger was holding his Bic to a Marlboro Light. He smoked for a while without speaking, and Rosalind thought that smoking might be Badger's way of tempering his speech, to avoid hurting anyone's feelings with a hasty remark. She waited, concentrating on the traffic funneled into one lane by construction work on that section of road.

Finally, he said, "Almost everybody on the team is new at this. It takes time to get it right. Besides, NASCAR isn't like it was in the old days. Now a driver can't make all that much of a difference. Now it's all about multicar teams pooling their research and about testing time in the wind tunnel. Engineering tricks."

"Well, we could use some engineering tricks," said Rosalind. "I wish I had some."

"Don't beat yourself up about it," said Badger. "Even if you get a great car, and the pit crew performs perfectly, we'll never be able to compete with the big dogs. Not to the championship. They have five hundred employees. What do we have? Thirty, maybe? And they have money to burn."

"Yeah," said Rosalind. "But if we could come up with some kind of an edge, we might be able to win one race, at least. Maybe on a track where driver experience still does count for something. What track would that be?"

Badger answered in a plume of smoke. "Darlington."

They didn't talk much for the rest of the ride. Badger asked where she was from and where she'd studied engineering, but when he told him MIT, he didn't even know where it was. Rosalind's shyness made her answers short and not very informative, and he didn't seem overly interested in her personal information, anyhow. She wasn't pretty enough to matter, and she had never been any good at keeping a conversation going, because she couldn't think of much to ask him in return. The biographical facts of Badger's life were posted on half a dozen Web sites, in varying degrees of adulation, and his life in 200 words was featured in slick racing magazines, accompanied by glamorous pictures of him in the firesuit and shades. If you wanted to know how the real person differed from the media image, asking questions wouldn't do much good. By now all his answers were well-rehearsed sound bites. It had probably been years since he'd heard an original question.

The only way to get to know Badger was by observation. Rosalind wasn't all that interested in him personally, anyhow. She thought motors were much more fascinating than drivers. As long as he handled her creation with reasonable skill and brought it back in one piece, he could be a werewolf for all she cared. And yet, because he wore a glamorous firesuit and looked like a catalogue model, people wanted him to sign pieces of paper, which they would treasure forever—or until they moved on to another obsession and unloaded their autograph collection on eBay. She thought it was a curious phenomenon, but since the fans' obsession with the sport and its stars had created a job for her, she wasn't complaining.

She took the highway exit for the hospital. "Last cigarette," she said to Badger, tapping the ashtray. "Want a breath mint?"

"Got some," said Badger, rummaging in the duffel bag he'd brought with him.

"I hope you've got a change of clothes in there, too, because you'll probably expect me to take you to lunch after this, and I'm not walking into a restaurant with Spiderman."

He looked down at his firesuit and nodded mournfully. "I hear you. Brought my jeans and a sweatshirt."

She gave him an appraising look. "So you don't want to run around in public wearing that getup, either."

"Well, it's kinda hot. Besides, I wouldn't get to eat if I went out somewhere like this. I'd be signing napkins the whole time."

"It must be tiresome."

"No, it's great to see little kids get excited when they see you. To make people happy for a couple of minutes. And, you know, for most of us celebrity doesn't last all that long. For Richard Petty and Dale Earnhardt, maybe, but for most guys . . . fifteen minutes of fame."

Rosalind pulled up at the hospital entrance. "Well, it's time for you to go make some kids happy. I'll park the car and be right in. As they say in show business, *Break a leg.*"

Badger looked out at the hospital sign. "This would be the place to do it."

Ten minutes and a dozen photographs later, they were in the elevator heading up to the children's wing, accompanied by a cadre of hospital administrators, who were either NASCAR fans or gamely hospitable to the celebrity du jour. Rosalind, whose longing in life was to be invisible to her fellow human beings, felt that she had never been so close to getting her wish. People almost stepped on her, so oblivious were they to her existence. Everybody wanted to get close to Badger. Shake his hand. Hug him. Get his autograph. Give him trinkets for luck. Tell him a story about their reaction to a race he'd been in, or about the time some friend of theirs had met him. Since it was a hospital, one enterprising female staffer even had an empty box of Vagenya, which she insisted on holding up when she posed for a photo with Badger. She had held up the box with one hand and grabbed him tight around the waist with the other.

"I hope you didn't take that stuff," he muttered to her behind the plaster smile.

"Don't need to with you around, sugar," she purred, inching closer.

As they walked down the corridor to the children's ward, Rosalind, who had overheard the exchange with the avid female fan, said, "I guess you're getting pretty tired of that remark about you being more arousing than Vagenya."

Badger winced. "Everybody thinks they're the first person who ever said that to me. I guess they don't mean any harm. Sark says people don't quite believe that I'm real."

Rosalind took a step back to look at the apparition in dark shades and a purple and white firesuit. "I can't imagine why," she said.

He shrugged. "Me neither. I just try to be polite and keep moving."

"Good, because I've never been a handler before, so don't expect me to fight off women for you."

Badger brightened. "No problem. Today is kids. Kids are great."

He grabbed a stack of autograph cards from Rosalind and rushed into the room ahead of the trailing hospital entourage. The shrieks of delight from many little voices billowed out into the hall, and Rosalind smiled. Badger had given up a $5,000 appearance to do this, and that had impressed her, but now she figured it would have been a bargain for him at twice the price just to feel that much love and admiration. She would never know what that felt like, but it was fascinating to watch it happen. She just hoped she'd brought enough autograph cards.

The children's ward was large and airy with a painted mural of a forest scene on the wall. If you looked closely enough, you could find rabbits, raccoons, and a fawn within the foliage, invisible until you looked closely. A banner taped across the top welcomed the NASCAR guest, but the name of the Roush driver had been covered over with tape and typing paper and Badger's name had been inscribed in black magic marker.

He went from bed to bed, shaking hands or letting himself be hugged, and he was smiling in genuine delight at seeing these kids. By now Rosalind could tell a polite Badger smile from the real thing, and this was genuine. Some of the parents had heard about the visit from a NASCAR driver, and they had come, too, armed with everything from videos to disposable cameras, so that the entire scene was bathed in the glow of flashbulbs and camera lights, giving Badger a celestial aura. Rosalind knew that some of the crew called him the Dark Angel, but today, she thought, he was an angel of light.

For an instant, Rosalind wished she had borrowed one of Sark's cameras, because a photo of Badger surrounded by smiling children would have been a publicist's dream shot, but then she realized that Badger himself wouldn't have permitted the taking of such a photo, anyhow. It would have embarrassed him. He would pose all day with a kid whose mom had a disposable camera, but he would never let his visit be exploited for commercial purposes. Rosalind almost smiled. The Team Vagenya driver might be a scrawny little redneck, but at least he wasn't a jerk. She was proud of him. She wished she could help him win.

Many of the children had NASCAR posters and die-casts featuring the Roush driver who had been scheduled to visit, and Badger duly admired these totems of his competitor, and even signed them if the owner insisted. Sometimes, if the child had a shaved head or looked particularly ill, Badger would turn away for a moment and rub his eyes with the back of his hand.

She heard one of the parents ask Badger about Victory Junction, the camp for chronically ill children that the Petty family had founded near their home in Randolph County. She heard him say, "Sure, I've been there. That place is awesome. I think they ought to let Kyle Petty win every third race just because he's a great human being." His eyes were glistening again.

While Badger was busy scribbling his name on everything thrust at him, Rosalind began to wander around the room, handing out autograph cards and purple Team Vagenya pins to anybody who wanted one, and answering questions directed at her.

"No," she'd explain, repressing a shudder. "I'm not his wife. I'm one of the team engineers."

"Awesome!" said the redheaded boy in a wheelchair.

Suddenly, Rosalind spotted something she had not expected to find: a Badger Jenkins poster. It was taped above the bed of a frail blond girl: a smiling image of Badger in his white and purple firesuit, standing next to the team Vagenya car he had driven at Daytona. Intrigued, Rosalind forgot her aversion to strangers and went over to the little girl's bed.

"You're a fan of Badger?" she asked, trying to keep the note of astonishment out of her voice.

The little girl had been staring longingly at Badger who was still posing for pictures on the other side of the room, but now she turned to Rosalind and nodded solemnly. "I love Badger," she whispered, glancing back over her shoulder, as if he could hear her from twenty feet away.

"He'll be over here in a minute," said Rosalind, sitting down in the bedside chair. "I promise he'll come over. He's going to be so glad to see you. What's your name?"

"Elizabeth Baird."

"Wow. That's a great name. I just hope Badger can spell it."

"Well, my dad calls me Littlebit."

"Mine's Rosalind."

"Can Badger spell your name?"

Rosalind nodded. "Six different ways. So, tell me, Littlebit, how did you happen to choose Badger Jenkins as your favorite driver? Are your folks originally from Georgia?"

The little girl shook her head. "My grandparents live in Berea, Kentucky. They like Mark Martin."

"But you like Badger instead, huh? How come?"

With a sigh of exasperation at having to explain something so obvious to a grown-up, Littlebit said, "Well, *because,* silly. My favorite color is purple. I want his hat."

"I think we can send you a hat," said Rosalind. "I'll bet he'd even sign it for you. Would that do?"

A slender man in a tweed jacket hurried over to the little girl's bedside, unwrapping a roll of film for his camera. "Littlebit," he said, "you shouldn't ask strangers to give you presents. It isn't polite."

"But she's not a stranger, Daddy. She's on Badger's team."

"Mike Baird," said the man, shaking hands with Rosalind. "We all appreciate your coming to visit the kids today. Are you Badger's publicist?"

"No," said Rosalind, "I'm Rosalind Manning. I'm the team's engine specialist, so I'm out of my depth today."

Mike Baird smiled. "I'm an engineer, too," he said. "Chemical engineering. I don't think I'd be very good as a celebrity escort, either."

They watched in silence for a moment as Badger made his way through the ward, signing autograph cards, chatting with the young patients, and posing for pictures with practiced ease.

"He's great," said Mike. "I don't think he needs too much help today, so you should be fine. I'm glad he's the driver who came. Badger is Elizabeth's hero."

"He's a nice guy," said Rosalind. "It's nice to know he has a supporter here."

Badger, who had finally seen the poster of himself, hurried over just then and enveloped the delighted girl in a hug. Rosalind stood up so that he could have the bedside chair. After snapping a few pictures of his daughter and her idol, Mike Baird went over to talk to Rosalind.

"He's great with kids, isn't he?"

Rosalind nodded. "Maybe it's because he's handsome. He never has to worry about people not wanting him around. But, yes, he really likes kids. And I did promise your daughter a signed

Team 86 hat. So if you'll give me your address, I'll make sure that she gets one."

"I don't think you need to," said Mike, nodding toward Badger. "He just took his hat off, and he's signing it for her. I'm glad he's a kind person. I wouldn't have wanted her to be disappointed."

"She's a feisty kid," said Rosalind. "I hope she's not here for anything serious."

"We hope not, too. They're running tests. We try not to let her know we're worried. Right now all she cares about is getting to see the NASCAR race on Sunday."

"Will she get to see it?"

"TV in the lounge. Any chance you're going to win this one?"

Rosalind sighed. "Not much of a chance, I'm afraid. We're a one-car team, and we don't have the resources or the research to really compete against the big teams. He's a good driver, but it takes more than that in motorsports."

Mike Baird looked thoughtful. "You know, I wonder if I might be able to help you out."

> Hey, Sark! How are things going with the Dream Team? Are you hooked on Vagenya yet?
>
> No, Ed, but thanks for asking. You'll be the first to know. I have been doing feature stories on some of the pit crew women. The media is interested in them, because they are an anomaly in a male-dominated sport.
>
> Oh, good. Is it true that you have a blackjack dealer and a former Miss Norway?
>
> No, Ed. What we have is Cindy, a bluegrass musician from Arkansas, and Sigur, a farm girl from Minnesota. No sensational stories there. Just nice people doing an unusual job. Actually, I'm kind of getting hooked on Badger Jenkins. He did his good

deed yesterday. Wish I could have been with him, but I took the day off. Just my luck. It would have made a great firsthand feature.

What did he do? Rob a gas station?

You wish. He visited the children's ward of a local hospital, filling in for some other driver who got sick at the last minute. And he turned down a paid gig to do it, too. Isn't that wonderful? Not everybody thought so, though.

Really? Someone does not approve of kindness to sick children? Do tell.

According to the team secretary, Badger's odious manager, who is variously called "His Restrictor Plate," the "Dominatrix," and other less printable epithets, was furious with him.

Sounds like she isn't popular with Badger's Angels.

You could say that. None of them would spit on her if she were on fire. And she treats Badger like dirt. She is also incompetent, if you ask me.

She must be beautiful then. Famous Cup drivers do not generally take crap from people, do they? Or even from each other if I recall the Bristol race correctly.

Cup drivers have short fuses, I think, but looks are not a factor here. The Dominatrix is certainly no beauty. Don't get me started. She has the manners of a hyena, the fashion sense of a circus clown, and the composition skills of a spider monkey. I think she has promised to make Badger lots of money, but even if she were competent it would be uphill work. Badger is not what you'd call motivated. Except on the track. He'll race his heart out on a speedway, but when it comes to everything else—appearances, interviews, sponsor events—you need a cattle prod to get him there.

That sounds like a promising observation for your article, Sark. "Slacker race car driver."

No, it isn't. So what if he's not perfect? He's a damn good driver. And at least he isn't an arrogant jerk. Which is more than I can say for his manager. Today I had some die-cast cars that I wanted Badger to sign so that we could send them to various charity auctions—we get a dozen requests a week, at least. Well, Melodie was with Badger when I asked him, and before he could break away to do it, she said she'd be in touch to negotiate his fee for signing them. I wanted to slap her. She is making him look like a jerk, but he really isn't one.

Sark, Sark . . . You are a journalist. We never slap anyone. We have other ways of making them suffer. This "Melodie" sounds like a very interesting person. Well, she sounds like she probably has a coat made of Dalmatian puppy fur, but as a journalist, I am bound to find that interesting.

Ed! Of course! I'd forgotten what a pit bull you are. Could you check up on the Dominatrix? Her name is Melodie Albigre, and she works for Miller O'Neill. Oh, please tell me she's wanted in six states for ax murders.

No promises, Sark, but if she has not led a blameless life, you may trust me to uncover the fact.

"Ax murderess" is a tall order. But we can always hope for the worst. Perhaps she has written a book of kitten recipes or has a brood of six unattended children who forage from Dumpsters while she's out working. Would that cheer you up?

Well, Ed, none of that would surprise me. I'll stock up on wolfbane and garlic and wait.

CHAPTER XX

Future Shock

"*Shark* oil?" said Julie Carmichael, wondering when the Excedrin was going to kick in. You might learn a lot by going out drinking with the boys, but it was sure as hell hard on your system. She groped for her coffee cup and tried to focus on what Rosalind was saying.

Rosalind shook her head. "*Shock oil*," she said. "I've been researching it since Monday, when Badger went to visit the children's ward at the hospital, and I went along as his minder."

Melanie Sark appeared in the doorway, waving a bag of doughnuts. "Bribe!" she said. "Can I sit in on the engineers' meeting?"

Julie turned even paler at the sight of the heavily sugared doughnuts dumped out onto a paper towel on the work table. "You can't report anything about car modifications. And you can downshift that cheerfulness."

"Okay." Sark lowered her voice to a soothing monotone. "I'll take notes, but I promise not to use anything without running it past you first. I wanted to ask Roz about the hospital visit. Badger did it for free, didn't he? That was nice of him."

Rosalind nodded. "He did. And apparently good deeds do get rewarded. A little girl in the children's ward was actually a Badger fan, and—"

"I thought Badger appealed more to *big* girls."

"Littlebit is six. Her favorite color is purple, so that was Bad-

ger's edge over, say, Jeff Gordon. Anyhow, it turns out that her father is Dr. Michael Baird, who is a chemical engineer with Carolina-
Petrochem. He was so grateful to Badger for his kindness to his
daughter that he offered to give us a little help on the track."

Tuggle appeared in the doorway, with herbal tea in a Bill Elliott
mug. "We could use all the help we can get," she said. "What is he
offering?"

Rosalind said, "I asked Tuggle to sit in on this, because she'll
know more about how this applies to racing. We can run it past
Jay Bird, too, next time he's here."

"Great," said Julie. "Tell me more."

"Dr. Baird is working on an additive for shock oil." Seeing
Sark's puzzled expression, Rosalind said, "We're talking about the
oil that lubricates the shock absorbers."

Sark blinked. *Shock absorbers?* It sounded trivial to her. "So
you want Badger to be more comfortable out there?"

Tuggle laughed. "He can sit on a thumbtack for all I care. He
was supposed to have lunch with Christine yesterday, but he blew
her off. Turns out she had a potential sponsor lined up to meet
him. She's not happy."

Julie said, "Shock absorbers aren't just for comfort, Sark. Shocks
do soften the bumps to keep the tire in constant contact with the
road, but for race cars, the important factor is that shocks control
the weight transfer of the car."

"Absorbing down force," said Rosalind. "They absorb the banking forces. Every time the race car hits a banked turn, there is
huge downforce acting on the tires, the springs, and the shocks."

"I'm a journalist," said Sark. "Keep it simple."

Julie tried again. "Turning a race car is all about controlling the
weight on the car. That's why we weigh it so many times and put
in different springs and different shocks. We build the inside of
our shocks to have certain characteristics. When the shock oil
heats up, it flows through the valve and shim stack at a different
rate, which changes the characteristics."

"That's one of the reasons we have to make adjustments as the
race goes on," said Tuggle.

"Complex turns are a factor at Darlington," said Julie. "If we can take those turns a hairsbreadth faster than anybody else, we stand a good chance of winning."

"Okay," said Sark, making notes on her legal pad. "What would make you take the turns faster?"

"Badger's talent," said Tuggle. "He's the key. But if the engineers can give him some technical help, it could make all the difference."

"Better shocks means that you have more control, especially in those turns where the downforce is such a factor," said Rosalind.

"Shocks also help take care of the tires," said Tuggle. "Darlington is hell on tires."

"Right," said Julie. "So, on every lap around the NASCAR track, Sark, there are at least four cycles on the shock: two for loading and two for unloading."

"It adds up," said Rosalind. "For a five-hundred-mile race, you're talking about two thousand cycles. Each instance of loading and unloading will generate heat in the shock."

"Heat," said Sark, writing it down. "Heat is bad?"

"It alters the performance of the shock. Cuts down on efficiency—not much, but some. And in this sport, a hundredth of a second counts. Improved heat transfer would keep the shock operating at maximum efficiency."

Tuggle said, "Shock absorber technology is an old shell game in NASCAR. At Daytona and Talladega the teams used to rig up shocks that would go down when the car hit the track and they never went back up, which made for good aerodynamics, but it made the car damn near impossible to control. NASCAR put up a stop to that. Now they issue the shocks to each team before the race at those two tracks."

"But not at Darlington?" said Sark. This week they were headed for Darlington.

"Right," said Tuggle. "Not at Darlington."

One thing about being a journalist—you had to catch on quickly. Sark cut to the chase: "And this guy you met in the hospital has figured out how to keep shock absorbers from heating up?"

"Well, not entirely," said Rosalind, "But he has developed an additive that keeps the oil cooler than it otherwise would be. He hasn't announced his findings yet, but he offered to let us try it out in the race Sunday."

"He's going to give us some?"

"I can pick it up today," said Rosalind.

"Is it illegal?" asked Sark.

Tuggle, Julie, and Rosalind all looked at each other. *"Not yet,"* said Julie carefully.

"Not this week," said Rosalind.

"But when NASCAR finds out it exists, they'll write a rule prohibiting it," said Tuggle. "But this week, anyhow, we've got an edge."

Sark set her wineglass next to the computer. It had been a long day, but she couldn't go to bed until she checked her messages. As soon as she had logged on, there was an IM from Ed Blair.

> Hey, Sark. Sorry I haven't checked in for a while. I got an assignment in Memphis—feature story on the jazz scene there. Probably not your cup of Quaker State these days, though. How are things going with the Dream Team?

> Sometimes it feels like I'm working for NASA, Ed. The engineers are always jazzing up some part of the car and worrying about modifying an obscure part to improve performance by a hundredth of a second or so. I bought my way into one of their meetings today with a bag of Krispy Kremes, and Julie and Rosalind were very patient about explaining things to me, but they refuse to let me do any articles about the technical modifications they're working on.

> Why should you care? Engineering is a very hard-sell topic in feature journalism. Too technical for the average reader. Even if you catch the team cheating, the explanation would be so convoluted that you couldn't make anyone care.

I wasn't thinking of ratting on them, Ed. They aren't doing anything that every other team in racing isn't doing. Car modification is a cat-and-mouse game that everybody plays—staying just ahead of the next rule change. Actually, I admire their expertise. Compared to the big five-car teams, they have so little to work with, but they're all keeping crazy hours trying to make the team competitive. They have a new trick this week, but I can't tell you what it is.

I wouldn't understand it, anyway. This is your story, not mine. What about Badger? Any dirt on him?

Not really. I have no complaints about Badger Jenkins. He can be exasperating, apparently, when he doesn't show up at the race shop or when he tries to get out of some dull but necessary bit of team business. Badger can't focus worth a damn except in a race car, but he's a sweet guy. He's not a jerk.

Ever thought about seducing him, Sark? That would be a juicy story.

I did think about it, but not for journalistic reasons. In that firesuit he is a very pretty pony. Anyhow, he affected not to notice my one tentative display of interest. (He gave me a hello hug here at the shop one time, and my response said a lot more than "Hello." He looked sort of surprised, but nothing came of it.) The consensus around here is that Badger Jenkins is not virtuous. He's just damned picky. Any *Playboy* centerfold who lost ten pounds and spent a week at a spa might have a shot with him.

I had those standards, too, but in my case they amounted to a vow of celibacy, so I've become easier to please. You can hug me anytime.

Thanks for the offer. I'll take you up on it when Badger asks me for *your* autograph. Meanwhile, I would like to put on a spiked vest and hug his manager. Spikes dipped in poison, that is.

"Malady" Albigre? Why? Have you had another run-in with her?

Yes, I suppose you could say that I've tangled with her. I am the team publicist. That is my *job*. But she seems to think that her job is to schmooze with sponsors and journalists on Badger's behalf. The problem with that is that she has all the charm of a cobra with PMS. She generally manages to annoy people in less than five minutes. She talks to the owner (Christine) as if Badger were doing the team a big favor by driving for them—bad idea in a profession with only forty-three job openings! She seems to think he could do better on a bigger team, which is probably true, but he is neither young enough nor famous enough for them to want him. Don't get me wrong: I adore him. We all do, but he's not NASCAR's golden boy. And *she's* no help to his situation. The team hates her. She e-mails me at least twice a week, usually to order me around as if I were her clerk, and despite the fact that I correct her after every message, she still spells my name "Melonie."

Well, *Melanie,* perhaps your perfume smells like cantaloupes? You know: Melon-ie.

Yeah. Or maybe the Dominatrix is dumber than a rock.

Hmmm. The Queen of the Badgers is beginning to interest me. Stay tuned while I call in favors, *Sarque.* I shall make inquiries.

*   *   *

There were legions of people—most of them female—who would have given worlds to know what went on inside the brain of Badger Jenkins, and most of the time it would have been very difficult indeed to pinpoint any particular train of thought inside the bundle of shiny bits *(appetites and instincts),* grass and twigs *(mannerisms of charm and defensive strategies),* and bits of colored string *(skill, shrewdness, and common sense),* that all woven together passed as Badger's mind.

But *when he put the helmet on . . . When the green flag dropped and the engines roared and the world flashed past at 200 mph . . .* Then one could read his thoughts like the ticker tape of a stock machine, because then and only then his mind focused into one single groove, zeroed in on the process of looping the oval faster than anybody else, lap after lap, until the checkered flag ended the exercise, and other thoughts were allowed to flow back into his consciousness.

He had raced at Darlington many times before. He liked Darlington. He had won the Southern 500 there. And while to the casual observer every circular race track may look the same, they aren't. This is how stock car racing differs—and becomes more difficult—than football or basketball, sports in which no matter where you compete the dimensions of the playing field are always the same. But in NASCAR, all the tracks are different. Every week presents a different set of challenges requiring different skills. The tracks vary in length from half a mile to more than two miles, which, among other things, changes the speed at which drivers race. Variations in banking change the angle and elevation of the turns at each track. Some tracks are not perfect ovals. Some tracks are road courses, so that even "left turn only" is not always the rule. A driver must master not one pattern of skills, but many—a different set each week.

Darlington.

The track is 1.366 miles long, and egg-shaped—wider on one end than on the other. Therefore, the turns on the narrow end of the egg are tighter than those on the wide end. Also, the banking in Turns Three and Four, the tighter turns, is two degrees steeper than on Turns One and Two, which means that every corner presents a different problem for the driver. As you hurtle up the track at nearly 150 mph, the walls seem to jump in front of the car. A second's inattention will put you in the wall. You are perilously close to the wall already. As you loop the speedway, the grooves in the track channel your car closer and closer to the wall as you go, so that at each revolution you pass only inches from disaster. The "Darlington Stripe," a long black mark down the right side of the car, attests to the times when you misjudge the turn and actually come in contact with the wall.

This was a driver's track, where skill mattered as much as expensive technology. The qualifying record had been set back in 1996 by Ward Burton: 173.797 mph. The record for speed during an actual race was much less than that: 139.958, set by Dale Earnhardt in 1993. Badger didn't think he had a shot at breaking either of those records this year, but at least he didn't hate Darlington the way some drivers did. He respected the "Lady in Black" as the track was called, and he knew that Dale Earnhardt had been right when he said that if you got fresh with her, she would slap you down.

When Sark was writing her team press release on the Thursday before the race, she asked Badger to explain his strategy for winning Darlington. "Just one sentence," she warned him. "All I want is a sound bite."

Badger thought about it for a moment between swigs of Gatorade, and then said, "To win Darlington: *Aim for the wall and miss.*"

Badger was not a chatty driver. Very seldom did his voice come over the headset, except in answer to a question from Tuggle, but if Sark, the novice at racing, had been allowed to tune into Badger's thoughts as he raced at Darlington, their telepathic dialogue might have gone like this:

A lot of times at Darlington a car will look loose on the back end . . . that's bad . . . if your car's nose won't turn, you're out of control, so you'll probably be getting a Darlington stripe. You know . . . scrape the wall, maybe wreck, even . . .

So you're saying that if the nose is not turned prop-erly, the car will wreck?

Right. You go straight when you get on the gas . . . Here at Darlington you've got four apexes to contend with, instead of the usual two . . . You use a diamond maneuver. . . . You go straight into the corner, and you exit on a straight edge the same way.

But what is an apex?

I'm coming into one now. It's the turn at the bottom of the banking . . . You let the car drift up to the wall and ease on the throttle at the top of the corner . . . you enter—Stay on it. . . . Stay on it . . .

On it? The throttle?

"Stay on it" means to stay on the throttle as long as your butt can stand it. Usually the pucker factor con-trols this issue. . . .

Until it scares the shit out of you?

Yeah, so stay on it as long as you can. . . . You're right on the wall, as you're going straight. Then you let off the gas; turn to the bottom of the groove. . . . If the nose is wrong, the car is still gonna slide . . . If the nose is pointed and you are *not* sliding, then you work up to the top groove, aiming for as close to the wall as you can get. . . .

Why?

Because the traction is at the top part of the track. As you enter the corner, you apply the throttle. See, I'm going up the hill . . .

She sees him going down the front stretch wide open. As he sets himself up for Turn One, he dives low near the white line, backs off the gas, grabs a little brake, drifts the car up the banking until it is almost touching the wall. *(This is called "walking up the track.")* Then as he comes off Turn Two, right where the wall wants to reach out and grab him, he eases the car a little to the left and points the nose down the backstretch.

> I'm at the top of the hill now . . . full throttle . . . There is a bad dip at the top of Turns One and Two. If the car is not pointed straight, the back end will come around. You got a *push-loose condition . . .*
>
> *Which is?*
>
> When the damn car is so tight in the front end that I have to turn the wheel so far left that it makes the back end of the car want to turn around on me. Sometimes the car is so tight that I have to put so much wheel into it when I get back to the gas that I lose the back end, and because of the car not being straight, I end up chasing the car up the hill.
>
> *So you fight your way through the Turn Two apex, balancing the turning of the wheel against back end's tendency to slide, so that you don't skid into the wall. . . . Then what?*
>
> Now the track gets really narrow, coming out off Turn Two . . . I'm going downhill . . . easing out of the throttle . . . Then I hit the apex. I'd not keep it out. I aimed right for it.
>   Early apex. Use bottom groove to make your car turn left.
>   Another big bump off of Turn Two the whole back end squats down . . . going into Turn Three—a lot of

guys would stay up high. I'd go down to the bottom, drive in really deep, and for the most part straight.

Heavy braking until you hit the apex, then ease off the brake . . . Then a second or two later, I apply the brake again just to slow the momentum. Now the car is walking up the track.

And that means . . . Drifting up the bank toward the wall, right?

Uh-huh. So you ease back on it, next to the wall. When the car is almost straight, go to full throttle . . . twenty or thirty yards on full throttle . . . Sharp turn . . . Ease up a little . . . then full throttle again . . . Oh, and the braking technique is used more in Turn Three than in Turn One.

Good to know.

Aggressive on entry . . . aggressive all the way around . . . if the car is set up right, you are sitting wasting time if you're not aggressive. Burning daylight.

Okay. Okay. I get it.

When the car is right, just before the middle of the corner, I go to the throttle hard . . . Also, when the car is right, you throttle up and go to the inside to pass . . .

On the inside? Why?

The inside is the preferred groove there. Because everybody else is running close to the wall, so most of the passing is done on the inside.

And the other cars have to get out of your way?

Look, Darlington is hell on tires. After about twenty
laps the good cars shine. If the set-up is right it cuts
down on tire wear. When your car is not right, every
lap can feel like an eternity; but when the set-up is
perfect, the other cars just become obstacles in your
way. When I'm running good, I can average passing
one car per lap. Do you get it now?

*Well, no. You might as well be saying the Lord's
Prayer in Comanche. But I'll take your word for it.
Aim for the wall and miss.*

But *only* if your race car is perfectly set up, and only if you have
the reflexes of a tiger, the courage of a teenaged rhinoceros, and
the focusing ability of an electron microscope.

Badger Jenkins was a superb driver—better than his win-loss
record would have showed, because he had always driven on
underfunded one-car teams, where talent was almost the only
weapon he had against the corporate giants of the sport. He may
have been hell on owners, sponsors, and people who loved him,
but he drove like an angel of light. For 367 laps at Darlington that
day, he etched his diamonds, double apexed his turns, aided by
augmented shock absorbers that didn't overheat, and his engine
held up, while he dodged the wrecks and lucked out on the caution flags, which always came just as he was in need of fresh tires
or more fuel. The pit crew was in top form at last—hopeful, confident, and comfortable in their roles in the intricate ballet that was
a thirteen-second pit stop.

Sometimes the universe simply aligns itself in such a way that
things go absolutely right for one person, and this was Badger
Jenkins's day. Two of the superstars had engine trouble, and another one lost a lap on a tire blowout. Another golden boy got
caught up in somebody else's wreck, damaging his car so badly
that he was out of contention. What it all boiled down to was the
fact that everybody who could have beaten Badger had a bad day,
while he had a phenomenally good one.

By the time the race had wound down to a ten-lap shoot-out

between Badger and the driver that the pit crew referred to as the "Prairie Dog," the 86 team was hovering between elation and the fear that even taking a deep breath could break the spell. *Eight laps* . . . Badger was holding his own, diving into every corner as if he were going to plow straight through the wall, and then at the last second cutting the diamond in the opposite direction, blasting down the straightaway, and then repeating the maneuver at the next turn. *Five laps* . . . He was keeping a one-second lead over the Prairie Dog, which didn't sound like much, until you consider that races can be won by thousandths of a second. *Three laps* . . . The Prairie Dog scrapes the wall in Turn Two, which costs him a fraction of a second.

"Prairie Dog's shocks are going," said Tuggle. "Yours are holding, though, right?"

"Doin' fine," said Badger. "I think we may be gonna win this sum bitch."

"Bring it home, boy," said Tuggle, trying to keep the catch out of her voice.

And he did.

Some of the younger drivers these days mark their wins in theatrical ways. The affable Carl Edwards does a backflip off the hood of his car. Two-time Cup champion Tony Stewart climbs the fence to collect the checkered flag from the official on the tower. Many drivers celebrate by cutting doughnuts in the infield or doing burnouts on the track. But Badger was an old-school driver, and mostly the old-timers did not believe in showing off.

So Badger's victory was celebrated in the restrained tradition of his predecessors. He let down the window net, collected the checkered flag, and took his Victory Lap, while the pit crew sprinted off to Victory Lane to join in the celebration, which was as much theirs as his. He couldn't have done it without them.

He drove the car into Victory Lane, climbed out the window, and hugged whoever was closest to the car. Tuggle. Christine. Sigur. Reve. Sark.

With microphones and television cameras thrust in his face,

Badger managed a grin, and launched into a carefully worded sound bite: "Like to thank my crew, and all the folks at Team Vagenya. We had a really good car, and they really came through for me out there. They've all worked hard to get this team up to speed, and I'm glad I didn't let them down today."

A simple speech. A variation of what everybody else said, week after week, from one Victory Lane to the next. But if the one who says it this week is your driver, and if it is you that he is thanking, then the words are more eloquent than Shakespeare.

Shortly after he exited the car, Badger was given something to drink—never mind what he wanted. He would be given the officially sanctioned beverage, whose makers have paid dearly for their product to be the one approved drink to be imbibed in Victory Lane.

As team publicist, Sark finally had the chance to assist for real in the Victory Lane ritual called The Hat Dance. The winning driver is photographed over and over in the aftermath of the race, and each of the team's sponsors wants a shot of the driver wearing their insignia. The purple and white Vagenya hat went first. *Pose. Smile. Click.* And then he swapped the first hat for another sponsor's cap. *Pose. Smile. Click.* On and on.

Then he posed with the trophy. The last time Badger had won at Darlington, the trophy had featured a crystal globe, but the track had recently rethought that design, and now they presented the winning driver with a layout of the Darlington Raceway mounted flat on a small pedestal. Badger hoisted the trophy over his head, while the team crowded around him, trying not to look astonished that they had won.

Most of the time the pit crew figured only as a jubilant crowd in the background of the celebration, but because the 86 team was a novelty—all female—they got more attention than Badger did. No one said anything more profound than his simple thank-you speech, but for almost exactly fifteen minutes, they were famous. And on Tuesday morning, "Littlebit" Baird would receive Badger's racing helmet, signed by the entire 86 team as thanks for her part in the victory.

ENGINE NOISE
Your Online Source for NASCAR News & Views

Endangered Species? Is it open season on "badgers" in Cup racing? *Engine Noise* is hearing that, despite the big win at Darlington on Sunday **(YOU GO, GIRLS!),** the Warrior Princess of the 86 team is getting pretty fed up with her unhousebroken Badger. He blows off sponsor meetings, weasels his way out of appearances, and almost missed the plane to last week's race. Hearing, too, that nobody likes having to deal with the person on the other end of the Vagenya driver's leash. He may be a badger, but by all accounts she is a skunk. He'd better fumigate his business office before the stench drives everyone away and costs him his ride. We love you, Badger, but "Unchained Melodie" is our least favorite song!

CHAPTER XXI

Teaser Stud

"You got a lotta sand," said Badger.

Instinctively, Taran reached down to brush off her jeans, before she realized that this expression was Badger-speak for possessing gumption and courage. "Thank you," she said meekly.

Badger grinned. "Bouncing around in the car back at Bristol. And you didn't scream once." He patted her arm. "Good job."

Wednesday night in Mooresville: Taran had been the last one left in the garage. She was working late because Tony had asked her to check out the wiring on the fans for his Late Model Stock race car to see if she could figure out why they weren't working. When Badger stopped by about eight on his way back from dinner, just to see what was going on, or to refute the accusation that he was never around between races, he had found her there alone at the workbench, peering at a tangle of colored wires.

She wasn't finished, but when Badger snared a blue Gatorade out of the refrigerator *(Taran herself made sure they never ran out)* and started to leave, Taran had walked outside with him. It was a clear, cool night with a quarter moon and the usual measly complement of stars visible in the haze of greater Charlotte. Taran's heart was pounding to the beat of *"I am alone with Badger Jenkins."* Unfortunately, it is difficult to think up any small talk when you have to keep reminding yourself to breathe.

"Thank you for paying my fine," she said.

He smiled. "You've already thanked me about six times for that, sweetie. Are you gonna thank me one time for every dollar of the fine?"

"It was so kind of you to do it, though," she said. "I'm so glad you turned out to be a nice guy. Before I joined the team, I was a Badger Jenkins fan."

He tilted his head back and peered at her, surprised. *"Was?"*

"Oh, I still am. It's just that sometimes I forget that you're *him.*"

She could see his face in the glow of the shop's outdoor security light. Badger looked bewildered, and Taran thought, *I may never have another chance to tell him. Let me just say it and hope I can make him understand. Nobody should be loved so much and not know it.*

Aloud, she said, "Do you know why I went to work on this team, Badger? Because I loved you." She waved away whatever reply he had been about to make. "Oh, not *you,* really, Badger. I didn't even know *you.* But I once stood in line for an hour in the hot sun at Atlanta to have you scrawl your name across a tee shirt, and you barely looked up when you signed it. It didn't matter, though. I loved you so much. Do you guys understand that? How much we care about you? That we cry when you wreck? That we know your dog's name. That every October there are birthday parties in your honor that you don't even know about, given by people you've never even heard of—celebrating *your* birthday."

Badger looked embarrassed. "Wa-all, thank you," he said softly.

She sighed. "No. Don't *thank* me. I didn't do it on purpose— care about you, I mean. One day I was watching NASCAR races without particularly caring who won, and the next moment *you* were all that mattered."

He tilted his head back and narrowed his eyes, the way he did when he was paying closer attention. "Which win was that?" he asked.

"You didn't win that day. You *wrecked.* Fourteen cars slammed into you broadside at Talladega, and I started crying, and after that I guess I never stopped, because you were having one lousy season that year. I was so scared that you were hurt, and I stayed scared for every single race after that. Sometimes I'd start crying during the National Anthem.

"But don't *thank* me, Badger. If I could have fallen in love with Tony Stewart, believe me, I would have. He had a great year, and being his fan would have been a much less painful experience, but fandom doesn't work that way. It just *happens.*" She shrugged. "It's like a cross between falling in love and typhoid fever. We can't help it. Do you understand?"

Badger shook his head. "It's just me," he said. "There's the fire-suit and the dark sunglasses, so I guess I look different, but underneath all that, it's just *me.*"

She looked at him appraisingly, marveling as she always did at the difference between Badger Jenkins in person and the Dark Angel who turned up on every autograph card, tee shirt, and coffee mug that featured him. "No," she said at last. "I don't think you are *just you* when you're out there. Not to your fans, anyhow." She managed a misty smile. "For one thing, you're taller."

"Well, those pictures make me look good, I guess. Better than I really look."

"It's more than that, Badger. It's as if ten thousand strangers loved you so much—loved the idea of you, anyhow—that they built you a soul, and the force of that collective belief made *him* more real than you are. If reality is a consensus of opinion, then he *is* more real than you are. How many friends do you have? A dozen, maybe? Well, there are ten thousand women who would sleep with him if he simply nodded in their direction. And a thousand people would die for him."

He shivered. "That doesn't have anything to do with me," he said. "Not really."

"No, I suppose not, but people like their dreams to be tangible, and so three hundred people wait in line to shake *your* hand . . . and they take *your* picture . . . and trembling women hug *you* . . . because it's the closest that any of us can come to touching *him.*"

"I try to be nice to people," he said simply. "I'm not anything special. I was just lucky."

She stared at him as if he were a stranger. It was like having a conversation about some absent third person. "I loved you so much," she said, wonderingly, as if she couldn't quite remember why. "Do you know why I took this job on your pit crew?"

He shifted uneasily, as if he expected her to lunge at him. Women did, sometimes, and this whole line of discussion was making him sweat. "Uh . . . To get to know me?"

"No. To *protect* you. I just couldn't sit there staring at a TV screen any longer, worrying about whether your tires were bad, or if your safety harness had been fastened right. So I decided to join the team for my own peace of mind, because I figured it was better to do something than to sit home and worry."

"Oh, I'll be all right," he said, giving her his aw-shucks grin. "Never been hurt bad out there."

She opened her mouth to say something and then thought better of it. At last she murmured, "It only takes once."

There didn't seem to be any point in saying what she had been thinking: *But you have been hurt out there. Lots of times. Bruises, sore muscles, cracked ribs—a whole catalogue of minor in-juries, but I wonder if someday they'll come back to haunt you in the form of arthritis. That isn't the worst of it, though. It's the concussions I worry about. All the times you slammed into the wall and lost an hour or a day, and walked around for two weeks afterward with a splitting headache and a tiny chunk of your life missing. Sometimes you even got past the doctors by pre-tending you were all right, and they let you drive a few days later. What's that going to cost you down the road? Parkinson's? Dementia? Nobody knows what repeated head injuries do long term. When you're old. When you're not famous anymore. When all those people who loved* him *have forgotten about* you. *Who will take care of you then?*

She didn't say any of it, though, and as much as she wanted to hug him, she didn't do that, either. He was too immured in his own fame—*sometimes he even mistook himself for the Dark Angel,* she thought. Badger would have thought she was hitting on him, and she'd have had to let him think that, because she couldn't bear to tell him that she was simply afraid for him, that someday it was all going to come crashing down, and she didn't know what would become of him after that. *Anyhow,* she told herself, *holding someone doesn't really protect him from any-thing, no matter how much you wish it could.*

Suddenly, and with a look of infinite sadness, Badger held out his arms, and Taran stumbled forward and put her head on his shoulder. She wouldn't exactly remember this embrace, because it lasted only a few seconds, while the duration of all her fantasies of hugging Badger Jenkins added up to hours and hours. There wasn't much similarity between the fantasy and the reality. For starters, it wasn't a passionate embrace. It was the sort of hug you would get from your grandfather if you fell off your bike. And she had to bend her knees a little in order to rest her head on his shoulder, which certainly hadn't happened in any of the thousand scenarios in her head. He felt as bony and insubstantial as a bird, she thought. Somehow she had assumed that underneath the firesuit his body would be muscular and solid, but now through the thin tee shirt she thought she might be able to count his ribs. He wasn't the Dark Angel, not even close. She had known that in-tellectually, of course, but now she could even *feel* it.

What was odd was what she *didn't* feel. In the thousand prac-tice laps in her head, this moment would be the starting point. . . . *And then I tilt my head up and kiss him. . . . And then I put one hand in the small of his back, and the other hand on his . . .*

But she didn't feel like doing any of that. It was like hugging your brother. *He's just being kind,* she thought. She barely had time to register these observations before he gently released her and stepped back peering at her with that earnest Badger expres-sion that people called his "retriever look."

"You're a great teammate, sweetie," he said. "You try real hard, and I thank you for all the worrying you do about me. I know about all that luck stuff you've been puttin' on the car, and you're a sweet girl. But don't put me on a pedestal."

Taran blinked at him. "What?"

"I'm just an ordinary guy. I'm not perfect. I'm not special. I'm just real good at driving a car. Don't make too much of that. Don't believe I'm more than I am."

Taran opened her mouth to remind him that she already knew all that. Hadn't she just said so? But before she could utter a word, her brain registered two salient points: he had barely heard a word of what she'd just said, and this speech of his sounded very well-rehearsed. As if he had said it hundreds of times. Maybe thousands. To the starlets and stewardesses who wanted to bag a race car driver. To all the adoring fans who thought they loved him when they didn't even know him. To the pit lizards.

"I won't," she said in a hoarse whisper, which was all she could manage.

"That's good. You take care now, and I'll see you tomorrow at practice."

She never thought she'd be glad to see Badger Jenkins walk away, but she was. She wanted to make sure he was out of earshot before she started to cry.

Fifteen minutes later, she was sitting cross-legged on the floor of the garage throwing lug nuts into a coffee can when Rosalind Manning found her. She had come back to see if she'd left her cell phone on the workbench, but one look at Taran's blotched and puffy face made her temporarily abandon that errand. Rosalind had seen Badger's Crossfire pulling out of the parking lot as she was coming in, so she knew that Taran's current emotional state had to do with him.

Inwardly, Rosalind cursed herself for being the one to find her. She avoided people whenever she could, and she hated emotional scenes. This had been a cataclysm waiting to happen. Everybody knew it. Little Taran with her Gatorade shrine for Badger and her magic amulets to protect him out there. Taran made her think of those paintings of the Virgin Mary that depicted her with her heart on the outside of her dress. That was Taran, all right. Everybody knew it—even Badger, thanks to Kathy Erwin, who, being a slightly malicious Good Samaritan, had made sure that Badger noticed. Kathy had told him, "You know, you ought to take care of Taran. She's dying for it, Badger. Hell, you could nail her and she'd pay for the room."

A spectrum of emotions—none of them good—had passed over Badger's handsome face like clouds across a landscape, but finally he settled on mournful sincerity. "I can't do it," he said.

"She's what the guys call a scary girl. She wouldn't look twice at anybody else in the world, but I could have her if I snapped my fingers. Thing is, though, then she'd *never go away.* Yeah. The Scary Girl. You don't ever want to mess with *her.*"

When she told the story to some of the team, Kathy had ended it with, "And then just because he is an arrogant, spoiled typical male *jerk,* he had to add, *'Besides, she's not all that hot, anyhow.'* " But nobody was ever going to tell Taran he'd said that. They all took a solemn vow. And she was pretty sure that Badger would never tell her, either, because he might be a jerk in sexual matters, but there was a gentle side to him, too, which Rosalind had never expected to find in a race car driver. Go figure. Oh, she wouldn't have wanted him if his kisses cured cancer, but at least she could still manage a grudging respect for him.

Now what was she going to say to poor Taran, crying her eyes out for somebody who didn't exactly exist?

Rosalind decided to go with the one recurring image she'd been having about the two of them. She sat down on the workbench next to Taran, and without preamble, she said, "Do you know anything about horses?"

Taran raised a tear-stained face and stared in bewilderment at Rosalind. "About h—horses?"

"Yes. Specifically about how they breed thoroughbreds."

Taran shook her head. "No. And if you're trying to take my mind off Badger, it won't work."

"No, I'm still on the original topic," said Rosalind. "See my mother's family was mad for horses. When I got interested in cars instead of show jumpers, they were all bitterly disappointed. So, horses are not my thing, but I couldn't help knowing about them, growing up in the family I had."

"Okay, but what do horses have to do with anything?"

Rosalind shrugged. "You just reminded me of something, that's all. When they're getting ready to breed a mare, they need to get her aroused so she'll be ready to be mounted by the stallion they want her to mate with. So they put her in a fenced paddock next to one that holds the teaser stud."

"The what?"

"Teaser stud." Rosalind smiled. "A sexy stallion to put her in the mood. She can see him and smell him, but she can't reach him, because there's a fence between them. Oh, but he's a good-looking little stud."

"A good-looking little stud," echoed Taran.

"Sexy as hell. Thinks he's God's gifts to mares. But—*get this*—the teaser stud is almost always a *Shetland pony!* He's beautiful. He's passionate. He's hot. But he's soooo tiny. One time I saw an aged Tennessee Walker brood mare back up to the fence separating her from a darling little miniature horse stud. It was hilarious because she was so hot for him and he was all for it, too, but even had they been in the same pasture, he literally would not have been up to the job. Now to anybody watching this, the little teaser stud is so ridiculous because he takes himself so seriously, and everyone can see how absurd it is—everyone, that is, *except* the mare who is the object of his attention."

Taran thought about it. "I'm the mare, aren't I?"

"I think so. And I see Badger as your teaser stud. You're hot for him, all right, but everyone except you can see that it just wouldn't work."

Taran's eyes welled with tears again. "Okay, but does the mare ever get to mate with the teaser stud? *Ever?* Just once?"

"Nope," said Rosalind cheerfully. "He's strictly there to do the prep work. But he's probably not as good as he looks, anyhow."

"Why are you telling me this? Are people laughing at me because of how I feel about him?"

"No," said Rosalind. "I don't see any of that, Taran. Okay, maybe some of us feel sorry for you, because we can all see how hopeless it is, but you're so sincere, and it's obvious that you care about him so much that only a heartless person would mock you for it. Badger is walking on eggshells trying not to hurt you. He's a little oblivious sometimes, but he's not heartless. I told you about teaser studs because we don't want you to lose the real thing while you're pursuing the illusion."

Taran wiped her eyes. "Have you ever noticed that Badger is always saying things to people like *'Don't like me too much,'* or *'Don't put me on a pedestal.'* It's strange, isn't it? Everybody else in the world is worried that nobody will ever love them enough, and here's Badger turning down offers of affection right and left. *'Sorry. I have enough love already, thanks anyway.'* I cannot even imagine what that would feel like. To have too much love."

"Don't look at me," said Rosalind. "I couldn't win a popularity contest even if nobody else entered. Fortunately, I don't like people enough to care. But in Badger's case, maybe he does have a point. Maybe you really shouldn't like him too much."

"I don't have a chance with him, anyhow," said Taran. "I'd be competing with models and movie stars."

Only until they got a good long look at Marengo, Georgia, thought Rosalind. She said, "I'll bet there's somebody you have more in common with."

Taran was silent for a few moments. At last she said, "There's Tony Lafon from the shop. I've been going to the track to watch him race for a couple of months, and sometimes we go out to dinner or to the movies. Not dating really."

Rosalind thought the smart remark, but managed not to utter it aloud. Instead, she said, "Tony is a great guy. He's about your age too. When I first came to North Carolina, I worked at one of the local speedways to learn about racing, and I got to know Tony there. He's a nice guy. Smart, too. He's got a real future, I think. At least a romance with him wouldn't feel like convoy duty. Being the significant other of a Cup driver is probably a species of martyrdom, if you ask me."

"Tony is my friend," said Taran.

"Exactly my point," said Rosalind. "Nobody ever sleeps with the Dark Angel, Taran. Nobody. He's either your friend or he's an airbrushed poster on the wall. There's no in-between."

"But Badger . . . I love him so much," whispered Taran.

"I'll bet you like him better when he's not around," said Rosalind. "Tell me something. What songs make you think of him?"

Like most people who spend a lot of time in their heads, Taran knew her own soundtrack pretty well. " 'My Sweet Lord' by George Harrison," she said. "And—well, it's a pretty mixed bag. 'I Don't Know How to Love Him' from *Jesus Christ Superstar.* Ummm . . . Some old ones my grandma used to sing to me . . . 'Abide with

Me' . . . 'In the Garden' . . . 'Precious Lord, Take My Hand' . . .
Let's see, what else?"

"Never mind," said Rosalind grimly. "Those will do. Taran, think
about it. Those songs are all *hymns.*"

"What?"

"Hymns. They're not sexy love songs; they are expressions of
religious devotion. Think about that." She laughed. "Oh, boy, the
ultimate teaser stud. Badger Jenkins is not a guy to you. He's the
Impossible Dream."

"That's another one of my songs," said Taran.

"Of course it is. If anyone ever loved purely and chastely from
afar, it is definitely you."

"How did you know?"

Rosalind sighed. "Oh, it takes one to know one, Taran. I'm not
very good with people, either. I'm not beautiful, which makes me
shy, and I have an engineer's brain, which makes me stand back
and examine everything critically, even my own emotions."

"No happy ending, huh?" said Taran, wiping her eyes.

"No, this *is* the happy ending," said Rosalind. "You walk away
and the dream never dies. If you ever got him, even for just one
night, that would be the tragedy, because you might get Badger,
but you'd lose the Dark Angel forever—and that's who you really
wanted, kiddo. The Dream. The Dark Angel."

CHAPTER XXII

What the Hell Happened?

Ed! We won the race at Darlington! That means we made the All-Stars!

Oh, good, Sark. I always liked baseball better, anyway.

Smart ass. The All-Star is next weekend's nonpoints race at Lowe's Motor Speedway. Home turf. The only people eligible to compete in this race are (I just had to look this up to write my press release) drivers who won races either in the current year or last year, or new drivers for car owners who won. Also eligible are drivers who are past Cup champions and/or are past winners of the All-Star race. Or whoever wins the All-Star Open. Actually, it's a little more complicated than that.

Surely you don't think I'm going to Google the NASCAR All-Star rules? You've already told me more than I wanted to know. But I get the gist of it, Racer Girl. Your team just became eligible for a winners-only competition, and you are unaccountably excited at the prospect. I suppose this is good for the greater glory of Badger, though.

You know, Ed, I've been thinking about that. When I first got into NASCAR, I thought that racing was all about one guy—the driver. But it isn't. To use your baseball analogy, on our team Badger is like the pitcher. He may be the highest paid person on the team and the one who gets the most attention, but he wouldn't get anywhere in competition by himself. Unless everybody does a good job at their own positions, he's going to lose.

Of course, he's going to lose! Oh, wait, he did win last week, didn't he? I actually found myself boasting of my tenuous connection to Team Badger to a sports writer from the *Charlotte Observer.* Get me a hat or something, will you?

Sure, if you buy me dinner. You don't want it signed by Badger, do you? Everybody has been complaining lately that he never does the autographing of items people send to the team. We're thinking of getting a cattle prod. Plus some of the Vagenya Pharmaceuticals people showed up at the race last week, and Badger was supposed to go do a meet and greet with them, but he never showed up. I got some of the blame for that one, because I was supposed to get him there, but I couldn't find him. They ought to hire him a nanny!

I thought he had one. That Albigre woman. By the way, I have some information about her that I'll bet you will find interesting.

You did? Is she an ax murderess?

No, but I believe she is dangerous nonetheless, and
for dinner and a Vagenya hat signed by the elusive
Badger, I shall reveal all.

The All-Star Race is held in May at Lowe's Motor Speedway, just
off I-85, about twelve miles north of Charlotte, within easy com-
muting distance of nearly every racing operation in the sport. This
race pitted the best against the best, competing for money, rather
than for points toward the Cup championship. The mile-and-a-
half tri-oval track had recently been resurfaced, but it had been a
fast track even before that. With only five degrees of banking in
the straightaways, drivers found it easy to maintain high speeds,
and easy to pass other cars. Lowe's was a popular track: a fun
place to race and an easy commute from home base.

Team Vagenya had no real hopes of winning a second race in a
row, especially not at a fast, flattish track that was usually dominated by the big team superstars, but at least the win at Darlington had put them into the race, and that alone was something to
be proud of.

Up in the spotters' position on the top of the speedway, Tony
Lafon watched the progress of the All-Star race with growing apprehension. Drivers who couldn't spell "invincible" were driving
as if they were. His current concern was with one of the more
reckless contenders, a fairly new driver who had managed to win
one race the previous season, despite the fact that he was considered both reckless and inexperienced. Generally, competitors are
referred to in spotters' conversations by car number, but this particular driver was universally known as the "Weapon." You didn't
want him anywhere near your car, because he would take you out,
sometimes on purpose, and sometimes simply because he seemed
to lack the skill to bump and run without leaving catastrophe in
his wake. "Driving over his head," the veterans called it.

As the race went on, the Weapon seemed to become progres-
sively more obnoxious, spinning out a former champion and nar-
rowly missing a collision with a couple of other drivers. Surely one
of the old-timers would swat this puppy into the wall before the

end of the race, Tony thought, but lap after lap went by, and the Weapon plowed on without retribution.

For Tony, the events on lap 76 seemed to unfold in slow motion below him. He realized that the lapped and damaged car directly in the path of Badger and the Weapon was moving much more slowly than they were, and that as they approached that point on the track, the Weapon was trying to overtake the 86.

Badger and the Weapon were running side by side going into Turn Two, approaching the lapped car on the inside. Badger held his line on the high side, but—true to form—the other driver, positioned in the middle, didn't back down, and he ran out of room.

Tony was shouting, *"Watch the lap car . . . Weapon on the inside . . . still there . . . still there . . . Holy shit . . . Bad-geerrrr!"*

With nowhere to go, the Weapon clipped the lapped car and got shot up the track into Badger and then the wall. Badger's car climbed the wall before slamming again into the other driver's car. Twisted together, two crumpled cars slid onto the apron.

Both cars were clearly out of the race. The concern now was whether the drivers were all right.

Badger dropped the window net, and as he climbed out, he looked over at the window of the other car, waiting for its window net to drop—but it didn't.

Badger didn't wait for the Weapon to show his face. He climbed out of the window and headed for the other car, which was sitting on the pavement a few yards away from the 86. Badger's clenched fists and his body language suggested that if the Weapon wasn't hurt, he soon would be.

Badger was one step away from his opponent's car, peering through the window net, which was still in place, when he seemed to realize that the driver inside was slumped forward in his seat, not moving. His fists unclenched, and he looked around, making sure that the safety crew knew he needed help. The helmet turned slowly toward the infield where the safety crews were just starting to roll. He waved one gloved hand and nodded.

An instant later, when he turned his attention back to the wreck, flames were engulfing the car inside and out.

In the pit stall, Taran started to scream.

Badger, still wearing all his gear, reached into the flames and lowered the window net, thrusting his body waist-deep into the burning car, searching in the darkness for the fire system plunger. He hit the trigger.

While the fire was held at bay by the spraying fire bottle, Badger backed out of the car, throwing off his helmet once he was clear.

"Why is he taking his helmet off?" asked Taran, who had covered her face with her hands and now was watching the scene through splayed fingers.

Kathy mouthed the words at her and pointed. "He's going back in."

Then Taran understood. Those cumbersome helmets hardly fit through the window by themselves, and they were hard to see and maneuver in. It could also be filled with smoke from the first time he went in. Besides, the Weapon was still wearing his own helmet, and two helmets trying to come out that car window at the same time would not work at all.

The smoke was thicker now, making it hard to see what was actually happening at the Weapon's car, but Tuggle didn't have to see to know.

Badger was getting him out. The safety crews were heading toward the wreck, but Badger wouldn't wait for them to get there. Firesuits protect against fire only for a matter of seconds. Taking a breath in the open air, Badger reached back into the burning car and removed the steering wheel. If he undid the driver's belts, the radio harness and the air hose could be ripped away, and the Hans device would come out with the injured driver.

Badger would tuck his chin over the Weapon's shoulder from behind and fall backward with his arms under the Weapon's arm pits and around his chest, pulling him partway out of the window. With the belts undone, the Weapon fell forward into Badger, who leveraged against the car and snaked the unconscious driver out the window and away from the flames.

From her place in the 86 pit stall, Reve Galloway was peering across the track through curtains of smoke to watch the rescue, when an odd thing happened. She should have seen a scrawny country boy in a tacky purple firesuit yanking a reckless jerk out of a bashed-in car . . . but somehow . . .

For just those few foggy seconds that it took for Badger to rescue the unconscious driver, everybody on Team Vagenya saw what Taran saw all the time. *Him.* The Dark Angel.

Someone taller than Badger Jenkins, and infinitely more graceful, had swung effortlessly out of his own car, which had crashed at nearly 200 miles per hour. Then without a moment's hesitation he had walked over to the other wreck and, it seemed to her, straight into a wall of flames. Now, instead of worrying about his own safety, he was risking his life to rescue someone he didn't even like. His movements were as deliberate and assured as those of a dancer. It was as if the danger did not exist. As if the wreck were simply a staged exercise in precision and movement. How beautiful he was, Reve thought. Why did we never see this before? Without any sense of irony, she found herself framing the scene in Hamlet's words: *In form and moving, how express and admirable. In action, how like an angel. In apprehension, how like a god.*

He was, indeed, a paragon of animals, but only for the span of perhaps a minute. Just as he pulled the unconscious Weapon out of the burning car, the rescue workers arrived and sprayed both drivers with fire extinguishers. Badger tottered for a moment in the smoke and mist, letting the Weapon slide gently to the ground. He staggered away for a few feet, as if he were heading back for the 86, but before he reached it, he came to a swaying stop, and then his knees buckled and he fell forward onto the track.

For Reve, the scene seemed to unfold in slow motion with the sound on mute, but as soon as Badger's body hit the pavement, the world went back to fast forward and the soundtrack in her head was scream after scream after scream. It was only the sore throat she had later that told her whose screams they had been.

Taran didn't know if the race was over or not. She was shaking with cold, although no one else had seemed affected. Badger fell . . .

She couldn't remember what had happened next. . . . Had she fainted? . . . Someone had led her to the hauler and wrapped her in a blanket. She had sat there—she didn't know how long—holding a Styrofoam cup of thermos coffee in both hands. Tuggle, recognizing the signs of shock, had wanted to send her to the infield care center, but she had refused to go, afraid that they would keep her, and then she would not know what had happened to Badger. They had taken him away in an ambulance. Concussion, Kathy Erwin had said. She had seen enough of them to know.

"Is he going to be all right?" someone had asked.

Kathy shrugged. "Probably," she said. "Head injuries are tricky, though. Sometimes they mess up your sense of balance or something. If it's bad enough, he'll never race again."

More time passed, and the voices faded in and out. The coffee grew cold.

She thought that Sigur had come in for a little while, or perhaps Cindy. And she thought she must have slept for a bit. But then Tony Lafon had appeared, looking worried. He cupped her chin in his hand and peered at her intently. "Are you okay? Reve said you fainted."

Taran shivered. "Where is everybody?"

"All over the place. Seeing to the car—what's left of it. Packing up to get out of here. Checking on Badger. He's going to be okay. Head injury. Smoke inhalation. They took him to the hospital. I think everybody forgot about you in all the chaos, so I figured I'd better come and find you."

Taran tried to smile. "Thanks. I'm okay. It's just that I've never seen him wreck before. Well, I mean, I *have*—back when he was just my driver, but now—" Her eyes welled up with tears, and she covered her mouth to hold back the sobs.

Tony looked away. "You're really torn up over him, aren't you?" he said at last.

Taran nodded. "That is exactly the right phrase to use," she said. If she had to put it into words—how she felt about him—the simile that came to her mind would be, appropriately enough, an image of torture from medieval times. She had found a description of it in *Henry V.* Fluellen had said of the robber Bardolph: *His nose is executed and his fire's out.*

The phrase was a reference to the one final indignity inflicted upon the prisoner before a medieval execution: the nose was slit with a sharp knife, *opened,* severing the cartilage between the nostrils and removing the anchorage that affixed the nose to the victim's face. The incision was not fatal, but it was cruel—both painful and disfiguring, resulting in fountains of blood gushing uselessly from the wound.

Over the years the term for that punishment "his nose is open" began to be used metaphorically to describe hopeless infatuation, when feelings spill out, causing a scene that is agony to the sufferer, distasteful to witness, and completely without purpose. And so it was with her feelings for him. She felt an overpowering wave of emotion, so strong as to cancel out everything else, and yet, painful, useless, and unpleasant to watch. It hardly felt like love, because it was so one-sided, so hopeless, and hardly voluntary.

"Do you want me to take you to the hospital to see him?"

The words were out of her mouth almost before she thought them. "Oh, no!" she said. "I don't really know him."

Several hours later Tuggle pushed open the door to the hospital room, knowing that Badger wouldn't care—and might not even know—that she had come empty-handed, but a strict sense of propriety inherited from an iron-willed grandmother made her feel guilty about it anyhow. But she'd be damned if she'd bring him flowers. Some sports reporters were sure to be loitering around in the hall somewhere, and a story about the "lady crew chief" bringing flowers to the handsome race car driver would be too good for them to pass up. No way in hell. Knowing Badger Jenkins, she thought he might have been grateful for a six-pack of Corona and a pack of Marlboro Lights, but she was pretty sure that his doctors wouldn't thank her for showing up with them, and she knew better than to give him a novel, so she ended up bringing him nothing—except some bad news she was in no hurry to give him.

Badger was looking even smaller and paler than usual, tucked under the white sheets of the hospital bed and surrounded by vases of flowers covering almost every flat surface, sent in by fans and by well-wishers who lacked Tuggle's horror of sentimental gestures. God knows where they had obtained them at that hour on such short notice. Wal-Mart, maybe.

He looked gaunt and weak, but at least he wasn't bandaged up. The one good thing you could say about smoke inhalation and a head injury was that they weren't messy conditions.

An article on one of the motorsports Web sites had likened the brain in a high-speed car crash to "putting a tomato in a cocktail shaker." The brain bounced around hitting the inside of the skull, and it got badly bruised and swollen, but with luck and care, it would revert to normal in a few days or a week. Now all they could do was wait to see how badly he was hurt—and how permanently.

Laraine was sitting in a straight chair at his bedside. Tuggle remembered her from the Atlanta race, but now she was looking exhausted and disheveled, as if she had been there for days without leaving, instead of only a few hours. Her clothes were rumpled, and there were dark circles under her eyes, but she had managed to smile when Tuggle came in. Then she touched Badger gently on the shoulder and nodded toward the door.

Badger's eyes lit up when he saw his crew chief standing there. That was good, Tuggle thought. At least he knew who she was.

"Hey, Tuggle!" he called out. "What the hell happened?"

Tuggle sighed. "Well, you were running second behind the 38 car—"

He brightened. "I was running second?"

"Yeah, it was looking good, but then you came up on a lapped car right after Turn Two, and the Weapon was running with you on the inside, and he got into you . . ."

Badger scowled. "The Weapon, huh?"

Tuggle nodded. "And you both went into the wall. Hard. How are you feeling?"

"I'm okay," said Badger. "Just a headache. I'll be fine. Ready to race next week."

Tuggle said nothing. She had noticed the stricken look on the face of Laraine, who was shaking her head very slightly, perhaps to forestall wherever the conversation was going next. Tuggle wondered what there was that she didn't know, and if it could possibly be worse than what Badger didn't know.

Which was that he had been fired.

They weren't going to announce it just yet. In fact, Tuggle suspected that the team owners had been relieved when Badger ended up in the hospital, because then they could get rid of him without seeming heartless. *"Let go for health reasons."* It wasn't true, though. They had been planning to fire him before he ever got in the car for the All-Star race.

Christine Berenson and a group of her fellow dilettantes had summoned Tuggle to a meeting in the skybox at nearly midnight. The race, which had begun at 7:40, was over, but the traffic jam of departing spectators would take almost as long as the race, so perhaps having nothing better to do, they decided to hold an impromptu business meeting.

Tuggle went in, feeling scruffy but morally superior, in her grimy purple coveralls and dusty Vagenya-86 cap. In skyboxes, the aristocratic fans sipped champagne and ate nouvelle cuisine from laden buffet tables, while beyond the plateglass window forty-three men played hit and run with Death. The Roman games must have been like this, she thought, and it made her shudder. Of course, the drivers these days were rich people, too, so maybe it wasn't quite as unequal as it looked, but it still felt wrong to her to sip champagne while you watched people risking their lives.

Badger could be dying for all they knew. Maybe they didn't care, but she sure as hell did. She thought of her first husband—the one who had taught her to put a restrictor plate on her heart. Maybe if they'd had a son together he would have been like Badger, who was a weasel, but so brave and beautiful that you couldn't help but love him. She was his crew chief. That made him *her* weasel, and she would fight for him. Because these people were up to no good.

"You wanted to see me?" she said to the assembly of elegant women.

"Grace Tuggle, so good of you to come!" murmured Christine,

using her name for the benefit of the assembled partners. "We wanted to know if you'd heard how Badger is doing?"

"They've transferred him from the infield care center to University Hospital," said Tuggle, using the locals' name for the Carolinas Medical Center-University. "I'll go down there in the morning. It's too late to see him tonight, but I'll let you know as soon as I hear anything."

Christine Berenson motioned her to a chair. "Sit down, Grace. That isn't actually the reason we called you here, although, of course, we are all terribly concerned about Badger."

Tuggle sat down in the chair, taking care not to get too comfortable, and eyed her employers warily.

"We have a situation," said Christine, dropping her voice to a steely purr.

"We may need a relief driver next week," Tuggle conceded. "Badger may well insist on driving with a concussion, but I'll be damned if I'll let him."

The women exchanged glances. Christine said, "You'll be glad to know that we already have a relief driver. A talented young woman who has been doing well on some local speedways in Virginia. Rookie of the Year at one of them."

Tuggle frowned. "Judith Burks? " She made it her business to know who was up and coming in motor sports.

"Oh, good. You've heard of her. And she's a lovely little blonde, too. Very photogenic."

"Nobody's prettier than Badger," said Tuggle.

"If you like the over-thirty-five redneck type," sniffed Diane Hodges. "He's no Rusty Wallace."

"Fans love Badger. He's kind to people," said Tuggle. "Besides, he may not need a relief driver." *The race has just ended and they already have a replacement lined up?*

The owners exchanged glances. "We've decided to let Badger go," said Christine.

Tuggle's jaw dropped. "But he just won Darlington!"

"Oh, nobody remembers who actually wins these races. There are so many of them. We think a woman driver would be a better image for the sponsor."

"True, Faye, but that's really beside the point," said Christine. "The fact is NASCAR is like a small town. If you misbehave, people know about it."

If she could have thought of anything to say, Tuggle would have said it, but fortunately no one was interested in being interrupted by incredulous protests, anyhow.

"One of the other owners clued us in, Grace. Badger has been working on a deal to change teams and take the sponsor with him."

"He's not that smart!" The words were out of Tuggle's mouth before she could think better of them.

Suzie Terrell, the team's attorney, said, "It's true, though. His manager Melodie Albigre has been talking to at least one of the multicar teams about his switching over to them for more money, and taking Vagenya with him as the primary sponsor."

At the sound of the Dominatrix's name, Tuggle's scowl became a snarl. "Have you talked to Badger?" she asked. "No. Of course, you haven't. I'll bet she is doing this behind his back. You need to hear his side of it."

"No," said Suzie Terrell. "They don't. His degree of involvement is really of no consequence. I'm sorry, Tuggle. I like Badger. We all do. But this is business, and the decision is made. Effective today. Judith Burks is the 86 team's new driver."

"How did you hear about her?" asked Tuggle.

"Jeff Burton saw her race at the South Boston Speedway, and he mentioned it to some of the owners, who in turn recommended her to us."

Tuggle nodded. She was thinking, *Judith Burks from Virginia. Not bad. Wonder if Brian Burton would spot for her.* But the fact that she approved of the replacement driver still didn't make it right about Badger.

"She's a college graduate from Amherst, Virginia," said Christine. "Quite well-spoken. And she has done some modeling. She's much more in keeping with the new face of motor sports. Let's face it, Badger is a throwback to the old redneck days of racing. He'll never change."

"Thank God for that," said Tuggle.

"Of course, we'll wait until he has recovered to announce this officially."

"*Engine Noise* probably has it already," said Tuggle. "But tell me, who's going to be your crew chief for the rest of the season?"

"Why, you are," said Christine. The others nodded emphatically.

"I'll finish out the year," Tuggle told them. "Because I gave you my word, and at least on my end, that means something. But after that, I'm gone."

Laraine's gesture had meant for Tuggle to follow her out into the hall. "We'll be back in a minute," Laraine promised Badger. She touched his shoulder, letting her hand linger there for a moment, and he smiled up at her and closed his eyes. "We're going to see about getting you some juice, hon." She closed the door behind them.

"Have you had anything to eat today?" asked Tuggle. "How long have you been here?"

Laraine summoned a wan smile and tried to smooth down her tangled hair. "I came up for the race. I don't think he knew I was coming, though. I sent a letter to his P.O. box and an e-mail, but he doesn't seem to be getting his messages lately."

"I think I know why," said Tuggle, who knew that Melodie had taken over Badger's correspondence on the pretext of "helping" him. Nothing got through to Badger anymore unless she approved of it. Unfortunately, she didn't check for messages as often as she should have, and as a result, Badger had missed vital appointments and opportunities. It had cost him dearly.

"I got to the hospital about the same time he did," Laraine was saying. "They let me stay with him. I told them I was family."

"You are, aren't you?"

Laraine shrugged. "Sure—along with everybody else in Marengo, to one degree or another. I think the law is the only one that sets a store by blood ties these days. The rest of us know that family is whoever you decide it is. I think Badger considers *you* family, Tuggle."

"Not for long," said Tuggle. She told Laraine what had happened in the owners meeting.

Laraine had listened without comment, but she had the same dark, sad eyes as Badger, and they said it all.

"So, as of now, whether he gets better or not, he's gone."

Laraine said softly, "You fought for him, of course."

"I did," said Tuggle. "What they did to him wasn't fair." *But I didn't fight very hard,* she was thinking. Maybe it wasn't Badger's fault that the Dominatrix had tried to pull a fast one on the 86 team, but that didn't mean that Badger was otherwise perfect. For starters, he should have been smarter in his choice of management, and he should have supervised her more closely. Besides, he never was much of a team player. He just wanted to race, but NASCAR had stopped being all about racing years ago. Now sponsors and fan base, image and publicity made the wheels go around. Lose your accent; get plastic surgery if you're not handsome enough; learn to project a bland and genial media-friendly persona. But Badger just kept on being himself, no more capable of brown-nosing and expedient insincerity than a racing greyhound. Which made him just as vulnerable as they were.

Laraine sighed. "Everybody gives up on Badger sooner or later."

"I didn't want to," said Tuggle. "I hope he never finds out how much I cared about him. He's all pride and courage—and not a lick of corporate savvy. Just skin and bones, but when he puts on that firesuit he thinks he's a lion. It made my heart turn over to watch him pulling that kid out of the wreck tonight. But I have to be realistic. I have a multimillion-dollar team to run. And you can't count on him anywhere but on the track."

"I know. He will break your heart and never know it. He never means to hurt anybody, though."

"Well, he's flushing a career down the toilet. He'd better clean up his act."

"That won't happen. He's been handsome all his life. People let him slide on account of that. Sure, people leave him, but somebody else always comes along to take up the slack."

"Not forever," said Tuggle.

"Oh, you can't explain to Badger about *forever.*"

"But you're still here. How come you never left him?"

Laraine blinked back tears. "Because I understand about *forever*," she said.

"Is that idiot awake yet? I need him to sign some papers."

Tuggle and Laraine turned at the sound of the corncrake voice echoing down the hall. Melodie Albigre, who looked as if she had dressed for vampire prom night, came tapping down the hospital corridor in her stiletto heels, wearing an expression that suggested that Badger had wrecked solely in order to inconvenience her.

"I don't suppose he's too badly hurt if it's only a head injury," she said to Tuggle, tapping her forehead with one finger. "Not much up there to get damaged."

Laraine's eyes narrowed and she took a deep breath, but Tuggle flashed her a warning look, and she said nothing.

Heedless of the effect of her personal charm on her audience, Melodie went on, "I might have known he'd screw everything up. After he won Darlington, I thought I might actually have some good business deals lined up for us. And now this nonsense!"

"Badger was a hero tonight," said Laraine. "He pulled that kid out of a burning car."

Melodie Albigre sniffed. "Grandstanding," she said.

"Don't you care how he is?" asked Tuggle in a dangerously quiet voice.

"Oh, I expect it's too soon to know. But I have made some contingency plans, anyhow." She dug into her oversized purse and fished out a thick sheaf of papers.

"Good thing he has me around to look out for him."

"Good thing," said Laraine evenly.

Something in her tone attracted Melodie's attention. "I don't believe I know you," she said, favoring Laraine with a patronizing smile. "I am Badger Jenkins's manager. Are you a fan?"

"Yes," said Laraine. "I am a fan of Badger. Always will be, always was."

"Laraine is family," said Tuggle. "Nobody gets in to see Badger without her okay."

Melodie frowned. "Well, I don't suppose anyone has told you, Grace, but I have it on good authority that Badger will be let go from the 86 team."

"Thanks to you."

Melodie took a deep breath and looked as if she wanted to dispute the point, but then she shrugged. "Oh, it's no great loss," she said. "There are other ways to make money. And lots of other rides out there."

Tuggle narrowed her eyes. "Well, no, there aren't. This is a non-union sport, with maybe a dozen or so team owners, barring the little independents. If you play fast and loose with one of them, the others will know about it before the end of the week. Just how much experience do you have managing drivers, anyhow?"

"Don't let her in there!" A woman's shrill voice echoed down the corridor of the hospital, and they turned to see Melanie Sark running toward them. She had clapped her hand over her mouth in a belated attempt to be more quiet. She had changed out of the power suit she'd worn as team publicist at the All-Star race. Now she wore Nikes, jeans, and a Team Vagenya sweatshirt, but she was still carrying her laptop case, and her labored breathing suggested that she had run all the way from the parking lot and up three flights of stairs with it.

Seeing the astonishment on their faces, she said, "Badger. How is he?"

"We don't know yet," said Tuggle.

"He's no longer your concern," said Melodie. "Badger has been released from the 86 team."

"I know," said Sark. "They want me to change the Web site tomorrow: put up a picture of Judith Burks and say she'll be the relief driver next week. But I still care what happens to him." She glanced pleadingly at Laraine. "I need to tell him something."

Melodie said, "You can tell me privately. I'm in charge of his business affairs."

"*That,*" said Sark, "is the problem."

"I think you'd better tell us," said Tuggle. "Laraine is family, and Badger is in no shape to make decisions right now."

Sark hesitated. "But here in the hall? I have papers to show you."

"Lounge," said Tuggle. "I think Laraine could use some coffee, anyhow."

Laraine shook her head. "I shouldn't leave Badger."

"Ten minutes," said Sark.

They walked down the corridor to the waiting room. Sark sat down in a chair next to the coffee table and pushed aside ancient copies of *Parents Magazine* and *National Geographic* so that she could spread out the paper trail.

"First," she said, "I have a confession to make. I'm a journalist."

"Publicists generally are," sniffed Melodie.

"Yes, but I didn't switch to being a publicist. I considered myself working undercover. I was planning to do an exposé of the 86 team for some national publication like *Vanity Fair.*"

Tuggle glared at her. "An exposé about what?"

"Whatever I could find," said Sark. "Badger's sex life. The team's incompetence. Drugs. Financial irregularities. Whatever was going."

"How very unethical," said Melodie. She had thought better of sitting on the sofa beside Tuggle and Laraine; instead, she was pacing in front of the snack machines, trying not altogether successfully to look bored.

Sark stared at her for a moment, took a deep breath, and said, "Yes, well, I decided not to write that article."

Tuggle's scowl had not lessened. "Why not?"

"I became a convert. Badger is pretty amazing. I was an expecting an arrogant jerk, and he's not one. And the team—everybody was trying so hard. Julie and Roz and the pit crew. It would have been like drowning kittens to make fun of them in a national article. I couldn't do it."

Tuggle grunted. "You're still fired."

"I can't afford to keep the job, anyhow," said Sark. "Doesn't pay enough, and it's rather a waste of a good journalist. Ed just got a book deal—Memphis jazz musicians—and he's asked me to go along as his research assistant. But there is another bit of research I wanted you to have before I go." She opened her laptop case and took out a stack of papers. "One thing about being a journalist is that you have friends who are good at finding things out. My friend Ed is one of the best."

"You had him investigate us?" said Tuggle.

"No. Not you. *Her.*" Sark nodded toward Melodie Alibgre, who was still pacing in front of the Coke machine.

"Why?"

Sark shrugged. "Mostly because she annoyed me so much. The way she orders people around. How rude she is to Badger. So Ed and I went on a fishing expedition."

Melodie stopped pacing. "You had no right!" She rushed to the table as if she meant to grab the papers, but one look from Tuggle made her think better of it.

With a grim smile, Tuggle said, "What'd you catch?"

"Barracuda," said Sark. "For starters, she isn't a sports manager. Oh, she works for Miller O'Neill, all right, but not as a manager. She's a clerk! They had stored all their old paper files in boxes from the past twenty years in a storage facility in Charlotte, and they hired her to go there and sort through the boxes to see which folders they needed to keep and which could be discarded. That's what Eugene Miller thought she has been doing all this time. Imagine his surprise to learn that she landed herself a client."

They turned to look at Melodie whose mulish expression did not indicate repentance. "I would have been a great manager," she said. "All I needed was a chance! It's not like you have to have a degree or anything to do it."

Laraine sighed. "Poor Badger. He always takes everybody's word for everything. Never checks."

"I did a good job," said Melodie.

"No," said Tuggle, "you didn't. This business runs on goodwill, and you cost him a ton of it. Badger may need somebody to ride herd on him, but the one thing in his favor is that he is kind and sweet-tempered, and people love him. But when they had to deal with a bitch like you, it cost him that advantage. Was she stealing his money?"

"Maybe," said Sark. "We had to put all this together in a hurry, so we can't really prove that. Besides, there's worse," said Sark.

"She really was trying to drum up business deals for Badger." She handed a printout to Laraine. "I think this would interest you."

Melodie blanched. "Where did you get that?"

"Ed hacked into your computer," said Sark, grinning. "We're hoping you'll sue him. It would make a great story."

"What is it?" asked Tuggle, seeing the stricken expression on Laraine's face as she read.

Sark saved her the trouble of answering. "Melodie has been negotiating the sale of Badger's land at the Georgia lake to a development company specializing in golf resorts."

Tuggle stared. "Badger agreed to that?"

"Of course, he didn't," said Laraine. "He'd die first. It says here that she has his power of attorney, and she's using it to broker the deal."

Sark nodded. "That's why I have to get in to talk to Badger. So that he can stop it."

"That won't be necessary," said Laraine. "I can stop it."

"You? How?"

Laraine sighed. "I've had Badger's power of attorney for years. I got my uncle the judge to draw it up for me, and Badger signed the form one time when he was down at the diner autographing posters."

"Did he know what it was?"

"Sure. He was all for it. He said if he ever got hurt real bad, he wanted somebody he could trust looking after him. And I mean to." She nodded toward Melanie. "What I'm wondering is how *she* got his power of attorney."

Melodie smirked. "Badger never reads what you give him to sign. Have you ever noticed that?"

Laraine nodded. "You can generally trust people where we come from. Not like here."

"So can you stop the sale of the land?" asked Sark.

"Oh, I already have," said Laraine. "I was afraid that some day some crook would try to screw Badger out of the land. I sorta thought it might be Dessy, but even she wasn't that cruel. So I talked it over with my uncle . . ."

"The judge?"

"Yeah. He suggested that we put a conservation easement on the land so that nobody could ever develop it. We figured that's what Badger would want."

Sark said, "But suppose he needs the money some day?"

"He'd starve first," said Laraine. "But he won't. I'll see to that." She turned a level gaze at Badger's erstwhile manager. "I don't think Badger needs a manager any more, ma'am. And if he finds out what you've been trying to do, he just might shoot you. And if he didn't, I would. So do yourself a favor and get gone."

Had she been dealing with men, Melodie might have burst into tears, but theatrics cuts no ice with furious women. As she left, she favored them with a final withering glare, and said, "Why would I want to stick around? It's not like Badger has a future."

Sark shuddered. "How could he let that horrible creature get control of his life?"

"Well," said Laraine, "when he was a kid, he used to keep snakes as pets."

They sat in the waiting room for a few more minutes, drinking bad hospital coffee and talking to dispel the chill of Melodie Albigre's visit.

"It's late," said Tuggle, glancing at her watch. "Or rather, early. But I'd like to go look in on Badger again before I leave."

"Don't tell him yet that he's out of a job," said Laraine.

"No," said Tuggle, "that can wait. How is he?"

Laraine glanced at the clock on the wall above the nurses' station. "We've been out here half an hour," she said. "Go back in and see."

So Tuggle pushed the door open and looked in on Badger. He was still lying there pale amidst the white bed linens, and his eyes were closed, but an instant later, he opened them and beamed a welcoming smile when he caught sight of her. "Hey, Tuggle!" he said. "What the hell happened?"

Tuggle stared at him for a moment. Then she said, "Um . . . In the race? Well, like I told you earlier, you were second behind the 38 car."

He brightened. "I was running second?"

"Yeah. It was looking good, but then you came up on that lapped car, and the Weapon was running with you on the inside right after Turn Two, and he got into you . . ."

"The Weapon, huh?"

Tuggle closed her eyes and willed her voice to become steady. "Yeah, Badger. You took a hard hit. But you'll be okay. Excuse me just a minute." She closed the door again.

Sark was still waiting outside in the hall. When Tuggle came back out she pointed to the door, but Tuggle shook her head. "He's not up to it yet, Sark," she said. "And he won't remember that you came."

Then she said to Laraine, "This is temporary. Happens to all of them at one time or another. It scares the hell out of you, but he'll get over this."

Laraine nodded. "I know. The doctors already told me that. I'm staying until he's well enough to go home."

"Figured you would," said Tuggle. "Let one of us know if you need anything. We're Badger's family, too, no matter what the team owners say. Get somebody to spell you before you get too worn-out. You've got my cell phone number."

When Laraine had gone back into Badger's room, Sark said, "I don't know what to say in this press release."

"Say whatever the doctor tells you," said Tuggle. "*Resting comfortably,* maybe. Don't say he has been replaced yet. Christine's orders."

"Is he going to be all right? Physically, I mean?"

"It's too soon to know," said Tuggle. "It will take a couple of days for the brain swelling to go down, and then if he's left with balance problems, he'll never race again. But I think he'll be all right. At least he has someone to look after him."

Sark nodded. "She loves him so much."

"More than he deserves."

"Do you think he'll stay with her?"

"Depends," said Tuggle, thinking about first husbands and restrictor plates on hearts. "He may never be able to drive again.

And if he does fully recover, maybe no other team will want him. He's not twenty-something anymore. So if he's done with NASCAR, then, yeah, I think he'll settle down with her. If he has any sense."

Sark shivered. "But if he does go back to Cup racing?"

Tuggle hesitated. She was thinking of a starry-eyed girl named Grace and of a race car driver who had put her so far into the wall she thought she'd never get over it. It was an old story. One that had happened many thousands of times. Maybe somewhere, just once, it ought to turn out all right. She said, "I think they're going to make it."

CHAPTER XXIII

Full Circle

Meet the Drivers. On the days leading up to the Sharpie 500 race in late August, the town of Bristol hosts a street festival dedicated to stock car racing. The Sharpie is the hardest ticket to get in sports: harder than the Super Bowl or the NCAA Finals. The Bristol Motor Speedway event is sold out every year, and race fans from all over the country begin turning up days in advance, clogging campgrounds and selling out motels in three neighboring states. To give the fans something to do in advance of the race itself, there are racing-related events nearby—hence the street fair.

Show cars are parked on the street for the public's inspection, and there are the sort of booths one might expect at any sports fair: food vendors, hat and tee shirt sales, NASCAR-themed artists displaying their work, and exhibit booths showcasing charitable organizations connected to motorsports.

Occasionally, for an hour or so in the afternoon, a Cup driver would appear at one of the booths to sign his name for the hundred or so fortunate people that the line would accommodate during his allotted time period. You could tell which booths featured appearances by Cup drivers, because those lines were a block long. But other drivers also turned up at the Bristol Street Scene. Local speedways or racing organizations with driver development programs often sent lesser-known drivers to such events to give them experience in dealing with the public before they became famous enough for it to matter much.

Like their famous NASCAR counterparts, these local luminaries would chat with fans, pose for pictures, and sign autographs on publicity photos of themselves. Often, they, too, would have dozens of people in line, because when you're giving away free stuff, autographed, many people don't care if you're famous or not. Besides, once upon a time every driver was an unknown: They had to start somewhere. Prudent fans collected the autographs of the aspiring NASCAR stars in hopes that someday these guys would turn out to be famous.

It was rumored that Roush driver Carl Edwards would be along later in the afternoon, but he had not turned up yet. Badger Jenkins was not driving in the Sharpie this year, and his fans missed him. Some passersby still proudly wore old Badger Jenkins tee shirts, and they would tell you in a heartbeat that one of these days he would be back out there. At his unofficial fan Web site *Badgers Din* there were conflicting reports: Badger was considering a ride in the Craftsman Truck Series; Badger would replace a driver at RCR next year; Badger was sponsoring a turtle rescue operation; Badger had married a girl from his hometown, and he was enjoying his time off at the lake; Badger was going to star in a Civil War movie. Nobody really knew for sure. They hoped he was happy. They missed him.

At the curb on State Street a line had formed at a table where three young men sat in front stacks of eight-by-ten autograph cards: photos of the driver in a brightly colored firesuit standing beside the vehicle he raced in local competitions.

Taran Stiles surveyed the crowd with the practiced eye of a recovering fan. She was here to see that her driver did not have to face the crowd unassisted. She wore a team polo shirt and a badge identifying her as a driver's assistant, but she had graciously volunteered to look after the other two drivers as well. Her job this afternoon was to hand out fresh bottles of water and new Sharpie markers for autographing, and to retrieve more autograph cards if anyone ran out.

The blue-eyed young man on the left side of the table had the longest line, mostly female fans, armed with cameras. Many of them wore the emblems of Cup drivers, but they were shopping for new talent, because, hey, nobody stays out there forever.

"They say he's a natural," said one dishwater blonde in a red #8 tank top to her frizzy-haired friend.

"Did you hear that he has a Busch ride next year? Grace Tuggle has just been named as his crew chief."

Taran smiled at the fan. This rumor was true. Tony had finally got his chance in NASCAR.

"I like the shape of his face," said an older woman. "He's got that cute cleft chin, and his haircut is really hot. Is he married?" They weren't bothering to lower their voices. Perhaps they thought that drivers weren't quite "real," that he was at most a robot or an animated poster with no life beyond his public persona.

Taran, who was handing out more marker pens, heard them, though. "Tony is engaged," she said sharply. She paused for a moment, letting the afternoon light catch the sparkle of the very small diamond on her third finger. She and Tony glanced at each other and shared a brief smile. Then it was back to the business at hand.

At the front of the line a dark-haired girl in a white sweatsuit handed her camera to the driver's minder. "Would you take my picture with Tony?" she said. "I've been following his career ever since he started driving around Mooresville. I swear I'm his biggest fan. Does he have a fan club?"

"He has a Web site," said Taran, trying to sound pleasant, or at least civil. These were Tony's fans, and he would need fans in order to succeed in racing. "The address is on the autograph card."

"He's gonna be a big star one of the days," said the fan.

"We hope so," said Taran. She lifted the camera and motioned for the dark-haired girl to pose with Tony.

Flashing a triumphant smile at the rest of the long line, the dark-haired girl walked around the signing table, leaned down to show off her cleavage to its best advantage, and snuggled up close to Tony Lafon, whose wary eyes would not match his public smile. Taran took the picture.

As the girl retrieved her camera, she smiled again at Tony, and said, "Would you like me to send you a copy of the picture? I will, if you give me your address."

"Just e-mail it to the Web site," said Taran briskly. "Who's next?"

The wispy young woman who was next in line was shaking. "I'm next," she said, barely speaking above a whisper. "I think you're wonderful, Tony."

Badger would have smiled and drawled, "Waal, thank you," but Tony Lafon was not yet accustomed to the kindness of strangers. He reddened and squirmed in his seat, and finally said, "I'm just lucky to be here."

Her pale eyes blinked at Tony through thick glasses, and she looked as if she might burst into tears at any moment. Tony smiled up at her reassuringly, scrawled his name across the autograph card, and held it up to her. She looked like a boiled rabbit.

"Thanks for coming out today," he told her.

Tears coursed down the woman's pale cheeks. "I love you, Tony, " she whispered.

AUTHOR'S NOTE

To the uninitiated, NASCAR looks like a solitary sport: one driver competing against forty-two opponents. In reality, racing is very much a team effort, with the driver occupying a place on the team analogous to that of the pitcher or the quarterback—an important, glamorous symbol for the team, but by no means its only contributor to the win.

Being a writer can be like that, too. I had to think up the plot, devise the characters, and spend many laps at the keyboard of my word processor to make this book happen, but it was by no means a solitary effort. I was blessed with a volunteer "pit crew" of the most generous, knowledgeable, and enthusiastic advisors that any writer ever had.

2002 Daytona 500 winner Ward Burton, who was "my driver" in NASCAR before he became my friend, is the soul of this book. Without him the novel would not exist. He swears that he does not remember receiving an offer to drive for an all-female team, but that is where this story began—not as a formal book project, but as a *jeu d'esprit* via e-mail to amuse Ward's posse. I wrote part of the first chapter in the hospital with an IV needle in my hand, laughing hysterically.

If you are going to write a novel with a Cup driver as a major character, it helps to have one on speed dial. During the writing of this novel, Ward has been remarkably patient and generous with his time and knowledge, telling me exactly how to drive the difficult track at Darlington, and sharing his racing expertise with me. It is because of Ward that I understand how people feel about their drivers, whether they are fans or friends or colleagues. In the novel Badger's kindness to fans and his rapport with children are traits he "inherited" from Ward Burton. Not only did Ward answer my questions about the life of a NASCAR driver, he also played the part of "Badger" in the movie in my head. Biographically, they are not alike, but in the sense that Harrison Ford is "Indiana Jones" *(but not in real life),* then Ward is the incarnation of Badger. No matter how exasperating I was in the process of creating this work, Ward was really nice about it.

My friend and fellow Virginia Tech grad, Adam Edwards, who has managed a Busch team, driven both Pure Stock and in the NASCAR Weekly Racing Series, and teaches for the FastTrack School of Racing, was my chief engineer, devising the 86 car's winning edge and his keen instinct for making the action scenes come alive for me was a key part of the narrative. In December 2005, Adam and I lived the scene in which Taran takes photos of Tony Lafon in his firesuit in Victory Lane at Daytona, and in July of 2006, he gave me my first ride-along in a race car at Lowe's Motor Speedway. In research, no matter how long it took or how complex the question, Adam always tried to make sure that I understood and got it right.

Jamie Bishop, former gasman for NASCAR legend Cale Yarborough and for other teams, was a wonderful literary crew chief. He helped set up my fictional pit crew, and he kept me straight on such technical matters as pit stop practice, ignition box changing, and the day-to-day operation of a Cup team.

My thanks to Lisa Kipps-Brown, site manager of www.wardburton.com, who answered the phone one day laughing so hard that she couldn't talk, and so began the train of thought that led to this book.

Tennessee author Jane Hicks, my NASCAR mentor from the outset, served as the sounding board for this story, keeping me focused and helping me work through the intricacies of a NASCAR story.

In the earliest stages of researching this novel, when I was trying to figure out how to engineer a winning race car, Austin Petty took me on a tour of the Petty Enterprises Race Shop and conspired with me about templates and air dams, and he was a great help in getting me started. Other engineering expertise was provided by Mike Mitchell and Dennis Duchene of NASCAR Tech in Mooresville and by Dr. Robert Sexton.

Many people generously shared with me their memories and

expertise on the subject of stock car racing past and present, and I thank them all, especially Cathy Earnhardt Watkins, Martha Earnhardt, Danny "Chocolate" Myers, Forrest Reynolds, Kate Lee, Ed Burton, and Brian and Judith Burton. I'm grateful for the assistance of Tabitha Burton, whose memories of coping with an injured driver formed the basis of the hospital scene in Chapter 22.

My thanks to H. A. "Humpy" Wheeler, for his encouragement and for his hospitality at the 2005 All-Star race at Lowe's Motor Speedway, to Mike Smith of the Martinsville Speedway, and to Jeff Byrd and Bruton Smith of the Bristol Motor Speedway for their kindness and hospitality.

For the information on the rescue of Badger's turtle, I am grateful to Carolina Wildlife Care (www.carolinawildlife.org), a nonprofit organization in Columbia, South Carolina, dedicated to the preservation of native wildlife and its natural habitat through rehabilitation, education, and environmental conservation. Carolina Wildlife Care rehabilitates sick, injured, and orphaned wildlife to return to its natural environment.

And Ricky Rudd. *I did not consult you on the writing of this book, but a key scene in this novel is based on something very brave that you did at Darlington on August 30, 1996, and I thank you for having done it.*

Sharyn McCrumb

ONCE AROUND THE TRACK
Sharyn McCrumb

ABOUT THIS GUIDE

The suggested questions are included to
enhance your group's reading of
this book.

DISCUSSION QUESTIONS

1. The central point of the book was the difference between "The Dark Angel" and "Badger." How do his fans perceive him, and what is he really like? Do you in fact ever find out what he is really like?

2. Has this book changed your perception of stock car racing as a sport?

3. What personality traits does Badger have that make him unsuccessful as a race car driver?

4. Do you think Badger and Laraine lived happily ever after? What adjustments would they have to make to stay together?

5. Would you want to get to know a celebrity that you admire? Do you care what he or she is really like, and would you want to know the private person?

6. At different times, three characters in the novel compare Badger to a horse. Discuss this metaphor as it is used by each of them.

7. Which character in the novel did you identify with and why?

8. What do you think happened to Badger after he left NASCAR?

9. Will Tony Lafon be more successful in NASCAR than Badger was? Why or why not?

10. *"Badger ain't the motor boat. He's the turtle."* In what way is this statement true in his career and in his private life? Or is it?

11. For a film version of *Once Around the Track,* who would you cast for each of the major characters?

Sharyn McCrumb Talks With *(fictional)* NASCAR driver Badger Jenkins

I read your book. It was a good one.

Thanks, Badger. I hope I didn't let too much daylight in on the magic.

I notice that in the book you never said what I was thinking or how I felt.

Well, there's a precedent for that. In her novels Jane Austen never wrote the thoughts of a male character, and she never set a scene in which two men talk without a woman present. In *Once Around the Track,* Badger, you were the great enigma. One of the themes of the book was that every character saw you in a different way. The fans thought you were an angel. To Tuggle you were a troublesome kid. Sark saw you as an exotic creature who provided her with adventures.

Like when she had to follow my pick-up down country roads to get to my lake house.

Right. For Sark being with you was like hanging out with Huckleberry Finn. And to Taran you were the Dark Angel, the wise and noble hero on the airbrushed poster. Her name is a clue to her nature. In Gaelic, a "taran" is the soul of an unbaptized child. Tarans are pure and innocent, but because they were never christened, they cannot ever go to heaven. In the novel Taran was an idealistic innocent—but she wasn't bound for any paradise with *you.*

I couldn't be the guy she thought I was. She wanted a plaster saint.

Yes, you would have broken her heart just by being yourself. Your fans and the team owner thought you were a sexy little stud, but I always thought you were a self-absorbed little boy playing Hot Wheels for real. What you needed was a motherly woman who would take care of you and put up with your thoughtlessness. Laraine was the only one who had a chance of being happy with you.

One time there Sark looked like she wanted to give it a try.

For the thrill of a short fling, maybe. But Sark was too smart for you. Sooner or later she would have minded that you thought that Madame Bovary was a type of dairy cow.

Was she that scientist that invented uranium ?

Never mind, Badger. The point is that Laraine was a warm-hearted woman who knew you before you became famous. She wasn't an intellectual any more than you were. You'd be okay with her, if you didn't let fame go to your head and leave her for some high-maintenance trophy wife. Because I made you a handsome race car driver, Badger, I think some readers expected you to be a conventional hero of fiction—but you *weren't.* You are a good person, but you are like Peter Pan: unchanging and unconnected to other people. I did that on purpose. You cannot be a romantic hero.

In *Once Around the Track* the people who love Badger the most know him the least. Women saw a handsome face on a coffee mug and built him a soul. Taran, who seems to love Badger the most, gives up on him and ends up with somebody else, but even then at the conclusion of the novel, the words "I love you, Tony," are *not* said by Taran, his fiancée, but by a tearful fan—a total stranger. That's not a romantic ending: it is a *creepy* commentary on the delusions of fans.

In the book you kept comparing me to horses.

I'm pleased that you noticed. Yes, Tuggle sees you as the practice pony who has to lose races to his thoroughbred running partner. Sark sees you as Boxer the draft horse in *Animal Farm,* exploited by the greedy owners. And to Taran you are the teaser stud, whom she will sometimes dream about, even when she's with someone else.

You never said what happened to me at the end of the book.

Well, I hope you lived happily ever after, but it's hard to know what would constitute a happy ending for you. You never wanted to leave your lake, which rules out a career as a TV commentator or a job anywhere in NASCAR. You'll never make much money again, but Laraine won't care, and somehow I don't think you'll mind, either.

Well, you could have given me a first-rate ride with one of the powerful four-car teams, like Roush or Hendrick.

They wouldn't take you, Badger. You're a unicorn in NASCAR, too. You're beautiful and useless. You won't go to the shop on non-race days. You hate doing publicity, and you aren't well represented on the business side of the sport. You can drive like a demon, but taxi drivers make about thirty grand a year. The few hundred thousand dollars above that which a race team pays you is for something other than driving. Tony Lafon is the future of stock car racing. You are its past.

Maybe I'll go on the pro circuit for bass fishing.

Good luck, Badger.

Thank you, Sweetie. Say, what year did I win the Daytona 500?

Well, *Ward Burton* won that race in 2002, but, Badger, you are not really Ward Burton. You resemble him, and he helped to create you, but you are a fictional character in a comic novel, and thus you are far less complex than he is.

Thass a good thang, right?

Yes. Yes, it is.